Robert "Bo" Forehand's

STEAMPUNKS

BOOK · 1

Robert "Bo" Forehand's

STEAMPUNKS

BOOK · 1

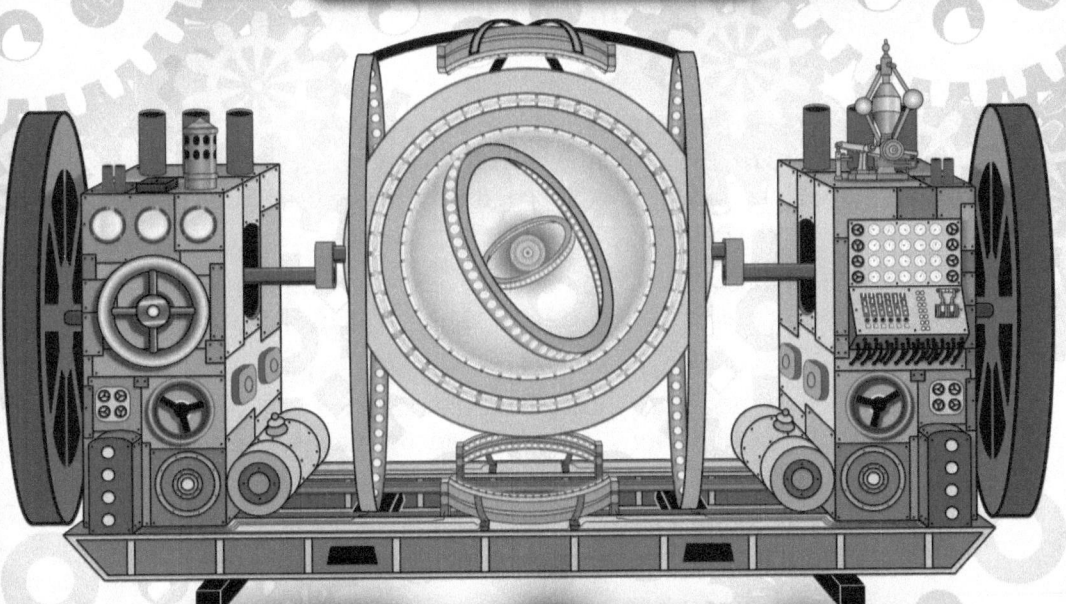

The Earthquake Machine

THIS NOVEL HAS BEEN RATED

	PRETTY GOOD(ish) times 12
PG-12	Also, **Parental Guidance** suggested for those 11 years and under due to: Mild Violence Semi-Mature Themes Childish Language Lack of Propriety Excessive Silliness

Some Material May Not Be Suitable For Children (or certain breeds of cats)

by the AUTHOR *and his nonsense committee*

Cover and all interior artwork created by Robert "Bo" Forehand. No A.I. was used in the creation of this novel.

Edited by Nicole Chapman-Leonard.

ISBN (paperback): 979-8-9928814-0-0
First Edition: 2025

Publisher: Steampunks Book Works
www.SteampunksBookWorks.net

Table of Contents

Dedication

To my parents:
who always supported me unconditionally
(mostly)
and loved me no matter what
(sometimes).

To Jessy:
my life, my love, my best friend.
My Jessy.
This adventure is just the beginning.

Additionally (because I can do what I want),
this book is dedicated to all of my
friends, family, and passing acquaintances
that helped encourage and inspire me along the way.
They know who they are.
If not, they might want to get checked out.
Amnesia is no laughing matter.
Except in soap operas.
Which don't contain nearly as much soap
as I was led to believe.
False advertising.

Forehand's

FOREWORD BACKWORD

& all those pesky

MIDDLEWORDS

Foreword is a bit of a misnomer. It is not the word before the book, nor is it a single word. The book cover has the first words, and if the foreword was before that, then it would be written on your hands, which is just odd. Backword, the thing I just made up, suffers from similar issues. Middlewords are where the real meat is located. Without the middlewords, you would be eating a bread sandwich. Your diet would consist of nothing but starch, which is more information than needed, thank you very much. While complex carbohydrates are fun and all, this word of the fore is meant to discuss our story and the tales behind it.

The Steampunk retro-futuristic sub-genre of science fiction has been around since the days of H. G. Well's 1895 novella *The Time Machine*, and if his story was true, it could have been around since the days of the dinosaurs. It's a wonder how a T-Rex could write with his little arms, but I digress. Well's work inspired generations of writers, but the term *Steampunk* didn't arrive until the 1980's as a play on the word *Cyberpunk*, which was an already established sub-genre of science fiction. Cyberpunk stories contain a dystopian, futuristic setting where the gleaming, high-tech wonders are mixed in with dark, gritty, realism. Steampunk is similar, except not really because it's different. While Cyberpunk travels forward to a bleak future, Steampunk travels backward to an optimistic past.

Considered to be alternate history or a different dimension, Steampunk stories are normally set in the late 1800's, most often in the British Victorian Era or the American Wild West. In these stories, inventors create wild, futuristic inventions for their time that employ some use of steam power to bring these wondrous machines to life. In reality, these inventions would have changed the world as it was known then, but in these fictional stories, they are an ordinary way of life.

"I'm taking the dirigible to work, darling," a man's voice crackled through the robot head's speaker box. "I'll be home later."

Over the years, piles of wondrous, incredible, jaw-dropping, Steampunk stories have spread across bookstore bookshelves like wildfires across... well, bookstore bookshelves, but I always felt there was something missing from the genre. While whimsy and creativity and silliness abounded, I do not remember laughing very much. Many stories seemed to focus on wars or torture or zombie cyborgs who tortured during wars. As a die hard (but mostly live soft) fan of *The Hitchhiker's Guide to the Galaxy* by Douglas Adams, which combines comedy and science fiction in a weird, wonderful, Britishy-humor kind of way, I felt inspired to bring that same fun to the Steampunk genre. (I also just enjoy adding an *S* to the ends ofs words.)

While I wanted to add *the funny*, I also wanted to subtract any fantasy elements. Though I absolutely adore fantasy, my inclination is for Steampunk science fiction to be filled with science. If there is someone flying around in the sky, I want there to be a jet pack attached to her and tooting out steam. If the city is suffering from unnatural earthquakes, I want an invention to be the cause, not a masked man speaking Latin and doing jazz hands. Personal preference, even though jazz hands are sometimes a crucial part of my morning breakfast.

Rebellion has become a common theme among the Steampunk genre, which is a natural cause/reaction during that time period. As the Industrial Age wound up, the people in power ground down the commoners beneath them. The concept of "cogs in the gears" applied to multiple levels of storytelling here. The oppressed would rise up to fight for equality and all that important stuffs, perhaps even leading to a happy ending or, at the very least, a five-day workweek. (Thank the Workers Union for that, kids.)

Adding it all together, 1800's Science Fiction + Comedy - Fantasy + Rebellion = my protagonist Adelaide, a runaway, teenage girl with a mechanical arm, a quick wit, and a habit of getting herself into strange situations. The location is made up, the history is imaginary, and the points don't matter. Specific years or timelines or cities or countries didn't matter to me. I just wanted to write a solid story that existed in its own world. Enter the fictional Parsons City in a timeline reminiscent of the late 1800's, but not really and quite different.

In conclusion, I have concluded that I tend to write a lot of silly nonsense, but if it brings some joy or inspiration to someone out there who has tastes as questionable as mine, then it was all worth it. I feel like anyone of any age from any stretch of life can find something to love about this story. Nonsense can make sense with the realization that time can be wasted well. The roundabout course filled with excess words and unnecessary footnotes can sometimes lead to a delightfully[i] fun journey.[ii]

---

[i] True, adverbs are bad and add *absolutely* nothing to the description, but I am also *involuntarily* kooky.

[ii] I've been told that footnotes in a novel are ridiculous. Yet, I've found that the way they break up the flow of reading the book in an odd, circular pattern is much like the spirit behind the steampunk sub-genre: inefficient, unnecessary, yet fun, inspiring, creative, and if done correctly, a marvelous one-of-a-kind experience. They can distract the eye and interrupt the reader's flow, but on the other hand, you have other fingers. And, after all, isn't that the pointer?

Chapter 1

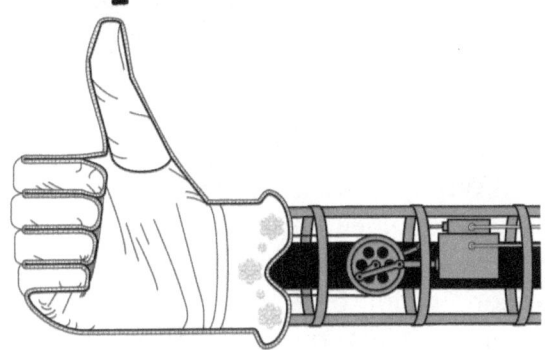

The Girl with the Mechanical Arm

As far as locomotives go, there had never been a more decadent enclosure of luxury than the United Exchange Engine No. 133.[1] On the inside, every item of hardware was gold-plated. Every piece of silverware and cutlery polished to a brilliant sheen. Every waiter and bartender in the dining car dressed in full tuxedos. Every guest wore the most lavish clothing, from glittering monocles to sparkling jewelry. On the whole, everyone thought themselves to be very shiny, everyone except for, of course, Miss Adelaide Wakefield.

Waltzing into the dining car, the bouncy thirteen-year-old girl was oblivious to the disapproving stares and glances following her every move. The most disapproving stares came from, doubly of course, her parents, Margaret and Franklin Wakefield. Wearing fine black clothing, the fussy couple sat in a booth much like a hen sits on a large, lumpy ostrich egg, which is, to say, uncomfortable and slightly confused.

---

1 Not even the Luxury Engine, Decadent Rover class could match it, and that was saying something because the Luxury Engine thought quite highly of itself.

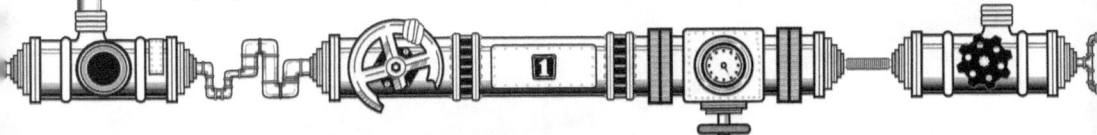

Mister Wakefield's facial expression never wavered from a mixture of shock and disgust as his daughter skipped her way over to sit opposite them. Or, at least, she attempted to skip in her black, combat boots, but she just managed to clomp around rather loud and bouncily.

"What in the name of all-that-is-decent are you wearing?" Mister Wakefield asked.

"What?" came Adelaide's reply. She glanced down at her dark purple, leather jacket over her lace-lined, yellow dress. Her bushy, uncooperative red hair shoved itself out from under a bright blue fedora atop her head. Stuck in the band, an extravagant, rainbow-colored feather poked and tickled the head of the elderly woman sitting behind them.

"Honestly, dear, why won't you wear the clothes I lay out for you?" Missus Wakefield implored.

"I think I look rather dashing." Adelaide smiled, knowing full well that her parents would prefer her dashing back to their private room. A little shake of her head tickled the elderly woman's head again, who scratched her scalp, ruffled her feathered shoulders, and went back to eating her platter full of escargot and peanut butter.

The most glaring piece of decoration adorning Adelaide's small frame was not even clothing at all. Years ago, her right arm had been amputated just above her right bicep. Now, a mechanical arm prosthetic poked out of her jacket's shortened sleeves. The skeletal creation of metal, gears, chains, and pistons worked well in an impressive display of engineering. The arm was attached to a harness strapped across her torso and shoulder with the straps and engine pack somewhat-but-not-quite-hidden beneath her oversized dress. The chains and pistons reacted to a counterbalancing system of Adelaide's own creation. The elbow and wrist joints would move in accordance to how she directed her residual limb, which Adelaide would lovingly refer to as her nub, her nubbin, or when she felt fancy, Colonel Cantankerous Von

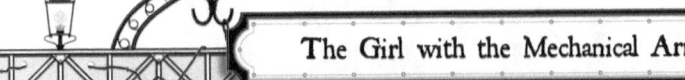

Puffingnub the Thirteenth. The controls of her currently stiff, metal fingers were another matter; however, even immobile, they did come in handy for nostril spelunking.

"You look like a degenerate," Mister Wakefield commented. "You will change before we arrive."

A waiter approached their booth. After a cursory glance and raised eyebrow at the extravagant girl, he showcased a tray full of elegant meals prepared on fine china with a generous helping of roast beef as the main course. He took the most delicate care in placing every plate and piece of silverware down before them in a precise presentation before bowing and stepping away like a dancing bear who just threw out his back.

Adelaide's good left hand snatched up a fork and stabbed at the roast beef. At least, she intended to. Her father slid her plate in front of himself, making her fork miss the target and jab the table instead. Mister Wakefield equipped himself with cutlery and began slicing Adelaide's plate of food into small, bite-sized chunks. Adelaide had no trouble with the concept of gnawing on her food until her teeth could rip it apart, but her father preferred decorum, whatever that was.

"Oh!" Her memory kicked back into gear. "I can cut it myself now. Check it. I built a new control panel to improve *dexterity*," she said with the air of importance of someone who just learned the word *dexterity*.[2]

Adelaide raised her right arm remnant, which in turn caused the mechanical prosthetic to raise and extend. The pistons working in unison helped reduce the weight on her across her shoulders. Rotating her arm would rotate the welded portion connected to her elbow. Her elbow and hand controls were located in a small device attached to her chest harness. Her previous control panel iteration could only command the fingers to fully open or close, which was useful, but not quite

---

2   This is what's called a "footnote," where a number points to itself and references something that the reader may want to know. This is not one of those, but here we are.

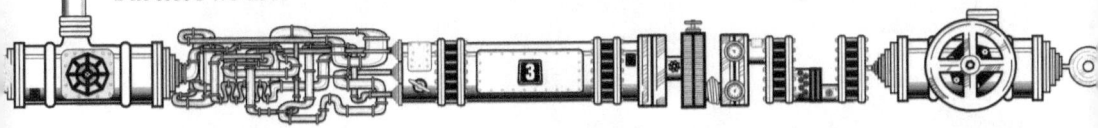

handy, as it were. Numerous cables snaked through the metal rods leading to the hand. Additional pistons connected inside the skeletal joints.

Adelaide slid her left hand inside a specifically cut flap on the front of her dress just below her collar bones. She worked a rotary dial control panel strapped on top of an old, grimy T-shirt. The entire circular plate design rotated to control the wrist, and five, individual sliders corresponded to each finger. A sixth slider would expand or contract her elbow.

In response to her good hand's commands, Adelaide's mechanical fingers rotated and extended as though the metal needed to stretch its muscles. The metal phalanges reached out and gently grasped her glass of water with a soft *tink*. Her parents watched in morbid curiosity as she brought the glass to her lips, but the digits lost traction on the slippery surface. The glass fell and spilled its contents all over the table.

"Adelaide!"

"I can fix that," she responded, more to herself than her parents. Adelaide tinkered with her control panel and twisted some knobs and slid some sliders until one of the whosiwhatsits did something entirely unexpected.

Adelaide's eyes widened in surprise as her mechanical arm slammed down on the table of its own accord, scattering the plates of food. The silverware did a joyful little flip in the air as the water glasses flooded the already wet table. Adelaide released her hand from the control panel, but completely unbidden, her mechanical elbow bent before extending and slamming her hand on the table once again.

"Whoops," Adelaide uttered, "uh..."

Her mechanical arm found its own rhythm, slamming up and down upon the poor, unsuspecting table. *Wham. Wham. Wham.*[3] Adelaide's good arm grabbed the metal one. She pushed down and attempted to hold it in place.

---

3 3/4 time, a favorite among elbow instrumentalists.

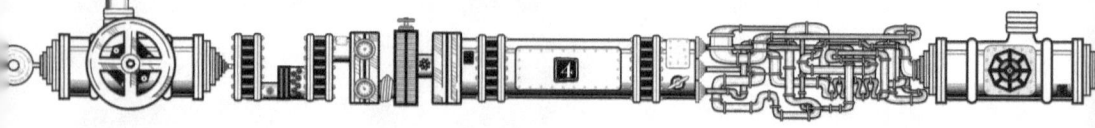

However, the superior torque and leverage of the pistons and hydraulics just rocked Adelaide back and forth along the bench. If she wasn't panicking with a side of anxiety, she might have enjoyed the ride. Her bouncing eyes found a glimpse of the surrounding passengers, most of whom were turned around or standing to watch her ridiculous display of table pounding.

"Could you control your daughter, Mister Wakefield?" a frowning, mutton-chopped man asked from behind them.

The gasps and harrumphs were nothing compared to her father's face, reddened with outrage. His hands tried to clamp down on Adelaide. The violent rocking rejected his cautious fingers as her metal hand tenderized the roast beef and mashed the potatoes.

"Adelaide..." her father's voice growled.

"Hold on," Adelaide gasped, "I got..." her head bonked onto the backrest, "it?"

She ripped out an air tube screwed into the pistons controlling her mechanical elbow. A hiss of steam sprayed the table. Her arm flopped down, lifeless. The steam generator backpack somewhat-but-not-quite hidden beneath her dress and jacket gave a soft toot from the exhaust pipe poking up from her collar. Adelaide slumped her concealed lump of a backpack against the backrest.

"I got it! I... uh... it's fixed. Or stopped anyways. No worries... uh... sorry..."

Her good hand waved sheepishly at the man with the mutton chops sitting behind her parents. His raised eyebrows and contorted face looked as though he thought Adelaide had just vomited a sack of dead rats onto the table. She thought he looked a little too judgmental for someone wearing a top hat that was two feet tall.

After a couple more moments, he and the affronted elderly lady and the shocked steward and the rowdy ruffles and the other civilized civilians turned back to their own meals with more than a few utterances of: *Absurd! Rude! Impertinent!*

Disgraceful! and Adelaide's favorite... *The Nerve!* She heard that one many times in relation to her antics, but she always thought it was funny since nerves were just the wires that her brain communicated with to her body. Although, that was probably what went wrong with her arm. The pulley system might have gotten wrapped around one of the wires and...

"Put that macabre thing away!" her father commanded.

Her father's throbbing vein in his forehead brought Adelaide back to the present. The waiter stepped back to the table to mop up the spilled waters and exploded bits of potato. Adelaide noticed how food-laden her metal fist was and promptly grabbed her napkin to wipe the largest chunks of meat and other brown things off her skeletal phalanges.

"Honestly, dear," her mother sighed. "We're in public."

Missus Wakefield withdrew a pair of long, white gloves from her purse as the waiter lifted the silverware and plates to mop up the table. Missus Wakefield handed the gloves over the working waiter to Adelaide. With a great, weighty, world-destroying sigh that only a teenager could possibly utter, Adelaide reluctantly retrieved the gloves before shoving and tugging the fabric over her metal fingers.

"May I bring fresh plates and drinks, sir?" the waiter asked when he finished mopping.

"No," Mister Wakefield said, "you may leave us."

The waiter bowed and stepped away. Mister Wakefield turned his slightly less throbbing vein toward his daughter.

"There is no reason to bring attention to your abnormality," Mister Wakefield said in a furious whisper. "Keep it out of sight. Use your manners, and eat what is left of your dinner."

He nodded toward Adelaide's plate. The ceramic somehow survived the great pounding, but the meat and vegetables were thoroughly mashed into paste. Adelaide didn't mind. Chewing was overrated. Though, her fork was a bit flatter than it used to be.

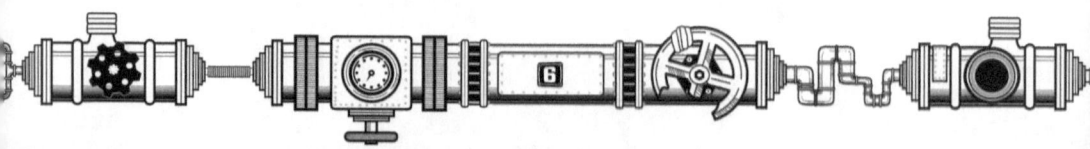

"Why must you make everything so difficult?" her father asked with a sigh.

Adelaide resisted the urge to answer his rhetorical question. She didn't intend to be *difficult*, but if her parents had it their way, she'd have as much personality as her prosthetic. They hated anything that was out of place, and that was exactly where Adelaide enjoyed putting things.

They ate the rest of their dinner in silence. As Adelaide took her last bite of the roast-beef-flavored toothpaste, which was actually quite tasty, she squeezed the goop down her throat and gazed out the window. Barren landscapes made way for hills, small mountain ranges, and little specks of towns in the distance. Dark clouds and smog rolled in. The slow, falling sun shone rays of purple and red, reflecting off the polluted vapor. She suddenly jumped in her seat, bumping the table and smooshing her face against the glass.

"Adelaide!" her father chastised.

"We're here!" Adelaide beamed.

In the distance, a great city emerged through the hazy smog. The train pulled up parallel, purposefully allowing a grand view on the approach. Churring and puffing buildings of all shapes and sizes dotted the landscape and comprised the metropolis of Parsons City.

The train approached the south district colloquially known as the Stacks because nobody felt like *Factory Land of Black Lungs and Hobos* really rolled off the tongue. Shacks and shanties packed every inch between the smokestacks and power plants billowing plumes of black. The shining Engine No. 133 did not even stop to consider the coal-covered train platforms before flying past. If the Engine had a nose, it would wrinkle in disgust at the dirty commoners.[4]

---

4 Train Engine Experimental Concept *Delta Echo Turbinate* #4 did, in fact, contain a nose as part of the design. It was scrapped, however, due to the engine sneezing every time it accidentally sucked up a squirrel on the tracks.

Right through the middle of the city, a shallow, black river cut a deep, sheer valley that, after a sudden drop, led to the ocean beyond. Mines, tunnels, steam pipelines, railroads, and makeshift houses and buildings covered the Gorge's three-hundred-foot walls. Bridges and tunnels connected the many and varied city districts at different elevations. The train sped along one such bridge as Adelaide watched the massive, mechanical lifts raising vehicles, cargo, train cars, horses, and people up the busy, sheer walls of earth. The train tracks rose and dove, back and forth across the valley in a design that must have made sense at one time, and that time was clearly long ago.

From the Stacks, they traversed over the Gorge and into the Lower District. Wrapped around the top of the Gorge and plunging through the abandoned mining tunnels, modest homes and cramped apartment buildings were pack- ed tightly together beneath a collection of tall hills. The top of the spacious hills comprised the aptly named Upper Districts, which extended all the way west to the sheer cliff facing the expansive ocean beyond the horizon.

Large, magnificent mansions claimed the best waterfront views, many of which were built into the cliff itself, all the way down to the short beach. Though the mansions had the same engineering and design philosophy as the abandoned industrial plants and overcrowded buildings covering the sides of the Gorge, these were different in every other way. While the Lowers clustered at the bottom of the rise and even below in a series of tunnels and underground dwellings, the rich built upwards with shining skyscrapers far above the pollution and grime. Here lived the people who ruled Parsons City. This was where the Wakefields belonged. Well, the adult Wakefields, at any rate. Grime was Adelaide's natural state of being.

Engine No. 133 came to a soft screeching halt at a massive, bustling train station underneath a rounded, glass

ceiling five stories above. The other passengers began to rise, and Adelaide shot off from the booth's bench.

"Wait," commanded her father, but Adelaide was already off the train. "Wait!"

Her heavy boots hopped down onto the fine wood planks of the massive platform. A wider variety of folks than the train's genteel passengers rushed about, but most were still well-dressed and highly impressed with themselves. Adelaide ran between them and across the wide walkway to a set of windows overlooking the city from the station's high perch. The artistry of the city's engineers and architects tickled her senses, but a sudden *clonk* turned her attention behind. A woman in her early thirties was pushing a luggage cart when the front wheel abruptly popped off the axle. The cart full of luggage screeched and dug into the floor.

"Cheryl!" a thin-faced woman in her late twenties looked back and called to the one pushing the cart. She brushed some imagined dust off her expensive dress.

"Sorry, ma'am," the other woman, Cheryl, called in reply. Her gray, well-worn dress had very real dust on it, which she gave no mind.

The thin-lipped woman turned to express her frustrations at the station attendant, who was seriously considering a different line of work. Along the busy platform, the loose wheel rolled into Adelaide's foot. She picked it up and skipped over.

"Well, that's a problem you don't see every day," she chuckled. "The lug nuts come off?"

"I couldn't tell ya," Cheryl said.

Adelaide scoured the wood planks for clues. She found a threaded nut with metal end cap. Her pinky and thumb held it while her index felt the smooth inside.

"Looks like it got stripped," she said. Adelaide studied the axle. "And just the one bolt? Could use three for support. Four would be ideal. Whelp, let me see."

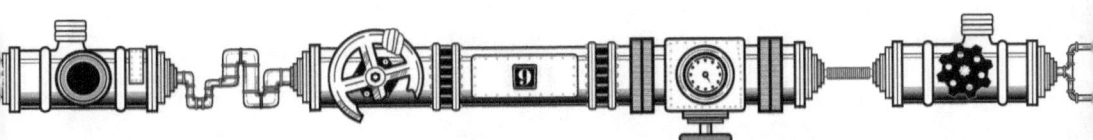

Adelaide ripped off the white glove covering her metal arm and tossed the expensive fabric to the ground. Cheryl's eyes widened in surprise, but she said nothing. Adelaide searched her floppy, metal arm and studied the screws and bolts and nuts. Her left hand tapped the metal wrist. She lifted up her metal arm and held it by the luggage cart's tilted axle to compare.

"Fifteen millimeters? Hmm. No, that looks like twenty-one." She lowered her arm into her lap, retrieved a pair of pliers from her jacket pocket, and unscrewed a nut from a prominent hinge on her elbow. She held up the free nut and measured it against the axle's bolt. "Ha! I was right! Here, help me lift it up."

"Adelaide!" Missus Wakefield called from next to the train. "Come here right now!"

Adelaide didn't hear, whether by purpose or accident. Cheryl heaved up the heavy luggage cart with surprising ease as Adelaide fit the wheel back in place. Her good hand screwed the nut onto the bolt's well-worn threads then used the pliers to tighten as best as they could.

"This probably won't last you too long," Adelaide talked while she worked, "but it should get you home. Need to cut new threads, or really just get a new bolt. Actually, just needs a new axle." She chuckled.

"Thank you, darlin'," Cheryl smiled. "And you take care of that arm now."

"You too. Well, take care, I mean. Not your arm. You have two. Though you can care for your arm if you want. I... uh... okay bye."

Cheryl nodded and waved as she rolled off after the impatient, thin-faced woman. Adelaide trudged toward her own impatient, thin-faced mother.

"What were you trying to do?" Missus Wakefield asked. "That's servant work, you know. Highly improper for a lady. Stay beside me. Oh, you're absolutely filthy now."

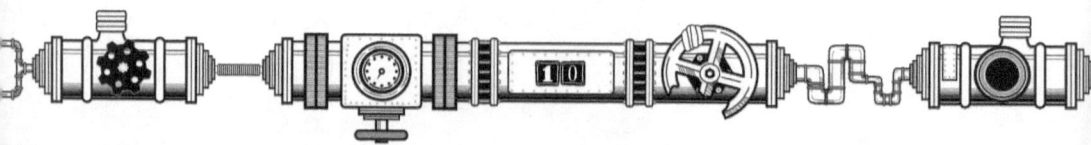

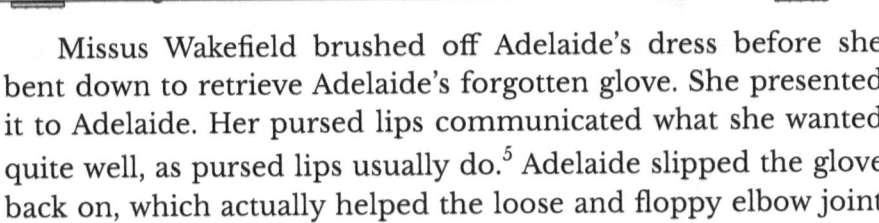
Missus Wakefield brushed off Adelaide's dress before she bent down to retrieve Adelaide's forgotten glove. She presented it to Adelaide. Her pursed lips communicated what she wanted quite well, as pursed lips usually do.[5] Adelaide slipped the glove back on, which actually helped the loose and floppy elbow joint that needed multiple repairs now.

A few cars down, Mister Wakefield met Luther, their sinewy butler in his mid-fifties. Despite his age, he was as strong as an ox with a face to match. His humongous, handlebar mustache waved in the breeze of his puffing nostril exhalations. He placed all of the Wakefields' luggage in a pile and lifted it with ease.

"Would you like any help?" Adelaide asked Luther.

"Of course not," he blustered in reply. "That would be improper, milady."

Luther marched away from the platform. Mister Wakefield followed and waved for his wife and daughter to do the same.

"You see?" Missus Wakefield commented. "Luther understands propriety. You would do well to brush up on the subject."

Down a flight of steps, Luther led them to a waiting vehicle. He stowed their luggage in the boot of the internal-combustion powered carriage.[6] The massive wheels reached up past the doors. Mister Wakefield helped the ladies up the steps and inside the carriage cabin before he followed. Luther climbed up the wheel spokes and onto the driver's bench. An engine compartment below resembled a small, snub-nosed train engine but with the smokestack and exhaust coming out the bottom rear, which was much like Luther himself.

The engine chugged to life and coughed smoke. The motorized carriage rolled away from the train station. Adelaide's

---

5 Despite common misconceptions, pursed lips are neither detachable from the face nor stored in handbags.

6 During the early days of carriage powering, an inventor named Harold Fjord created an external-combustion powered carriage. It made one very fast journey. It did not make two.

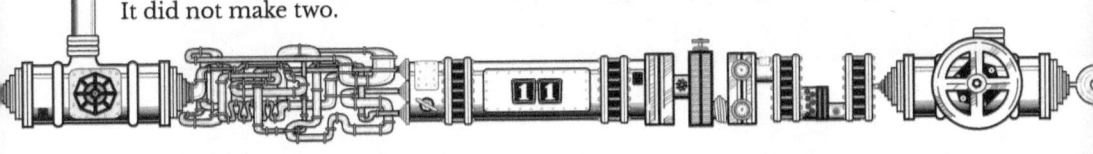

attention quickly shifted from the carriage to the streets themselves. A mechanical marvel, the metropolis of Parsons City seemed to come alive with whirs and clanks as though the roads and buildings were part of one, giant, clockwork mechanism. Moving sidewalks ferried pedestrians past storefront windows. Outdoor lifts rocketed guests up the sides of buildings or even over the rolling elevations in the city built upon hills.

The carriage stopped before a spacious, multi-street intersection as a large tram on rails stopped in the middle of the crossing. Colossal gears and mechanisms built into the asphalt near the intersection's corners rattled and spun. The entire intersection before them rose into the air as a geared platform. Adelaide tilted her head to catch a glimpse of the powerful, hydraulic piston lifting the chunk of street. The teeth hanging off the edge of the raised intersection met with the vertical gear teeth of the outer mechanisms. The raised intersection turned in place, a perfect circle. With the tram rotated to face another street, the intersection lowered back into the road, lining perfectly to match. The tram puttered off, following the rails lining the city. Adelaide smushed her entire face against the window to try and take in everything.

Three stories up, a pair of catwalk drawbridges clanged and lowered to meet high above the intersection. Safety gates unlocked, and pedestrians walked across the drawbridge, glancing down at the traffic below. As their carriage drove ahead, Adelaide rolled down the window to get a better look. She watched pedestrians ride up to the third-story shopping areas and catwalks. They used sets of heavy chains with loops on the end. A woman put her foot into the loop, and a geared mechanism raised the chain into the air, stopping at the catwalk.

Adelaide smiled with her mouth open wide enough to catch a bird. In fact, she might have if there were any birds that lived in the city. Many thought it was because the city

was too polluted, but really they just couldn't stand the strangeness of it all. The city's delightfully bizarre construction exemplified organized chaos. Adelaide thought she might be comfortable here after all.

They rolled to a stop at another intersection. On the sidewalk, a shabby-looking man with a wild beard and torn coat was approached by two police officers with shiny bobby hats. The man spotted the officers and raised his hands in surrender. The first officer kicked the man's knees down as the second retrieved handcuffs. The Wakefield carriage chugged past.

"Adelaide, roll up the window," Missus Wakefield implored. "We don't need to assault ourselves with all the odors at once."

Adelaide huffed and did as she was asked. Missus Wakefield retrieved a bottle of perfume from her purse and sprayed the air, which made Adelaide's nose tickle. She shook her head to beat a sneeze. The city smells were far less pungent than whatever was in that bottle.[7]

Thinking about science making weird stuff, Adelaide asked, "Where's the school?"

"The university?" Mister Wakefield asked in response. "Two or three kilometers from here, I believe."

"Kilometers?" Adelaide wondered aloud. "What happened to miles?"

"Civilized societies are switching to the metric system as the new standard. Best to adapt if we want to fit in."

Adelaide wrinkled her nose. *Fitting in* had never been one of her strengths. Since Adelaide's accident when she was six, that never even seemed like an option anyway. Perhaps proving her engineering abilities and enrolling in one of the country's top universities would help with that. She smiled at the thought of learning from a real teacher and not just from a crazy amount of self-inflicted trial-and-error.

---

7 In fact, Adelaide did not realize that she was allergic to ground-up bits of a honey badger's colon, but then again, most did not realize what was in the different aroma squirts that the refined ladies sprayed in their faces.

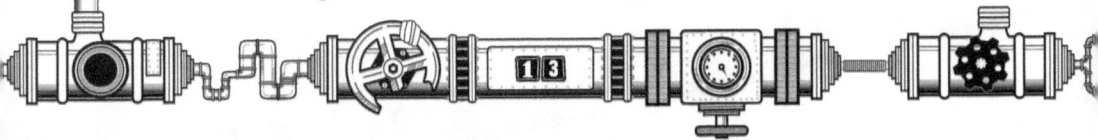

The carriage pulled into a gated driveway leading up to a large Victorian mansion. In a city composed of concrete and metal, the spacious grass lawn in front seemed like quite a luxury, which it was. What better way to show off that you're better than your neighbors than to grow small, green plants on top of rusted metal and polluted soil?

Luther pulled them up along the circle driveway, passing a fountain in the center with a stone angel peeing a stream of brownish water into the pool. The discontented stone face looked like it challenged anyone to judge it. Immediately after they came to a soft stop, Luther hopped off the driver's bench and opened the passenger door. Mister Wakefield stepped down without acknowledging the butler. Luther extended a hand for Missus Wakefield.

Adelaide hopped rather than stepped down, and she couldn't help but stare up at the imposing building before them. The dark brick and black turrets did little to alleviate that symptom. In fact, the jutted, eyebrow windows and spiked dormers made the entire mansion seem like it was looking down upon her, disapproving of her presence. Adelaide felt like her eyebrows weren't nearly impressive enough to be here.

Luther stepped up to the heavy, front door and opened the lock with a *clunk* that seemed to echo for miles within. Mister Wakefield beamed at the building as though it was the child he always wanted. He glanced back at Adelaide.

"Welcome home."[8]

---

8 This is the end of the chapter. You can tell it's the end of the chapter because this is where the chapter ends. If you continue reading, a new chapter will begin on the next page. That's how books work.

Chapter 2

A Cold Housewarming

The girl with the mechanical arm stepped through the front doorway. The wide foyer seemed to extend upwards for several miles. On her left, a living room was packed with velvety furniture that no one had sat on. To her right, a family room was adorned with decorations and fancy things galore that was someone else's idea of luxury. Ahead past the spiraling staircase, a hallway plunged into darkness.

Their first house, a much, much, much smaller place out in the country next to her father's first train yard, had a quick little add-on room that was filled with splinters.[9] Every floorboard creaked and croaked more than the frogs that Adelaide insisted to her mother that she absolutely did not have tucked away in five different shoeboxes in her closet. Train engines constantly rattled beside her old window too. And bits of dust rained down from the ceiling periodically. She quite missed it.

---

9 Side effects of an unplanned-for baby include: nausea, heartburn, splinters, uncontrollable crying, explosive diarrhea, and also, a baby.

Their second house on the hill was okay. The third in the steel mill was too loud. She didn't even remember the fourth. The fifth was big and boring. But that first house was special. Enough ingenuity and imperfections to make it feel like home. Almost like it was built with love. It may have just been the memories of a six-year-old, but Adelaide felt that her parents were more carefree and loving before the accident. She had always gotten the impression that her parents would have wanted more children, but Adelaide was such a hassle that they decided against it.

"Adelaide," her mother called. "Your bedroom is down this way, fourth door on your left."

The new floorboards didn't creak as Adelaide made her way down the hall. She instantly didn't trust them. Four doors of thick lacquer later, a bright pink room assaulted her eyes. It was like cotton candy got in a fistfight with a field of flowers, who were both demolished by a ruthless swarm of bad taste. The overabundance of doilies looked like they were trying to smother the white and pink polka-dot furniture. Adelaide slumped against the pink four-poster bed. This was her life now, she supposed. She tried not to throw up, though she didn't think it could possibly hurt the decor.

Her eyes meandered until the rolling orbs landed upon a vanity desk and mirror by the window. Lipstick, jars of face powder, mascara brushes, and various instruments of hiding one's face littered the desk top.[10] She opened a jar of face powder and looked inside at the white dust. Perhaps she could use it to dust for fingerprints at all the imaginary crime scenes she was going to create just to annoy her parents.

---

10 An inventor by the name of Doctor Floyd Humdinger created a face cream that caused mild paralysis, medium drunkenness, and the occasional spicy fit of mind-numbing hysteria. Naturally, the face cream was quite popular at family gatherings.

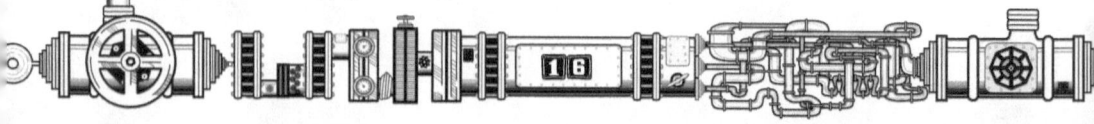

Her eyes spotted an enormous trunk taking up space inside the closet nearby. Adelaide's face brightened as she lifted the lid. Inside, a chaotic conglomerate of machinery, devices, wrenches, and tools greeted her. Adelaide yanked out and heaved up a massive, vice-like contraption and clonked it onto the vanity. She did the same for the other devices and tools and boxes, taking over the desk and shoving the makeup and mirrors aside.

Her good hand unbuttoned her dress, revealing a grimy T-shirt underneath, a pair of oversized cargo shorts, and her mechanical arm chest harness with a generator pack. She unstrapped herself from the harness and plopped the metal arm onto the vanity. Her fleshy hand viced the metal hand in place as she began maintenance.

A new nut was in order. Also needed to troubleshoot the cable and pulley mechanism. Didn't want another table slapping incident. At least, not an accidental one. Might as well check the springs, pistons, gears, and coils while she was at it.

Globs of grease oozed near the joints and many of the moving parts. Adelaide dumped some makeup powder on the grease and used the mascara brush to scrub the metal somewhat, but not entirely, clean. Mainly, the powdery goop mixture just flicked off onto the desk.

"Oh, doesn't it look just lovely in here," Missus Wakefield said as she stepped into the room.

She opened the window before fawning over the doilies and flowers.

"Just beautiful. The movers first said it might take 'til the morrow, but your father told them, in no uncertain terms, that was unacceptable..." Missus Wakefield's words trailed off as she looked at the mess that was her daughter.

If her nose could turn up any more, her nostrils would lie flat against her cheeks.

"I see you are finally using the makeup I keep buying for you."

"Oh, yes." Adelaide smirked. "It's quite handy."

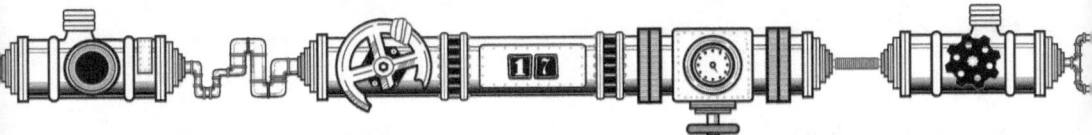

"And... oh!" Missus Wakefield's face lit up as her eyes spotted a small, gold-plated jewelry box on the vanity. The well-crafted piece seemed to glitter amongst the white powder and chunks of rusted metal bits.

"What's this?" Missus Wakefield picked up the box and studied it. "I didn't know you had such a lovely jewelry box. Wherever did you get it?"

"I made it," Adelaide said.

"Truly?"

"For Lillian."

Her mother's beaming face drooped, then her skin tightened its grip on her skull.

"See. Look." Adelaide retrieved the music box from her mother's hands. She set it down on the vanity and turned a spring-loaded crank on the back. Instead of playing music, the box jerked and shivered to life.

The lid opened of its own accord. Tiny metal arms unfolded, rolled out from underneath the lid, and locked in place over the side. One hand held a broom, the other a small dustpan. Four, tiny, metal legs extended out from the bottom and lifted the box, wobbling as it tried to both walk and keep itself upright. The little box robot attempted to clean the desk with its tiny broom. It occasionally dumped the dustpan inside the box. Even less occasionally, it actually panned some dust.

"She taught me how to carve wood, you know. I thought this might help her with my '*many, many messes,*' as she liked to say," Adelaide chuckled. "Though she never seemed to mind."

"I would think not. She *was* your nanny, after all, and she was paid well to clean."

"She was far more than that," Adelaide countered. "To me."

Missus Wakefield's eyes narrowed. "Yes, well... she is not here anymore, is she? So, no need to mention her again. In

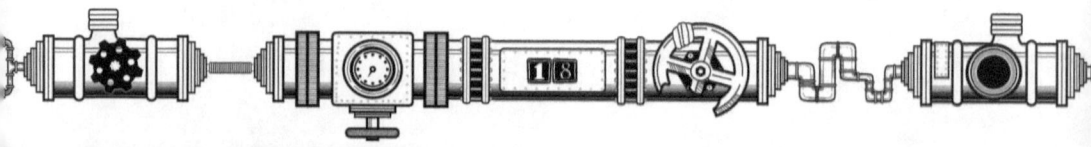

fact, we should just go ahead and get rid of this thing." She grabbed the wobbling jewelry box from the vanity. Its sad, little legs flailed about.

"No!" Adelaide yelled as she snatched it away from her mother.

Adelaide held it close to her chest. Missus Wakefield's stern face opened her mouth then closed it. She turned on her heel and stepped away, but Adelaide's voice made her stop.

"We should have gone to her funeral."

Missus Wakefield paused for a few moments before she turned around. A sharp inhalation carved her nostrils razor thin. "Adelaide, certain classes do not mix. It is vitally important for us to maintain our station—"

"What does it matter what other people think of us?!" Adelaide interrupted.

Her mother waved her hands to calm down her daughter. "Listen now. Your father and I worked so hard to be where we are today. No, no, just *listen* for a moment. Now... I came from nothing, and he had to rebuild his entire family legacy. Coming back to the city was just one of his ambitions, but we are living on the edge of a razor. Our investments could fall apart if the right people get the wrong impression of us. So much depends upon these next few weeks. If we do not fit in here, we will be forced to go back to living at the train yard."

"I liked the train yard."

"That place has too many..." her mother traced her hand along Adelaide's shoulder, above her amputated arm, "terrible memories." Missus Wakefield shook her head and gave a near imperceptible shiver. Adelaide percepted it, as she always did. Her mother slid over to the closet and rifled through the many dresses that Adelaide never wanted to wear. "Now, that is why it is essential for you to be clean and pressed and on your best behavior tomorrow night."

"What's tomorrow night?"

Tomorrow night was the grand housewarming party.[11] At the appointed time, a cavalcade of visitors swarmed the Wakefield mansion. Many arrived on horse-drawn carriages, others by steam-powered vehicles. Some walked there, but no one else talked to *those* people. While the transportation varied, one thing did not. They were all well-dressed and highfalutin.[12]

In the foyer, Franklin Wakefield jovially greeted all the incoming guests as they arrived. He seemed almost genuinely, but not quite happy that they were there. Adelaide was unfamiliar with that notion coming from her father.

Escorted by her mother, Adelaide entered the foyer from the rear hallway. Both women wore fine dresses woven of the finest fabrics and enormous hats woven of all the other fabrics. Adelaide kept trying to blow a piece of dangling lace from the wide brim out of her face. She was unsuccessful. On the bright side, it did make her look like she had a vertical mustache.

Adelaide lost the argument about wearing the audacious apparel, as she usually did, but she did earn a small victory by convincing her mother that she could wear comfortable shoes underneath. Missus Wakefield relented on that subject mainly because she thought Adelaide had terrible balance when the girl was walking around on her bare feet, let alone with a two-inch heel. Adelaide thought she had the balance and reflexes of a three-legged cat, which was, to say, wobbly but decent.

---

11 Did you like that segue? Smooth.

12 *Highfalutin*: affectedly genteel. *Genteel*: marked by refinement in taste and manners. *Manners*: qualities Adelaide did not possess. *Gent-eel*: a long, slimy fish that enjoyed wearing top hats.

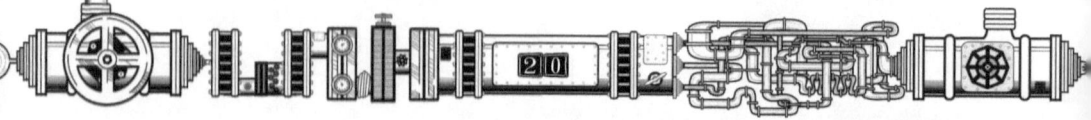

Her mother handed her a white glove. To her credit, Adelaide's eyes only rolled a few degrees before she slid the glove over her mechanical arm.

"If you insist on wearing that thing instead of a more believable prosthetic," Missus Wakefield began, glaring at the mechanical appendage, "it could, at least, be smaller in size."

Adelaide struggled pulling the fabric over a protruding screw head. "I need room for the pistons, or I can't lift anything heavy."

"What heavy objects would you possibly need to lift?"

"Definitely not a regulator valve from a locomotive engine, I can tell you that."[13]

Missus Wakefield ignored Adelaide as a woman with an outrageously puffy dress floated into the foyer.[14]

"Mary!" Missus Wakefield exclaimed. "So good of you to come. This is my daughter, Adelaide."

Adelaide sauntered over to the humanoid puffball. Her arm's generator backpack that was mostly-hidden beneath her dress suddenly chugged to life, stopped, and gave a soft *toot* from the exhaust pipe poking out from her collar. "Pardon me."

Across the house, in the living room, another person mixing with the guests seemed out of place. Zadie Stanbury, a sixteen-year-old girl, strutted about while wearing what appeared to be a dark-colored drapery wrapped over a leather jacket. She passed through the various wealth-on-legs and shouted out various greetings, such as: "Ahoy! Top o' the mornin'! Good lookin' out, mate! Oiy, pleasure to see you again! 'Ow ya doin', guv'nah!" She nudged a stuffy man whose shirt ruffles extended up to his chin. "If this party ain't a puff off the ole' pipe, eh?!" He looked highly affronted as her elbow nudged him quite painfully in the ribs.

---

13 It's my party and I can take my arm off if I want to.

14 Not literally floated. It's creative license. Unless her dress was actually a hovercraft. That would be neat. Be on the lookout: hoverdresses will be the wave of the future.

Zadie sauntered over to the buffet table, which was absolutely loaded with feasts and beasts and pastries and schmastries. Her face broke into a wide grin as she viewed the treasure trove. She quickly stuffed both her face and the pockets of her pants underneath her drapery shawl. Her cheeks full of frosted filling, Zadie glanced around to check that no one was looking before she swiped a few pieces of the fine silverware.

On the other side of the house, Adelaide blew the dangling lace out of her face yet again. She hid herself for as much as her large hat would allow against the doorframe to the living room. While her parents enjoyed the company of the so-called "high society" members, Adelaide couldn't give two flips about it. *Stand up straight. Smile. Speak only when spoken to. Curtsy. Nod. Bow.* She had to remember a thousand little slices of pomp and circumstance only to listen to the most boring conversations of all time. Like this goober, for example: Clayton Bamonte.

Standing at the edge of the bar on the other end of the living room, the 16-year-old with the puffed-out chest decorated with ruffles wore a monocle, just like his father, Mister Philip Bamonte, who worked with her father and was chatting him up right now in the foyer. The boy didn't need to wear a monocle. He just thought it made him look dashing. It didn't. The teenager also liked to declare how he detested machinery and preferred his servants to do the work for him. Worst of all, he seemed to like Adelaide.

With his palm up, Clayton gave a pompous "finger wave" to Adelaide from across the living room. Already absentmindedly playing with her control panel, Adelaide returned the finger wave with her gloved, mechanical hand. She smirked as sudden inspiration swirled in her mind. *Had he ever seen her prosthetic without a glove on it?*

Her left hand turned the control panel dial. Her right wrist and hand spun violently. The white fabric glove twisted

around in bunches. Adelaide's face widened in mock, silent horror. She stared at her hand as her fingers slowly bent backwards. The digits hinged back and touched her forearm. Clayton's look of horror was far more genuine. Apparently, he had not seen her mechanical arm undressed, as it were. An involuntary dry heave caused his hand to cover his mouth. He looked faint and sat back on a stool, almost falling right off.

Mister Bamonte looked at his son and stepped to his side in concern. Adelaide dove around the corner so Mister Wakefield wouldn't see his daughter and step to her side with something less than concern.

Adelaide snorted and chuckled and took cover behind a couch. On the other side, an elderly woman chuckled and guffawed at something that undoubtedly earned neither chuckles nor guffaws. Adelaide peeked around the cushiony edge. The woman sported an outrageous hat with a brim that curved so far upwards it looked like she was wearing a giant bowl on her head. Adelaide contemplated what things she could throw in there until the lady would notice the extra weight. What finger foods did they have around here?

Bowl Hat bawked to the two ladies she was chatting with on the couch. Adelaide decided their names were Rooster Head and Feather Cap for fairly obvious reasons. "Oh, no. That was his father, *Walter* Wakefield," Bowl Hat declared. "The drunk who lost the family fortune."

Adelaide stopped searching for discarded shrimp tails and turned to eavesdrop.

"I knew him since he was a boy," Bowl Hat continued. "The Wakefields used to be respected, admired even. Their home was on Leupold Road. It was nice despite being on the south side." Bowl Hat sloshed her glass of wine. "But he drank and ended up gambling away everything. Their home too. Scurried out of the city with his tail between his legs. As far as I am aware, he died a shillingless fool. Somehow, his son, Franklin here, got it all back."

Rooster Head crowed, "Oooh, that sounds suspicious, that does."

Feather Cap chirped, "They say it has something to do with trains. Built an empire, he did."

Bowl Hat slurred, "Codswallop, if you ask me. Once a family falls out of grace, they never recover. Once a worthless fool, always a worthless fool. Back in my day, the Wakefields would not have been allowed to purchase a home in the Upper District. They would have been relegated to the Lowers or the Gorge."

"Or the Stacks!" Rooster Head guffawed.

"Oh, my," Bowl Hat giggled. "You are too cruel, my dear. I love it."

Adelaide changed her mind. She was going to find whole shrimps to throw at that lady's head. Maybe whole pieces of fish. Like a swordfish. Or a whale. As Adelaide searched for inspiration near the buffet, a newcomer approached the front door. Mister Wakefield bustled off in a bluster to welcome him.

Douglas Godwin swept his top hat off his head as he entered. An extravagant coat with far too many buttons decorated the 58-year-old man's frame as he walked with an ornate, decorative cane that was seemingly unneeded for support.

Franklin greeted him and shook his hand. "Mister Godwin! Glad you could make it."

"Please, call me Douglas," he said. "It is heartening to see the Wakefield family back on their feet, as it were."

"Thank you, sir. My father always thought quite highly of you."

"Yes, if only the feeling were mutual. Now, one of these days, you must let me examine your new mining drill. Three heads attached to a locomotive engine, yes?"

Adelaide stood in the doorway. She didn't quite like what she heard over there either. She wondered what kind of

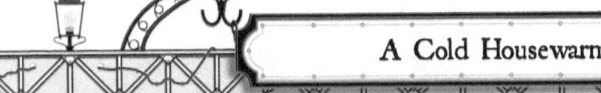
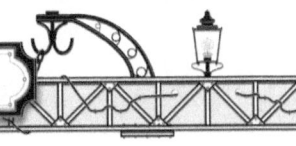

finger foods she could toss in *his* top hat before Luther shuffled past her.

"May I take your hat and coat, sir?" Luther asked Douglas and bowed.

"No need, servant," he replied.

Douglas presented his cane, twisted the middle section, pressed a button, and it extended with the pop of a spring. Three legs clanked open on the bottom; the top half extended upward to head height; and three arms protruded out. He topped the cane rack with his top hat and hung his coat on one of the arms.

"Good show!" Mister Wakefield congratulated with a single clap of applause.

Douglas smiled. "I hope this does not dampen your foyer's ambiance, but one does like to show off new inventions."

Adelaide sprang over to goggle at the cane rack. "Wow! Is that a spring mechanism?"

Douglas looked slightly taken aback by the curious girl. "Oh, um, yes."

"Held in place by..." she studied the cane, "pressure and... screwing the midsection together to hold it down?"

"Yes..."

"The extension is bending under the coat's weight." She pulled on one of the arms. "What kind of metals are you using?"

Mister Wakefield blustered. "Adelaide, where are your manners? Please excuse her. This is my daughter: Adelaide. Adelaide, this is Douglas Godwin, the Dean of Newcomen University's Engineering Department."[15]

"The Engineering Department? Then have you considered using a thicker alloy and a sliding mechanism?" Adelaide's attention quickly shifted back as she interrupted him. "Allow for a higher weight capacity."

---

15 A *Dean* is an administrator in charge of a division of a university or college. They are incredibly important people who collect information, such as: admissions, financials, what's for lunch, when can I go golfing, how many paperclips can I stack to make a perfect replica of my vacation house, etc.

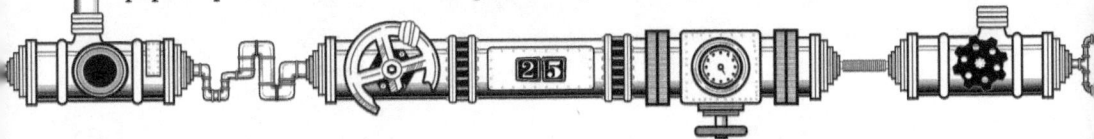

Dean Douglas did not seem pleased with her assessment. The corners of his lips drooped further than his horseshoe mustache.

"My apologies, Douglas," Mister Wakefield said. "My daughter enjoys tinkering with toys, and it looks to be well past her bedtime."

"Is not. Hey, when does the school take new students? I can show my knowledge of engineering. Look." Adelaide extended her mechanical arm and slid her glove down to the wrist. Her arm nub rotated, and the pulley system rotated in accordance with her movements.

Adelaide didn't notice as her presentation got the attention of several nearby guests.

"Built this myself. Steam-powered. I got a pressurized tank and a small generator on my back. Wanna see?" She turned to show him the slight bulge from beneath the back of her dress.

Taking no effort to hide her eavesdropping, Bowl Hat lady gasped, "Oh my." Her wrinkled lips gave a morbid smile as her eyes ravished the scene.

Dean Douglas shook his head. "I believe there has been some misunderstanding, my dear girl. You see, we do not accept female applicants at Newcomen University."

Adelaide stared at him in confusion. The steam generator on her back let out a soft *toot*. One could hear a bowling pin drop in the silence, mostly because bowling pins are large and rather loud when they smash into the floor.

"What do you mean?" Adelaide asked very slowly.

"It is our policy," Dean Douglas replied.

"But why? I don't get it."

Nearby, a haughty-looking gentleman with a horseshoe mustache crossed his arms at the scene and frowned, though that might have just been the horseshoe mustache. Mister Wakefield glanced around at the guests who were taking more than a little notice.

"Adelaide, time for bed," her father attempted to interrupt.

"Do you think girls aren't as smart as boys?" she asked rather loudly as she stepped toward the affronted Dean.

A curly-haired blonde chuckled quietly and tugged on the tuxedo of her husband. "Impertinent," the husband said. Mister Wakefield gave the room a forced smile.

"There are a great many reasons for the traditions at our school," Dean Douglas said.

"Yeah?" Adelaide scoffed. "Well, your traditions are garbage."

"Adelaide!" Mister Wakefield gasped.

Bowl Hat scoffed to Rooster Head. "You see?"

Her father grabbed Adelaide's left hand and pulled her away from the foyer and the affronted, genteel guests to the dark hallway leading toward her bedroom.

"Father! That's a load of horse—"

"You will learn your place, young lady!" He stopped and spun around to face her, bending over until their noses were practically touching. "You will speak only when spoken to. Do you understand me?"

"Why? So the empty suits won't get mad if I ask a question?"

Her father looked away, struggling hard to contain himself. He turned back to her and spoke every word through his teeth. "You will stay in your room and not embarrass me any more tonight! Do I make myself clear?"

Adelaide finally relented their silent stand-off. "Transparent."

"Good."

He pulled her along to her bedroom door. He opened it, pushed her not-too-lightly inside, and closed it behind her. Now, it was Adelaide's turn to grit her teeth and clench her fist. She paced back and forth until she realized something.

She wasn't alone in her room.[16]

---

16 This is what's called a *cliffhanger*, a teaser non-ending that makes you want to read the next chapter immediately. Did it work?

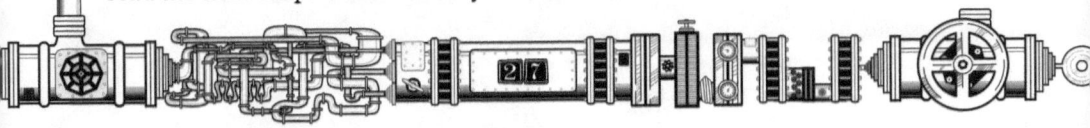

Chapter 3

An Uninvited Guest

hat are you doing? Who are you?" Adelaide spluttered when her voice finally returned. She inadvertently stepped back toward her closed and locked bedroom door.

Zadie held Adelaide's jewelry box creation in her hands and rubbed her finger over the inlays of gold upon the lid.[17] She opened it and looked inside. Her nose wrinkled in confusion. "Thought there might be something good in here, but it's just dirt. Is this where you keep your dirt?" Zadie played with the spring-loaded, mechanical leg popping out of the bottom.

"Put that back," Adelaide said.

"That's gold plating, yeah?" Zadie shrugged. "Guess it's not a complete loss."

---

17 Zadie Stanbury was quite a bit less shocked than Adelaide to find another person in a room in which she thought she was alone, mainly because it wasn't her room and it was quite difficult to shock Zadie in the first place.

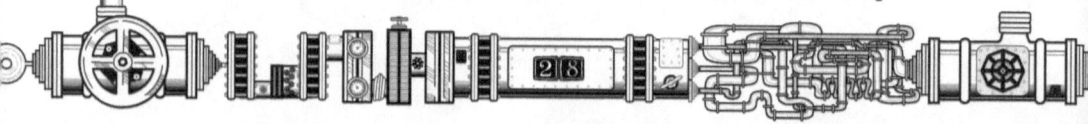

"That's mine!"

Adelaide rushed toward Zadie, who sidestepped and, with a quick snap of her free hand, grabbed Adelaide by the scruff of the neck, used the girl's momentum against her, and tossed her to the floor.

"Don't worry, high class." Zadie smirked. "I'm sure you can buy more."

Adelaide looked up from the floor. "I made it for someone!"

"Well then, you can *make* more."

Adelaide rushed to tackle Zadie again. Zadie tossed her aside again. Adelaide could not get a handle on this girl and was beginning to get tired of feeling the floor, as one does.

"Tell you what," Zadie began as she rummaged through a satchel. "I'll leave you somethin'. You were born with one a' these in your mouth, right?" Zadie pulled out a silver spoon and tossed it on the floor in front of Adelaide. "Take it easy, money bags. Not that you take it any other way."

Zadie strolled to the open window and cast aside her shawl, which Adelaide realized was actually a drapery. In fact, it was Adelaide's drapery. The little thief must have stolen it right off of her window earlier.

Zadie slid her leg over the window frame and hopped out, clearing the small bushes and landing on the lawn outside. Adelaide ran to the window. She watched Zadie skip across the grass. Adelaide's mind reeled, which was a feat since there wasn't much left in there except pain, frustration, rage, and a hint, just a little itty bitty hint, of curiosity.

"Adelaide!" her father's voice was accompanied by a rapping at the door.[18] "Quiet down that ruckus! Go to bed!"

Adelaide's hesitance vanished in an instant. She ripped off her dangling, lacy hat and attempted to exit with grace, but her oversized garments were not her friends. She crashed into the

---

18 Yo yo, I'm Mister Wakefield. I like my 'tatoes peeled. I deal my meals in veal, for real.

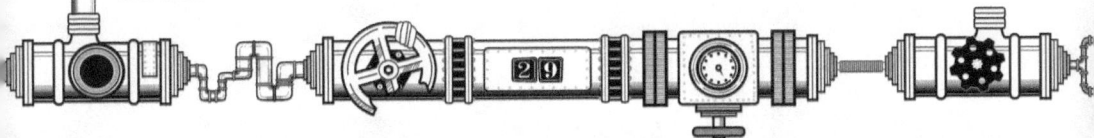

bushes outside her bedroom window, ripping her frilly dress in the process. After trudging and clawing and fighting her way out of the frenzied foliage, Adelaide gave chase.

A fair distance away, Zadie ran to the five-foot-high, brick wall enclosing the property. With a bound and a surprisingly strong pull up maneuver, she climbed over with ease. Adelaide stopped at the base of the wall. Using her good arm, she climbed up with much less ease, scraping her elbow and kicking her feet wildly to gain any sort of momentum that she could.

Adelaide heaved herself over and crashed down onto the sidewalk on the other side. Down the street, Zadie hopped onto the back of a slow-moving horse carriage trotting along the asphalt, away from the Wakefield manor. Zadie glanced back and gave a mock salute.

"Don't try to follow me, baby privilege! You'll only get hurt!"

Adelaide's incredulous look of defeat shifted to determination. She gave chase on foot, dodging the occasional kerfluffled pedestrian.[19] The carriage horses accelerated. Adelaide churned her legs as fast as they could go, but it wasn't fast enough. She jumped onto the rolling belt of a moving sidewalk. The motorized belt wobbled on top of wheels built into the concrete. Her legs found their balance and ran on. Still, she lost ground.

A block ahead, the carriage stopped as a lone street guard with a bright, yellow vest waved the carriage to halt at a massive, multi-street intersection. Colossal gears and mechanisms rested near the corners. Adelaide recognized the place from the day before.

Zadie hopped off the back of the carriage and ran past the idle horses. The lone guard yelled at her, but he wasn't paid enough to do more than that. He did enjoy the yelling

---

19 *Kerfluffled*: to fluffle with extra *ker*.

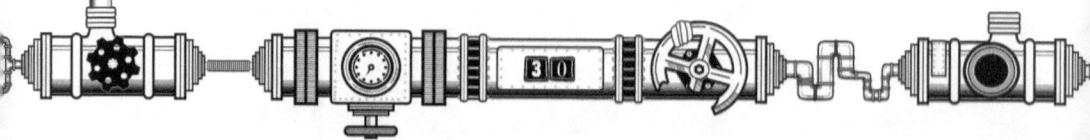

part though. And the waving. Standing around was fine too in decent weather. But the loneliness... the loneliness could get to a man...

Anyways, a tram rolled along the tracks built into the asphalt and came to a stop in the middle of the intersection. Adelaide gained ground and followed the thief into the street. The yellow-vested guard yelled at her too, but he just shrugged and stared at the horsies. Zadie sprinted past the tram. The colossal gears and mechanisms near the corners rattled and spun.

The entire intersection's asphalt center rose up as a geared platform. The outer horizontal teeth of the street section met with the vertical gear teeth of the outer mechanisms. Zadie had no trouble keeping her balance on the rising piece of concrete, Adelaide less so. Lifted above the rest of the street, the intersection rotated in place. Zadie paused and braced herself. Adelaide fell right on her face.[20]

Near the middle of the spinning circle of land, Zadie followed the radius and ran outwards. Near the outer edges, Adelaide made zero progress running in the wrong direction on the moving ground. Zadie hopped off the elevated platform and onto the street below.

The rotation stopped and lowered. The platform's teeth met the ground below and locked in place. The tram rolled off in the opposite direction, and Adelaide finally made it across.

On the sidewalk opposite, Zadie lifted a heavy, metal hatch leading down into the earth itself. She hopped inside the dark abyss and disappeared.

Adelaide caught up and caught the metal hatch just before it hinged back closed into the sidewalk. She grunted and lifted the hatch to peer below. The thought of trudging around the sewers didn't appeal to her, if that's where this led, but she made it this far.

Why not keep the bad ideas rolling?

---

20 Because it's physically impossible to fall left on your face.

Adelaide jumped inside the dark, spooky hole.[21] The hatch closed above her with an ominous clang. Once her eyes adjusted to the darkness, she discovered that she landed in an old, utility tunnel. Further down, a single, sad, flickering light bulb revealed water pipes, steam pipes, and cables running overhead in the circular tunnel formed of concrete. Even further down, the flickering light revealed the back of a thieving, teenage girl. Adelaide gave chase.

The tunnel sloped drastically. Adelaide struggled to keep her footing on the slanting stone, which eventually gave way to soft dirt at an intersection with another tunnel. Much older and much more haphazard, this passage appeared to be an old mining tunnel with cart rails traversing the middle. Not only was it clear that any sort of mining operations in the past had stopped long ago, it was clear that the present generation adapted the tunnels to their own devices. Steam and water pipes ran vertically, horizontally, diagonally, parallelelly, and even grammatically all over the place.[22] Generators along the walls whirred, hissed, and tooted.

Down the way, Zadie held onto the back of a motionless, metal, mining cart. The old wheels had rusted so much onto the rails that it looked like they were made of orange stone. Adelaide slowed at the sight of Zadie and used the chance to catch her breath. Her sides burned, but she was happy to see that the thief had to catch her breath as well, though her breathing difficulty was only a fraction of Adelaide's.

"Give..." Adelaide panted, "it... back..."

Zadie smiled. "Still followin' me? You ever even been down here before, rich girl?"

"Give it ba—"

---

21 Kids, when someone tries to trick you into a dark, spooky hole, ask if they have candy first.

22 Did you look up how a pipe could run grammatically? Because I'm not quite sure how to picture that either.

Zadie didn't wait to hear Adelaide's wish list and sprinted away yet again. After a few steps of running momentum, Zadie jumped onto the mining cart rails. In between the heels and balls of her feet, Zadie's shoes had a metal concavity built in, allowing her to grind on the rail down the slope.

The incline leveled out, and Zadie sprinted onwards with her significant advantage as Adelaide struggled to keep up with her stupid, normal shoes. The metal rails led right into an opening in the wall. Wooden frames built into the earth revealed an open elevator shaft. A rickety, old, metal lift waited within. It did not look safe or operable in the slightest.

Zadie jumped right in and kicked an ancient, rusted lever built into the floor. The lift groaned. The floor shook. Finally, it dropped free a foot before it lowered at a steady pace.

Adelaide ran down the slope and caught sight of the open elevator just as it dipped Zadie's head below the level of the floor. Adelaide closed the distance as the elevator disappeared. She braced herself on the wooden frame of the open shaft. She watched as the lowering lift descended into the earth. For the eleventh time tonight, Adelaide decided not to think about her actions first. She jumped into the shaft.

Her feet landed on top of the elevator as it clacked and screeched down. Zadie jumped in surprise and looked up. Only a rusted-but-still-rather-strong metal grate comprising the elevator's ceiling separated them. Also, Zadie's viewpoint gazed right up Adelaide's dirty dress.

Zadie chuckled. "I see Parsons. I see Fort Lance. I can see your underpants."

"I'm wearing pants," Adelaide replied dryly.

"Wait, really?" Zadie craned her neck for a better look.

"Would you..." Adelaide blustered and gathered her dress. "Just... give it back!"

Adelaide shoved her good hand through the metal grate, reaching for Zadie's face. She was a good two feet short. Zadie just smiled and stared up.

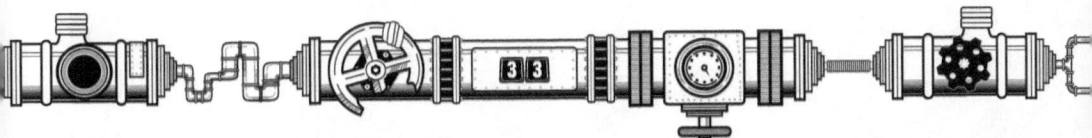

"Why is this empty box so important to you?"

"It's all I have left of her!"

Zadie chuckled. "Guess not anymore."

Adelaide growled and ripped off the white glove covering her mechanical hand. Her right arm nub lowered, and her metal arm followed the movements with its pistons and levers. Her good hand unfolded a metal lever tucked into her forearm until it was perpendicular to her elbow. She shifted the lever forward to her wrist.

Air hissed out of the small, steam generator on her back. Spinning motors vibrated her entire torso beneath her torn dress. A puff of steam issued from an exhaust vent just below her collar. Air pressure flowed into the pipes and tubes lining her mechanical arm.

Adelaide straightened out the arm and used the guide lever to aim the closed, metal fist toward an opening in the ceiling grate.

"What is that?" Zadie asked.

The hissing and whirring stopped, indicating the air pressure was at maximum. Her good thumb pressed the button on the end of the guide lever.

In an explosion of steam-powered propulsion, her metal hand shot out of her arm like a rocket, trailing a cable behind its wake. Adelaide's aim was off, and Zadie also dodged backwards. The flying hand missed her by several inches.

"Is that a metal hand?" Zadie chuckled. "You got a metal hand?!" Zadie snorted as the trailing cable looped and spun down behind it, helplessly spooling everywhere. The cable finally stopped at the end of its length. "You need to work on your aim, rich girl." Zadie grabbed the loose cable trailing from Adelaide's arm. "I'll admit though, that is a neat trick."

She yanked the cable down, hard. Adelaide's entire body slammed down onto the metal grate. Her head bonked off some rust in a cloud of red dust. Her bushy, red hair didn't soften the blow in the slightest.

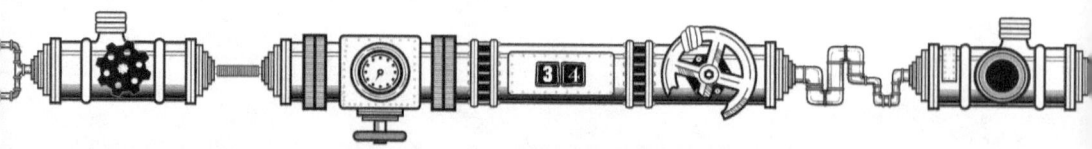

The lift cleared the entrance to the bottom floor. Zadie hopped off into the earthy tunnel before the elevator stopped. The lift clanged, caught itself on a chunk of unaligned shaft, and tilted alarmingly to the side. Adelaide's eyes widened as she slid a few inches along the top. Then the elevator remembered where the floor was and scraped back into place at the bottom.

The top of the lift had three feet of clearance with the tunnel's ceiling, which Adelaide recognized immediately. What she didn't recognize as she jumped off the lift and into the tunnel below was that her mechanical hand was still disconnected and inside the lift's car. Adelaide's arm cable followed the leader, and the hand zipped up inside. At least, it zipped for a while.

Adelaide sprinted off down the tunnel after Zadie. Her mechanical wrist joint caught on the metal grate built into the lift's ceiling. Her arm's momentum came to an abrupt halt while feet and legs kept going forward. Her feet flipped so hard that her shoes almost flew off. After floating parallel to the floor for a surprised moment, Adelaide was yanked back down hard into the dirt. Naturally, the sharp reaction snapped the hand free of the lift's grate. Even more naturally, Adelaide thought, her hand sailed through the air, took a few gracious-yet-completely-unnecessary somersaults, and flew right back toward her face. Luckily, Adelaide's fleshy hand was able to catch her metal hand in the most curious case of a *self high-five* that's ever been recorded in Parsons City.[23]

Adelaide shifted her mechanical forearm's guide lever back toward her elbow and folded it down. The cable retracted inside the arm. She locked the metal hand back into place before

---

23 At least, officially. Unofficially, the most curious case of the *self high-five* was, of course, the scientist, Walmenowitz Barnes, who invented time travel and broke the space-time continuum simply to give himself a high-five from his future self to his present self over a particularly bad joke that no one else enjoyed at the time. Immediately afterward, he and all those in attendance were violently disintegrated in a space-time collapse, thereby destroying all knowledge of time travel and of this particular event in question.

slowly rising to her feet on top of the long-abandoned mining cart rails buried in the dirt. She shuffled along to an intersection with another tunnel, giving her three directions to go and no idea where Zadie had run off, except for the fact that Zadie was waiting at the end of the left tunnel.

Zadie smiled and disappeared down the far intersection. Adelaide followed, barely remembering why she was doing so in the first place. She gazed at the haphazard tunnels of dirt with wooden beam supports strewn about. Adelaide couldn't help but be perplexed at the engineering behind these utility tunnels carved deep into the earth.

Occasionally, a metal pipe venting steam or some other gas that was jutting out of the wall would make a turn after a few feet and stick right back into the wall again. Other times, pipes and cables and all sorts of metal nonsense would travel from one wall to the other, whether along the ceiling, the floor, or every which way in between.

Adelaide ducked under and stepped over a strange pipe duo crossing the tunnel. Zadie stood at the tunnel's end, waiting for her. As Adelaide came closer, she realized the tunnel's end didn't end so much as it dropped into a hole in the floor. Sounds of r water echoed below.

"Ever been to a water park?" Zadie smiled.

"Do you actually want me to keep chasing you?"

"Well, sure! Isn't this fun?"

Adelaide wasn't sure how to respond. She didn't want to even think about such a ludicrous idea, mostly because, deep down, she thought it actually was.

Before Adelaide could approach within striking distance, Zadie jumped into the dark hole. Adelaide peered inside. She could only see minor details from the flickering lights along the walls in the tunnel above. It looked like a metal trough with a fast current of shallow water rushing down a slope.

Zadie expertly balanced on her feet and slid down the current, out of sight. Adelaide jumped. Unlike Zadie,

Adelaide quite inexpertly slipped onto her rear and flew down the trough on her back with her feet in the air. Her momentum was out of control. In fact, if she wasn't completely terrified, she would have been having a great time. The trough twisted and turned and topsyed and turvyed and, little did Adelaide know, ended abruptly with a steep drop into a massive chamber.

Zadie was ready for the drop, in more ways than one. She jumped off the end and grabbed onto a metal chain hanging from the ceiling. It was almost as if someone put that there specifically for this purpose, mostly because Zadie did put it there on purpose earlier. In a well-practiced maneuver, she swung over the empty space and hopped off onto a raised platform on the side of the tall chamber.

Unlike Zadie, Adelaide flew out of the pipe and dropped three stories into five feet of water. She clonked onto the metal channel's bottom and swirled along the waterfall current. Disoriented, Adelaide reached the surface and gasped for air.

Multiple pipes poured streams of water into the basin from varying heights in the four-story chamber. It all funneled down into a singular pipe at the bottom that the current was now pulling her toward. She was glad the water down here was warm, at least, though she tried not to think of why. There were too many answers to that question that she did not enjoy.

Three stories up, Zadie glanced down from the metal platform to the girl floundering in the water and called, "Hey! Can you swim?! If you can't, I'm sorry 'bout killin' you and all! Didn't mean to!" She saluted and exited the chamber.

Adelaide spit out a mouthful of water. She could swim, in fact, but the ripped, lacy dress and skeletal, mechanical arm and bulky, generator backpack was not helping her case. She flailed around as the current pushed her down toward the exit pipe. The liquid churned around a thirty-foot-tall water wheel built into the side of the wall beside the platform.

Adelaide finally found her bearings. They were inside her head all along. It didn't help that the sources of illumination for

the entire chamber were a collection of lone bulbs hanging by wires from the ceiling, and Zadie's chain swinging shenanigans had sent them twirling. The pendulums of poor lights were rather disorienting.[24]

Adelaide squirmed, kicked, and used the swirling, confused currents to her advantage. Floundering to the water wheel, her good hand attempted to grab the slippery surface, but the paddles smacked her back. The water swallowed her again before she trout-kicked back over.

This time, Adelaide let herself fall in the water a bit so her good hand could work her chest's control panel. Her mechanical hand reached out and grasped onto the wheel with a vice-like grip. The metal phalanges dug into the thick wood as it rose into the air. Her straps and chest harness pulled the rest of her along as her hand held through the curve. The wheel turned up, and the water splattered down.

As she reached the apex, Adelaide blinked her eyes enough to spot the platform Zadie had previously been standing on. Adelaide slipped on the paddles, adjusted, then skipped and jumped her way onto the metal platform.

After pushing herself up and sweeping her not-so-bushy-anymore hair out of her face, she trudged along to the only tunnel connected to the platform. This one was formed out of concrete. If the engineers had the proper equipment, it might have even been somewhat circular, but the bumpy and lumpy cylinder served its purpose well enough, she guessed.

She wasn't sure why she was so judgmental over the little things like that. Shoddy builds were a particular kind of pet peeve for Adelaide. Why would you spend all that time and money on making something only for it to be a big 'ole shiny turd? She suspected a lot of this animosity came from her

---

24 Although, the copper-wire bulbs felt the whole experience was rather fun and thought, "*Wheee!*"

father's work. Her ideas on improving his train engine designs, for example, no matter if they were more coal efficient or safer, were always shot down because of either her age or because it was more expensive. But she wasn't bitter about that. Nope. Noooo. Not at alllll. Nope nope nope nope... nope.

It didn't take Adelaide long to come upon an intersection with another identical tunnel. Her eyes scanned two empty tunnels before they found the bemused form of Zadie waiting down the third. The young thief smiled and tilted her head toward another intersection at the end of that tunnel. She disappeared down it.

Adelaide followed. After that intersection, Zadie led her to another intersection. And another. This one had pipes crisscrossing over the entirety of the tunnel. The girls ducked and crawled through the webs of pipes. Zadie wasn't even attempting to run anymore, most likely because Adelaide could barely accelerate faster than a llama with narcolepsy.

Zadie slithered over a four-foot pipe at waist height and then took a sharp left. A hole in the wall, right next to the pipe, led inside and down. It looked like someone had a very cathartic day with a sledgehammer on that spot. The hole was in such an odd place, Adelaide was sure she would have missed it if she hadn't seen Zadie crawl over and inside.

The wet girl incidentally gathered clumps of dirty mud onto her frilly dress by plopping into the hole. Cables upon cables and pipes upon pipes melded overhead. This makeshift, emergency, utility tunnel was clearly not in the original designs and nearly pitch-black. Bent over, Zadie squished her way down and up through an opening on the other side. Adelaide fully caked herself with mud before squeezing out the other small exit.

This opened into a previously thought-out, concrete tunnel. Steam pipes hissed and vented overhead. The entire area had a hazy, humid weight to it.

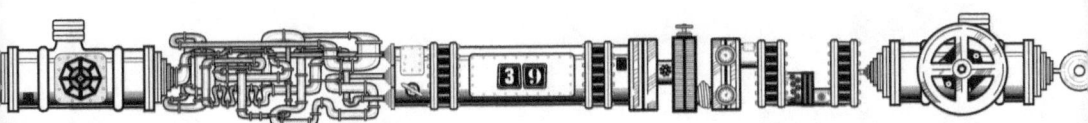

Zadie brushed herself off and skipped ahead. After a short distance, the tunnel opened into a partially illuminated, gigantic, five-story chamber serving as an intersection of steam pipes. Massive machines built into the walls and bolted to the floor whirred, clanked, and issued forth puffs of heated air. One of the generators built into the wall hummed before it shook violently. It clonked and bonked and coughed out a toot of black smoke. Then it went back to humming contentedly.

"We're almost there," Zadie said.

"Almost where?"

As Adelaide stood at the entrance, staring blankly at the assortment of machines that might have served some purpose, Zadie stepped toward one such generator standing stoically and tooting out steam two rows in. It contained, among other things, the end of a long, metal cable. It wrapped around itself in a small loop. The cable extended far overhead and seemed to go up for four or five stories. It was hard to see from the bottom of the chamber with the limited, copper wire, lamp lighting, but overhead, a much brighter source of illumination poured from a platform near the ceiling.

Zadie inserted her foot into the cable's end loop and tugged on it hard. A motor overhead whirred and retracted the cable, pulling Zadie along with it up high into the chamber. Adelaide staggered over to where the thief was moments before.

From the silhouette, it looked like a small crane arm pulled her up to that platform with the lights two stories above even the tallest machine on the floor of the huge chamber. Whatever that platform was, it appeared to be attached to three of the walls and jutted out nearly halfway across the entire chamber before ending abruptly, leaving the beleaguered, fourth wall out of whatever festivities were happening up there. If walls could talk, it would probably be

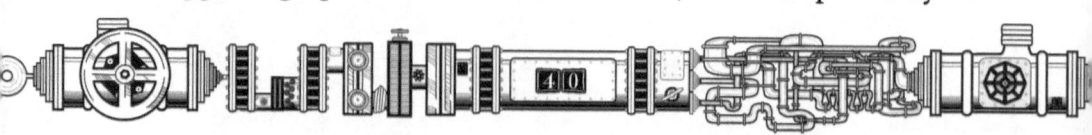

quite cross at not being included in all the fun with the other three.

Adelaide's left hand worked her mechanical arm. She wasn't sure if she was supposed to wait for the cable to return or climb up herself, but she had something better anyhow. Her hand withdrew the forearm lever and twisted the cylinder clockwise. The metal fingers clanked outwards, bending and locking in the shape of hooks pointing back to her arm. Air pressure flooded the tubes as she shifted the lever forward. She aimed. Her thumb jammed the button.

Her mechanical hand fired upwards through an explosion of air pressure. The hook-like fingers sailed over the platform before falling down and catching the ledge. Adelaide pulled on the cable to make sure her grappling hook hand was secure before she shifted the guide lever back toward her elbow. Her arm cable retracted, pulling her entire body up into the air. Her droopy and drippy and limp body swung back and forth as her altitude increased.

As she got closer, she could see the platform was a giant, metal grate much like the one in the water wheel chamber, but this one was far larger and had some sort of padding on top, masking and covering all the openings. The bright lights were almost blinding after racing through the poorly lit tunnels for who-knows-how-long-now.

Her arm cable retracted into her wrist. She was still dangling precariously, so Adelaide's good arm reached over the platform. Her elbow pushed until both she and her wet dress flopped over. Battered, bruised, soaked, exhausted, but determined, Adelaide turned to face the thief.

What she found was four sets of eyes staring back at her.[25]

---

25 I know I used that ending for the last chapter, but hey! Look over there! ➡

Chapter 4

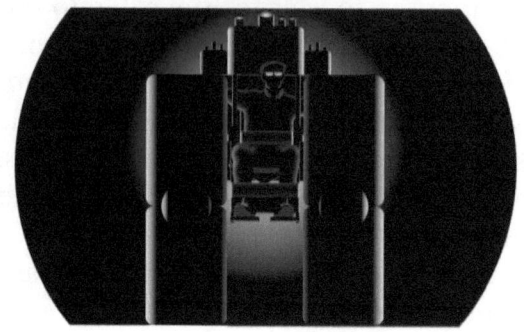

The Steampunks

Adelaide wasn't sure what she was expecting, but it was definitely not this. The other people on the platform were not sure what they were expecting when they heard Zadie generating a ruckus below, but it was definitely not an intruder able to reel up to their hideout through a hooked, mechanical arm. The only one who remained unsurprised was Zadie, who was quietly laughing to herself.

The giant, metal platform was welded into the wall and suspended from the ceiling near the top of the massive, five-story chamber. Unlike the previous platform, this one was decorated to the max. Carpets, rugs, and various scraps of reclaimed wood covered the floor, giving it a somewhat cozier existence. Couches, chairs, tables, desks, devices, lamps, and suspended hammocks covered the rest of the area in a makeshift, scavenged sort of home. Clusters of stringed, light bulbs and bulbed, light strings crisscrossed and crosscrissed all overhead.

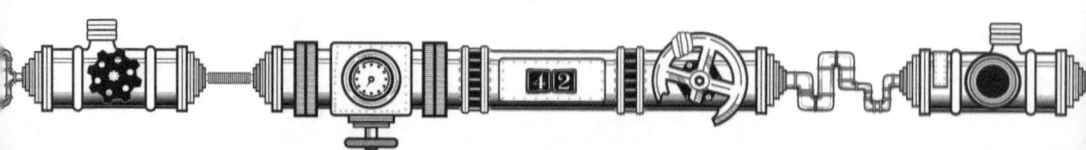

Zadie was sitting in a plush, somewhat-fuzzy, cushioned chair. She leaned back and put her feet up on a small, overturned garbage can. An amused sigh escaped her lips.

"I gotta admit," Zadie admitted, "that was pretty smokin'. Did you build that?" She pointed at Adelaide's mechanical appendage.

Adelaide struggled to her feet. "Yeah, just like I built that box you stole from me."

"Hmm, well, look on the bright side," Zadie shrugged, "at least I didn't steal your arm. That'd probably fetch a fine price."

"Why don't you come over here and try it?" Adelaide twisted her metal forearm's guide lever counter-clockwise. The wrist rotated and locked the hand in place. The hook fingers clanked back into normal phalange formation.

"Zadie?" a soft voice spoke. Neither girl noticed.

"Nah, I don't feel the need to kick a cripple when she's crippled."

"That's a rude term," Adelaide scolded.

"I'm a rude person."

"You shouldn't label people by what they can't do."

"Yeah?" Zadie smirked. "Wanna challenge me to a pull-up contest?"

"Zadie?" the soft voice spoke again. Neither girl noticed again.

"Are you *trying* to be a terrible person?" Adelaide asked.

"I don't have to *try* at anything," Zadie said.

Seeing the smirking thief emboldened the wet, beaten, and exhausted Adelaide even further. She stomped right up to the reclining trickster.

"Give. It. Back." Adelaide demanded.

Almost before Adelaide had even finished, Zadie withdrew the stolen jewelry box from her satchel and tossed it at her. Adelaide caught it against her chest with her good hand.

"Here, you earned it," Zadie said.

Adelaide studied the jewelry box to make sure it was undamaged. Aside from some scratches and scuffs, which she wasn't confident that weren't already there to begin with, she was surprisingly satisfied with the condition. After all, it was much less soaked in strange water than she was. Adelaide crutched the box in the crook of her metal arm to secure it.

"Zadie!" the voice from the side yelled, which finally got everyone's attention.

Adelaide turned to see the three other faces staring at her, not all of which were smiling like Zadie, especially not the young, blond-haired boy of fourteen who went by the name of Baxter Forge. He absentmindedly adjusted the goggles squished against his brow as he shook his head in confusion and shock at the two girls.

"What the frack is this?" he asked.

The third girl in the mix and the second one of the unmet three was the one named Harriet Ashdown.[26] She giggled. Fifteen years of age, she brushed back her perfectly-curled, brown hair as she dangled her legs off the picnic table she was sitting on.

"Are you going to introduce us? Or shall we just start making guesses?" Harriet snorted.

"It'd be as good as mine." Zadie shrugged. "I don't know who she is either."

"And you just let her strut into our hideout?!" Baxter's head steamed.

"Technically, she zip-lined," Harriet thought aloud. "Or was it reeled? Grappled?"

"Is the right word important right now?" Baxter blustered. "Hello? Guys? We have an intruder! Sound the alarm! Man the battle stations! Jules, help me out here, man!"

---

26 Maths is confusing. It's also confusing if it's *maths* or *math*. You'd think all those smarty pants could figure out if it was supposed to be plural or not. Much like this book series' title.

The last member of the surprised group on the platform leaned back against the wall with his arms crossed. The eyes of the silent guardian studied Adelaide from behind his full face mask. It was difficult to tell his age behind the coverings, but the young man in his late teen years had youthful, long, black hair hanging over thick goggles with dark lenses. Deep scars mangled his visible left ear. A concoction of part gas mask, part bandana covered his nose, mouth, and neck. It looked like a device of his own design, as though a gas mask was not enough coverage for him, so he sewed and attached until he was properly hidden.

"Well?" Baxter implored him.

Jules looked in Baxter's direction and gave a half-hearted shrug.

Baxter blustered out a frustrated, "Gah! Am I the only one who thinks this is a problem? It's called a *secret* hideout for a reason!"

"Oh, was it a secret?" Harriet smiled at Baxter's continued annoyance. "I probably shouldn't have put up all those flyers giving directions then, huh?"

"Harriet!" Baxter harrumphed. He looked away from her, attempting to brush her off, before his paranoia got the better of him. "You didn't... *actually* do that, did you?"

Harriet laughed in his face. Baxter turned around and dove face-first onto a crusty, brown couch. He shoved a stained, half-frilly pillow over the back of his head.

"Do you guys like... live here?" Adelaide asked the room at large.

Zadie scooted down into her chair and clasped her hands behind her head. "Free from all rules, laws, and oppression. We do what we like, when we like."

"In the sewer?"

"In the steam tunnels, ya snob hob. This is where the power of Parsons City is generated. Can't you feel it in the air?"

Adelaide could certainly feel the warmth and the moisture in the air along with faint vibrations coming from the vast

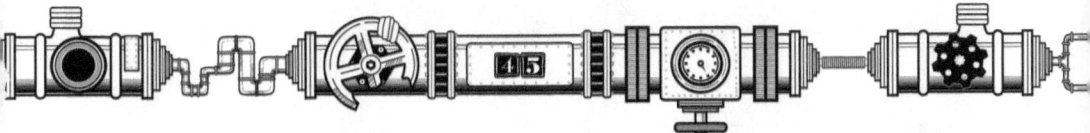

amount of generators in front of and behind the walls and ceiling and floor all around them. She couldn't imagine anyone wanting to actually stay in this industrial sauna.

"Being this is where the actual work gets done in the down and dirty city," Zadie continued, "naturally, no one wants to come down here."

"The poor girl looks exhausted," Harriet chimed in. "Do you want to spend the night?"

Baxter jerked up off the couch. "Harriet!"

Adelaide stared at them all in surprise and confusion. "I'd rather not spend the night with a bunch of thieves, thank you very much." She turned away.

"Then you won't want to go back to your parents' place," Zadie said.

Adelaide stopped and turned back. "What's that supposed to mean?"

"You don't get rich by doing honest work. You get rich by stealing. If not overt like me, then more stealthy-like." She wiggled her fingers like they were possessed by ghosts.

"You don't know what you're talking about." Adelaide shuffled and then pointed her nose at Zadie. "*Goodbye!* Or... well... I would say 'goodbye,' but I don't mean 'goodbye.' I hope it's a *bad* bye. Because you're a thief. Who stole from me. *Badbye*, I say!"

Adelaide stepped away from Zadie. She glanced around, searching for an exit. The platform connected to three separate tunnels. She picked the closest and marched inside.

Concrete foundations fortified this curved passageway. Dangling, small, and rather pathetic filament light bulbs burned sparsely overhead. The wires connecting them were frayed and liable to fall apart at any moment. Adelaide followed the wires, hoping they'd lead somewhere, which they did. The wires went through the wall over a heavy, closed door. Adelaide had to shove her entire weight against it just to creak it open a crack.

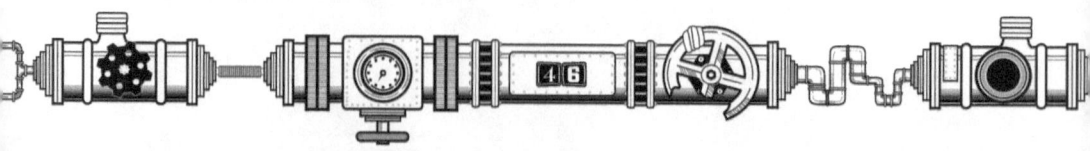

The sound of generators thundered even louder here. And sure enough, after two more heavy doors and a stairwell leading down, she came upon a bank of the ten-foot blocks of chugging machines. The old, well-worn steam pipes, venting out the spare exhaust, warmed up the room to a near unbearable degree. When she had a moment to think in between gasping for breathable air, Adelaide was more upset at the old, lackluster, poorly-maintained engineering of the place than the high temperatures. She quickened her pace out of there as she felt her soaked dress start to steam itself dry, even as her skin sweat more moisture onto it.[27]

Adelaide didn't much pay attention to where she was going while she was wiping sweat off her forehead and brushing back her matted hair. Anywhere that was cooler was bound to be an improvement. This tunnel curved around and seemed to slope upwards. She hoped it might eventually slope all the way to the surface. More heavy doors built into the sides led to places beyond. All of them were locked. Adelaide trudged on past.

Finally, she could see light at the end of the tunnel. A lot of light. And voices. And... couches? It wasn't until her foot landed on a crusty rug that the bleary-eyed girl realized where she was. Adelaide had made a full circle to stare at the faces of the thief and her friends once again. Her exiting tunnel was not even the one she had initially started down.

"Bugger," Adelaide sighed under her breath.

"Hi again!" Harriet beamed.

Zadie laughed. "You want some help, silver spoon?"

"Not from you," Adelaide grunted and blustered.

She trudged down the third tunnel, sure that this was the actual way out. Her surety didn't last long. The curved, concrete passageway looked the same as the others, but it contained a vast collection of pipes running overhead, sidehead, underhead, and

---

27 Her dress didn't literally steam itself dry. She clearly obviously wasn't actually literally adverbily boiling.

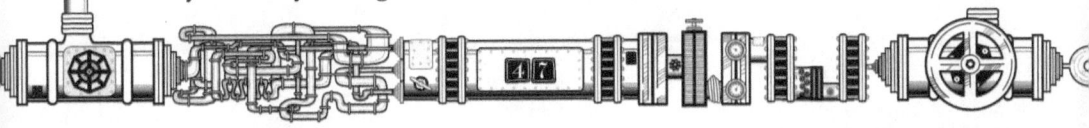

all the other heads. It made for such a confusing hydra, she thought it would be all too easy to lose her bearings in here.

She ducked under a low-hanging bundle of pipes going across. She sidestepped pipes running diagonally. She started climbing over a large one traveling two feet off the ground, but the heated metal burned her fingers to the touch. Steam hissed from a junction between that pipe and another. Adelaide did her best to hop over without touching it. Her best tripped her feet and landed her rear on the pipe's other side.

Shortly thereafter, a three-way intersection greeted her. All of the pipes leading from all of the ways joined together in an overloaded junction of engineered nonsense. Valves, gauges, levers, and, for some reason, ropes gathered together in the middle of the junction for a meeting of the mechanical minds. Adelaide tried counting all of the gauges and valves monitoring the bundles of metal. It was more than a few but less than a bushel.[28]

All of the gauges were running hot. The little needles bouncing over the half circles were far from the green good zone on the left and were dancing along the red bad zone on the right. In the dim light, Adelaide's eyes followed the very hot pipe from the floor on to its gauged intersection. That needle was slowly rising to the very end. Before she thought any more, it maxed out. A piercing whistle exploded from the pipe's junction over her head. The seal joining the two pipes together ruptured. Steam whistled out in a rush of boiling air.

Adelaide ducked to the ground to get away from it. While this junction was new to her, she understood the basic concepts. Without thinking, her hand started turning valves. The pressure lowered. She yanked on some levers to redirect

---

28 A bushel is equal to four pecks. A peck is what birds do to your head when you don't compliment their feathers.

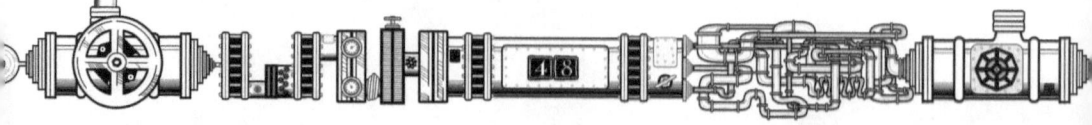

the stream. She turned more valves. The piercing whistle lessened to a warm raspberry as though the ruptured joint had a tongue it was sticking out at her.

"Tarnation!" a voice yelled from down the tunnel.

Far down the dark, winding intersection, a massive shape appeared around the bend. Two monstrous, colossal arms supported the lumpy, square shape and clomped its way down the tunnel. Adelaide stumbled and fell on the ground as the monster enclosed upon her. Adelaide's eyes snapped closed of their own accord. By the time she could force open a slit for a peek, the monster was so close that she could look at its face. Its head bumped into the sad, swinging light bulb dangling from the ceiling. Its monstrous face looked just like... a normal old man?

The tough and grizzled and barely-shaved face of the seventy-two-year-old fellow analyzed the whistling steam pipe. He sat in a chair harness supporting his frail, skinny, withered legs. Attached to the harness was a pair of gargantuan, mechanical, gorilla-like arms, which comprised the shape that frightened Adelaide.

The old man used those huge arms to traverse distances like a metal primate. His bulky, muscled, human arms reached inside the metal arm skeletons to control the movements from within. He didn't need his frail legs dangling from the chair harness to move him about at all, which probably worked for the best since it appeared as though he couldn't stand. Turned out, he couldn't stand a lot of things.

He swung himself up onto the higher pipes. His human arm snaked out from behind his arm harness and yanked on a release valve on the tunnel pipe junction. Just as Adelaide was wondering why he wouldn't have mechanical legs to walk around instead of mechanical arms to lumber around, his eyes snapped back to Adelaide.

"What did ye do to this, eh?!" he yelled. "What did ye break?!"

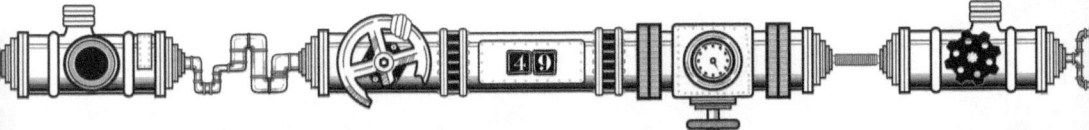

"I... I..." she began, "I didn't..."

A piercing whistle exploded from a second pipe's junction over their heads as a seal joining those two pipes together ruptured.

"Conflabbit!"

The frightening man turned his attention to his newest threat. Adelaide took that as her opportunity to run in the opposite direction. Her adrenaline allowed her to easily hop over the floor pipe this time. It wasn't until she reached the end of the tunnel that she realized her error. She should have run the other way. Because now, she was right back where she started. Again.

Adelaide stared into the faces of the thief and her friends. She was at a loss for words as she stood, once again, on the crusty rugs topping the platform hideout.

"I... uh..." she began.

An earthshaking, clomping noise thundered down the tunnel. Adelaide ducked as the old man launched himself up and over the girl. He swung up over the furniture and string lights and kids. His monstrous arms grappled onto the pipes overhead and pulled him to a breaker box suspended above the floor five stories below. His human hands and metal appendages quickly began turning controls and flipping switches and pulling levers and pushing buttons and tapping and rapping and scrapping all along the many machines and gears and devices around the chamber. His movements were seamless between swinging around, one arm holding his entire harness up, and then his other metal hand or both human hands manipulating all the controls. Adelaide realized why he used mechanical arms instead of legs.

"Darn punks!" he blustered out to no one in particular. "Messin' with me babies."

"We didn't do nothin', you old coot!" Zadie yelled at him.

"Oh yeah?!"

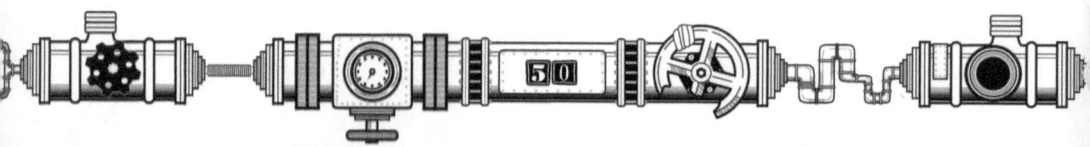

He pulled on a release valve wheel and swung himself over to the platform. His monstrous metal arms clanked onto the floor. The entire platform shook under the sudden and sharp increase in weight. He stared at Zadie in the eyes. She stared right back.

"What about this one?" he asked.

He snapped his head to Adelaide and approached. His chair harness was imperfectly balanced as his monstrous arms jiggled and shook everything on their way over.

"What did ye do to me babies?"

"Your..." Adelaide's confusion made her hesitate. "What?"

"Why did junction four-two whistle in pain?"

"They're steam pipes," Zadie replied for her. "They do that."

"Looked like it overheated," Adelaide replied for herself. "Popped a gasket, I think. I shut down the pipe, redirected the flow, and adjusted the exhausts for the others. Looked like no one had maintained the ratios in quite a while."

"I do the maintenance in these tunnels!" he shouted in her face.

"Not very well then." The words slipped out of Adelaide's mouth before she realized what she was saying. Her face sunk into the bottoms of sheepish legend. Her wide eyes stared into his wild pupils. His gritty face gritted his teeth.

"Ha!" he blustered as a smile erupted on his face. "Too true, that!"

He guffawed with such gusto that Adelaide was taken aback. In fact, at this point, she was so aback from the entire night that she nearly went full circle into being taken afront.

He glanced back at Zadie. "So what's this one about, eh? Pick up another troublemaker to clog up the place? Another punk in me steam tunnels?"

"They aren't your steam tunnels, old coot," Zadie replied.

"Bah!"

"I'm just trying to get back home," Adelaide sighed.

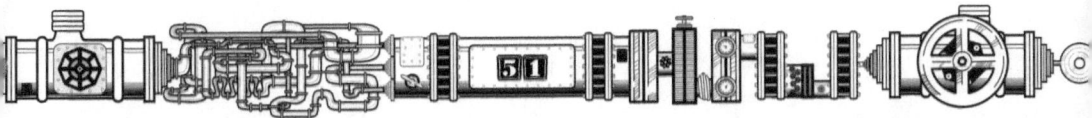

"Oh, and what's this?" The old man's massive metal hand pointed at Adelaide's much smaller metal appendage.

He towered over her, but this time, not in an intimidating way. His eyes darted over her creation and studied her arm.

"Pistons..." he mumbled as he went along, "counterbalanced... extensions... generator?"

"Umm..." Adelaide began, "steam pack."

She pointed to her back and the pack protruding from beneath her dress. The old man nonchalantly and non-gently pushed her over to get a better look. He studied the parts poking out by her neck. She couldn't help but crane her neck around to try and look at his own backpack generator. Compared to Adelaide's, it was massive. He probably needed those colossal arms just to lift the heavy thing off the ground.

"Recessed exhaust," he analyzed. "Compact size. Highly efficient. Manufacturer?"

"Umm... me."

"Ohhhhh," he pushed them both straight up and looked her in the eyes. "And you are?"

"Adelaide. Adelaide Wakefield."

Harriet nudged Baxter in the ribs. "I would have guessed she looked like an Adelaide."

"Oh yeah," Baxter rubbed his side, "me too."

"Phineas Vinge," the old man said. "A pleasure to make yer acquaintance."

His human hand tipped an imaginary top hat. With one metal arm holding his entire frame above the floor, he put his human hand into the other metal arm and grabbed onto Adelaide's metal hand. An unusual, grinding handshake ensued.

He leaned in to speak in her ear, "Don't touch anything else." Phineas turned away, and his massive arms swung himself off the platform and down below into the chamber.

After a moment, Adelaide's thoughts caught up to her mouth. "Wait!" she called down to him. "Can you show me the way out?!"

He paused at the entrance to a tunnel five stories below. "I'm workin'! Ye got yerself down here! Find yer own way out!" He turned and disappeared down the tunnel.

Adelaide sighed. She stood straight and took a deep breath before looking back at the other teenagers around her.

"I'll help you find your way back home in the mornin', genteel," Zadie said. She leaned back in her plush, incredibly old recliner. The chair's back cracked and flopped backwards. A metal spring within plucked and vibrated loudly. Zadie put her feet back up on the garbage can ottoman and closed her eyes.[29]

Adelaide's toe tapped in her shoe. Her courage rose up in her throat. "Now," Adelaide declared. "You'll help me now."

Zadie's eyes cracked open. She smirked at her. "Nope. It's late. I'm gonna find a sleep. You should do the same." Zadie adjusted herself and scooted down in the chair. She slid her hat down over her eyes. Within five seconds, she started snoring.

Adelaide turned to find Harriet's face directly next to hers and jumped in surprise.

"I wish I could do that," Harriet said. "Always takes me forever to get to sleep."

Adelaide found her heart and put it back in her chest.

"Oh!" Harriet continued. "You can take Zadie's bed! She never sleeps in it anyways. Clearly. Even though I made one 'specially for her. With *my own hands*!" Her last words were pointedly thrown at Zadie, who continued to snore. Harriet shrugged at Adelaide. "Well, stolen with my own hands, you know what I mean? But still, it's the thought that counts."

Harriet directed Adelaide's gaze to the four, ratty, cloth hammocks suspended by chains off the platform, dangling forty

---

29 Technically, anything is an ottoman if you put your feet on it. That's why the empire lasted so long.

feet above the ground. Jules leaned back in one, seemingly comfortable and completely at ease in the swinging bed.

"I'm Harriet, by the way."

Harriet's right hand awkwardly tried to shake Adelaide's metal right arm. The effect was much like someone using an old-timey water pump to fill up a jug.

"Adelaide."

"The talkative one is Jules." Harriet pointed out the relaxed fellow with the face mask. "Mister Grumpypuss over there is Baxter."

Baxter sat on the table with his arms crossed. His cheeks warmed up to bright red. He responded by blowing a raspberry at her.

"And you've already met Zadie." Harriet nodded to the snoring thief in the chair. "And this is the Steampunks Hideout,"[30] she continued. "Not much, but it's home."

"Steam what?" Adelaide asked.

"Punks of the steam tunnels, they call us. So we just leaned into it, you know?"

"Who calls you that?"

"Everyone really." Harriet shrugged. "I think one of the other gangs started it."

"Other gangs?"

"Sure."

"So you're a gang?" Adelaide glanced at the teenagers.

"Sure." Harriet shrugged again. "Depends on your definition of gang, really. It's really a broad term, you know? Zadie keeps telling everyone our gang name is the Grinders, but hasn't really caught on. Hey! You want some new clothes? You're rather... moist."

"I'm fine, thank you."

"Sure? We got a pile of stuff over in the corner. They're mostly clean, I think. And dry. Probably."

---

30 Roll credits. Also, that's with two S's, one *tea*, and extra *mpunk*.

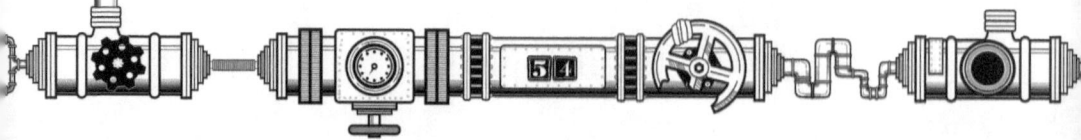

"I'm fine, thank you." Adelaide was uncomfortable enough without the thought of changing clothes in the presence of this strange group of thieving teenagers.

"Alrighty. Well, let's call it a night then, yeah? You are probably super duper exhausted. I chased Zadie through the city once. I couldn't lift my arms up for two days." She snorted in laughter then looked suddenly worried. "Oh, I'm sorry! Is that offensive?" Harriet clutched her chest and stared at Adelaide's mechanical arm.

"No?"

"Oh, okay. Alrighty. Whew! Come on then! Your bed awaits, *your majesty*!" Harriet led Adelaide to the hammocks suspended off the platform's side, dangling over the fifty-foot drop.

"I just..." Adelaide studied the swinging bed of terror, "you want me to..."

"Yeah! Just hop in!" Harriet grabbed the chain and put her arm around Adelaide's waist.

"No." Adelaide instinctively recoiled. "No. I got this." She took a deep breath and spoke to herself more than to anyone else, "I got this."

Harriet shrugged her shoulders and stepped back, but she couldn't hide her smile. Adelaide grabbed the leading chain with her good arm. One foot snaked into the hammock. She lifted her other foot on the platform but then thought better of it. The hammock swung back and forth as she slid and kneeled one leg into the hammock. She raised her other foot. The hammock swung around so much it was like it needed to go to the bathroom really bad. After much grunting and panicked shimmying, Adelaide settled in the suspended bed.

Just as Adelaide started to relax into it and catch her breath, Harriet grabbed the chain and popped her head over. "Good night!"

Adelaide jerked in surprise, giving the hammock another wild swing. She calmed herself and relaxed back. "Umm... yeah," Adelaide replied. "You too."

Harriet popped her head out of sight before climbing into her own hammock right next door. Adelaide checked the jewelry box cradled in her metal arm. Her fleshy hand patted the wooden lid.

"This is a bad idea," Baxter mumbled to no one in particular.

Adelaide quietly agreed.

He trudged over to a large, metal desk against the wall. On top, a large orange button connected to the wires upon wires leading to the stringed lights overhead. Baxter smashed the button with his fist. All of the stringed lights on the platform clanked out.

Adelaide finally settled into a comfortable swinging rhythm in her hammock. Her soaked dress was actually a nice source of coolness in the sauna-like heat of the chamber. Her exhaustion and bruises and sore muscles begged for sleep, but Adelaide knew, without a doubt, that she would never be able to find a single wink for the entire night. It would be impossible for her to rest. So naturally, she fell asleep immediately.

Chapter 5

Home Sour Home

Built into the sidewalk, a metal hatch suddenly clanked upwards, forcing two pedestrians to jump back in surprise. Zadie's head popped out of the passage. She glared at the pedestrians and stuck out her tongue. They took that as an opportunity to shuffle away without a word, but not without a derisive sniff in her general direction. Zadie scoffed and raised herself onto the warm sidewalk.

Behind her, Adelaide climbed the ladder with her good arm. Zadie extended a hand to help, but Adelaide promptly turned her nose up at the offering, reaching the sidewalk herself and basking in the sunshine.

"Just go down this street," Zadie said as she pointed down the way, "and take a right. In a mile or so, you'll be at your house. You'll know it because it's big enough to fit a couple dozen families in there, but I guess that's just the right size for you and your parents."

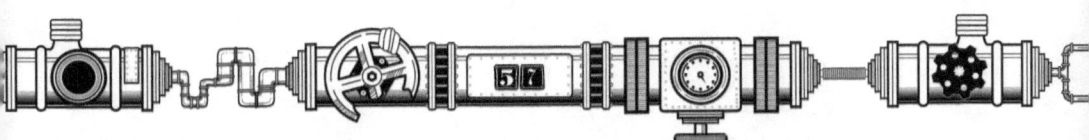

If Adelaide had feathers, she would ruffle them at her. For now, she contented herself with pursing her lips and giving Zadie the stink eye.[31]

"You know," Zadie began, "you're not too bad for a genteel. And you kept up with me, which is even more impressive."

Adelaide searched for the insult but couldn't find one.

"Civilized folks don't like people like us. We don't fit in their box." Zadie climbed down the ladder, leaned back, and propped her elbows up on the sidewalk behind her back. "I don't think you fit in at that big, fancy house with their big, fancy parties any more than we do."

Adelaide glanced at the jewelry box crutched in her mechanical arm and said, "That's my home now."

"Ain't look that way from where I'm standin'."

"You're standing on a ladder."

"Point is: if you hunger for freedom, you're welcome back anytime, fancy hand."

"My name's Adelaide."

"I know." Zadie winked, hopped down into the depths, and disappeared from sight.

The front gate leading to the Wakefield manor was open. As Adelaide made her way to the door, she noticed a fleet of vehicles and horses were stationed outside. Adelaide thought for sure the party would be over by now, but maybe they were still having fun. And maybe, just maybe, with a bit of luck, her parents would never have noticed she was gone.

"Adelaide!" her mother's voice called.

---

31 *"The stink eye"* is a global phenomenon. Scientists have attempted to study the origins of the chilling gaze, but all studies have ended abruptly due to excess amounts of sheepishness, constant apologies, and the incessant desire to telephone their mothers.

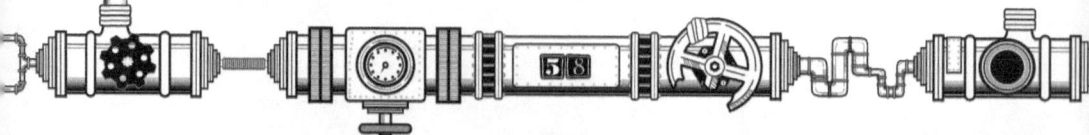

Adelaide stepped into the open doorway, stopped, and blinked her eyes. There were a lot of people in the foyer and the living room and that other room that Adelaide wasn't sure what to call. These weren't the fancy folks from the housewarming party the previous night either. She recognized an assistant to her father and a small handful of others that must be working for him. The rest of the gathering were, quite clearly from their attire and shiny badges protruding from their chests, police officers. It was at that moment that Adelaide's stomach plopped right out of her bottom.

Missus Wakefield rushed over to embrace her daughter, but she stopped abruptly at the sight and smell. Adelaide's face was bruised, her bushy hair stuck out in every single direction, her dress was torn and dirty and disgusting, her left leg had a slight limp, and her general aroma was an incredibly strong whiff of you-don't-wanna-know.

"Oh, Adelaide," Missus Wakefield began, "what happened to you? Are you all right?"

Police Officer Otis, the man in charge, had stopped taking notes from her father and marched over to the girl. Adelaide could tell he was important because his bobby helmet was the bobbyest of them all, which only made Adelaide silently question why police officers were also called bobbies. Was the first policeman named Bobby? Did they just keep naming them that, even though the second policeman might have been named Gerald or something?

"This is your daughter, ma'am?" the head-bobby-not-named-Bobby asked. "I'm going to need to take a statement from her."

Adelaide rubbed her bleary eyes at the tall man with the bulging mustache. "Alright. Well... umm... I'm hungry."

"Not that kind of statement," he replied. "Do you know the names of the men who kidnapped you?"

"Men who... kidnapped me?"

"Oh, my dear girl," Missus Wakefield doted, "she's quite clearly traumatized. Can't we do this later?"

"I am not. I'm just hungry. And I wasn't kidnapped."

They all stared at her. "You weren't?" Officer Otis asked nearly at the same time as Mister Wakefield demanded, "Then what on earth happened?"

"A girl at the party stole my jewelry box," she began rather sheepishly. "I ran after her to get it back." She lifted up her mechanical arm still clutching the jewelry box in the elbow.

"*You ran after...?*" Mister Wakefield blustered and chuffed and looked away, unable to even complete his question.

"You were gone all night!" Missus Wakefield reasoned. "We had thought—"

"I kinda got lost in the tunnels."

"The tunnels?" Her mother looked pale.

"Beneath the city."

Missus Wakefield gasped and put her hand over her mouth in shock.

Officer Otis waved at his men and twirled a finger in the air. "Alright, boys. We're done here. Pack it up." As the officers bustled about and grabbed their most important equipment, like half-eaten sandwiches and bobby helmet polish, he scribbled something across a piece of perforated paper and handed it to Mister Wakefield.

"What's this?" an exhausted Mister Wakefield asked.

"A ticket for filing a false kidnapping report."

"I... what? Of course I thought she was kidnapped! Do you know how much I'm worth?! Do you know who I am?!"

Officer Otis smirked and tipped his bobby helmet. "Welcome to Parsons City."

He marched outside, and the other gaggle of totally-useful police officers followed. Mister Wakefield looked like he wanted to say something, to shout even, but the only thing that escaped his mouth was a short squeak.

Mister Wakefield's face turned bright red. His fist clenched and crumpled the ticket. After a pause to breathe and calm the bulging vein on his forehead, he glanced at his wife while not even looking at his daughter.

"Clean her up and put her in her room," he ordered.

Missus Wakefield reached to put her arm around Adelaide, but she stopped and placed two fingers on the dirty girl's shoulder instead. She led her from the foyer down the hallway.

Nearly an hour later, a freshly-washed Adelaide wearing clean clothes was sitting on her bed once again in her room. Her mother dried her hair with a towel.

"I can do it myself, you know," Adelaide said.

Chef Charlemagne, a new employee of Adelaide's parents, strutted inside while carrying a silver platter in one hand. His outrageously-twirly, handlebar mustache was so thin, Adelaide wasn't sure if it was actual hair or simply drawn on his face with a pencil.

"Breakfast for the little one," he said. "Enjoy."

He bowed. His toque blanche chef's hat was so tall, it nearly swatted Adelaide in the face as he leaned over. He pranced out the open doorway without another word.

Adelaide slid her head out from the towel in her mother's hands. Her red hair instantly exploded out in all directions. She ripped the top off the silver platter. A plate of eggs, hash, biscuits, gravy, toast, and orange juice greeted her. Adelaide's face dove in.

It was a tad more difficult to eat once her mother began trying to brush her hair at the same time, but Adelaide was so ravenous, nothing could impede her progress. The only thing that brought her from the engorgement was a loud noise outside her window. A pair of grumpy men hammered a set of iron bars over the window pane outside.

"What's that?" she asked with chunks of biscuit exploding from her lips.

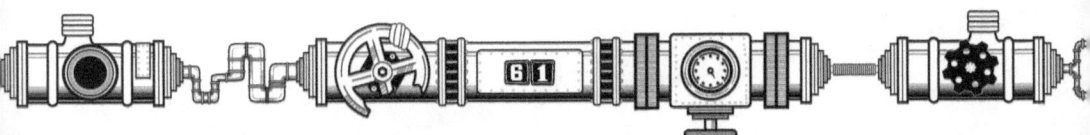

"For your protection," her mother replied, frowning at her daughter's poor eating habits. "So no more thieves or bad people can sneak into your room."

"Oh," Adelaide swallowed and thought for a moment. "For a second there, I thought that might be there just to keep me in." She gave a slight chuckle.

Her mother said nothing and brushed a large knot from her bushy hair. Adelaide's grin faded. Her mother's brushing yanked Adelaide's head back and forth with a little more force than Adelaide thought was necessary.

That was yet another thing that made Adelaide miss Lillian. The kind eyed woman with the curly, white hair would sit with her and brush Adelaide's hair with the gentlest touch. She would always find knots in Adelaide's red bushel of tangles, but Adelaide never felt her hair being yanked out. Lillian's soft demeanor and patience would just make the tangles fall away. Her mother just gave Adelaide whiplash with a side of bald spot.

Another pair of grumpy-looking men carried opposite sides of a wooden door and stepped inside the bedroom. Adelaide just noticed that her bedroom door must have been removed while she was in the bath. One man held the door up while the other inserted the bolts into its hinges.

Mister Wakefield approached and studied their work. The first man handed him a key before they both shuffled away.

"What happened to my old door?" she asked her father.

"This is your old door," he replied. "Though it is still brand new, I must add."

"Was something wrong with it?"

"We just made a few additions."

Mister Wakefield fit the key into a brand-new, deadbolt lock on the door. Adelaide didn't remember any kind of lock being there before at all. Her head bobbed as her mother seemed to brush her hair with even more vigor.

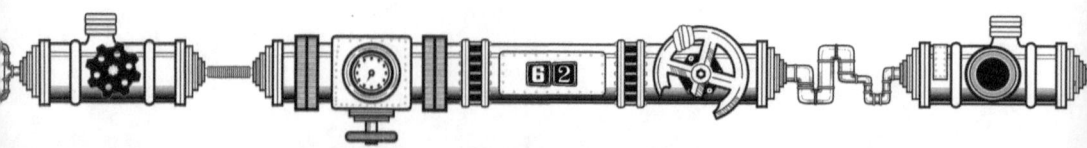

"A new lock? But... there isn't a latch on the inside."

"For your protection."

"But how would I get out?"

"Simple. You ask for permission."

Adelaide balked at him. She stood up and shook off her mother to stop her from the incessant brushing. "Are you going to lock me in all the time?" Adelaide demanded. "Am I to be your prisoner?"

Mister Wakefield brushed off his shoulders. "Do not be so dramatic."

"That's a fire hazard, you know."

"Pshh," Mister Wakefield inadvertently sounded like a fire extinguisher.

"Am I even allowed to leave?"

"Of course," he replied. "With us, or with one of your guards."

"Guards?" Adelaide balked. "I'm to be watched now?"

"Of course not. You are simply to be escorted if you are to leave the house."

"I can take care of myself!"

"Clearly not."

"I am not some fragile thing!" Adelaide stared him in the face.

He stared right back, matching her intensity. "Do you have any idea what we went through when we couldn't find you after the party? Do you have any idea what it is for a parent to not know where their child is? To not know if she's alive or dead?"

Adelaide rocked back on her heels at that. "I didn't... I didn't mean to..."

"I canceled the party early and nearly made a scene with the Trevithicks. Your mother couldn't even speak. I thought... we thought the worst."

"I... but... it was one time. I won't do it again."

"It only takes the one time," he replied. "It only took the one time for you to lose your arm. That happened on my train yard!

On *my* watch! I carried you, bloodied and broken to the surgeon. I ripped off my own shirt and used it to staunch all the blood."

"You never told me that part."

"You may not remember it, but your mother and I shall scant forget."

Her father put his arms on his hips and refused to look at Adelaide. Her mother's eyes filled with water and refused to stop looking at Adelaide.

"I'm sorry."

He inhaled and glanced back. "Yes, well, for now, this will be for the best."

Her mother grabbed Adelaide's head and kissed her noggin once. It was the most affection she had seen from her mother since... well, probably since before the accident.

Her father ushered her mother out the door, closed, and locked it behind them. Through the wooden portal, Adelaide could clearly hear the furious whispers pouring from the other side.

"Franklin," her mother's voice said. "Are you sure we're not overreacting?"

"Margaret," her father's voice said, "you know what she is like. She needs boundaries, otherwise she will be running all over, getting herself hurt, getting into trouble. It must be either this or we send her away."

"But to keep a young girl in her room all the time..."

"Margaret, we are *this* close to having everything we wanted. It could all fall apart with the smallest of prodding. Trust me, I know. This is for the best."

Footsteps sounded and grew quiet. Their voices faded. Adelaide's thoughts jumbled. Her guilt from disappointing her parents plus her shame of failure plus her disdain of confinement plus her sadness from being misunderstood: all of them clashed together in an all-out cage match. The winner received a few moments of being the primary

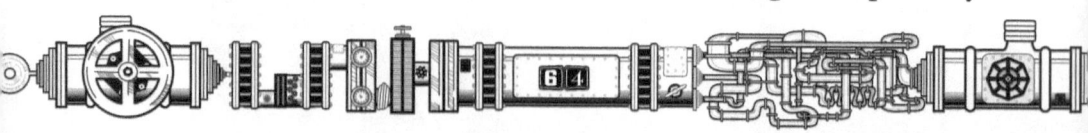

emotion she was bombarded with until they repeated the process and all clashed together again.

Over the following hours, she tried keeping herself busy. Her mechanical arm needed adjusting and cleaning. Lots and lots of cleaning. The steel and metal alloys were unlikely to rust, but she always wanted to make sure by wiping it down and keeping it as dry as possible, when she wasn't swimming in an underground fluid system anyways. She was sure that there were improvements to be made to her arm, but she couldn't think. Her mind felt suffocated. This was her life now. Here in this room. All alone. With just these pink doilies to keep her company. At least she had her own bathroom. It would have been awkward trying to pee in the corner.

Adelaide fiddled around until it was time for lunch. Her mother unlocked the door and invited her down to the dining room. Being escorted through your own home was a bit of an odd feeling, even if it was a new home that already felt odd. She sat across from her father at the massive table. He said nothing. Her mother said no more. Adelaide wasn't sure she remembered how to speak at all.

The crystal chandelier dangled overhead. She stared into the sparkling, rainbow facets. An image of Adelaide knocking down the chandelier and using the chaos to run away and escape briefly flitted through her imagination.[32]

After eating her fill of the various meats and cheeses and breads and fruits arrayed on the ceramic dishes, her mother escorted her back to her bedroom. The deadbolt lock clicking behind made Adelaide flinch.

She fell onto her bed. Her squished face turned to the side. She watched the world outside her window. Clouds floated by. Smog floated by. Smoke floated by. While their home had the luxury of grass in the yard, there wasn't much visually

---

32 *Flitted*: not to be confused with *Fluted*, which is when your past self plays the flute.

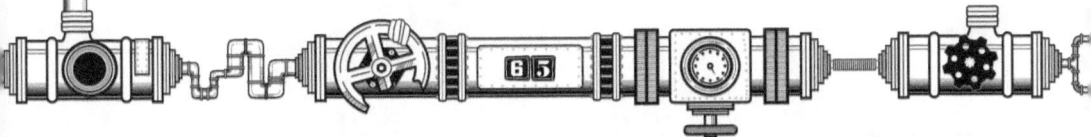

interesting about staring at it. The blades of grass waved in the breeze from the house to the surrounding brick wall. Tall buildings and the various colors of air and gasses were all that she could see beyond.

She pictured growing a luscious beard on her face, suitable for those on solitary lockdown. Really sell the image. Make her parents rethink her imprisonment. She might like having a big, fluffy beard, actually. Could braid it. Or maybe put some little pouches in there and store some food for later. Could she put something in her chin hair so that she wouldn't even have to move to eat meals? Just stick her tongue down there and scoop up some morsels. *Could you put my dinner in my beard tonight, Mister Charlemagne?* she thought. Goodness, it was less than a day, and she was officially losing her mind already.

In whatever the opposite of "before she knew it" was, the sun began to set. Most of the colors of the rainbow made an appearance, shimmering off the different plumes of vapor and smog and pollution. Industry made a rather interesting canvas. Adelaide couldn't tell what color green that was. Olive? Lime? Regurgitation?

Dinnertime rolled around. Her mother escorted her to the dining table. They ate in silence. Her mother escorted her back to her bedroom. And so it was.

The next day was the same routine. And so was the next day. And the next day.

On the evening of the seventh day, Adelaide's mother escorted her to the grand dining room. Her father sat at the head of the massive, exquisitely-crafted, wooden table and read the evening newspaper. Her mother sat at the other end. Adelaide joined, sitting in the single chair in the exact middle on the side, as usual. She thought about scooching the chair down toward her mother at about a tenth of the table's length and wondered if her father would notice.

In the corner, a large, glass cabinet housed all of her mother's most expensive china, displayed and propped up to look but never touch. Another large, glass cabinet in the next corner showed off all of the tiny statues and crystal thingamabobs that her mother so loved. Adelaide never could quite wrap her head around why her mother needed two dozen crystal ducks, but who was she to judge someone's strange taste in items?

Expensive paintings of portraits of fancy people lined the walls.[33] Behind her father, an oil rendition of a smirking man with a trimmed beard wore dress military vestments, a monocle, and a fez atop his head. Next to it was a smaller oil painting of a stern-faced woman with a hooked nose and hair curled to the point of overindulgence. The woman judged them all from a much smaller canvas and frame, but she was still somehow ten times as imposing as the other paintings. Those were her grandparents, apparently one of whom was a terrible gambler.

She had heard her father shouting about his father on multiple occasions when they were at their first home and their hardships were highest. After Adelaide's father's father's wife died from heart failure, the not-completely-distraught man didn't have a care in the world, not even for his son. He drank all the alcohol he could find and gambled away everything else. That bowl hat lady from the party was right about that part, at least. He had simply laughed when the debt collectors collected all their furniture and prized possessions. He had said it was "just stuff" and "now he was free." Adelaide's father sounded incredibly bitter when she first heard him yell the story years ago, but Adelaide just thought it meant that her grandfather was incredibly unhappy while he was married and made her feel a bit sorry for him.

After the gambling man passed from a brain aneurysm, the only inheritance left was a dry iron mine. Though, her father

---

33 Portraits are for fancy people. Non-fancy people get poor-traits.

eventually discovered that it wasn't dry after all. The veins were buried beneath deeper rock that was near impossible to dig by hand, but he reclaimed an abandoned locomotive engine and built a new type of mining drill from the scraps. The motorized monstrosity revolutionized the industry and gave her father all the precious metals he wanted. Then he built a railway empire to transport all the goods and machinery he was making.

Adelaide was always proud of her father for that. He earned back the family fortune through ingenuity and hard work, which was something she always aspired to, even though her father was never quite the same man after his wealth returned. He valued profit margins and shortcuts more than anything else now, but she felt that he still had that ingenious engineer inside of him somewhere. And that... that gave Adelaide an idea.

Chef Charlemagne burst into the room with a "Helloooo!" His beaming face showered them all. From his silver platter, he distributed plates of pasta, bread, and salads. He gave a little twirl as he finished and exclaimed, "Bon appétit!" And then he was gone.

Adelaide's mind attempted to puzzle together the perfect plan, but before that went anywhere, her mouth ran ahead and blurted out, "I want to go to school!"

Mister Wakefield set down his fork. "What?"

"The university, I mean. I want to learn engineering."

"Nonsense," her father replied immediately. He unfolded his napkin and placed it on his lap. "You do not require an education. You are to stay here, where you are safe."

"I want to build stuff! Like you!" Adelaide crumpled her napkin in her hand. "When your father lost everything," she continued as his mustache furrowed past his lips, "you saw a need, applied your knowledge of engineering, built something new, and succeeded."

"That was only part of the story," Mister Wakefield snorted.

"I want to do the same. I loved watching you work at the train yard."

"Playing at the yard and falling on the tracks is how your arm was amputated."

"Okay, true... but watching you and reading books and experimenting was how I built my new arm! And I love stuff like that. Building new things."

Mister Wakefield grumbled, "You do not require schooling. You will stay here. You will be safe. You will stay out of trouble and not embarrass the family any further. Our social standing is hanging by a thread as it is, not to mention the volatility of the railway contract."

"Adelaide," her mother added, "it is improper for a lady of status to go to a school or work on machinery. Those are for men. We are in high society now. They expect better of us."

"Is it wrong for me to want to be something more than just your daughter?" Adelaide looked to her father. "Like you are more than just your father's son?"

"I will hear no more of this!" Mister Wakefield slammed his hand down on the table. The silverware clanged and skittered away, also uncomfortable with this conversation, the spoons especially.[34]

After the ringing died down, Missus Wakefield reached her hand toward her daughter across the table that was far too long, but her fingers fell short. "Oh, Adelaide," her mother cooed. "My sweet girl. Of course you are more than just our child. One day, you will be a wife. And then, a mother. And that is the most gratifying feeling in the world."

Her mother smiled. Her father ground his teeth on his pasta. Adelaide's eyes went dead.

---

34 As we all know, spoons are the most emotionally sensitive of all silverware.

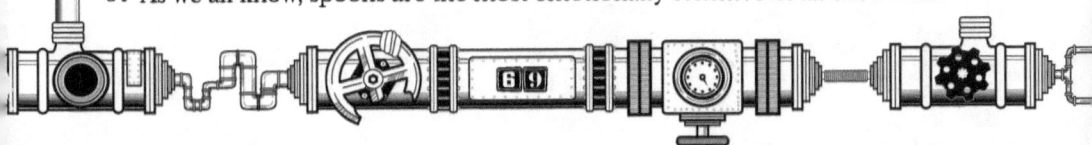

Chapter 6

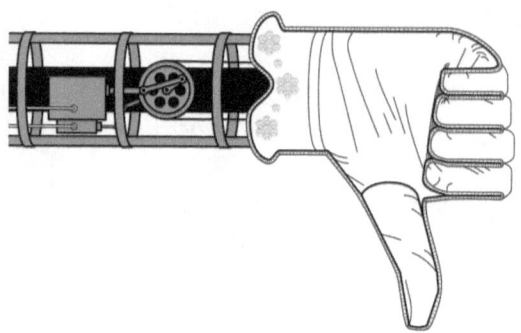

Hunger and Hinges

oonlight filtered in through the barred windows of Adelaide's bedroom.[35] Sprawled out on top of the covers, Adelaide absentmindedly played with her chest's control panel. Accordingly, her mechanical fingers began to tap together in a steady rhythm.

Her mind kept going back to one phrase, over and over again, *"If you hunger for freedom, you're welcome back anytime, fancy hand!"* The thief wasn't disturbed by Adelaide's mechanical arm. She didn't think being different was a bad thing. How many people had Adelaide met that felt the same way? She thought of the future her parents wanted for her: imprisoned, only let out for meals and to be shown off at parties, destined to be wife'd off to the nearest boy or the highest bidder.

---

35 "There's no place like home confinement," says the doughnut with a surprising amount of nut.

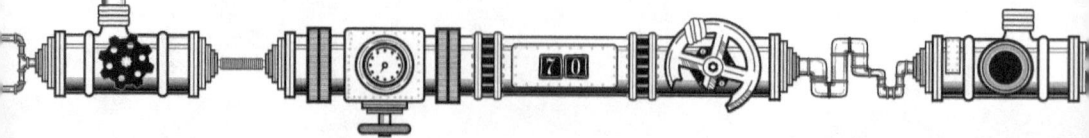

Adelaide rose out of bed. She stepped to her closet and began rummaging through, pulling out clothes and tossing them around the room. Pants, shirts, underwear, and socks got stuffed into a duffel bag.

Adelaide adorned herself in faded blue jeans and a dark brown leather jacket. After a moment of grunting and shoving, her mechanical hand poked out from her right sleeve. The leather jacket tugged and restricted her movement. Adelaide grimaced at the obnoxious thing. Her parents had that specially tailored for her along with a softer, less noticeable prosthetic filled with goose feathers.[36]

After a few moments of indecision, Adelaide retrieved a pair of scissors and cut her right sleeve off near where her bicep would have been. She tore into the fabric with an almost animalistic growl. Beneath the leather, the skeletal, metal rods shone in all their glory. She ripped and tore the sleeve off of herself with great relish.[37]

The elbow bent and rotated with full, free moment. She could feel a breeze on her shoulder and arm. It felt quite nice.

She took another few moments to embrace that feeling before she slipped her feet into some socks and her trusty, comfortable, running shoes. She looked into the mirror above her vanity. Something was still missing. She dug through her closet again. A rugged, dark blue, ladies' top hat (which was more bottom than top with its small, squat, and squashed shape) completed the ensemble.[38]

Adelaide threw the duffel bag onto the vanity. She tried to think of everything she wanted to take. There was quite a lot. A few of her many books on engineering could go. The vice grip

---

36 Goose feathers are far more comfortable than moose feathers, who really don't enjoy being plucked. Especially since they don't have any feathers. At least, not since the incident.

37 With great relish comes great picklebility.

38 After all, one cannot steampunk without the proper headwear.

wouldn't be practical. Wrenches, screwdrivers, and ratchets she could take though. Air compressor, not so much. Welding torch, nope. She'll have to do generator maintenance on the fly. Just a handful of her most common screws. Didn't want to bring too many for risk of stabbing herself repeatedly.

So much she might need. So little space in the bag.

And the jewelry box she built for Lillian. Her fingers touched the lid, and the spring-loaded leg popped out from the bottom. Happier memories flooded her brain. Lillian reading her a bedtime story. Lillian calming her down after she had a nightmare. Lillian and Adelaide rolling around with uncontrollable flatulence on the giant dirt pile at the train yard. Adelaide laughed. That last part may have just been herself. Her mother was so mad at the both of them anyway for getting so filthy.

Adelaide's mother had become rather distant after the accident. She even seemed a bit squeamish in trying to clean Adelaide's residual limb once. Adelaide remembered feeling that anything different was wrong. She remembered feeling that *she* was wrong, but Lillian never acted that way at all.

Lillian taught her how to manipulate objects with one hand, how to use her core and prop things up with her legs. How to be proud of who she was and all that she accomplished. All of her favorite memories from growing up had Lillian in them. She would just have to take those with her too.

Adelaide wrapped the duffel bag strap around her shoulder and shifted until it felt like the weight was closer to fifty-fifty between it and her mechanical arm. She stepped toward the door.

Oh yeah. It was locked.

Whelp, that was why she brought tools. What would get her through? Adelaide dug into her duffel bag. She had just packed this thing, and already it was completely

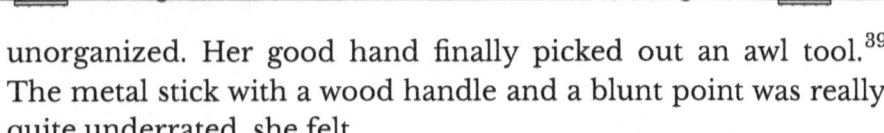
unorganized. Her good hand finally picked out an awl tool.[39] The metal stick with a wood handle and a blunt point was really quite underrated, she felt.

Adelaide stepped up to the door's hinges. She shoved the pointy end of the awl tool into the bottom and, with some finagling, pushed the bolt out through the top.[40]

Once all three hinges were out, the door needed a bit of prying from the side and the bottom. She tried to be as quiet as possible in the scraping of wood against wood. The deadbolt was just a little loose in its new fitting, so she was able to rotate the door just enough to let it slide completely free. And with that, she was free too.

Adelaide skipped out into the hallway and gave a little happy dance, but the metal tools jangled around inside her duffel bag, breaking the silence. Adelaide stopped and listened. Nothing. After she was sure the toast was clear, or whatever that saying was because she couldn't fathom how bread could be see-through, she gave another little jig of joy and tip-toed down the hall.

She passed her parents' bedroom. Her father's rhythmic snoring could be heard through the door. Adelaide stopped. A sudden wave of guilt washed over her.

Trembling fingers turned the handle, and she peeked inside. Her parents were both asleep. Adelaide had walked past their room dozens of times, but she had never been inside before. Even in the dark, everything glitzed and gleamed off the sparse sources of moonlight scattered here and there and willy nilly. Her mother had not skimped on the decorations, even in a room where other guests weren't allowed.

One of the especially glitzy items was her mother's vanity. Gems sparkled within necklaces, rings, bracelets, bangles, tiaras,

---

39 Owls were different than awls in that one did not appreciate being stabbed into things and the other said, "What?"

40 The noun of *finagling* is *finagler*. That's it. Just wanted to say that.

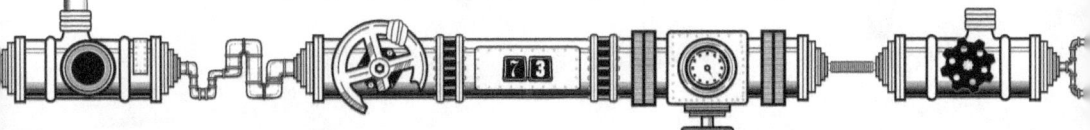

and other shiny things that Adelaide didn't even know what they were called. She spotted a fully gold-plated, jewelry box. It was quite a bit larger than her own. Even with the jewelry scattered along the vanity and hanging up on the mirror, the box was filled to the brim with extravagant pieces.

Adelaide remembered the many, many times her mother would always say that she had no jewelry to go with her outfits. Or no dresses to go with her jewelry. And so her father would buy her both. Many, many times. Even at the housewarming party, her mother said that her jewelry didn't match her ensembles. Adelaide scoffed. *Then she probably won't miss them being gone*, Adelaide thought. She made some space in her duffel bag and tucked her mother's jewelry box inside.

Stacks of papers and books rested on the top of the desk by the window. *A window without bars on the outside*, Adelaide noted. That gave her a bit of extra gumption.[41] She crept over to the desk and unfurled a blank piece of parchment. Her fingers pulled a quill out of the ink bottle. With a drop of ink dabbing the page, Adelaide realized she didn't know what to write. How could she possibly condense all of her thoughts, her feelings, her misgivings, her wants, her regrets, into paragraph form? Finally, she decided simple was best.

Dearest Mother and Father,

I hunger for freedom, and I know that I won't find it here. Goodbye.

Love,

Adelaide

---

41 *Gumption*: fortitude through being sticky, chewy, and covered with saliva.

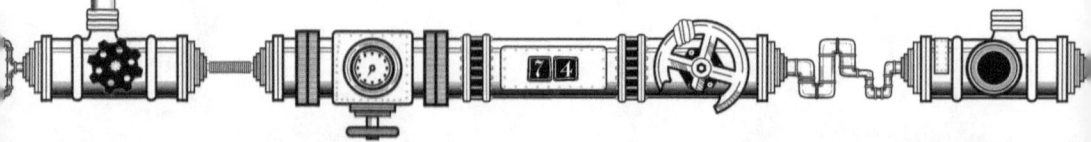

It didn't seem sufficient, but then again, she didn't think it ever could. She watched the sleeping forms of her parents, their chests rising and falling with each breath, or each snore in her father's case. Adelaide's eyes watered, but she knew it wasn't regret she was feeling for what she was about to do. It was regret for what might have been.

She left. As she made her way through the manor, she came upon a gas lamp illuminating the kitchen doorway. Adelaide peeked inside. Chef Charlemagne quietly hummed to himself as he sprinkled spices into some sort of sauce. He brushed the goop onto slabs of meat.

"Oh!" he exclaimed as his eyes spied her by the door. "Why, you nearly startled me out of my fluffy pants, Miss Adelaide!"

"I'm sorry."

"Don't be! Don't be!"

Adelaide put her finger over her lips. His voice lowered in volume.

"Oh, yes yes," he whispered. "Mustn't wake the Wakefields. Wouldn't hear the end of that. No, Charlemagne would not."

"Why are you cooking at this time of night?" Adelaide asked.

"I was sleeping, and then? Inspiration struck! Specially marinating prime cuts of brisket and letting them smoke for thirty-six hours. I've been meaning to try it for ages, but I've never had the proper equipment. But now? Voila! The Wakefields have all of the things! So much to play with. So much to experiment with. So much artistry to create. Oh, shall I create something for you, my dear?" Chef Charlemagne wafted sizzled smoke into his nostrils. His tongue waggled in the air as though he was trying to lick the vapor.

"Create?"

"What would you like to eat, Miss Adelaide? You are going on a trip, no?"

"Oh, umm, yes."

"And a bit late for an average departure, yes? Or early?" He gave a knowing wink.

"I won't tell if you won't," she said.

"My dear, my only concern is making exquisite cuisine to fill empty bellies." He guffawed and added, "Mieux vaut prévenir que guérir."

Adelaide turned a confused expression toward him.

"Ah, this means, 'It is better to prevent than to heal.'" He smiled and gestured to the entirety of the kitchen. "Now, how can Chef Charlemagne serve?"

Adelaide looked around and returned the smile.

"How much can we fit in my bag?"

[42]Zadie had been having the most lovely dream. Unfortunately, she couldn't remember any of it. Had something to do with money. Or food. Or food filled with money. Either way, the dream bubble was punctured by a sound. It wasn't from Baxter's sporadic snorts and wheezes. Nor was it from Harriet's random sleep talking. It was most definitely not from Jules' complete silence. It was a noise of metal clanking on metal, but not from the clanks and cranks and hisses and thumps that normally surrounded them in the Steampunks hideout. The sound jerked Zadie instantly awake.

The platform suspended high up in the massive chamber was completely dark. Zadie smashed a button built into the side of her reclining chair specifically for this reason. The overhead lights thunked into life. Jules hopped out of his hammock and landed on the platform without a sound. Baxter snorted himself awake.

---

42 Fun fact #42: A paragraph divider, like my little awl tool drawing, is used in novels to denote when a period of time has changed or the Point Of View is different. When three asterisks or bullets in a row are used as a paragraph divider, that is called a "Dinkus." You know that now, because that's a thing. It's a Dinkus. You're welcome. Enjoy all of my original Dinkuses. Dinkusi? Dinkususesssiessusseriesy... and also... dinkus.

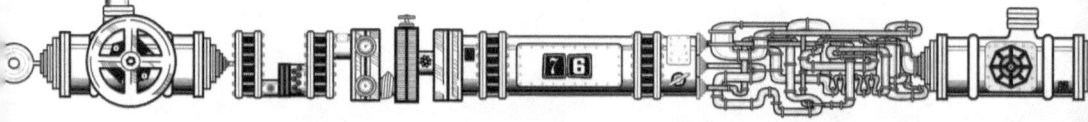

"Huh what who? Gimme back my possum." Baxter drooled on his chin.

Zadie tossed an old orange peel, or what she thought was an old orange peel, at Harriet. The girl didn't move an inch. Zadie pointed to Jules then to Harriet. While he went about gently shaking her hammock, Zadie went about looking for the source of the noise.

The sound of a small, distant generator chugged, followed by a metal cable whirring. Zadie squinted her eyes, starting to understand. She found the mechanical grappling hook hand caught on the platform's edge.

Adelaide's mechanical arm cable retracted up. Her good hand grabbed onto the platform, and she heaved herself over the lip. Her mechanical hand locked back into her mechanical wrist. After wobbling for a second, she rose to her feet and adjusted her wide-brimmed hat.

"Greetings," Adelaide said.

Zadie tilted her head up and smirked. Baxter's bleary eyes and drooping mouth had nothing to say. Jules simply stared. Or he was sleeping. It was hard to tell through his dark visor. Harriet finally shook herself awake.

"It's Adelaide!" Harriet cheered. She flipped and turned and rocked and flopped herself out of the hammock before running over to grab Adelaide in a bear hug. "What'd ya bring me?!"

Adelaide plopped her bulging duffel bag onto the table and took off the strap. She unzipped it and started unloading wrapped piles of meat, pastries, fruit, bread, vegetables, nuts, and screws, but she didn't mean to unpack the screws.

Baxter's eyes finally sharpened after they found the meat. "Food!"

He swung out of his hammock and dove upon the smorgasbord. From a face full of meat, the muffled sound of the word "thanks" fluttered out. Zadie picked up an apple and tossed it in the air before catching it again.

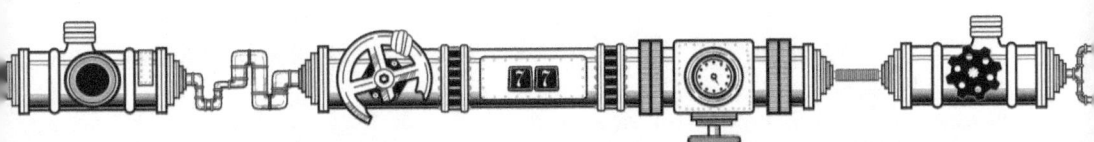

"And what'd ya bring *me*?" Zadie asked. "Need tribute if you wanna be part of the gang."

"No, she doesn't!" Harriet laughed.

"Shh!" Zadie shushed. "Don't ruin it."

"I got that covered too," Adelaide said.

Adelaide pulled out her jewelry box with the wooden lid and the gold-plated bracings that she made for Lillian.

"Isn't that empty?" Zadie asked.

"This one is still mine," Adelaide replied with one raised finger while the others set down her prized possession. "But this one..."

She withdrew her mother's fully gold-plated jewelry box. Zadie's eyes widened into tiny, envious suns. Adelaide placed the box on the table and opened the lid. The gems, diamonds, and jewelry within sparkled up to the brim.

Zadie's eyes could have fallen right out of her head. Meat plopped right out of Baxter's mouth. Harriet drooled a little. Jules' dark visor was dark and visory.

"All yours," Adelaide finished.

Zadie's eyeballs finally had to blink from dehydration. A wild, mischievous grin creased the entirety of her face.

"Let's have some fun."

Chapter 7

The Bizarre Bazaar

Very few tried and true methods existed for obtaining friendships. The first was establishing an honest bond between people with mutual respect, complementary chemistry, and just generally enjoying each other's company. The second, more superficial, method was to shower the other person with money or gifts. The third was to feed them, which worked very well on animals, including humans. The second also worked well on humans, to no one's great surprise. However, only the first led to long-lasting, meaningful, heartwarming relationships. But, when a person was able to apply methods two and three together, no one remembered to care about the first method. And so it was with the Steampunks. In the grand scheme of things, honest bonds and mutual respect didn't matter all that much anyway.

Zadie led the troupe of five through the steam tunnels, all of them chatting away, minus Jules, about anything and everything. Adelaide realized that, though she's been through this tunnel

maze three times already, this was the first time she did so
without fear or adrenaline. She never really had friends
before. Much of what she was experiencing now was quite
new.

"This way you have to duck under some pipes," Harriet
explained, "but it's *way* better than the dirt tunnel on the
right. That clay gunk takes forever to scrape off your shoes."

"I found a crocodile in there once!" Baxter boasted.

"You did not," Zadie said.

"Did too!" he replied. "Twelve feet long, it was! Missing
an eye too!"

"*Anyways*," Harriet continued, "just up a ways is the Lower
District. It's a bunch of tunnels like we got down here, but
they're nicer and got some shops and apartments and such.
You go up a couple levels to the surface on the top of the
hills, and that's the Upper District."

"On Savery Street, there's this bakery sandwiched
between two big old buildings, right?" Baxter's eyes glowed
hungrily. "The old tosspot never locks the back door. Ooh,
can we go?"

"You just ate," Harriet said.

"But doughnuts! You can always eat doughnuts."

"Pipe it down," Zadie ordered. "We're almost here."

"Aren't we always where *here* is?" Harriet asked.

The sparsely-lit tunnel took a 90-degree bend. Built into
the corner laid a small but heavy-set, metal door. Zadie
shoved against the door with all of her weight, and it scraped
open. Hot steam wafted in through the opening.

"Whoo, that's hot," Adelaide mentioned.

"Relax, we'll be through it in a few seconds," Zadie said.

"I would say that you get used to it," Baxter began, "but
you don't."

Adelaide followed the rest of the punks inside. The
warm, metal, steam ventilation pipe extended out for a few
feet before it dropped suddenly into open air. They

crouched and squatted before hopping out. Harriet and Zadie helped Adelaide down the five-foot drop to the dirt.

Even though Adelaide could see sunlight from the open air, she couldn't actually see the sunlight or the open air. There were cloth coverings and tents and shacks all over the place. Even the dirt floor outcropping she was standing on was behind some sort of shanty.

Jules was the last one out of the pipe. Once all five were on the ground, Zadie marched up to the cloth wall and peeled it back. Inside, Adelaide realized the shanty was some sort of makeshift shop. There were multiple fold-out tables with goods and all sorts of weirdness hanging from the walls/ceiling of the tent/wood house. Dangling in front of her was a dream catcher made out of an old hubcap with some purple feathers sticking out.

"Oi!" the shopkeeper yelled at them from behind a table. "Where'd you lot come from?"

Zadie scoffed at him. "Yo momma's lady business!"[43]

The shopkeeper groaned and waved them away as Zadie exited through a tent flap. Adelaide followed and immediately had to blink her eyes against the assault of pure sunlight. Once she could see again, she couldn't believe what she was seeing.

The world opened up into a massive, strange marketplace built into the side of the cliff face on a wide outcropping. Shacks, shanties, stores, stalls, tents, tables, single-level, two-level, three-level, boss level, colors and nonsense spread out all before them. It looked like every small business owner, or stolen goods hawker, wanted a space here. The more daring salespeople had their shops set up right next to the cliff.

Over those and beyond the hanging tapestries, sunlight and clean-ish air wafted over the Gorge. The now small, rather sad river far below must have been a roaring behemoth at one point

---

43 You see, kids, when a man business and a lady business fall in love, they make little baby entrepreneurs, which are both expensive and highly prone to failure. Always use protection when venturing into new monetary ventures.

in the past in order to cut the solid rock into these three-hundred-foot-high walls. Pipelines, railroads, and power lines crisscrossed over the wide chasm.

The others stepped around Adelaide to exit the tent. She stood wide-eyed and wide-mouthed, trying to take in all of the sights and sounds. And smells. Although, those she didn't try to take in as much. Yep, she made a note to definitely try and avoid the smells.

"Is it a gorge or a valley?" Harriet asked to no one in particular.

"Everyone calls it *The Gorge*," Zadie replied.

"Yeah, but what's the difference?"

Zadie shrugged.

"Who cares?" Baxter chuffed.

"Language is important, good sir," Harriet said. "Otherwise, we're all just making noises at each other."

Zadie looked back at Adelaide, whose eyes were still darting from one shiny thing to the next. Zadie smirked at her. "Welcome to the Bazaar. I take it you've never been before?"

"We only moved here a few days ago," Adelaide replied as their group melded into single-file and pushed through a crowd of people.

"Can find most anything here, if you know where to look," Zadie said. "Just keep an eye on your pockets. There's folks down here that're almost as disreputable as us. Speaking of—"

As Zadie stepped past a wooden barrel, a child's hand reached out from behind toward Zadie's satchel. With lightning fast reflexes, Zadie grabbed the hand and yanked out the owner.

"Nice try, Winston!" she said.

"Maybe we should start calling him Loses-ton?" Harriet asked with a smile.

"Get off me!" the little boy replied.

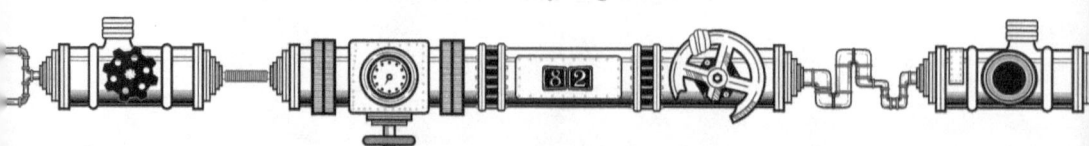

Zadie let him go. He scowled at her. She scowled back and said, "Don't put your hand in anything you can't snatch it back out of real quick. And don't pick the first one in a group, ya knob. Pick the one in the back. Less a chance the others will notice."

"Bah! I could've gotten ya!" Winston said.

"Not in this lifetime, twerp. Run on back to your master." Zadie looked behind the boy. "And I see you snot faces back there too! Get goin'!"

A collection of rag-tag youngsters looked on from around a tent flap back by the cliff wall. Winston ran back to them. As one, they all stuck out their tongues and blew raspberries at Zadie. She returned the favor, following up by picking her nose and flicking a booger at them. They scattered, and Zadie chuckled.

"You're such a role model," Harriet commented.

"I know right?" Zadie said. "I should be a friggin' school teacher or something."

"You know those kids?" Adelaide asked.

"Yeah. Winston and Wally run with the Caretaker. Creepy old man takes in orphans and feeds 'em so they can run around and pick pockets and beg for scraps to give him all day long."

"That's awful."

"It's a livin'. You do what you gotta do to make do."

"Have you thought of giving them a place with us?" Adelaide asked.

"Oh, it's *us* now?" Zadie laughed.

"She tried, actually," Harriet said. Zadie's eyes shot daggers at her. Harriet shrugged.

"Yeah, well," Zadie began, "most folks aren't cut out for our kind a' life. We got freedom, but we don't have all the other things usually."

"Like food," Baxter added.

"Or comfort," Harriet multiplied.

Zadie frowned at them then continued, "We can't take care of everybody, high class."

Adelaide let it go at that. Zadie trudged ahead, and they followed along through the crowds and the strange aromas. Adelaide's eyes watered from trying to take in everything all at once, and also because of an aroma that could best be described as flowery perfume stuffed inside a hot dog.

"Top of the line!" a street merchant called out. "Top of the line!"

Next to the cliff's edge, the merchant stood behind a table with the head of a gargantuan, metal golem sitting atop it. Its blank, lifeless eyes stared at nothing. The weight of it bent the wooden table top beneath it. Adelaide stepped in for a closer look. The eyes blinked, giving her a start so bad she nearly had to change her pants. Adelaide jumped back and bumped into an elderly woman sitting in an uncomfortable-looking chair next to the inner wall.

"Oh, sorry," Adelaide said.

The woman with a buzz cut said nothing. A small, metal trumpet protruded from where her left ear should have been. An eyepatch covered one eye. The other, bloodshot one would not stop staring at Adelaide, following her every step.

"Nice day, isn't it?" Adelaide muttered.

The woman lightly smiled at her with nothing left inside but three silver teeth.

"Bax?" Harriet called.

A few tents back, they spotted Baxter standing beside a coat rack filled with goggles. A lone mirror dangled from the top. They backtracked beside him. Adelaide couldn't help but glance back through the towers of people where the old woman's single, bloodshot eye kept following her.

Baxter tried on a new pair of gold-plated goggles. His reflection in the mirror smiled back at himself. "Check it out," he said while showing off the sparkly gold bits.

"You don't need gold goggles," Zadie said to Baxter. "You don't even wear the ones you got around your neck."

"You never know when you might need a good pair of goggles," he said. "Eye protection is very important. You wouldn't want me to go blind, would ya?"

Zadie crossed her arms and stared him down through the shiny lenses. "Yes."

"Harsh. Just for that, I'm buying 'em. Gimme some coin."

"No."

"You don't carry your own money?" Adelaide asked.

"He's not allowed to anymore after the rooster incident," Harriet replied for him.

"Mister Gizzard was there to alert us of intruders or poisonous gasses!" Baxter protested.

"The first day," Zadie explained, "it crowed, woke us all up at sunrise, then fell off the platform and died."

"Yeah," Baxter sighed, "I really should have put up a chicken fence around the edge."

"Oh yeah," Zadie responded, "because *that* was the problem."

Baxter looked to Adelaide. "I was so sad, I didn't even eat him for lunch."

"He *was* a bit chewy," Harriet commented.

"So now I hold the money," Zadie said. "You want somethin', you come to me and we talk about our budget."

"So official," Adelaide snorted.

"More like: I got tired of working hard on gettin' loot only for some goober to blow it all then we gotta eat scraps out of the garbage again. No goggles!"

Baxter deflated and sulked as he put the golden gift back on the display.

"Those work just fine." Zadie pointed at the pair around his neck. "If they break, then we can discuss getting you some new ones, alright?"

Baxter nodded his head and perked up.

"And no breaking those on purpose so we'll buy you gold ones, yeah?"

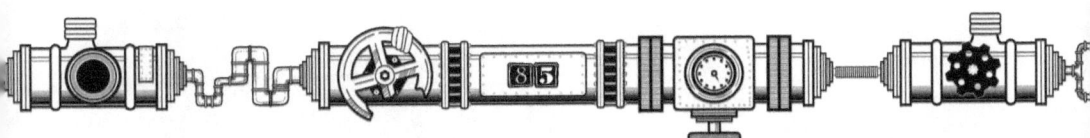

Baxter scowled, his plans immediately foiled. He snapped his old goggles over his eyes a little more forcefully than he intended.

"Come on, Bax," Zadie grunted. "You be a good boy and maybe we'll get you a fried rat on a stick, yeah?"

Baxter's face immediately brightened.

"Get you a what now?" Adelaide asked.

"Don't forget to eat the butt." Baxter nudged Adelaide in the ribs. "It's the juiciest part."

Adelaide clamped her lips together with a *hurp*.

Jules, with his limited vision from his own tinted visor, elbowed a goggle display as he attempted to walk past, but his reflexes were so fast, he caught the stand with his foot, one pair of goggles with one hand, and two pairs of goggles with the other. He kicked the stand upright and tossed the goggles back into place like it was nothing. Adelaide stared at him, but Jules just shrugged. The others walked on, apparently used to this sort of thing.

"Jules, may I ask about your mask?"

"No," Zadie answered for him.

Adelaide looked to her in confusion. Zadie simply shook her head. Jules shrugged.

"Okay," Adelaide said. "Well, I enjoy your quiet company anyway, Jules."

Jules bowed his head in thanks toward her. The fivesome trudged and skipped and oogled their way to one of the more well-kept shops in the bazaar, which wasn't saying much, but this shop had walls that were made out of wood and were also standing semi-straight. Although, instead of glass, the windows just had boards nailed across. Painted in bright colors across the sign next to the door were the words: "*Mister Pawn's Pawn Palace.*"

They entered inside the store filled with so many devices, shinies, and knickknacks that it was difficult for them to make their way through to the counter in the back.

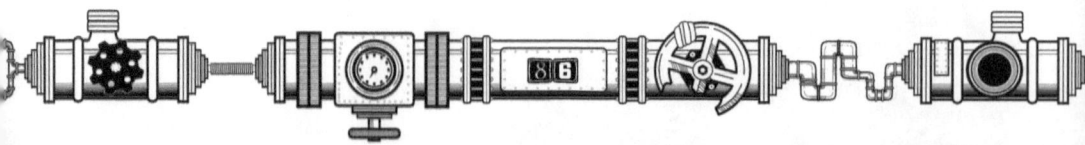

Bookshelves lined the floors. Metal shelves lined the walls. Thin filament bulbs dangled illumination overhead. "Sale" signs, toys, and more random things lined the ceiling and dangled down by wires. Every inch was packed with nonsense, and every piece of nonsense had a price tag on it.

On the other side of the counter in the back, Mister Pawn looked up and watched them through a jeweler's microscope, which was attached to a metal faceplate bolted into the older man's skull. He grinned with a mouthful of gold teeth.

"What tha' punks gots for me today?" he asked.

"We're the Grinders," Zadie grunted.

"Sure, sure, sure."

Zadie withdrew Adelaide's mother's jewelry box from her satchel and plopped it on the counter. Mister Pawn opened the gold lid and gazed at the collection of fine jewelry inside.

"Nice haulses. Very nice indeeds."

"Yep," Zadie said. "Let's talk price."

"For the lots and the box, I'll give yous—"

"No, no, no," she interrupted. "Each piece. Fair price. For each."

He smirked with a sparkle of gold. "Very wells. As the lady wishes."

"I know your game, old man."

"Oh, miladys, we have yets to even play."

Baxter and Jules wandered down the aisles. Harriet followed and nodded at Adelaide.

"She's gonna be a while," Harriet said. "She likes haggling just as much as he does."

Adelaide squished herself through the cramped space and past a collection of dusty jackets hanging off an impromptu rack. The frills and lace of one dark brown duster in particular almost made her sneeze. Unbothered, Harriet looked through the jackets with interest as though they weren't all enveloped in the dead skin cells of previous shoppers.

Adelaide browsed the bookshelves that didn't contain any books. Small baskets were filled to the brim with differently colored and shaped ballpoint pens. Adelaide picked up one with an unnerving clown head on the end. She clicked the button. The clown head shot out from a small, metal spring. The head rolled with, what Adelaide swore was, a disturbing cackle underneath a bookcase.

Jules knocked over a coat rack. After catching it and putting it back up, he brushed off his hands and walked away all nonchalant-like.

"Oh, by the by," Harriet mentioned to Adelaide, "don't steal anything here. I know it's tempting with all these small little goodies, but don't."

"I figured you guys didn't have any rules," Adelaide said.

"We don't, but if you lift from the best fence in the city, he'll know. I don't know how he knows since he's always looking at other stuff in the back, but he'll know. Then you'll have trouble selling anything you pick again. Ever. Because the other fences will blacklist you too."

From the other side of the shelves, Baxter added. "Used to be a gang called Bone Broth did that. Other gangs kicked 'em out of the city just by not lettin' them buy or sell anything."

"Honor among thieves?" Adelaide questioned.

"Guess so," Harriet replied. "Order in the chaos and all that."

"How many gangs are there?"

"Oh, like a dozen. Cogs are the biggest. They got the whole Stacks."

Harriet browsed the old hats. She delighted in picking up a rather atrocious wide-brim with a stuffed rooster dangling atop it and shoved it on her head.

"What do you think?" Harriet presented the stuffed-bird, fashionable monstrosity.

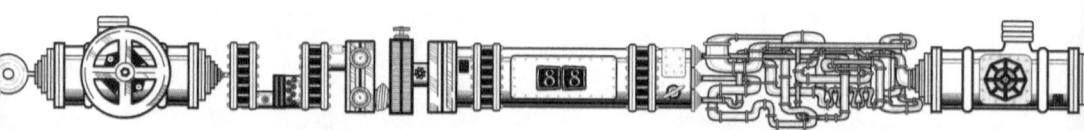

"I think it'll bring back painful memories for Baxter," Adelaide said.

"Oh frag. Good point. Though, that could also be fun."

"You talkin' bout me?" Baxter's voice filtered through the other side of the bookcase.

Adelaide joined Harriet in a laugh. The girls went back to browsing. Adelaide picked up a stick with a series of cog wheels attached. She spun one. The wheels turned and rotated up and over and around each other in a dizzying pinwheel. Jules walked past them both and held a rubber chicken in his hand. He squished it to make it squeak with each step he took.

"So what brings you here?" Harriet asked Adelaide.

Adelaide pointed to the girl haggling at the counter. "Zadie."

Harriet snorted. "No. What brought you to the city?"

"Oh. Well, my parents, I guess. My father specifically. He's wanted to move back to the city since he was a kid. And he just got the contract to redesign the rail system."

"That's nice." Harriet tried on just about every single gold bracelet that Mister Pawn had in his collection, which went up past her elbows. She had trouble putting on more because she could no longer bend her arms.

"Not really. His designs have a bunch of flaws. But they're cheap. So he makes everybody money." Adelaide mesmerized herself with the pinwheel, turning the gears over.

Baxter strolled into the aisle. He wore no less than six sets of goggles: one for his eyes, his forehead, his head, his nose, his chin, and his own pair hanging around his neck. Baxter tried on a mechanical bow tie and snapped the sliding metal pieces above his goggles around his neck.

"Leaving the grunts to fix the problems as the rich get richer, eh?" Baxter commented.

"I overheard his lawyer tell him that it's cheaper to pay lawsuits for wrongful deaths than to spend the money to fix the trains up properly."

"That's a bunch of bollocks—" The mechanical bow tie suddenly tightened around Baxter's neck. The metal bow spun of its own accord, twisting the belt noose. Jules grabbed the metal collar and unattached it from him. Baxter gasped for breath. "What the frag was that?"

"A gag gift?" Harriet smirked at her own pun.

Baxter stuck out his tongue at her and rubbed his throat.

Adelaide picked up a cylindrical device with three, sharp prongs on the end. She pressed a button on the side. The prongs spun around in dangerous fashion.

"What's this for?" Adelaide asked.

"You don't wanna know," Harriet replied.

Adelaide's mechanical arm suddenly spun around at the elbow's rotator, spinning three-hundred degrees before it spanked her on the rear before flying and smacking into a bookshelf. A box of cuff links scattered onto the floor. Adelaide grunted and tried holding it before it slapped her in the face before finally bending over and clamping her arm between her legs. She unscrewed the air hose connected to the rotator piston. After tooting out all of her hot air for an extended period of time, Adelaide slowly stood up with a limp, mechanical arm dangling by her side.

"I'll uhh... fix that later." Adelaide blushed. She gathered the fallen cuff links and knickknacks as one final toot punctuated the event.

"You okay?" Harriet asked.

Adelaide nodded. "Yeah, still got a few kinks to work out."

"Oh, kinky."

"So what's the deal with your arm?" Baxter wondered aloud.

"That's a rude question, Bax," Harriet scolded.

"Is not. She got a metal arm. I'm a curious person." He placed his hand on his chest and gave his most upturnious upturned nose his nose could possibly nose.

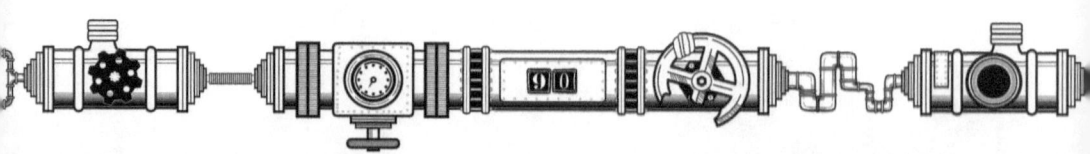

Adelaide chuckled. She absentmindedly played with her mechanical forearm lever. "It's okay. I lost it when I was six. My dad used to bring me to his train yards when he worked. I've always liked the big engines." Adelaide unscrewed her metal hand and tossed it to Baxter. He juggled it in the air before he finally caught it. The attached cable trailed loosely between her hand and arm and spooled along the floor. "When he wasn't looking," Adelaide continued, "I went out to the tracks. Hopped up on a running engine to see how the gears turned. I slipped and landed on the tracks. Next thing I remember..." Adelaide shrugged. "I woke up with one arm."

"I'm so sorry," Harriet said.

Adelaide withdrew her arm cable into her forearm until the cable was taut. She retrieved her hand from Baxter, retracted the cable, and reattached the hand. "After that," Adelaide said, "my parents weren't comfortable letting me out of their sight. Or the house. Or my room."

Jules poked his finger into an old, shoddy, metal clock. A cuckoo bird popped out from behind the faceplate. Aside from the spring loaded entrance, the sad display was silent and dead.

Adelaide continued, "Which is why I was looking forward to moving to the city, you know? First time I got to ride a train again in years."

"You ever get them ghost pangs?" Baxter asked.

"The what now?" Harriet asked back.

"You know, the things where you can still like... feel your hand even though you don't got one anymore. Like a ghost hand."

"Phantom pains?" Adelaide corrected.

"Yeah! That's it."

"Sure, but not so much anymore. Since it happened when I was really young and all."

Zadie approached the group with a large sack full of money. She nodded toward the exit, and they shuffled their way through

the crowded shop together after putting back all the various bits and bobs and roberts.

"You haggle him good?" Harriet smirked.

"I haggled the shillings[44] out of him," Zadie said. "He gonna be walkin' funny for weeks." They stepped outside into the smoggy, open air and stood on the rocky outcropping. Zadie jingled the coin bag. "Who wants to go shopping?"

"Food," Baxter said.

"You just ate."

"Oh," Adelaide looked around at the various shops, tents, shacks, and whosiwhatsits, "do they have any one-by-two air compressor pneumatic cylinders here?"

"Do they have a who-the-what-now?" Zadie replied.

"You can't eat those," Baxter grumped.

"Could," Harriet thought aloud, "but you'd wreck your teeth."

"And your bowels," Zadie added.

Approaching fast from the shadows of a nearby tent, a young man bumped hard into Zadie's shoulder.

"Watch it, pig rectum!" Zadie yelled at him.

The man smiled a yellow, toothy grin. A red tattoo of an eagle's claw displayed proudly on his neck. Two large, muscular men with the same tattoos flanked him.

"Looky here," the man said, "if it ain't the Punks. I thought you liked it rough, Zadie."

He chuckled and reached a hand toward Zadie's face. Jules snapped his hand out and grabbed the man's wrist, holding him tight in a strong grip.

"Don't start nothin' you can't finish, Johnny," Zadie said coolly. "And we're the Grinders."

---

44 A *shilling* was a type of coin currency used back in the day. Back when money was heavy and laws were light. Also the origin of the term *shill*, a person who does something only for money. Also the origin of the game known as *hilling*, where you curl yourself up like a coin and roll down a hill until someone vomits.

The man named Johnny attempted to twist his wrist free, but Jules' grip was iron tight. The two cronies behind him started to move, but they froze at the intense, icy stare behind Jules' semi-opaque visor. All Johnny could do was bluster in Zadie's general direction.

"This is our territory," he spat. "Gotta pay the toll to pass."

"Blood Claws got the Gorge, but ain't nobody got the Bazaar. Neutral territory."

"We're branching out."

"Oh yeah? How 'bout we go have a chat with Kaylock? He can sort this out."

Johnny's flushed face turned white. His struggle against Jules relaxed, and Jules released him. He gritted his teeth in Zadie's direction and opened his mouth to speak.

"Are you three in a relationship?" Adelaide asked, much to everyone's confusion.

"What?" Johnny asked.

"The matching tattoos." Adelaide pointed at their necks. "It's very cute."

"It's the mark of the Blood Claws, punk!"

"Well, it makes you three look adorable."

"It's a gang tattoo!"

"You even have little matching outfits."

"What?" Johnny glanced at his comrades. They inadvertently did dress alike, though all black leather was a rather common fashion statement. "I—"

"Guess you can't call yourselves a couple. You know, since there's three of you. Or would you be a thruple?"

"Are you out of your gourd?" Johnny blustered.

"I don't have a gourd, so I guess so?" Adelaide shrugged.

"That's not..." Johnny had trouble finding words, "it's not..." He glanced at Jules. Jules cracked his neck bones. Whatever Johnny was thinking of saying, he thought better of it and replaced it with, "Bah... whatever. Stupid kids."

"You're like two years older than we are," Harriet muttered.

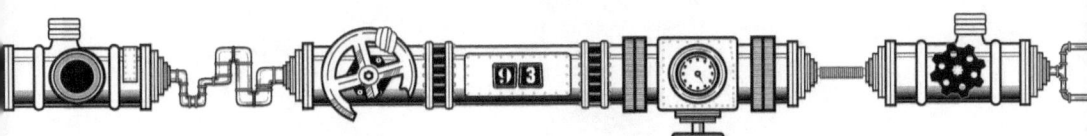

With a twirl of his finger, Johnny's overly loquacious buddies turned to follow. He stepped backwards so he could call out one last time, "Catch you later, punks," he said. "Remember, the Blood Claws strike without warning."

"But you just warned us!" Adelaide called back. "That doesn't make sense!"

The gang of three growled and walked out of sight. That was Zadie's cue to burst out laughing. Harriet and Baxter shortly followed with rowdy guffaws. Even Jules' muscled chest puffed up and down with silent giggles.

"I can't tell if you're a danged genius or a ditzy idiot," Zadie admitted.

Adelaide shrugged and grinned. "It's a fine line I like to walk." She beamed as they shared another laugh before she added, "Were they one of those gangs you mentioned?"

"Yeah," Zadie replied. "Blood Claws, overreaching little turd nuggets. Seem to forget the Bazaar is neutral territory,[45] but none of 'em would dare cross Kaylock. He's the leader of the Cogs, the biggest of the lot. Well, if you don't count the bobbies. Them cops are really the biggest gang in the city, but even they don't mess with Kaylock."

Zadie glanced into the Gorge and the sky above. Pinks and greens mixed in with the clouds. Rays of sunlight peaked through at a low angle from the clouds to the west. Across the Gorge, the Stacks with their black smoke coughing towers and chugging machines looked like they were trying to block the sun from sunning.

"Gonna be dark soon," Zadie commented. "Let's take the long short way home."

"What's the long short way?" Adelaide asked.

---

45 The long and bloody gang wars over the Bazaar came to an abrupt end after years of conflict when a beloved bakery was caught in the crossfire and set ablaze. A ceasefire was declared, and united funeral services were held for the famous éclair, making it the sweetest ending to a conflict in the history of Parsons City.

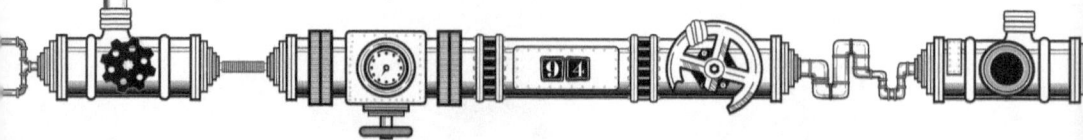

"The train."

"Zadie," Harriet chastised, "that's insensitive."

"What?" Zadie asked.

Harriet nodded toward Adelaide then pointedly glanced at the girl's mechanical arm. Zadie shrugged her shoulders in confusion. Harriet made the jarring head motions again.

"Oh, no," Adelaide began, "not because of me. I love trains."

"Really?" Baxter wondered. "I'd a figured you wouldn't like trains, since your arm got the chop and all."

"It wasn't the train's fault," Adelaide replied. "I find all sorts of things fascinating while also not wanting to be run over by it."

Baxter nodded while Harriet added, "Understandable."

Zadie led them through the Bazaar after she bought Baxter a cursory fried rat on a stick. Adelaide tried not to heave at his chewing and crunching as they weaved their way through the parting crowds. She looked out over the Gorge and followed the train tracks and the power lines and the bridges and the ziplines. The closest railway bridge carried a traveling engine chugging smoke from its stack and towing three passenger cars. Its whistle blew. Zadie picked up the pace.

They delved into claustrophobic roads tightly packed with all manner of housing and apartment buildings covering the top of the Gorge. Steep slopes and hills did nothing to stop the original builders from shoving buildings into every available inch, and some of them were even level. Those rare few that lived there felt particularly fancy at their flat floors.

As they rounded a corner, Adelaide saw the train tracks built three stories above the streets below, snaking its way between the clustered buildings. Ahead, a set of stairs led up to a platform connected to the tracks above. She could barely make out the small crowd settled around a barred barrier and ticket taker on the platform raised over the street. As they reached the middle of the stairs, Adelaide looked past the others and ahead to the platform where two people waited in line for the ticket taker.

"How much does it cost to ride?" Adelaide asked.

The others laughed at the question. Adelaide looked to Harriet. Harriet pointed to Zadie, who hopped off the stairs and onto the precarious footing of the cross braces supporting the raised train tracks above. The others followed along on the metal beam. Jules lagged behind.

Adelaide eased her legs over the railing and gently shuffled across the beam. It actually wasn't bad if she didn't look down. But if she didn't look down, she didn't know where to plant her feet. And if she didn't know where to plant her feet, she would look down and see the ground coming up to smash her skull into tiny bits. And if she didn't die from the immediate shock, her death would be slow and agonizing as her brains oozed out all over the asphalt while everyone around her watched.

On the other side already, Zadie climbed up the braces. Within moments, she was up onto the train tracks. Baxter and Harriet followed close behind.

Adelaide shuffled over to the end of the beam. Jules, with perfect balance and poise, stood behind her with his arms spread out, ready to steady her if needed. Her pride wanted to tell him that she could do it by herself. Her common sense told her pride to shut the fudge up.

With her one good hand, she began the climb, which actually wasn't difficult. The cross braces and decorative moldings made for a rather strange, but easily climbable, ladder. Zadie and Harriet helped pull Adelaide up to stand on the wooden beams comprising the platform.

"Hold on," Zadie said quietly to the group as Jules climbed up next to them.

Zadie's shortcut had them standing next to the train, on the other side of the station and ticket taker. Adelaide stood up on her toes so she could peek over the rim of the passenger car's window, through the spotty glass. On the other side of the car, a portion of the populace departed. A new group of passengers began entering.

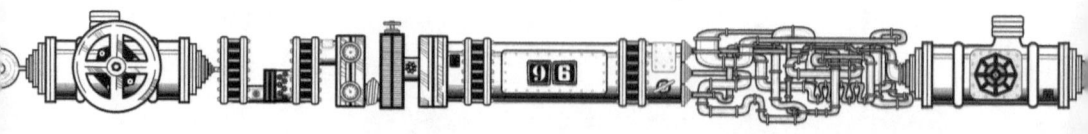

"All aboard!" shouted the unseen train conductor.

The train's smokestack puffed. Adelaide turned to look at Zadie, but she was gone. Baxter and Harriet climbed up the side of the train car, where Zadie was waiting on the roof. They used the railings and small ledges around the windows as hand and footholds.

Adelaide followed the leader. This makeshift rock-climbing wall was far more difficult than the cross beams below. Apparently, she was taking too long, because Jules grabbed her by the trunk and lifted her up. Zadie and Harriet grabbed her good arm and pulled her onto the roof. Jules leaped up with ease behind them.

Adelaide panted for breath as the train car lurched forward. The axles clacked. The wheels clanked. The smokestack chuffed. The sounds she so loved calmed Adelaide. She remembered why she wanted to take the train in the first place. She loved the artistry and engineering behind making several tons' worth of metal glide from one location to another.

With their ride gaining a bit of speed, Zadie rose to her feet and gave a mock salute to the shocked ticket taker back on the platform. She smiled down at Adelaide.

"Ain't nobody can stop you from riding the train this way!" Zadie laughed.

Adelaide gave a nervous chortle. The rushing wind whipped through her bushy hair. She blinked her eyes against the walls of buildings moving past. Baxter, Harriet, and Jules joined Zadie in standing up, gaining their balance and surfing on top of the train's roof. Slowly, very slowly, Adelaide found her feet underneath her. Her squat wobbled up into a standing position.

The train turned and rocketed up a hill. Adelaide shook and nearly lost her balance. Jules was ready to catch her, but she adjusted and caught herself. Her eyes studied the others and how they moved and shifted their weight in accordance to the train's direction. After approximately forty-two seconds, Adelaide understood how it worked.

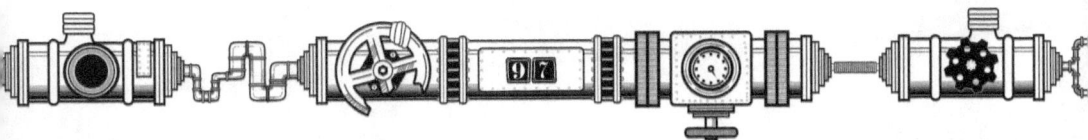

She surfed on the top of the speeding tube of metal along with the others. She imagined it was quite like riding on the back of a humpback whale. Or a metal dragon soaring through the sky. Only completely different. And much less strange. She grinned and blinked back tears from the onslaught of wind in her face.

After yanking left, then right, then right, then left, then up, the train entered the Upper District and reached the apex of a hill. From the top, Parsons City sprawled out across the landscape before them. All its construction, artistry, engineering, and beauty wafted over Adelaide like a rush of inspiration.

Adelaide closed her eyes and spread her arm out wide, taking it all in.

Chapter 8

First Day of School

With her eyes closed, Adelaide stretched out on an old, musty couch in the corner of the Steampunks' hideout, purely content within her new world. Her left arm draped down onto a rug and tapped out a steady rhythm, not even aware she was doing it. Her fingers had a mind of their own sometimes, always wanting to fiddle with something. Her rhythm was about as good as any rich girl from the Uppers who never learned any kind of musical linguistics, which was, to say, always, but not completely, off by a little bit.

Standing next to a blank stretch of wall, Harriet held a lunch tray in one hand and a paintbrush in the other. A variety of color globs spread out on the tray. Her hand brushed out what appeared to be an impressionistic view of the night sky.[46]

---

46 Impressionism is an art style that falls into two categories. One: it is a creative viewpoint of the world expressed with vivid colors, quick brush strokes, and purposefully vague detail work. Two: it is a creative viewpoint by artists who never quite got the hang of painting hands.

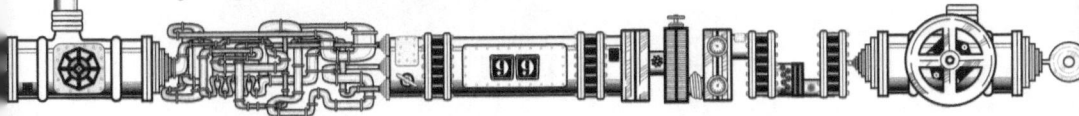

Jules laid back in his hammock, dangling off the hideout's ledge, fifty feet off the ground far below. He was reading a book, or, at least, he appeared to be reading a book.

Baxter sat cross-legged on the thin, uncomfortable rug next to the hideout grate's front edge. He dug into the inner workings of the wire pulley mechanism that lifted any stray punks from the ground below up onto the platform. He unscrewed a screw with a screwdriver. Inside the case, a rectangular piece of metal swung down and stuck itself into a rusty spring. Baxter immediately questioned his decision to unscrew that screw with a screwdriver.

With her feet propped up next to a metal lamp atop a small table, Zadie leaned back sideways in a plush, fuzzy chair, opposite the couch and Adelaide. A sigh escaped Zadie's lips so forcefully that she blew a raspberry. Her eyes darted around the hideout. They finally rested on Adelaide's jewelry box sitting on top of the coffee table in between the two girls. With a glance full of mischief, Zadie snatched it.

"So what's the deal with this box anyway?" Zadie asked.

Adelaide's eyes popped open. She jumped to her feet and grabbed the jewelry box from Zadie, who simply smirked at her. Adelaide clutched the object close. Memories of Lillian flooded her conscious and subconscious. All the consciouses. Adelaide glanced at Zadie. Then back at the jewelry box. Then back to Zadie. Then back to the box. Her mouth opened and closed as she wondered what she should tell them. Lying, much like organized rhythm, was never her strong suit.

"She was..." Adelaide began, "my nanny."

Zadie snorted and burst out laughing. Baxter and Harriet immediately joined in.

"Of course you had a nanny," Zadie chuckled.

"Yeah, yeah," Adelaide droned. "Ha, ha."

"Did baby's widdle nanny fix your booboo's?" Zadie wondered.

"No no," Harriet chimed in. "She done gived her a spot o' tea and some biscuits whenever she felt a tad peckish."

"Yeah!" Baxter wanted to join in too. "She like... wiped her nose and... and her butt."

He laughed. Zadie and Harriet turned their judgmental eyes to stare at him instead.

"She was more than that to me though," Adelaide explained. "She took care of the house and me, yeah, but... she taught me how to read. And she encouraged me and-and made me believe in myself." Adelaide plopped down on the couch. She gently set the jewelry box down on the table and gazed into it. "She made me feel loved. I had my mom, but Lillian was always the one who cared about me. The real me. More than my parents ever... anyway, never got a chance to give this to her."

"Why?" Harriet asked.

"She died. About a year ago. You know, I wasn't even allowed to go to her funeral. My mom said our *classes* shouldn't mix."

"Class?" Baxter asked. "Like maths?"

"No," Zadie answered. "She means the poor and the rich."

Adelaide's gaze shifted to the floor. She sighed herself deeper into the cushions.

"Buncha bollocks," Harriet said. "Family isn't determined by money or blood." Harriet strode over to the couch and plopped into the flattened cushions right next to Adelaide. Harriet wrapped both of her arms around her in tight hug. "Family's what you make of it!"

Even with her eyes getting a bit juicy, Adelaide couldn't hold back a slight smile beneath the grip of Harriet's oppressing shoulder. A hug when she was sad. That reminded her of Lillian too. A sudden, loud clank made Adelaide jump and Harriet release her. The wire pulley clonked and bonked and hissed, and the cable inside unspooled itself on Baxter's feet.

"Bah!" Baxter shouted at it. "Frag it!"

"What is it?" Zadie asked.

"It's a pulley, derp."

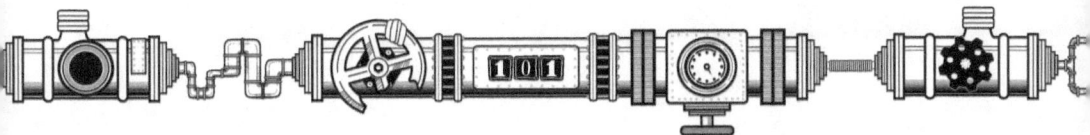

"What's the problem, doof?"

"The ratchet gear keeps slipping."

Adelaide raised herself from the couch and stepped over to take a closer look. She reached her good hand inside the pulley case and took off a metal piece.

"The pawl spring is rusted together," Adelaide deduced.

"Great," Baxter sighed. "We got any owl springs?"

"Pawl spring."

"What did *I* say?"

"Why don't you go look for yourself?" Zadie grumped.

Baxter whined, "But it's so far away."

"Really?"

"Hey! I'm doin' this for all o' youse. Where's *my* help when I'm fixin' junk?"

"Oh, fine."

"What's so far away?" Adelaide asked.

Zadie paused and smiled at her. "Have I never shown you the stash?"

Adelaide shrugged and shook her head.

"With me then. You're gonna like this."

Zadie led Adelaide out toward a side tunnel. After a couple of minutes of brisk walking, they came upon a cut-open section of the wall. Pipes and cables diverted inside where a small passage led to an intersecting tunnel. Zadie climbed in with Adelaide right behind. The passage traversed over an uneven, unlevel, unsafe, metal-grated floor, which looked down on a flowing trough of water below. Pipes and loose cables crisscrossed the extremely short ceiling overhead. Zadie and Adelaide ducked under a broken pipe and crawled along the creaking metal floor.[47]

---

47 Emergency Redirection Services had to be called numerous times in Parsons City over the years to repair pipelines and tunnels due to collapse and erosion. Emergency Redirection Services also specialized in spinning news after a politician would inevitably put his foot in his mouth, and once, in the case of Senator Gilderoy Pockmark, putting his foot in someone else's mouth.

"Is this stable?" Adelaide asked.

"Girl, ain't nothin' stable in the steam tunnels."

"I can see why no one really bothers you down here."

"It's perfect, right?"

Adelaide thought how they must have very different ideas of "perfect." For Adelaide, it was: a picturesque sunset, or a finished project she could be proud of, or maybe having good food with good friends, which was a more recent discovery. For Zadie, it appeared to be: dangerous things that no one else in their right minds would even consider doing. Adelaide couldn't pinpoint what it was about Zadie exactly, but no matter the amount of crazy that girl got her into, it didn't take Adelaide long to want more.

They hopped down from the passage into an intersecting utility tunnel. The pipes led out from the passage and out and around and eventually over to a circular chamber built into the circular wall. A large, circular, metal door barred the way. It was far too many circulars.

A hand wheel locked the door closed. Zadie leaned on the wheel and practically hung off it in order to turn. She grunted and shoved her entire weight against the door before it finally scraped inward to sounds of objects falling and crashing within.

Zadie stepped inside. Her hand pulled down a switch dangling from the wall. A collection of sparse light bulbs flickered to life.

"You can put your junk over here," she continued, "or keep it by your spot in the hideout. Don't matter."

Adelaide gazed around in wonder. The massive, metal, circular, holding container was overwhelmingly full of furniture, sewing machines, shoes, hats, bolts, chains, doors, wheels, anything and everything the mind could imagine. Her eyes couldn't decide what to land on next.

An old drapery draped over a rusted bank of levers and pulleys. A wood-fired grill gathered spatulas and tinker toys. What looked to be a half-collapsed collection of scaffolding laid

against the wall. A steering wheel hung from a chain attached to the ceiling, and an enormous amount of objects dangled from that as well, thirty feet off the floor. A rectangular banner read: "*Happy 70th Birthday, Grandma Gertrude.*"

"What-the-what is all this?" Adelaide wondered aloud.

"Years worth of stuff we've lifted," Zadie answered. "Some we had grand plans for but never got around to." She spun a tire attached to an axle stuck on a wooden dresser. "I think this used to be a water tower or something, why there's all the pipes and stuff coming in it. And that drain in the floor. Oh, can't really see it anymore underneath the horse carriage."

"Is that what I think it is?" Adelaide asked.

"I ain't no telepather."

Adelaide pointed up. Hanging from the ceiling was a large piece of fabric sewn onto a metal support structure that loosely resembled the wing of a bat. "Is that a glider?"

"Oh yeah," Zadie said as she gazed upward. "Part of one, at least. Couldn't figure out how to finish it. Or even make it work. Probably why we found it at the bottom of the Gorge."

"I've only ever read about those." Adelaide stared at the fabric, transfixed. Riding on top of a moving train was one thing, but the mere thought of flying made her ears tingle.

"You can mess with it if you want. Since you're smart and all."

Zadie stepped next to a desk topped with a dozen different lamps, some with shades and even less with bulbs. She opened the large bottom drawer, which was filled to the brim with every kind of screw, nut, bolt, washer, nail, hinge, pin, doorknob, bottle cap, and spring imaginable. Zadie was about to dig her hands in there but thought better of it. Her fingertips lightly shuffled around the pile of protruding metal pointy bits.

"We're bound to have one of those wall springs in here somewhere," Zadie muttered.

"Pawl spring."

"Sure that."

After twenty seconds of poking and prodding and haphazard searching, Adelaide approached and immediately picked out an only slightly-rusted pawl spring from the top of the pile. She blinked her eyes slowly while waiting for Zadie to catch on.

"Ah ha!" Zadie cried. "Right where I thought it was!"

Zadie plucked the spring from Adelaide's fingers and marched toward the exit. Adelaide hadn't moved from within the treasure trove of whatchamacallits.

"You comin', fancy hand?"

Adelaide's face had the exact expression of a kid who just got the keys to a candy factory. Endless possibilities encompassed every inch of her wet, squishy brain.

"I wanna build something," Adelaide finally gained the cognizance to say.

"Build what?"

"I don't know yet."

Zadie chuckled. "Alright." She turned around but stopped and turned back. "Oh, if Harriet comes by and locks you in as a prank, just turn the wheel on the inside panel there. It unlocks from the inside too."

Zadie strolled out of sight. Adelaide mostly heard what Zadie said. Part of the first part, at least. But her mind was even more obsessed with spinning out ideas, blueprints, and illogical concepts. What did she want to build, indeed? What *didn't* she want to build would be the easier question.

Adelaide had lost all sense of time. The stash was a mess, and she was going to organize all of it. She had made significant progress in rearranging the furniture and polishing the fireplace and setting up different containers for all the parts and pieces

when Zadie returned with the other Steampunks in tow in what must have been hours later.

"Havin' fun?" Zadie asked.

"Oh, you have no idea," Adelaide replied with an inadvertent snort.

Zadie tossed a large bread roll at her face. Adelaide didn't have the awareness to catch the flying food before it bonked on her nose and fell on the cold grill topped with scarves.

"Don't forget to eat, nerd," Zadie said with a smile.

Adelaide's eyes finally focused on the roll. She shrugged, nodded, and took a bite.

"So," Zadie began, "we discussed it and came to an agreement."

"Well..." Harriet countered.

"Shush," Zadie cut her off. "We think it's time for your initiation."

Adelaide raised eyebrow and asked through a mouthful of roll, "Initiation?"

"Yeah. Gotta initiate you all proper and junk into the gang."

"Yeah yeah!" Baxter cheered.

They all looked hungrily at Adelaide. Well, everyone except for Jules. His dark-tinted-goggled face seemed to be more interested in a rubber glove nailed to the wall. He yanked on it and watched it bounce back up.

"Is this gonna hurt?" Adelaide asked.

The others laughed, which did not reassure Adelaide in the slightest.

The Steampunks stood out quite plainly in the Upper District. The glass buildings shined against the gang's dirt. The potted flowers bloomed besides their dust. Even the rusted, clanking, moving sidewalks seemed to have a bit of

sparkle to them as horse-drawn carriages and automobiles chugged along the street before the smudged-nosed teenagers.

Across the street, a sprawling campus greeted them. Concrete walkways and metal structures and glass buildings scattered all over in a bit of organized chaos. A brick wall surrounded the property, accented by a sturdy, metal gate at the front. The steel-plated, arched gateway itself was welded to form letters that all looked like they were balancing on each other, and a plaque on the gate's right column bared the school slogan.

Elite School of Engineering,
Applied Physics,
and Mathematics
Where All Newcomers Are Welcome

Adelaide scoffed as she read the last line. "All newcomers are welcome, my amputated arm nub."

Zadie smiled and said, "They're gonna welcome us today, whether they want to or not. This is that school you wanted to go to, yeah? The one that made you yell at that guy at your parents' party? That was pretty funny, by the way."

Adelaide gazed at the University sign. She really did still want to go to school, but not quite in this fashion. They crossed the street and passed through the gateway and walked the grounds spattered with grassy lawns, concrete walkways, and a surprising amount of metal-plates providing structure or cover for whatever was below the grounds. Or the metal was just decoration. It was hard to tell. The only thing missing was the students. The Steampunks were quite alone.

"I'm surprised that it's empt—" Adelaide cut off her sentence as Zadie extended a hand back toward the rest of the punks.

Across the metal-plated yard and some bushes and a fountain and a confused area that was waiting to decide what it wanted to be once it grew up, a group of students in their late teenage years strolled out from behind the grand, dome-topped building in the center. The Steampunks took cover beneath the closest abstract statue. After a few moments, the students vanished from sight.

"Not completely empty then," Adelaide said.

Baxter looked up to the statue and the various bits of metallic, geometric shapes welded together in a conglomeration of other shapes and blobs.

"What the frack is this?" Baxter asked.

"Art." Harriet smiled.

Baxter's eyes crossed when he attempted to study the statue. "Fancy people are weird."

Jules paid no mind to the art. Instead, he adjusted Baxter's haphazard shirt collar. Zadie stared at a metal cube dangling by a chain off of the statue. In one move, she ripped the flimsy creation off of the larger flimsy creation.

"Want a souvenir?" Zadie smirked and tossed the metal cube to Adelaide, who juggled it with her good arm before finally catching it.

"Aww," Harriet whined, "you messed up the art."

"Really?" Baxter muttered. "How can you tell?"

"Umm, I don't know. It's the spirit of the thing, yeah?"

"It looks like the same piece of junk that it was before."

"That's because you're uncultured." Harriet put her hands on her hips.

Baxter crossed his arms. "Well, what do you think it looks like then?"

"It's art. It doesn't have to look like anything."

"So I can put a bunch of crap together and call it art?" Baxter asked.

"Well, there's like..." Harriet tapped a finger to her lips, "more to it than that. I think."

"Like what?"

"Like... spirit?"

"You don't have to make up answers to look smart."

"No, really. Look." Harriet presented the structure with grand flourish. "Doesn't it make you feel something?"

"You want me to touch it?"

"No, in your heart. Doesn't it inspire you? Doesn't it make you *feel* something?"

Baxter paused as he studied the shapes of metal. "I feel... hungry."

Harriet sighed. "So uncultured."

"I'm a realist. I don't waste good metal by plopping it in a clump to stare at."

Zadie groaned. "If you two lovebirds are done bickering..."

"We are not," Harriet and Baxter said in unison. "Stop it," they continued simultaneously. "No, you stop it." They both harrumphed, crossed their arms, and looked away.

"You want me to keep this?" Adelaide asked as she presented the metal cube.

Zadie snatched it and casually tossed it in the air before catching it again. She nodded for them to follow. Zadie strolled past the statue and to the side of a large, nondescript, rectangular building. In between the exterior beams made of metal, the brick walls gave way to windows. Zadie peeked through one pane of glass and saw an elaborate classroom on the other side.

"Good art can get you into places," Zadie smirked to herself. She firmly placed the cube into Adelaide's palm. "Initiation time." Zadie strolled over to the classroom window. Her finger tapped on the glass as her eyes studied Adelaide. "Smash."

"You want me to..." Adelaide trailed off as she looked from Zadie to the window.

"Smash. Smash. Smash." Zadie chanted with a wide grin on her face. Baxter and Harriet joined. All three chanted in unison, "Smash. Smash. Smash."

Adelaide glanced at all of them then back to the window. Butterflies flew into her stomach.[48] Jules ignored them all and watched actual butterflies flying by.

"Smash! Smash! Smash!"

Adelaide never thought that this would be the way she was finally going to get into school. Her brain couldn't decide if she was scared or excited. She didn't want to break anything, but the thought of disappointing her new friends grabbed her intestines and twisted.

"SMASH! SMASH! SMASH!"

Her anxiety boiled over to the point where her faculties slipped away. With an equal mix of confusion and determination, Adelaide wound up a pitch and threw the metal cube at the window.

It *thunked* against the glass and plopped down to the ground. The window survived completely intact with only a mild scratch. After an awkward silence, Harriet giggled and snorted. Baxter laughed as well.

"Maybe the spirit behind the throw counts?" Harriet asked between giggles.

"Maybe the spirit needs to build some muscle." Zadie plucked the cube from the ground.

Adelaide simply shrugged like the sheepiest sheep that ever did sheep.

"We'll work on your follow through later." Zadie dug into her satchel and pulled out a foot-long crowbar. She reeled back, but Adelaide leaped in front of her and held out her good hand. Zadie stopped and blustered. "Geez! What?"

"Wait," Adelaide replied. She placed her hand on the glass, and slid the frame upwards. It was unlocked.

Zadie gazed at her and the open window. "That's less fun... but quieter, I 'spose."

---

48 The first case of *butterflies in a stomach* was quite literal and led to so many questions.

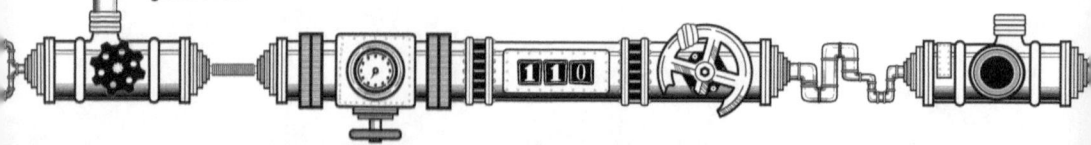

Harriet and Baxter laughed. Zadie waved her hand down. Their laughs softened. Meanwhile, Jules had no less than four butterflies sitting on his forearm.

"Let's see what they got." Zadie hopped through the window.

Baxter scrambled up behind her. Harriet held out a hand for Adelaide. She and Jules hoisted Adelaide inside before following afterwards.

Adelaide gained her feet on the tile floor and looked around. Desks and chairs formed perfect lines facing a chalk blackboard. A powerless projector stared at the wall by the desk up front. The thin-filament bulbs inside the chunky machine looked like it couldn't project much. Various plaques denoting special achievements covered the walls. Motivational posters were painted with phrases like: *"There's no 'I' in Steam!"* and *"If you see something, say something. If you don't see something, clean your goggles."*[49] Next to bookshelves and cabinets by the walls, several pieces of strange machinery hummed in the otherwise silent room.

"What do we do now?" Adelaide asked.

"Take it, break it, mess it up," Zadie replied. "This is your initiation." Zadie handed Adelaide the crowbar. "Grind the gears. Throw a wrench in the corrupt machine."

"That's a crowbar."

"Close enough. Go on." Zadie nudged Adelaide. "Grind the gears."

She stared at Adelaide. Everyone stared at Adelaide. Adelaide stared at Adelaide. Her head shrunk down beneath her shoulders. She glanced around.

---

49 Motivational posters first came into prominence in the city during the infamous Bread Riots, which historians disagree as to the whether the cause was the lack of bread availability or the lack of bread variety during a wide surplus of exotic cheeses. It was believed that motivational posters would alleviate tempers and ease the populace back to work, thus saving the boards of directors from having to pay out living wages. While the riots ultimately concluded with the return of the guillotine, and thus a more well-fed workforce, motivational posters themselves still remain popular to this day.

In a moment of peer-pressured panic, Adelaide shoved over a desk. The other Steampunks simply stared at her as it clonked onto the tile floor.

"Well, that's a start. I guess." Zadie snatched the crowbar out of Adelaide's hand.

Adelaide shrugged. "I don't wanna break anything."

"But that's part of your initiation," Zadie argued.

Adelaide's mechanical hand suddenly released itself from its wrist joint and fell to the floor with a *clonk*. Her eyes sheepishly glanced around.

"Breaking yourself doesn't count," Zadie stated simply.

Adelaide fiddled with her forearm lever until her hand reeled back into the wrist. She adjusted a couple of screws and said, "But Zadie, I just wanted to look around and—ooh books!" Adelaide rushed over to a bookshelf. "They have a copy of *Centrifugal Force and the Power Within*!" She opened it and thumbed through the pages. "I left mine back at my parents' place."

"Oh yeah," Baxter muttered. "Me too."

Zadie watched Adelaide for a moment before sighing and walking away. "Whatever." Jules followed her, but not before walking into the teacher's desk, knocking over papers, and picking them up quickly.

Baxter dug into the projector's underbelly, which was really just a box with lights and mirrors inside. He yanked out a string of copper wiring. "Oh, we can always use this," he said. Baxter began pulling the wire out. He pulled out some more. Then some more. He kept pulling out more like he was an illusionist performing a trick. "How did they fit all this in there?"

Harriet dug through the cabinets next to the blackboard. "Ooh," Harriet ooh'd. She retrieved a can of red paint and a fluffy, well-used brush. "I do think this place needs some color," Harriet said as she got to work painting the wall.

Baxter gathered a spool of copper wire in his hand and attempted to yank the final bit out of the projector. "Well, the art around here is rather gray," he grumbled. "And stupid."

"So's your face."

Harriet stuck out her tongue. Baxter stuck out his tongue. They both smiled at each other.

Adelaide stepped from one foot to the other. She looked around nervously. "We should go. We shouldn't be here."

"This's your initiation, ain't it?" Baxter asked.

"But I don't... we shouldn't... we're gonna get caught..."

"Not if we run fast," Baxter said with a chuckle. He looked into Adelaide's darting eyes. "Hey, slow your motor. It's all good. We're all in this together."

"That's what I'm worried about."

Harriet presented her work with a resounding, "Ta-da!"

Adelaide and Baxter looked up and gazed upon the huge, red letters that spelled: "*Girls Were Here.*" Her painting began with massive letters upon the wall next to the blackboard, proceeded onto the blackboard itself, then as she ran out of room, the letters became smaller and smaller. She finally ended up painting around the corner with the final "E" on the other wall.

"Just ran out of paint," Harriet said. "Well, what do you think?"

Adelaide tried to bury the sinking feeling in her gut. Her poker face refused to bluff.[50]

Baxter glanced at the paint. "It's just letters?"

"*Girls were here!*" Harriet chirped with a grand gesture across the painted words. "Funny, right? Since they don't let girls in. Buncha bollocks. Serves 'em right."

Adelaide thought Harriet had a point. People who do bad things should expect bad things in return, but she also felt the same about their own actions. Wasn't breaking bad peoples' stuff and writing all over it also a bad thing? Her brain hurt. Ethics

---

50 Her face also wasn't good at Parcheesi.

and sociology were never her strong suit, not when she could read about controlled explosions that powered pistons.

In the hallway outside the classrooms, Zadie strolled around with her crowbar on her shoulder. Her eyes locked on a glass display at the end of the hall. As she got closer, she saw that it was a trophy case. Partitioned into three glass sections, the case was filled with trophies, plaques, photographs, medals, and other awards, such as: "*Top Engineering School*" and "*Best Mathematics Program*" and "*Miss Grizzle's Barbecue Cookout First Place Award.*"

In the middle, a showcase was given the utmost space and respect. A golden plaque shined next to a photograph displaying the Mayor of Parsons City cutting the ribbon leading to a new wing of Newcomen University. The bearded man with a top hat and a fake smile had eyes that were a shade of dark auburn nearly identical to Zadie's wild, angry orbs. Zadie ground her teeth against each other with a scraping noise that would have made anyone else's skin crawl. Zadie's skin, however, felt nothing except red hot rage.

Her crowbar unleashed a sudden fury against the glass and the awards within. Zadie smashed and crushed everything she could see. Her eyes blazed. The shelves, plaques, and tin trophies didn't stand a chance. Not content with simply tearing apart the photographs, her crowbar pounded into the golden plaque given by the Mayor. She didn't make much progress in destroying the metal, but the scratches and scuffs and dents began piling up.

Zadie growled as a hand touched her shoulder and threw it off. She reeled around, ready for a fight, but instead, she found Jules' comforting, stoic figure. Zadie blinked her eyes. She shook her head, panted, and paced back and forth. After several moments, she caught her breath.

"I'm alright," Zadie said as she waved her hand at him.

"Zadie?" Adelaide asked as she, Harriet, and Baxter cautiously stepped over.

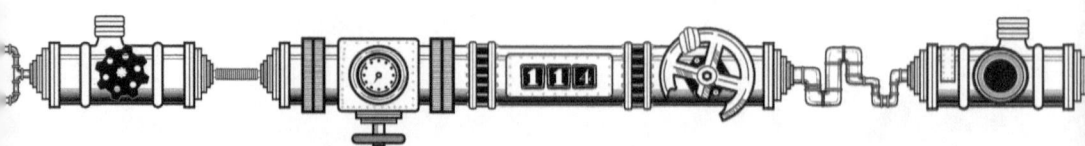

"I'm alright. Just... uh... just grindin' the gears, you know?" Zadie rubbed her nose with the back of her crowbar-wielding hand. Her other hand pointed at Adelaide. "How 'bout you? You break anything yet?"

"I..." Adelaide stuttered, "I-I didn't..."

Zadie growled. "You gotta get tougher, rich girl. If you're not willing to get your hands dirty, you ain't never going to change nothin' you don't like."

"Trashing a school won't exactly enlighten them on the matter," Adelaide argued.

Zadie smirked and glanced up at a canvas banner stretching over the trophy case. It read: *"The Future is in our Hands!"* Zadie ripped it off the wall in one motion. Her feet stomped the banner into the broken piece of wood, glass, trophies, and photographs. Her hand dove into her satchel, and she retrieved a box of matches.

"W-What are you doing?" Adelaide asked in a quavering voice.

"Enlightening them," Zadie replied as she tossed the lit match.

Chapter 9

Hot and Bothered

As it turned out, dry canvas material covered with a rather flammable brand of paint tended to be quite combustible. Fire spread across the remnants of the trophy case. The photograph of the Mayor stuck out from beneath the banner. His fake, plastered smile didn't quite match the setting anymore as the blaze enveloped the celluloid and charred it black. His smile smiled no more.

Adelaide stood still out of shock, not knowing what to do or where to go.

"Let's motor!" Zadie called.

Zadie, Harriet, and Baxter ran down the hallway toward the first classroom. Jules stood motionless beside Adelaide. After the flames danced in her eyes for several more moments, Adelaide's brain kicked back in, and she ran down the hallway in the opposite direction.

Zadie peeked her head back around the corner of the classroom. "Jules!"

He didn't respond. His dark, visored face just stared at the flames.

"Frag it," Zadie said as she ran toward him. "I'm sorry, J." Her hand grabbed his, and she pulled him away toward the classroom. "Come on!"

Down the hallway, Adelaide found a junction box bolted into the center of the wall. Pipes snaked down from the ceiling and gathered for a meeting of the metals within the box. Adelaide flipped open the lid. Inside, the pipes joined into various valves and crank wheels.

Her eyes traced the pipes back to their sources. One went into the wall. Another looped around before diving into the ceiling of a nearby classroom. A third just stopped for no reason whatsoever.

She finally found a pipe that ran along the hallway ceiling and connected to a series of sprinklers. Her good hand tracked the pipe to its valve and cranked the wheel. It seemed to do nothing.

Just as Adelaide questioned her ability to trace pipes back to its source, the sprinkler head over her head puffed. It squished out a lumpy mess of mold and sneezed out a stream of brown liquid. One by one, the sprinklers on the ceiling followed suit. A snort, a sneeze, and the sprinklers sprinkled bits of gloop. The pipes clearly had not been used in years.

Adelaide ran back to the inferno blazing upon the wreckage of the trophy case and threatening to overtake the wall. The brown water showered on her face, and she even managed to beat the slow stream to the flaming banner and wood. The sprinkler head above cracked and exploded. Old, moldy water fell over the area, or, at least, that's what Adelaide hoped it was. The brown shower doused Adelaide's hair, clothes, and the fire.

The flames slowly withered and died as the sprinkling waters extinguished the blaze. Her good hand manipulated her chest's

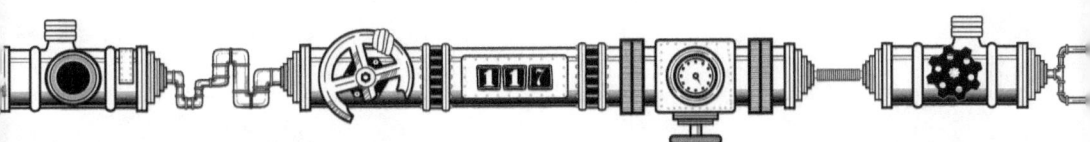

control panel, and her mechanical arm patted down and smashed any remaining remnants of smolders.[51]

Adelaide covered her mouth as black smoke poured upwards from the demolished case and mixed with the brown liquid pouring down from above. She coughed and staggered away. Her frizzy hair matted itself to her forehead. She wiped it away as her shoes squished and squeaked and slipped on the tile leading into the classroom.

As far from graceful as one can get, Adelaide flopped one dripping leg and then the other out of the open window frame. Her hip bone smacked into the ground. Jules, Zadie, Baxter, and Harriet stood safely outside with panic-stricken faces and/or gas masks.

"What the frag was that?" Zadie yelled as she studied Adelaide's wet, sopping form.

"I should ask you the same thing!" Adelaide yelled back.

"Stop right there!" a voice called. Behind them and around one hundred yards away, a grumpy-looking man sporting a bowler hat stepped out of the building opposite.

He blew into a shrill whistle that pierced the smoggy sky. The Steampunks ran for their lives across the campus. The forms of two, large men ran out of the classroom building's front entrance behind them. "Stop!"

They didn't stop. They passed underneath the gated archway. Adelaide glanced back. The men were keeping pace. She saw a glint off one man's metal helmet. A bobby. They were in it now. Adelaide would have felt regret had her head not been filled with the pounding of her wet, running feet squishing into the concrete, leaving a brown, liquidy trail behind.

---

51 The most unstoppable and untamable smolder belonged to, of course, "Handsome" Harry Plonkinulater, the famous hand model from the mountains of Boe. His smolder was said to make a woman swoon at fifty paces. His looks were revered until the day he died due to his being crushed by the world's largest mirror.

Zadie led them down the sidewalk. They turned a corner, leaped down a stairwell, rounded a bend, and sprinted through the underground. The concrete gave way to dirt, and the sounds of pursuit lessened. It wasn't until they made several more twisting turns that sloped down deep into the earth that Zadie finally relented their pace. Everyone seemed to appreciate that as all five of them panted for breath and held the stitches erupting along their ribs.

The Steampunks stopped in a massive, tunnel intersection of the ways. No less than seven different directions spread out before them in the circular chamber. Zadie turned her flushed face to Adelaide and pointed a tired finger at her.

"Alright, what's your deal, rich girl?" Zadie asked.

"Mine?" Adelaide panted. "You set a fire!"

"To send a message. You don't like it?" Zadie stepped up in front of Adelaide's wet, muddy face. "Tough."

Adelaide stood straight and stepped even closer to Zadie's face. If their noses had any hair, they would be tickling each other. "I don't like it."

"Tough."

"Schools should be safe spaces."

Zadie scoffed. "And why's that? 'Cuz they're rich?"

Adelaide softened. "Because knowledge is precious, and we should protect it."

"Hogwash."

"I thought *you* were making a safe space where... weird kids like us could belong and... and find freedom. I'm not going to be a part of any destroying stuff or hurting people. I'm just not. And if you don't like *that*, then I'm out."

Zadie wrinkled her nose and stared at Adelaide. "You want out?" Zadie spread her arms out at the conjunction of the tunnel entrances. "Take your pick."

"Zadie, stop," Harriet said. "That's enough. Let's just go before we get caught."

Harriet marched down one of the tunnels. Baxter and Jules followed. Zadie and Adelaide stared at each other.

"Fine," Zadie said. "You guys go your way. I'll go mine." She turned and walked away.

"Zadie..." Harriet called.

Zadie backhanded the air in their general direction. She strolled into a separate tunnel.

Harriet nodded toward Adelaide. "Come on. Let's go."

The four of them traveled back to the hideout without much to say, which seemed like a first for the group. Harriet checked on Adelaide and the others. Baxter made some grumbling remarks, but Adelaide was too wrapped up in her own mind to make much conversation. The peace and freedom she first felt from spending time with her new friends suddenly seemed fragile and not at all what she thought it was. Even Jules seemed more quiet than usual, which was seemingly impossible.

After they arrived back at the hideout, Harriet softly-but-not-so-subtly encouraged Adelaide to take a shower and wash off all the muddy, gooey liquid that covered every inch of her body. The shower turned out to be a boiler room filled with hot machines, a drain in the floor, and a tepid water pipe with a spray nozzle built into the wall, but it did the job. Adelaide washed out her clothes and put on new ones.

She retreated back to the stash to clean out her mechanical arm and generator pack, but she also just wanted to be alone for a while. Her brain couldn't comprehend talking about anything, and for the first time, she felt more alone with her new friends than without. It wasn't a good feeling, and she was suddenly rethinking all of her recent choices.

An hour or two or five or so later,[52] Harriet popped by and asked, "Want anything for dinner?"

---

52 It was difficult to keep track underground, after all.

120

Adelaide shook her head. She couldn't stomach the thought of eating right now, let alone literally stomaching something.

Harriet let her be, and Adelaide stirred restlessly and alone for many hours after. Her brain couldn't sleep. She just tried to keep herself busy and let her mind work in the background. She didn't know what to do or how to feel. So she just worked.

Zadie knocked on the metal, circular door of the stash, jolting a sleeping, drooling Adelaide awake. She wiped saliva and metal shavings and various indentations from her cheek.

Zadie sighed and leaned against the doorway. "Hey."

Adelaide brushed back her hair and nodded. "Hey."

"You, uh..." Zadie began, "I see you fixed up the stash."

The cluttered cacophony of chaotic crap around them was completely changed from the day before. The furniture was collected and upright. The tools were organized. The lamps were lit. The draperies hung straight and decorated the walls. Organized sets of drawers were labeled for every kind of screw, nut, and bolt that they had. It looked like there was an actual purpose to the stash. Adelaide herself was sitting at a makeshift workbench comprised of a wooden desk and an old stovetop.

Adelaide glanced around and replied, "Yeah, I tend to organize things when I'm upset."

The two avoided each others' gaze in several moments of awkward silence.

"So," Zadie began, "I'm told that I might have gotten a bit... carried away... back there."

Adelaide raised an eyebrow at her.

Zadie sighed. "Wanna take a walk?"

Adelaide searched her expression. Given that her own cluttered mind had refused to give her any answers, or any proper questions for that matter, she shrugged her shoulders and followed Zadie.

They walked the tunnels for a full minute in silence before Adelaide asked, "Where are we going?"

"I wanted to show you somethin'."

"Do we have to break anything or set it on fire?"

"No." Zadie snorted. "Unless you wanted to, then I'd be down for it." Adelaide frowned at her, so Zadie chuckled and said, "Kidding." She sighed and softly muttered, "Sorta."

They walked the tunnels. Adelaide still had a lot on her mind, but walking around again and getting some fresh air felt nice. Well, it was the freshest air she could get underground, sticking on the walls of muggy tunnels. After a few minutes though, Adelaide just had to know something.

"Do you really like destroying things?"

Zadie cocked her head. "Sure. Doesn't everybody?"

"No, I mean really." Adelaide sighed as she tried to find the words. "Like just... angry... *I-wanna-destroy-the-world...* stuff."

"I mean..." Now it was Zadie's turn to sigh and try to find the words. "I don't know."

The girls took a turn and crossed through a generator room. One row of boilers faced a row of steam-powered generators. Pipes and hoses and wires and cables traveled every inch of the place, so much so that they had to duck and step around them to get through.

"Here, let me show you something."

Adelaide's good hand grabbed Zadie's empty hand, and she led her over to the steam turbines. She placed Zadie's hand on the warm, vibrating metal roaring up a storm.

"You feel this?" Adelaide asked above the noise.

"It's vibratey," Zadie replied.

"This is beautiful. The boilers boil the water, make steam, push it through nozzles, the differing air pressure pushes the turbine blades, that spins the shaft around the magnets, and that sparks the electricity that turns on the lights."

"Did you just make all that up?"

"That's incredible! Whoever thought of doing all that before? You feel this concrete beneath our feet? The ingredients by themselves are nothing, but you mix water and hydraulic lime and dirt and brick powder and stuff together and lay it out until it dries and it makes this!" Adelaide jumped up and down. "That's beautiful!"

She skipped over the last two cables crossing the room and stepped to the lighter air of the tunnel beyond.

"Beautiful?" Zadie questioned.

"And these tunnels! Look at these tunnels." Adelaide stretched her hand and gestured to the ceiling. "Concrete block walls and metal braces and support beams and look how much weight they can support all at the same time. Tons and tons of it! We're a hundred feet below the ground! Isn't that amazing?"

"You are way too excited about dirt."

"Just think of everything they needed to build this place. All the knowledge and experience and engineering. Look at those pipes pumping water into the boilers. Just think about where all the water comes from and how far we'd have to go just to have something to drink. Just think about the plumbing! Genius."

Zadie shrugged as they meandered their way down the tunnel. "I do like my toilets."

"Exactly! See, it's just like with the university. I don't see just a place where ignorant people come to spend time. I see all the brilliance and inspiration behind the work. The sheer artistry and thoughtfulness that goes into this stuff is just... incredible."

"Yeah? And what about if all those ignorant people just use this incredible stuff to beat down others? What then?"

Adelaide sighed and looked around, buying time for a suitable answer. "I think... I think everyone deserves the right to learn from their mistakes and improve themselves. That's how we grow."

Zadie scoffed. "You're an optimistic little sod, aren't you?"

The two girls smirked at each other. Soon, the mugginess of the warm steam tunnels cleared. The lights became brighter.

They took another stairwell up, which ended in a pair of cellar hatch doors. Zadie opened them up.

Blinding sunlight blasted into the stairwell. Adelaide staggered up onto an alleyway in the Upper District by a sidewalk. Numerous pedestrians shuffled past as horses and automobiles chugged and tooted along the street adjacent. After her eyes adjusted to the onslaught of sun, Adelaide recognized the gated archway of Newcomen University a-cross the street.

"You wanted to take me back to the school?" Adelaide groaned. "I still feel bad about that."

"Nah," Zadie replied. "Across the street."

Zadie nodded her head to the side. A variety of shops and apartment buildings encompassed the area surrounded by moving sidewalks and trams. One in particular instantly caught Adelaide's eyes and refused to let go.

The front face of the nearby, multi-story building had an alcove in the front that broke the monotony of its straight, brick walls and shiny windows. Within the alcove was a twenty-foot-tall, metal-plated, clockwork-geared, spiky-headed dragon statue. Bits of reclaimed metal pieces of all shapes and alloys had been welded together to form the colossal shape. Adelaide marveled at the artistry and wonder-ed how sharp those massive fangs were. Suddenly, a burst of fire shot from a pair of nozzles in its mouth. The flames swirled and evaporated on the wind.

A metal-lettered sign attached to the dragon's belly read: "*The Book Wyrm*."[53]

"I thought you might like the bookstore," Zadie said.

---

53 A wyrm is a dragon. A worm is a worm. A stern term for a burn wyrm is a pachyderm to squirm your dern learns. And a book is what you're reading, in case you forgot.

Chapter 10

The Book Wyrm

The three-story store had floor to ceiling, floor to ceiling, and floor to ceiling bookshelves filled from top to bottom. Adelaide squeezed through the entrance hall marked by piles of free-standing books that hadn't made it onto the shelves quite yet. Zadie squeezed through looking as though touching one of the books might scald her skin right off.

Adelaide looked up through the atrium, the heart of the place that looked up onto all three stories. The top two floors were built from the same metal grating that seemed so popular in the tunnels below, but here, Adelaide thought they were magnificent.

"Greetings, readers," called a man behind the front counter. The lenses of his half-moon spectacles made the bottom half of his eyes appear to bulge and twist. He didn't wear a hat as was common among men of a certain age in the Upper District. Instead, he let his hair stick out wildly in all directions as though he just suffered a tremendous shock.

Upon the counter was even more books. He seemed to be sorting through them. His wrinkled, paper-cut hands placed one volume onto a metal contraption with a flat top. The machine sprang to life. Literally. A large spring within launched the book like a mini catapult. It flew through the air above their heads and landed somewhere upon the third floor. Adelaide had to blink her eyes several times to make them change focus back to the clerk.

"How can I help you ladies today?" the Book Wyrm clerk continued before bowing his head toward them. "Boregard Waunderlust at your service. Looking for anything specific?" Before Adelaide could think to respond, he replied to himself, "Too bad!" He cackled and snorted. "That's not how I do things. You'll find no ordering or cataloguing 'round here! Books go on the shelves. You browse and find what tickles your fancy." He placed another book on the catapult, and it launched somewhere into the second floor. "Wheee!"

"You don't separate by genres or categories?"

"Poppycock!" he snorted. "The best discoveries are made by accident. Wander the aisles. Finding a wondrous treasure that you weren't searching for is what it's all about. Tootle-loo! Off you pop!"

Zadie and Adelaide shrugged at each other and stepped away from the counter. The clerk returned to his sorting. Another book catapulted through the air and crashed onto the third floor, knocking over a pile.

Adelaide just shook her head and decided to simply start at the nearest bookshelf. As the clerk said, there didn't seem to be any rhyme or reason to the filing system. "*Parsons City: From the Mining Age to the Industrial Revolution* by Bernard Bagginhoten" was right next to "*Discovering your Inner Clockwork Mechanisms* by Nigel Stewart" and "*Advanced Alchemical Solutions: 7 Uses for Rat Intestines* by Rudolph Leopold Jericho Hoffinstuffins the Fifth."

"I'll be up on third," Zadie said. "Think they got chairs there."

She stepped over to a cable with a handle on the end, dangling from a motorized pulley somewhere up near the ceiling. Zadie gave it a slight tug, and the cable yanked her upwards through the atrium. Her feet found the third floor railing and stepped off down the short steps to the grated floor welded for that purpose.

With Zadie's weight released from the cable, the mechanism released the lock and unspooled it once again. Adelaide watched and waited as the cable extended down to her on the first floor. She followed suit. Her left hand grabbed and pulled, and she was yanked skyward. Adelaide's eyes and stomach sank down to her bottom, but they popped back up at the third floor. She dangled her feet over the open air and kicked around until she found the third floor railing. Her hips hoisted her over, and her feet clomped onto the tiny steps. As Adelaide grabbed the railing behind her and watched the cable descend once again, she made a mental note to find the stairs next time.

Adelaide lost Zadie through the twisting maze of bookshelves and towers of books, but she didn't mind. The minutes flew by as she crutched her metal arm and stacked volume after volume in the crook of her elbow. "*The Forgotten Fallacies of Ancient Mechanics* by Albert Meningrad" and "*Magnetic Influxes and You* by Eric Lennysure" and "*How to Tame your Generator* by Asterid Hicklelumps" were just to name a few. She even found another copy of "*Centrifugal Force and the Power Within.*" The clerk downstairs was right. What she found was a wondrous collection of knowledge that she didn't even know she wanted.

In her rambling yet focused meanderings, Adelaide finally found Zadie sitting in one of a pair of plush, cushioned chairs next to a massive, circular window overlooking the grand campus of Newcomen University across the street below. The top of the horned dragon was visible near the bottom of the window frame. A burst of fire exploded from the wyrm's mouth

outside. Zadie snorted herself awake as Adelaide flopped down into the chair next to her.

"Oh," Zadie smacked her lips, "find some stuff, did ya? Don't spend it all." Zadie tossed her the pouch of shillings. Adelaide failed to catch it with her good hand, but it landed on her pile of books crutched in her metal elbow. "It's all we got for now. Until we find another score, at least."

"You aren't gonna give me a budget?" Adelaide asked.

Zadie shrugged. "It's uh... consider it a peace offering."

She crossed her arms and leaned back in her chair. She gazed out onto the campus. They could see a work crew gathered around one of the classroom buildings, dragging out damaged goods and hauling in new items. Adelaide wanted to question her, pick her brain. After all, this was the first time their leader-in-thief seemed vulnerable, but Adelaide held her tongue and waited for Zadie to open up if she felt like it, which she apparently did.

"I can go overboard sometimes," Zadie admitted. "I know that. Sometimes I may need somebody to... hold me back. But sometimes I see something that reminds me of..." She sighed and stared out the window. "My father is one of those rich big-shots, and I was a bastard child. Him and the maid. Kept it quiet a few years. Protect his marriage and reputation and all. 'Till I was about five or so. Best I remember, he was makin' a run for political office. Wanted to get rid of the skeletons in his closet, so to say. He got a big ole' waterfront mansion on the ocean cliffside. Stabbed my mom. Tossed her over the edge. Stabbed me. Tossed me over the edge."

"Holy smokes!" Adelaide gasped. "And you survived?"

Zadie raised an incredulous eyebrow toward her. "No. I died. Clearly."

Adelaide blustered, "Oh, I well..."

Zadie lifted up her shirt and showed a thin but nasty scar by her ribs. "That's from the knife." Large scar gouges crossed the side of her belly. "That's from the rocks, I think."

She traced marks on her cheekbone and jaw that Adelaide had not really noticed before. "Some folks picked me up and patched me up. Still got this weird noise in my arm though." She extended her elbow with a *click*. She retracted and extended, again and again, each time with an audible *click*. "I feel like I should make music out of it and charge people to listen."

Adelaide grimaced. "Feel free to stop that anytime now."

Zadie stopped and shrugged her shoulders instead. "Bad elbow-related memories?"

"Nope. Just kinda creepy."

"Huh. I should do it more often then."

"Only if you want to pop your elbow out of socket."

"Hmm. Noted."

After a moment, Adelaide asked, "Who were the people that saved you?"

Zadie shrugged. "Didn't ask. After I could walk, I scarpered. Been on my own since."

"I guess that's why you have so much trouble trusting people, huh?" Adelaide deduced.

"Hey, don't go shrinkin' me now, yeah? I just thought you should know why I get a little... anyways. Just thought for if you wanted to stick around, is all." Her eyes glanced at Adelaide then looked away.

Adelaide smiled. "Yeah, I guess I could."

"Alright then." Zadie sat back and faced the window.

"Alright then." Adelaide sat back and faced the window.

A flying book launched by a catapult knocked over a pile of books on the aisle next to them. A soft train whistle tooted from above. Adelaide looked up and saw a toy train following tiny tracks built into the top of the bookshelf behind them. The cargo cars dragging behind the engine and wooden tinder box were filled with various books of different sizes.

A complex, three-fingered, mechanical arm was built into the caboose. It extended downwards several shelves and looked like the collapsible limb could extend much farther still. A

rotating flap on what could only be considered its elbow dragged along the books on the third shelf down from the top as the train drove along the top. The flap appeared to be counting the books. As it reached an empty space, the train engine stopped. The arm reached up, plucked an unfiled book from the toy cargo car, flipped it downward, and placed it on the empty space along the shelf. The train engine tooted its whistle and started off again.

Just as Adelaide marveled at the design philosophy and engineering behind such a device, the toy train bumped and took a sharp turn down an adjacent bookshelf. The book cargo flew off and rained down on their heads.

Zadie grumbled, "Alright, I'm done with this place," after being clonked on the skull with "*Sweating It Out: The Healing Power of Steam Baths* by Clarence Clearwater."

"Yeah, let's get out of here," Adelaide groaned after getting hammered with a flying copy of "*Love Among the Cuckoos: A Clockwork Romance* by Matilda Muffinhouse."

They retreated down to the first floor, by the spiral staircase this time. Adelaide made her purchases from the bespectacled clerk.

"A pleasure spreading knowledge with you today," Boregard Waunderlust said. "Do come back soon. And oh, would you file this on your way out? Anywhere will do."

He placed a book on top of Adelaide's head and nodded toward the shelf by the entrance. Adelaide didn't know why he put the book on her head or if she was supposed to balance walk it all the way over, but she decided to just roll with it.[54]

---

54 "Learning through osmosis" was a scientific strategy employed by many during the Intellectual Resistance. Though it mainly resulted in whelps and concussions, one scientist successfully absorbed the knowledge of the entire encyclopedia into his skull, which unfortunately caused others to shun him for the rest of his life due to his being an insufferable know-it-all.

A toy train traveling along the top of the bookcase behind Boregard tooted, derailed from its tiny tracks, and crashed into the floor. He gave absolutely no notice and said, "Ta ta!"

Adelaide slowly balanced and tip toed her way over to the shelf. With her mechanical arm crutched with several books, she used her good hand to shove her balancing head book randomly into the fourth shelf by the door, which seemed to be in spirit with the place. Zadie shook her head in confusion and couldn't seem to get out fast enough.

Once her brain finally relaxed, Adelaide realize she was hungry since she hadn't eaten in a full day. Zadie led her to the "*Catwalk Cuisine*," a bistro on a fifth-floor rooftop. Adelaide ordered a Butternut Squash Burrito, and Zadie got a Carrot Country Cornpop. Adelaide's meal of wrapped, orange goop was surprisingly tasty, but she wasn't sure she could get used to the fizzling. All the same, her stomach was empty, and she ravished the poor thing.

Afterwards, Zadie took them a different way home this time. They found a lift built into the sidewalk close to the entrance to Newcomen University. It lowered through the earth for the better part of a minute before the concrete walls gave way to dirt then gave way to open air. Adelaide gazed through the protective gate and into a massive monopoly of naturally-formed caverns beyond.

Large lamps and bulbs were wrapped and strapped and tied around every nook and cranny and stalactite in every part of the cave ceiling. Or, at least, every part of the cave ceiling that Adelaide could see. Seven stories, eight stories, science fiction stories of towers and piles and complexes of homes, apartments, dwellings, and other wellings were stacked up into nearly every single speck of space.

Stringed lights were stapled along under roofs and eaves and pergolas. First floors jutted out beneath the second on some buildings. Other second floors were more prominent in a bucktooth-like situation. There was no rhyme or reason for the overall design of the place. Every multi-story structure seemed to have been built at a different time than the rest, and every story of every building was seemingly built at different times as well. Sometimes the fourth floors came before the thirds. Sometimes they skipped the fifth and went right to the sixth. With the multiple levels of varying elevations, angles, and directions, it appeared as though hundreds or even thousands of families and groups decided to come down here and hammer their own little block of home in the cavern. The cacophony of packed dwellings made Adelaide's mind whirl.

The lift lowered, and Zadie led her through the maze-like alleys that hooked the whole place together. Front doors of one building were next to the back doors of another as everything pointed in its own direction. They walked past a group of shabby-clothed individuals huddling around a metal barrel with a fire going inside.

"Where are we?" Adelaide asked.

Zadie glanced back. "This here's Lower Central. Most blue collar folks live down here so they can work up in the Uppers above."

"Why wouldn't they just live in the Upper District?" Adelaide asked.

Zadie laughed. "Ain't nobody got money for that. They got the room up there, sure. Lots of unrented places. But these folks can't afford that."

Around a few but-less-than-a-bushel more twisting alleyways, Zadie nearly marched headfirst into a large group of both shabby-clothed and definitely-not-shabby-clothed individuals gathered outside a tower of residences. She stopped dead in her tracks. Several of the men were police

officers. Their shiny bobby helmets turned toward the two teenagers.

"If it isn't my favorite punk of the steam tunnels," said a tinny, gravelly sort of voice that sounded like it echoed from within a metal container.

The five-foot-tall, trenchcoated man Zadie had nearly bumped into turned around to face her. He leaned on a heavy, metal cane. Wisps of black hair floated out beneath his raised, black hood attached to his black trench coat that looked like it had been sewn together entirely out of pockets. Dark, black, reflective goggles hid his eyes. Most notably, a molded block of metal completely covered the lower part of his face and jaw, if he still had a jaw under there. A pattern of holes were drilled into the place where his bottom teeth would have been.

"Good morrow, Zadie," his voice echoed through the metal jaw. It moved slightly as though he still had limited control over its movements.

"Caretaker," Zadie greeted with a tone more metal and devoid of life than the man's jaw.

A bobby marched out of the residence tower that had been cobbled together from a variety of rooms that had no business being stacked on top of each other. The officer threw a chair onto the small patch of clay and limestone comprising what might be called a yard. A woman and two children huddled near the broken, picket fence surrounding the property.

"What's goin' on?" Zadie asked.

"Just serving an eviction notice," the short yet imposing man known as Caretaker replied.

Next to the part of the broken picket fence where all the planks had fallen off, Adelaide placed her hand on a solitary, wooden brace. She stared across the clay yard at the family. Adelaide recognized the woman from the train station platform: Cheryl, the kind-eyed lady who pushed the cart with a broken wheel.

"Why are you throwing them out?" Adelaide asked.

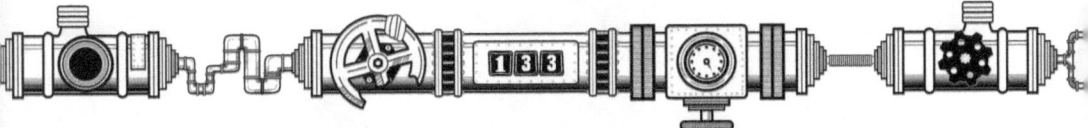

"Failed to pay their dues," Caretaker said simply.

"How much do they owe?" Adelaide asked.

"It's not about the amount," Caretaker replied. "I've a reputation to uphold. Without order and rules, humans devolve into chaos." He spotted Adelaide's mechanical arm. "Ah, a fellow amputee." He lifted his heavy cane and tapped his right foot. It clanged as the metal cane hit a metal boot. "Just a solid piece, I'm afraid. But yours! So intricate. Slim. Functional. Who built it for you?"

"I did," she replied.

"Truly? Tremendous work. Simply tremendous. Perhaps you would like to come live at the orphanage with me and my other children." He gestured to the opposite side of the alley. A group of three, ragged-clothed children stood by and watched Caretaker. They nodded their heads in unison to his beckoning.

"Not interested," Zadie replied for Adelaide.

"Oh? But you could have your own room. A warm bed. Safe. All the food you could eat. And you wouldn't have to eat scraps from the garbage anymore."

Zadie jabbed her finger into Caretaker's pocketed chest. "Back off, old man."

"Such fire, Zadie. Think of all the profits we would make if you worked for me."

Zadie growled and walked away. Adelaide looked back to the clay yard and broken fence. An officer threw a wooden dresser off the second-floor balcony. It shattered into splinters on the clay below. Cheryl held her two, young sons close to her chest. Adelaide stepped around Caretaker and a couple of completely-useful-and-not-just-standing-around-and-doing-nothing police officers. She stood on the other side of the fence by the family.

"Do you have anywhere to go?" Adelaide asked. "I'd have to ask, but we could make room. Maybe find a couple more hammocks."

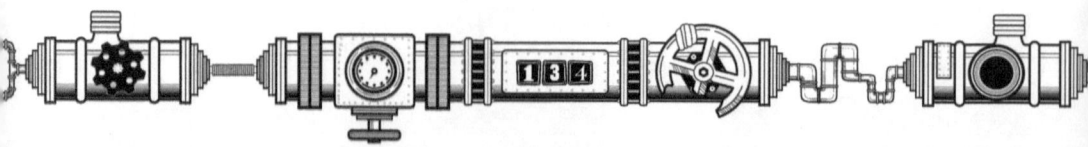

"That's awfully kind of you, but no, thank you, darlin'," Cheryl replied. "We'll find our way, just like we always do. Ain't that right, boys?" She jiggled the shoulders of her sons, who nodded and continued to stare transfixed at the dirt. They all jumped as an officer tossed another box of belongings off the balcony. After a few moments of quiet, she continued to her boys, "Come on, we've got all we need right here. Let's go."

They walked around to the gate, stepped past Caretaker, and without another glance, made their way down the twisting alleyways. Adelaide watched until Cheryl and her boys disappeared beyond a corner. Caretaker stepped up behind her.

"It's just business," he said. "In this city, there are the *haves* and the *have-nots*. If you want to be one of the former, I suggest you get away from Zadie. Don't let her drag you down into the gutter too."

Adelaide looked up into the face of one of the orphan boys. His eyes looked like they had seen too much. The lights were on, but nobody was home. Adelaide finally turned away and shuffled past the Caretaker.

"Think about what I said, girl," he called.

With a backwards glance, she saw Caretaker handing a pouch of something to one of the officers. Adelaide turned back and walked in the direction she saw Zadie go. After a turn down one of the alleyways/roads/passageways, she found her. Zadie waved her along.

"Don't listen to that old fart," Zadie said. "He's just another money grubber. Take you in, work you to death, then kick you out when you can't pickpocket enough 'tribute.' That's where Harriet was when I first met her. Ain't nothin' good 'bout that orphanage of his."

They made their way across, and Zadie heaved her weight against a metal door built into the cavern wall. They entered yet more tunnels and twisting passageways. Even out here were many scavenged sorts of homes that had been dug into the

corners of the dirt tunnels.[55] Wooden pallets formed the walls. Blue tarps covered the roofs. Cloth towels flapped over the doorways. Power cables draped along the top in what were clearly fire hazards waiting to happen. Adelaide had had just about enough of fire hazards.[56]

"Do people have to pay rent for these too?" Adelaide asked.

"Everything costs money," Zadie replied. "Everybody thinks they own everything. Unless you go a mile underground, avoid the cave-ins, hide, cover your tracks, and live in the sweltering heat next to the boilers and generators like us."

"I'm surprised more don't."

"Never be surprised at what people will do for a little bit of comfort or security, even if it's only imaginary."

The two punks walked through the packed tunnels until they transformed from sparsely populated to none at all. Adelaide looked back.

"I wish there was something we could do to help," she said. "I wish I could build something to help everybody. Make everyone's lives easier, you know?"

Zadie looked at her for a moment as they trudged their way down a slope. "I've tried to get Caretaker's kids to join us, but it's hard to compete with three square meals and your own bed. And when they get tired of him, if he even lets them go, they'll just join one of the bigger gangs that actually have space and sunlight. Everybody does what's best for them, that's all."

"Do you wanna be like one of the bigger gangs?"

---

55 Digging a corner into a cylindrical tunnel was a "perfectly sound engineering structure," according to Professor Hopstead Wingledom the Fourth. It reinforced the location by confusing mathematicians, which appeared to be Professor Wingledom's primary purpose in life due to a traumatic incident in his youth involving a protractor.

56 I hadn't had haddock who had had a hadron hadrosaur.

Zadie shrugged. "It'd be nice to have respect. Maybe we wouldn't have to struggle so hard all the time. Maybe even get a slice of territory up above. That's why I keep trying to get us into the Gear Games."

"The Gear Games?"

"Oh, that's right. You don't know nothin'."

"Rude."

"Gear Games is the best entertainment a bunch of street rats like us can find. All the city's top gangs gather together and compete for money, prizes, and street cred. Leader of the Cogs puts it all together. He calls 'em all in to the games once or twice a year, depending on if he can get the bobbies to look the other way or not for a night. I really wanted to build an auto to race in the games again, but Bax said we're about fifty parts shy. And also shy a motor. And wheels."

"It's an automobile race?"

"Sort of. It's different every time. First time we went, it was a race. Then it was like a relay. Then it was a scavenger hunt." Zadie giggled. "That one was funny. Bunch of dumb gang bangers trying to solve riddles." She snorted and wiped her eyes. "Good times."

"Did you participate in that one?"

"Naw, we tried our hand when it was like a slalom one. Kind of like a race. Ran around to different gates and all. That... didn't work out."

"They had automobiles?"

"That and... they mugged us and knocked Baxter out cold."

"That's not against the rules?"

Zadie scoffed as they rounded a corner. "Ain't no rules in the Gear Games. Why it's filled with a buncha dirty lowlifes like us. But even so, we lost a ton of rep that day. *Reputation*," she explained for Adelaide's arched eyebrow. "Nobody respects us. That's why they call us the punks of the steam tunnels. I wanted our gang name to be the Grinders, but no one calls us that. Steampunks stuck real quick though. Still, could be worse. Heard

of one small gang that got stuck with the nickname: *Skidmarks*. No one wanted to join them. Don't think they're even around anymore."

"I like the name."

"Skidmarks?"

"No!" Adelaide giggled. "Steampunks."

"Like I said, could be worse. They mostly just call us *Punks* though."

"So you want an automobile for this competition?"

"I mean, it don't gotta be. Just need somethin' fast to keep up with the rest of 'em. They're always some kind of race, or it helps if you're fast at any rate."

Adelaide tapped her finger on her lips as they hopped down a stairwell.

"You know," Adelaide thought aloud, "you got lots of stuff in the stash."

"Yeah."

"Engines, generators," Adelaide counted off on her good hand's fingers, "bits of chassis, axles, wheels," she counted on her mechanical hand's fingers, "hose, wiring, pipes..."

"Yeah?"

"Can't build you an automobile," Adelaide reasoned. "But I could build something else."

Zadie cocked her head and looked at Adelaide.

"Several somethings, in fact," Adelaide continued.

"Like what?" Zadie asked with more than a bit of interest.

"Depends."

"On?"

Adelaide looked Zadie in the eye and asked, "How fast do you wanna go?"

Zadie's entire face curled into a mischievous smile as she replied, "Yes."

Chapter 11

The Gear Games

Gangs flooded the streets bathed by an air of nighttime mischief.[57] In a swath of flat concrete surrounded by oddly-shaped buildings, a conglomeration of unsavory-looking characters gathered. The fierce men, women, and all-manner-in-between filtered into separate groups and all appeared to have their own color-coordinated, matching uniforms, of a sort.

This area was the Stacks, a nickname given to the southern district bordering the Gorge. Shacks and shanties packed every inch between the smokestacks and power plants billowing plumes of black. While the residents of the Upper District enjoyed the wealth of electrical power and water that flowed from the Stacks, they enjoyed having the Gorge separate the two districts even more. The bridges and tunnels connected them, but one man connected the two districts above all else.

---

57 Nighttime mischief air tends to smell, unsurprisingly, like canned beets with just a hint of flatulence.

"Enoch! Enoch! Enoch!" the gang members chanted in unison. Most of the noise came from the largest group of ruffians who were all wearing cog-themed glasses and apparel. While they all had their differences, one thing was for sure: they sure seemed to like their metal wheels with the pokey bits. One older un-gentleman displayed an actual gear cog strapped over his face as an eye patch. It looked highly uncomfortable.

"Enoch! Enoch! Enoch!" chanted gang members here and there from within the other groups. They joined in, not really knowing or understanding why they were chanting, but from their experience, a good mob stampede was always a fun time. And in the end, there was usually some sort of alcohol involved afterwards, so all the more reason to join.

"Enoch! Enoch! Enoch!" The cadre of cog-themed comrades parted to allow a single, colossal beast of a man through. A pair of monstrous chain guns retracted behind his broad shoulders and onto the back of his bulky, chest armor. His outrageous top hat was lined with metal, which formed it into a protective helmet of sorts. Retractable, shaded monocles extended down from the hat and over his eyes. Being nighttime and all, these were highly unnecessary, but the effect simply oozed cool over his many admirers, so much so that they could overlook his occasional bumping into objects and people from being unable to see where he was going.

"Enoch! Enoch! Enoch!" While there were many random objects and furniture strewn about the haphazard, concrete-covered cul-de-sac in between the various homes, buildings, tiny factories, and one, solitary ice cream shop, a massively-oversized anvil easily outshone them all and took up a good portion of the center. The large man stepped on top of the anvil pulpit and towered over the chanting crowd. He smiled with chompers spattered with silver teeth here and there. As to whether he was missing those teeth or simply adored the taste of silver in his mouth was a topic under hot debate.

There was a rumor floating around that he used those teeth to bite the heads off of his enemies. He did nothing to dissuade those rumors, and also may or may not have started those rumors himself. He raised his arms, and a respectful hush fell over the crowd.

"Ladies and gentleman! Thieves and degenerates!" the legend known as Enoch Kaylock boomed over the crowd. "Welcome back to the Gear Games!"

A great roar erupted from those gathered, even from the other gangs. Enoch Kaylock earned that respect. He was the leader of the Cogs, the most successful gang that ever did gang in Parsons City. His underhanded dealings reached all the way into the Upper District, but the Stacks were undeniably his territory. Everyone there existed solely for the pleasure of Enoch Kaylock. He knew it, and they knew it.

"Tonight," his booming voice continued, "we have an extra special event! First off, I want to thank myself for funding and coordinating this grand spectacle." He sparkled his silver smile and winked, but no one noticed because he was wearing shades in the dark. "You're welcome!"

Spatterings of laughter filtered through the crowd. A few whoops and cheers came from the Cogs. One of the main reasons Enoch Kaylock rose to such a high prominence within the city was his ability to inspire that aforementioned respect in both his allies and enemies, almost as much as his ability to inspire both fear and horror. He could be a warm adoptive father that helped someone into their first home, or he could be the brutal landlord that set fire to it after a mild slight. His charm was such that one could be delighted to hear that he had invited them for dinner, or terrified that he had invited them to *be* dinner. There was a rumor floating around that he was a cannibal and ate his dead enemies so that their bodies would not be discovered. He did nothing to dissuade those rumors, and also may or may not have started those rumors himself.

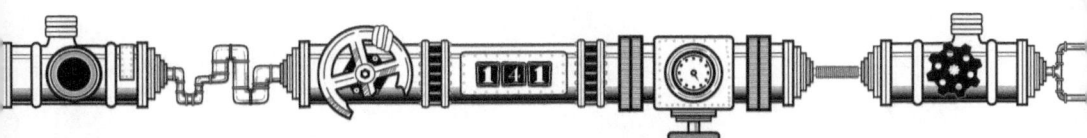

"I would also like to thank all of you for coming out tonight for this grand competition! The streets are empty! The bobbies are paid! And the pot is full! The only question left is: which of these fierce competitors will go home with all the riches and glory?!"

Roars and cheers echoed, all of them wanting riches and glory. Not many of them knew how to spend glory, but they certainly knew riches would buy them plenty of alcohol.

"First up to the starting line, we have: The Cogs!"

Enoch gestured to the group of gang members huddled together who all wore cog-themed apparel. They cheered and whooped. They whooped and cheered. Excitement was had. The older man with the cog eye patch drooled a little bit.

"Don't worry! I promise not to be biased. Well..." his hand covered his cheek as though he was going to whisper, but his voice boomed out all the same, "not *too* much anyway!"

His laugh boomed out as loud as his voice, but it was less with a giggle and more with a hardy har har. It was this kind of behavior that always kept everyone on their toes. Was he serious? Was he joking? It probably didn't matter anyway. This was his show, and they were all spellbound within it.

"But no no, I assure you that my Cogs have just as much chance of winning as... those plunderous pirates along the waters' edge: The Scallywags!"

A gang of tricorn hats and eye patches yarged and roared in approval. Their eye patches looked much more comfortable, mainly because they were made of actual cloth; although, their actual purpose was much more ambiguous. A dirty, young man in his early twenties had his eye patch over his eyebrow and not over his working eyeball, but still, one can't fault one for trying. It's really a person's spirit that determines their pirateyness.

"Or maybe the spoils will end up going to... those flying foes within the Gorge: The Blood Claws!"

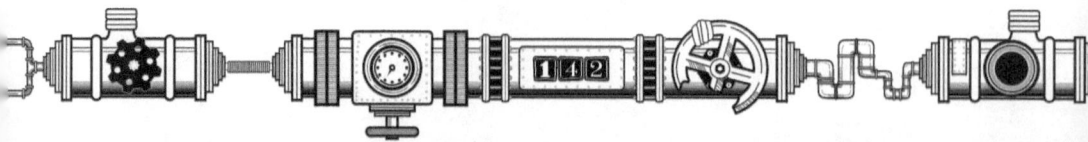

A gang with red eagle's claw tattoos and dangly talon earrings and feathery caps screeched. Blood Claw Johnny was present, right up front. He flapped his arms and crowed like a rooster, undoubtedly unsure what an eagle actually sounded like. But still, it's really a person's spirit that determines their birdyness. And Johnny's just happened to enjoy waking up at sunrise and strutting about the farm.

"We all know the deep pockets from the Lowers have a good chance of winning. I give you: The Goldens!"

A gang of well-dressed jewelry cheered. Ostentatious was a perfect term to describe these fine examples of refined refuse, and it was also a term where only ninety percent of them had to look up the definition. Many of the members were descendants of inherited wealth who enjoyed walking on the wild side to gain their thrills. Others just liked shiny things and were easily distracted—ooh a ruby.

"Perhaps the prize will go to the unknowns, those who step out of the sewers among the shadows and go bump in the night: The Faceless!"

A gang of masks and bandannas yelled. Going bump in the night was a trait not limited to the Faceless gang, as Enoch himself couldn't help but running into things in the dark. Their gang philosophy started with the common sense of not wanting their faces to be seen while committing crimes, but they also liked taking roll calls and carving their names into the walls of locations they recently looted, so their common sense may have waned over the years.

"Or the grand prize could go to our final gang competitors, those broken blades striking out from the Slums: The Rippers!"

A gang of scars and knives shouted. If ostentatious was a perfect term to describe the Goldens, the opposite of that described the Rippers.[58] So dirty even the dirt had dirt on it, the

---

58 They were *suoitatnetso*, if you will. Not exactly a palindrome, but there you have it.

Rippers liked to brandish all sorts of rusted, broken, bladed weapons. They were less adept at handling them as the many scars and bandages would attest. One older woman in the front seemed to misunderstand the gang's theme as she waved around a spoon in the air.

"With all our competitors present and accounted for—"

"Wait!" Zadie's voice cried out from behind the mass of flesh and smells. "Get outta the way, horker!" Blood Claws and Faceless stepped aside and parted for the group of marching youngsters from behind.

"Excuse me," Adelaide's meek voice squeaked. "Sorry."

Zadie, Adelaide, Harriet, Baxter, and Jules stomped up right in front of Enoch Kaylock and his anvil pulpit. Zadie announced, "We're here!"

Enoch and the dead-silent crowd studied them. Enoch snorted and chuckled. "If you're looking for the daycare, the other babies are sleeping in the grocery mart."

Everyone roared and guffawed at their expense. Knees were slapped. Tears were wiped. Snot dripped into cackling mouths.

Adelaide's confidence took an instant nosedive into the concrete. She and the others spent weeks planning and building new devices for this moment, not to mention all of the parts-stealing they had to do, but actually being here under this oppressive derision, she forgot why they wanted to come in the first place.

Winston and a collection of other orphans sat on the edges of balconies overlooking the scene below. They jeered and laughed and booed the hardest.

"Oi!" Zadie yelled above the din. "We're here to compete, ya buncha loud-mouthed, water-brained, stuck-up, quarter-witted, butt stanks! Ya wanna laugh?! Do it after we win and crush yer stupid faces into the dirt!"

The laughter died down to chuckles. Enoch kneeled down to look Zadie in the eye, but he still towered over her.

"This ain't the kiddie pool," his gravelly voice cooed like a bucket of rocks scraped over a metal pan. "You play with the big boys, you're gonna get hurt."

"Oh, we're here to play, and we're here to win. Any gang that can pay the ante can join, yeah?" Zadie said more than asked. She lifted a small sack full of money and plopped it on the anvil in front of Enoch. He looked at it then back to Zadie.

With his voice as soft as he could possibly make it, Enoch said, "This didn't go so well for you last time, little girl."

"This ain't like last time, *little boy*," Zadie added with a voice as loud as she could possibly make it.

A chorus of gasps and "ooh's" flowed around the clearing like a wave. Enoch's unreadable face was... unreadable. Zadie's determined face of unyielding stubbornness matched his. Enoch's cheeks finally lifted into a grin.

"Correction!" Enoch called out to the crowd as he rose to his full height. "We have one final entry! And maybe the grand prize will even go to... this unassuming slumber party of orphans from the steam tunnels: The Steampunks!"

Unlike the other announcements, this one was followed by a round of scoffs and mutterings and chuckles.

Harriet took that as an opportunity to toot their own horns. "Whoop! Whoop!" she yelled. "Yeah! Whoo!"

Adelaide's steam generator backpack took that as an opportunity to literally *toot* out a wisp of steam. The resulting silence afterwards swaddled them like the most oppressive weighted blanket that ever existed.

"I told you," Zadie objected to Enoch, "our gang name is the Grinders."

"No, it isn't. Now," Enoch's voice raised and called out, "as the *Punks* reminded me, time to ante up! You gotta contribute to the pot if you want to win it all!"

The other gangs shuffled about and searched for money to donate. The Goldens were, of course, the first up with coinage prepared and ready to spend. The Steampunks took that

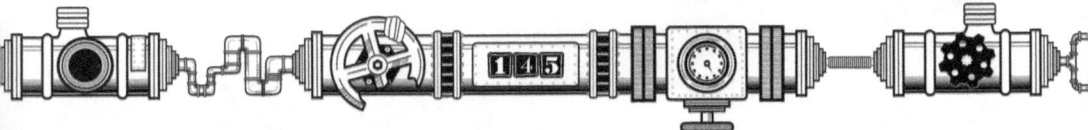

opportunity to carve out their own little spot in the crowd and huddle together.

"Are we sure about this?" Baxter whispered to the others.

"My stomach hurts," Adelaide admitted.

"It'll be great!" Zadie replied. "We're prepared. We're ready. We got thingamajigs."

She gestured to the odd assortments of new devices strapped to their small bodies. Jules wore a massive backpack with long, metal rods folded into the sides. Harriet and Baxter both sported smaller backpacks. Inside, mini-generators came equipped with tubes and pipes extending out into metal pipes strapped across their forearms. Zadie and Adelaide's shoes were surrounded by an elaborate metal structure that almost, but not entirely, resembled pairs of boots. Pipes and tubes extended from those as well and up to their own backpack generators.

"So you really think it's gonna be capture the flag?" Harriet asked.

"Yeah," Zadie replied. "Gotta be. They done all the other games already. At least, it's as good a guess as any. 'Sides, we're prepared for most any game. You and Bax will be the blockers, me and Addy will be the runners, and Jules will be the scorer. It's just like that game with the sticks and balls."

"Croquet?"

"No no, the one where you hit people with sticks, and the ones without sticks grab the ball and kick people in the face."

"What in the clockhead are you talking about?" Harriet asked.

"Oh..." Zadie stroked her chin. "That might have just been a dream I had... but hey! It'll work! We fight together to capture the flag, defend our spot, and return with the booty. We got this in the bag."

"Were we supposed to bring bags?" Baxter asked.

"I feel like I'm gonna throw up," Adelaide admitted.

"Swallow it," Zadie said. "Or point it at the Blood Claws."

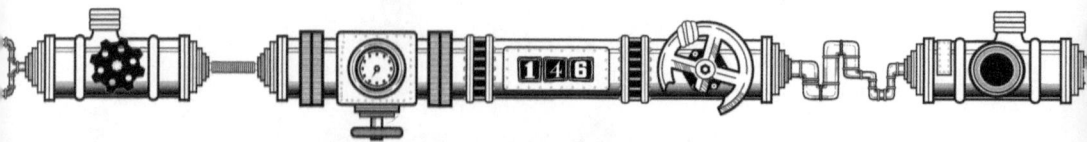

"Tonight!" Enoch Kaylock's voice boomed out and echoed over the clearing. "Will be a brand new game!"

"Crap," Baxter muttered softly.

"It could still work," Zadie whispered.

"Tonight will be..." Enoch paused for dramatic effect, "a foxhunt!"

"See." Zadie nudged Baxter in the ribs. "Same thing. We pick it up and bring it back. Only the flag is gonna move around."

Harriet added with a smile, "And be an adorable little animal!"

"And probably tear out our eyes if we touch them," Baxter subtracted with a frown.

The Cogs brought out three large cages into the clearing and up to the anvil pulpit. Three mechanical foxes laid motionless inside. The three-foot-long, metal creations were fairly sleek and shiny along their main bodies, and different metals composed all three. The heads appeared to be just for show as the spring-loaded eyes and free-flapping jaws seemed to serve no purpose whatsoever, other than an attempted form of engineered cuteness. The legs were the interesting parts. A collection of pipes, pistons, gears, and metal claws formed four sets of fierce paws.

The first cage opened with a screech as Enoch pulled out the first mechanical fox formed out of primarily white silver alloys. "This one, I call Billywinkle!" he called out and smiled like a proud papa. He gave an unnerving, grating, little giggle. The crowd in attendance couldn't tell if he was serious or not, so deadly silence was the agreed-upon reaction.

Enoch flipped the static creature on its back and opened a compartment on its belly. Enoch managed to shove his massive fingers inside and cranked a rotating gear. An oscillating engine inside the torso whirred to life. The entire fox body shook as the engine picked up to operating speed. The short, stubby, metal tail revealed itself to be a simple exhaust pipe as black smoke tooted out.

The little clawed legs moved and spun in circles. Enoch flipped it right side up and let it go. Billywinkle, the white silver fox, fell to the ground and staggered about on its unsure legs. The spinning, metal appendages finally forced the body level with the asphalt, and it took off. The frenzied creature sprinted off into a connecting street leading to the north. Its head bonked into a street light before it adjusted, rotated, and spun off away. Its head bonked into the wall of a building before it adjusted, rotated, and spun off away again. A few of the gang members looked eager.

"Don't chase him yet!" Enoch called out. "I have yet to start the games!" He reached into the second cage and grabbed the second, motionless fox thing. "Your goal will be to capture them all!"

"Okay," Zadie said, "we may need a new strategy."

"That's what I said," Baxter said.

"That's what *she* said," Harriet said.

"How the foxes come to be in your possession is irrelevant!" Enoch shouted over the rising din. "Catch them and bring them back here!" Enoch's harsh expression suddenly shifted to unbridled joy as he gazed upon the mechanical creature with red copper folded over its body. "This one's name is Fizzlesticks!" Enoch chuckled and beamed as he brought the second fox to life. He even gave him a little kiss. "He's a wily one!"

Fizzlesticks, the red copper fox, chugged and scraped and flung itself into a street leading to the east.

"I'm not sure about this, you guys," Adelaide revealed. "What if something goes wrong? I didn't have near enough time to properly test and retest all of these. We didn't do enough stress tests on the wings or monitor updraft reactions or map out air current routes..."

Her voice trailed off as Jules placed a comforting hand on her shoulder. His eyes beneath his visor/gasmask/banana combo could just be seen within, illuminated from the light

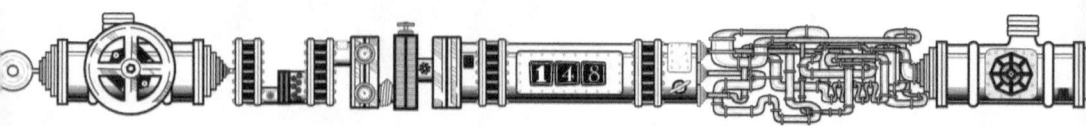

bouncing off a nearby streetlamp. He nodded and looked at Adelaide.

"He does have a point," Baxter translated.

"Besides," Zadie added with her own air of nighttime mischief, "it'll be fun!"

"One rule!" Enoch's voice echoed. "Deadly force is restricted unless your opponent possesses a fox! If they have one, they are open game! If they do not, non-lethal force only! If you break this one rule, your life will be open game! We want to avoid a bloodbath like the last time! I'm looking at you, Rippers!"

"Ohh," Baxter moaned. "We're gonna get murdered." His free hand grabbed the pipe strapped to his arm, and he stared directly down the barrel. Adelaide ripped it away.

"Don't point it at your face," she said.

Zadie grabbed Baxter by the back of his neck and stared him in the eye. "They hurt you, you hurt 'em back."

"The team who catches the most foxes..." Enoch yelled and paused for his most unnecessary dramatic effect, "wins!"

With less enthusiasm than the first two fox releases, Enoch cranked the third fox to life and let it go. Clad in black iron metals, fox number three scampered away and spun headfirst into a doorway. The closed portal seemed to confuse and confound the fox's balancing countermeasure mechanics. It scraped its head into the left side of the doorframe until it corrected and scraped its head just to get stuck on the right side of the doorframe. It scraped into the left side. It scraped into the right side. It scraped into the left side.

Enoch sighed. "And that's... why I call the last one Idgit! A papa's not supposed to have favorites, but there's a black sheep in every family, I suppose." He waved down a specific Cogs gang member. "Steve. Steve! Would you..." he sighed again, "just handle that please. Hold!" Enoch yelled at a group of Faceless starting down after Fizzlesticks, the red copper fox. "Do not start yet! Or I will break your heads open on the pavement for trying to cheat in my games!"

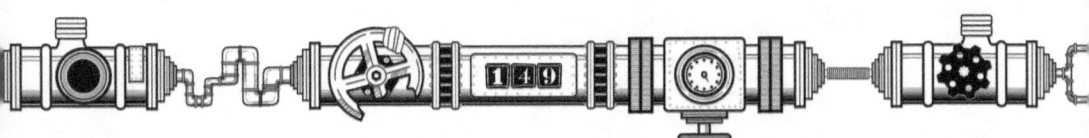

The Faceless immediately stopped and shied back into the clearing.

Enoch's wild eyes from his sudden outburst calmed and turned jovial. "Everyone's gotta play fair, lads!" He beamed a smile, flip-flopping his personality in such a way that always kept those in his presence on their toes and sometimes, even off their toes completely. Enoch sighed as he stared at the black iron fox. "A little hint..." Enoch's robust voice added, "Idgit was always a little slower than his brothers, Billywinkle and Fizzlesticks! Plan your pursuit parties accordingly!"

"What is this naming convention?" Zadie whispered to no one in particular.

"I feel bad for Idgit," Harriet said.

"You feel bad for an unbalanced, mindless, tinker toy?" Baxter asked.

"He's still cute. Not his fault his brain is leaking oil."

Jules ignored them all and played with the fringe dangling from the jacket of a Faceless gang member standing beside them. He flicked the fringe back and forth with his finger until the Faceless turned his masked face toward Jules' masked face. Jules turned his masked face away.

The legend known as Steve picked Idgit the black iron fox off of its doorframe limbo and shoved the poor creature down a connecting street leading west.

Adelaide's stomach rumbled audibly. Her throat uttered a rather warm, chunky burp. "Oof, uhh."

"Keep it in, stumpy," Zadie said. "We all know what we gotta do. Stay safe. And aim for the squishy bits."

Enoch Kaylock gazed at the enraptured crowd, reveling in how they followed his every movement. A trigger-like controller on a spring extended from his sleeve to his hand.

"With that..." Enoch boomed over his admirers and despisers. He pulled the trigger, and the dual chain guns strapped upon his back fired a mass flurry of bullets into the sky. "Three-two-one-GO-GO-GO!"

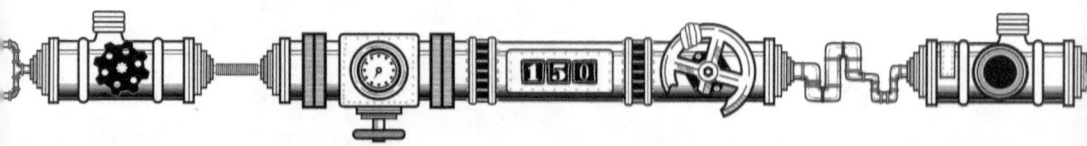

Chapter 12

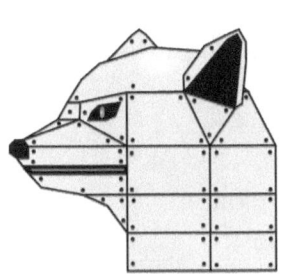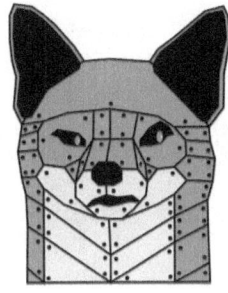

Billywinkle, Fizzlesticks, and Idgit

Keeping with tradition, the start of the Gear Games was a mixture of excitement, adrenaline, and absolute chaos. Tracer rounds from Enoch's chain gun fire lit up the dark, night sky enveloped by black smog. All of the gang members staggered and stumbled into each other. The incidental contact between the Blood Claws and the Faceless quickly led into shoving. And the Faceless shoved the Rippers. And the Rippers shoved other Rippers because it was easy to forget where you were in the crowd. That led to punching, and kicking, then escalated quickly into a full-out brawl. It was chaos. It was bedlam. It was pandemonium. It was a thesaurus.[59]

The Steampunks avoided the mosh pit altogether and took cover by the anvil. Enoch stood atop, guffawing at the fighting.

"Careful now," Enoch's voice overpowered the din, "the foxes are getting away!"

---

59 Not to be confused with *The Saurus*, king of all dinosaurs. That winged creature could soar. It could fly. It could aviate. It could synonym.

A gold-covered tooth knocked out of some poor fool's mouth, popped onto the ground, and rolled over into Adelaide's foot. She gingerly poked it with a single finger.

"Ew! Don't touch it!" Harriet protested.

"Free money!" Baxter suggested.

"We gotta split up!" Zadie shouted over the noise of fists smacking faces.

"Great," Baxter sighed. "You guys get the foxes, and I'll go home."

"Bax and Harrie," Zadie continued unabated, "go for the fox going west."

"Idgit," Harriet corrected.

"Excuse me?" Zadie harrumphed.

"Idgit, the black iron fox, went to the west."

"Oh whatever."

"Wait, aren't we the blockers?" Baxter asked. "We can't go fast."

"That's why you're going after the gimpy one." Zadie looked at the tall, silent type of the group. "Jules, go for the fast silver one running north."

Jules nodded in agreement.

"Billywinkle," Harriet corrected.

"I don't care what their names are," Zadie groaned.

"It's rude to not use their proper titles."

"They're not alive though," Baxter chimed in.

"They are too! They're just... life-challenged."

Zadie snapped, "We don't have time for this. Addy, you're with me. We're going to the west after..." she looked at Harriet's pleading face, "frazzlerocks?"

"Fizzlesticks."

"Oh I don't care!"

"How're me and Harrie 'sposed to keep up?" Baxter asked. "The other gangs got autos!"

"I don't know! I'm making this up as I go. Steal one or something. Now let's motor!"

The Steampunks split up and ran around the edges of the clearing in between the buildings, keeping to the edges of the brawl. They chased after their appointed foxes as the fight began to break up and/or continue into the adjoining streets. Several staggered away from their opponents and ran off. A portion of the Golden gang pointedly hung back and took strategic positions near the courtyard.[60]

Harriet and Baxter sprinted off west along the general direction that Idgit, the black iron fox, haphazardly traveled. They glanced around for clues. Along the sidewalk, little droplets of oil marked a faint, breadcrumb-like trail that could have come from the fox. Harriet noticed that a touch of green coloring mixed with the brown oil. Unfortunately, the trail led into the road, mixing with the older splotches of oil stains from the large amount of automobiles that traveled the streets every day.

Harriet stopped and yanked Baxter off the street as a group of Rippers cut them off while riding monocycles, single giant wheels six-feet in diameter with a seat and motor attached to the inside bottom of the rim. While those machines looked highly unwieldy to drive, they were overflowing with piles of coolness, so it made up for the fact that turning the monocycle and just the simple act of seeing out the front was difficult, at best.

The Rippers driving the monocycles in the front of the pack glanced back and jeered at the Punks. A smattering of Cogs in automobiles chased the Rippers, and a spattering of Scallywags, all crammed into a single auto and all swinging around cutlasses, chased the Cogs. Hauling up the rear far down the street from the others, a lone Ripper wobbled and tooted his way over. Clearly unsure about how to drive the thing, his monocycle zigged and zagged in his eventual pursuit.

---

60 This information might be useful later. *wink!*

Harriet spun a metal dial attached to her backpack strap. The small generator inside whirred to life. She aimed the metal-piped air cannon attached to her forearm. "Load!" she yelled for Baxter.

Baxter pulled a potato out of a side pouch from Harriet's generator backpack. He shoved it into the metal pipe. Harriet aimed at the wobbly monocyclist. Just as he pulled in front of them, she pulled a small lever on the cannon. Air pressure exploded forth and shot out the potato missile. She missed and smashed a window across the street.

"Nice aim, punk!" the Ripper monocyclist jeered and laughed at them.

The momentary distraction, however, was more than enough. His monocycle hit the curb, lost control, and crashed into a building. His body flew off the seat and ate pavement. He laid unmoving in unconscious bliss as the monocycle tilted and rotated against the wall, coming to balance itself at an angle over him.

Harriet and Baxter ran over. Harriet pulled the heavy monocycle upright and gingerly hopped onto the seat. Her much shorter legs tip-toed the rather weighteous machine straight and backed away from the wall.

"Do you know what you're doing?" Baxter asked.

"When has that ever stopped me?" Harriet replied.

He shrugged. She motioned for him to sit behind her on the seat. He hopped up and settled against her back. His arms wrapped around her midsection. A furtive[61] smile curled his lips as he pressed his cheek against her shoulder.

"Hold on tight, derpface," she said.

Harriet revved the monocycle's engine. They took off down the street, highly wobbly and unstable but still an improvement over the last driver. Though that meant little

---

61 A smile so sneaky and mischievous that it was covered in fur, or something like that. What am I: a dictionary?

to nothing as Harriet drove on the curb, narrowly missed a lamppost, and careened back onto the road.

Baxter screamed, "Person! Person!"

Harriet swerved the monocycle away from nothing, bounced off the curb, and rolled back onto the street.

"Stop backseat driving!" Harriet accosted.

"We're on the same seat!"

"Then stop same-seat driving!"

They caught up to a gang of monocycles darting in between horses, carriages, and even more unfortunate pedestrians. Harriet's eyes caught a glint of liquid shining on the hood of a parked automobile. She cranked the brakes and brought them to a sudden, awkward stop. Her feet barely reached the ground enough to keep them from tipping over.

"What are you doing?" Baxter asked.

Harriet didn't answer. Instead, her eyes studied small, almost imperceptible droplets of oil along the street. The trail ran up on top of the hood of a parked automobile, down the sidewalk to their right, and off into an alley between two buildings. Within the oil droplets, a touch of green glittered from underneath the street light overhead. Harriet smiled, and she tippy-toe-walked the monocycle backwards.

"Umm..." Baxter uttered, "they went that way." He pointed to their left.

"Good," Harriet replied. She revved the monocycle, and they took off to their right and down the alley, following the oil trail from Idgit, the black iron fox.

Billywinkle, the white silver fox, scarpered down a road leading north out of the Stacks and ending abruptly at the cliff face overlooking the Gorge. The shining silver fox bonked into a street lamp and sprinted through the guard rails, falling off the cliff.

Two eye-patched Scallywags and one normal-eyed Scallywag, who thought he was too good for covering up his perfectly-working eyeballs, were in hot pursuit of the fox. They ran into the railing and looked down helplessly as the fox fell fifty feet through the air below before bouncing onto the roof of a building built into the cliff face.

Billywinkle promptly fell off again and crashed into other buildings, homes, roads, smokestacks, train tracks, knickknacks, paddywhacks, and gave that dog a bone. On the balcony of an abandoned factory, the fox rotated, got its legs under it, caught its balance, and promptly ran off the edge anyway.

"Well, now what?" the infamous Scallywag Bob said.

The three Scallywags looked back just in time to see Jules sprinting toward them. The four-eyeballed group of three jumped out of the way as Jules barreled between them, stepped onto the rail, and jumped off the cliff.

Falling through the open air of the valley, Jules yanked a pull cord on his chest. His massively oversized backpack opened up the sides. A pair of glider wings extended outward. The instant the structure locked into place, Jules felt his momentum slow considerably. The tail section extended and locked into place. His feet shoved into the pair of stirrups hanging below, and his hands grabbed the metal holding rods above his head.

Still falling at a higher speed than nine out of ten doctors would recommend, Jules pushed his body straight. Every muscle in his body tensed as his glider wings caught a plume of hot air rising from a smokestack below. He banked and soared up into the sky. His goggled eyes darted around. It took only a handful of moments for Jules to master one of the most extreme forms of travel ever invented. For the first time in many times, sound came from Jules' throat. From beneath his mask, joyous laughter echoed throughout the Gorge.

In a modest, low-income home nestled within the Stacks, a father, son, and daughter giggled over a joke.[62] They sat at a dining table and finished up a lovely family dinner. A mother brought over a Bundt cake from the kitchen.

Fizzlesticks, the red copper fox, leaped onto the table, scratched the bejeezus out of the wood, and scrambled off before running to the back of the house. The fox leaked droplets of oil with just a hint of green along every step of the way. Several Blood Claws barged into the dining room and chased after it. One accidentally knocked the father over in his chair. The rest of the family jumped up and backed away in surprise. Two Scallywags followed close behind. Adelaide and Zadie followed close behind their behinds.

"Sorry!" Adelaide exclaimed between pants of breath and looking sheepish. "Excuse us!"

"You should really close your doors!" Zadie advised on her way out.

The two girls burst out of the home's back doorway and into a neighborhood cul-de-sac, which was formed, not due to structure or logic, but out of haphazard planning and sheer chance. These houses faced their butts together like a strange, domestic dance.

Zadie and Adelaide followed the crowd chasing after the fox. Blood Claw Johnny and his two cronies sprinted out of a nearby alley and smashed into Zadie, knocking her to the ground.

"Watch it, punk!" Johnny yelled.

Adelaide stopped to pull the grumbling and cursing Zadie back to her feet. They continued the chase out of the cul-de-sac and up a main street rising upon a hill. The two girls stopped at the precipice and gazed at the downward slope, descending

---

62 It's an inside joke. You wouldn't get it anyway.

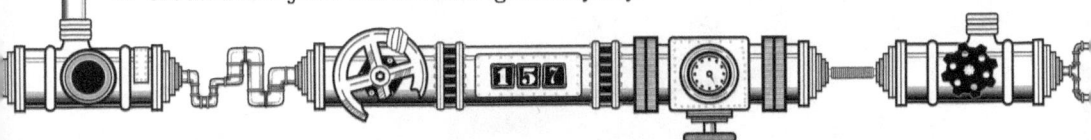

steep into the Stacks. At the end of the road, the pavement dove down into an even deeper tunnel carved into the earth. Fizzlesticks sprinted down the hill, then tripped and tumbled into a little flying ball of metal claws. Without missing a beat, its still-churning legs caught itself upright and sped down the hill again toward the tunnel.

The other gang members in pursuit hopped onto horse-drawn carriages that didn't belong to them or grabbed onto steam-powered vehicles screeching out from the side streets. Some were driven by their fellow gang members. Some were driven by highly confused citizenry that immediately regretted their decision to go out on the town tonight.

On the hilltop, Zadie nodded to Adelaide. "Let's roll."

Zadie lifted her metal boot and pulled a small lever on the ankle. The wheels built into the sides lowered below the soles. Adelaide did the same, and they balanced on their makeshift roller skates. The girls each turned a dial on their respective chest plates. The steam engines in their backpacks whirred to life. The transparent portions of the tubes and pipes leading from their packs to their shoes filled with the semi-transparent, white smokiness of steam.

Zadie kicked off and rolled her skates down the hill with Adelaide close behind. The exhaust vents poking out the top of their generator packs whistled, the cue for the air pressure filling the container and maxing out. Zadie pushed the button on the center of her chest dial.

Air pressure burst forth through nozzles built into the metal boots just below her Achilles. The escaping steam rocket-propelled her down the hill. Zadie waved her arms frantically and caught her balance.

Adelaide pushed the button on the center of her chest dial. Her steam rocket boots propelled her down the hill as well, but suddenly, her right boot nozzle stopped. Just when Adelaide began to question if it was clogged, all of the air pressure diverted and exploded out of her left boot. Her

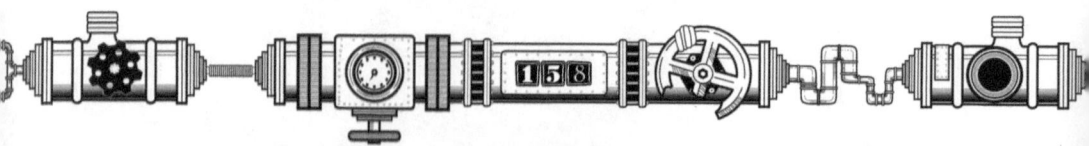

entire body snapped to follow her careening foot. She slammed her right boot's wheels down on the ground behind her, trying not to fall. Adelaide gained some semblance of balance while skating in almost a full split with her feet pointing in opposite directions.

Zadie's far more balanced posture and double-firing rocket boots double-fired her ahead and down the hill. She quickly caught up to the sprinting Blood Claw Johnny and his cronies.

"Broadside!" Zadie yelled. Johnny looked back as Zadie's elbow slammed hard into his face. His falling body tripped up his fellows.

Adelaide swerved out of control. She managed to avoid the tangle of Blood Claws by veering off to the curb. Her fast boots barely felt the bump. She barreled through the few remaining pedestrians on the sidewalk who all saw their lives flashing before their eyes.

"Sorry! Excuse me!" Adelaide swerved into the street. Her body slammed into a horse pulling a carriage with two Cogs holding onto the back and hitching a ride. "Sorry, horsey!" The startled animal reared, whinnied, and slowed to a stop with the Cogs cursing behind.

Zadie skated between the carriages and vehicles bottled up in a cluster of traffic at the bottom of the hill. Just before the tunnel entrance, her boots' nozzles whistled to a stop. She skated under her own power and gained distance. She could see Fizzlesticks within reach.

Adelaide's wild left boot continued to fire strong. Her flailing form skated and bounced between the traffic and the surprised onlookers. She bonked on the side of an automobile and kept going, catching up to Zadie. Out of control, Adelaide tackled Zadie and barreled them both off the street, away from Fizzlesticks, and onto the sidewalk. The two girls crashed into a freight elevator built into the side of the tunnel. They landed on top of two pedestrians who were tired of the city and were just trying to make their way home.

Everyone in the tangle of bodies and limbs and generator packs groaned.

"I can fix that," Adelaide's muffled voice filtered out from somewhere within the pile.

Her left boot, sticking up in the air, finally puttered out its last wisp of steam and died. Fizzlesticks, the red copper fox, scampered along the street outside. Zadie reached her hand out, but the lift's doors closed of its own accord and clanked downward.

Harriet's monocycle sped through the aisles of factories, power stations, and flue-gas smokestacks. She scoured the dark asphalt with the dark stains in the dark night for traces of dark oil splotches from Idgit, the black iron fox.

Baxter held on as Harriet leaned into a sharp turn. They rolled onto the grounds of a screw factory. Baxter was quite comfortable holding onto the abdomen of the attractive girl, a little too comfortable, in fact, but he was getting antsy too.

"Where is it?" Baxter asked.

"I'm lookin'," Harriet replied. "I'm lookin'."

Their monocycle screeched to a stop. Harriet tip-toed them steady and craned her neck around, searching for something. Anything.

"Did we lose it?" Baxter asked. "Maybe we should go back to where we last saw—"

Harriet shushed him. "Listen."

Faint scratching noises tickled in from the west. Harriet slapped Baxter's hands around her bellybutton, prompting him to release her. She extended the first kickstand and kicked out the second. They both hopped off the monocycle.

Their ears led their feet in a vague direction toward the sounds. Harriet pointed out a spot of oil with just a touch of

green on the ground. Then another. Then a whole heap of droplets.

A flue-gas smokestack reached up into the dark, smoggy sky that it helped create. A tall, open platform of metal supports, pipes, tubes, and gears comprised the base. Idgit, the black iron fox, with its head and body wedged between the metal braces, helplessly flailed its legs around in the air.

"It's stuck," Baxter chortled. He kneeled down and pulled on the fox. "How did you...?" Baxter wondered aloud as the fox's torso refused to budge. "Frags, he's really stuck. How did you even get in there?" He yanked on the mechanical fox with all of his weight, but he might as well have been trying to pull on the entire smokestack. "Your name really fits, you know that?"

Harriet gazed around everywhere else. Ominous, man-sized shadows floated past the surrounding corners bathed in darkness. Her hand reached around to her backpack, withdrew a potato, and slid it down the barrel of her air cannon.

"Hurry it up," Harriet whispered. The sounds of revving monocycle engines echoed in the distance. Idgit flailed its legs and scratched Baxter's arms.

"It'd be easier if it'd just stop—"

A Faceless gang member emerged from the darkness behind Baxter and grabbed him in a chokehold. A second Faceless appeared and grabbed for Harriet's neck. However, her reaction time put Baxter's to shame. She spun around and punched her assailant in his full-face gas mask. Aside from moving his head back, it did not appear to hurt him much, unlike Harriet's hand, which was throbbing from the impact against the hard plastic.

He returned the gesture and slugged Harriet in the face, hard. She staggered and fell to the ground. Her feet shuffled her bum backwards along the asphalt as he stalked after her. Harriet raised her forearm's air cannon, aimed, and fired. The potato projectile smashed into his face, shattering his gas mask's goggles. Pieces of spud exploded everywhere. If it were under different circumstances, it would have been delicious.

Struggling under the tall man's grip, Baxter remembered he had a weapon too. He pulled a potato from his pack and loaded the cannon. He shifted the lever into gear, aimed the pipe over his shoulder, and fired. The Faceless dodged his masked head to the side. Baxter began to lose strength beneath the tight chokehold. Then he lost some oxygen to the brain parts. Only one good shot. Missed. Hungry. Time for bed. Sleepybye.

Harriet smashed her air cannon pipe across the man's head. The Faceless fell unconscious to the concrete. Baxter fell to his knees and gasped. The rush of oxygen opened his eyes again.

Harriet leaned back against the smokestack's base and exhaled. She flexed her sore hand and stretched the muscles. Baxter stared at her, unsure how to voice the multitude of swirling thoughts in his mind. He thought of a word that probably summed up his emotions well enough.

"Thanks," he said.

"Yep."

Baxter looked back at the flailing, mechanical fox. He wrapped his arm around the stuck rump and squeezed the two rear legs against his own chest. The flailing cut down by half. He squeezed his head over the tiny metal body and studied the damage. Looked like the exposed metal chassis on the fox's belly had gotten hooked on a pipe junction and valve. Baxter slid it backwards to unhook one part, sideways to unhook another. With a shove forward then back, he pulled Idgit, the black iron fox, free of its bondage. He chuckled in triumph and turned back to look at Harriet.

A Rippers gang member, who went by the name of Riptide for no discernible reason, held Harriet from behind and pointed a knife at her throat. Two more Rippers approached. They stood over the two Faceless, who were just rousing from their quite pleasant dreams of winning the house championship and becoming Headboy. Waking up to

headaches and the sights of Rippers brandishing blades in their directions, they promptly pretended to go back to sleep.

"Hand it over," Riptide snarled. "This don't gotta be messy."

With the air cannon strapped to his right arm and his right hand holding Idgit by its exhaust pipe tail, Baxter reached back with his left hand, retrieved a potato, loaded his cannon, and aimed at Riptide's face over Harriet's shoulder.

"How accurate are you with that spud shooter, kid?" Riptide scoffed.

"Shoot him," Harriet ordered.

"You can't kill her," Baxter reasoned. "She doesn't have a fox."

"Who said anything about killing her?" Riptide said. His sharp knife cut a tiny line of blood on Harriet's throat.

"You hurt her, I'll throw this fox, and you'll have to chase it all over again."

"You do that, I'll hurt her."

"Potato his stupid face," Harriet ordered.

"Give us the fox," Riptide commanded, "and you can take your girl home, safe and sound, back where you children belong."

Baxter looked from Riptide to Harriet and back. Idgit spun its legs in the air. The muscles in Baxter's arms felt like they were about to give out. He needed to make a decision.

"Okay, here!" Baxter tossed the fox toward them. It hit the ground next to the prone Faceless with the shattered gas mask. The Ripper standing guard above him snatched up Idgit and held it tight in his muscular arms.

"Pleasure doin' business, kid," Riptide said. He shoved Harriet toward Baxter.

She stumbled, but Baxter caught her. The three Rippers retreated. The two Faceless decided that they rather liked the ground and took another nap. Riptide punched his fellow holding Idgit in the arm until he handed over the fox. Riptide grinned at the fox before stopping at Harriet's parked monocycle.

"Children shouldn't be driving yet. It's not safe." He stabbed his knife into the massive, single tire and tore it open. He smiled, and they sauntered over to their own parked monocycles.

"Joke's on you!" Harriet shouted at them. "That was one of yours!"

The flat-tire monocycle fell down to the asphalt with a clonk. Riptide frowned in confusion and shrugged his shoulders. The three Rippers revved their monocycles and raced away. Harriet turned her frustrated face on Baxter.

"Why didn't you take the shot?" she demanded.

"I would rather lose a thousand foxes than one you," he replied.

Baxter seemed to realize what he said only after he had said it. His eyes widened, and his pupils sheepishly looked away. His cheeks flushed red with embarrassment. A slight tinge of red tinted Harriet's cheeks as well, and a small grin curved her lips.

"Come on," she said. Harriet held Baxter's hand and pulled him along behind her.

Jules glided through the open air between the walls of the Gorge. He soared over the buildings and caught an upstream through a cloud of smoke. He leveled out and rocketed down.

Billywinkle, the white silver fox, sprinted across the roof of a cable factory built into the side of the cliff face. Jules banked and aimed himself. One of his hands cautiously let go of the holding rod and reached out as he soared toward the roof. In one fell swoop, Jules' strong hand snatched the fox by the tail exhaust just before Billywinkle charged off the roof's edge.

Winston and a collection of other orphan boys ran up to a ledge nearby protruding from the Stacks far above. They whooped and hollered and cheered. "Go Jules!"

The strange creature flailed its legs and wobbled about in Jules' grasp. He grunted and struggled to control the glider and the clambering fox. The glider sank lower and lower, unable to gain altitude. Near the valley floor, Jules had to bank in between the plethora of tall buildings constructed hodgepodged and willy nilly all over the river bank and into the dark, grimy, pollution zone of the river itself.

A train chugged along near the base of the cliff. Jules turned sharply and flew over the tinder car. His glider continued to lose altitude until he reached the train's smokestack. The black smoke made it hard to breathe, but the hot air pushed his glider back upwards into the air.

The train tracks ramped up the side of the cliff. Jules' glider bobbed up and down, gaining bursts of altitude by following the smokestack and flying above. It didn't take long for him to clear the Gorge and soar into the Stacks.

Scattered members of the Golden gang dotted the rooftops leading back toward Enoch and the finish line.[63] They formed a perimeter of sorts, and they all wielded rifles. While most were focused on the streets and alleyways below, one hawk-eyed Golden scanned the skies and spotted Jules approaching fast. He yelled out to his fellows.

As Jules glided closer, four sets of rifles opened fire. Jules banked and dodged, but bullets ripped into the wings. He jerked and groaned as one bullet tore into the side of his lower abdomen. His love handle turned into a hateful holster.

The glider's gained height was quickly lost. The tattered wings kept him flying but at a steep descent. He soared past the buildings and careened into the courtyard. Jules dove for the

---

63 Remember when some of the Goldens held back by the clearing? Remember? That's called foreshadowing. This writer is brilliant. Brilliant, I say!

great anvil and the three cages on top. His hand still grasping the holding rod pulled down to aim the glider. With his other hand still holding onto the flailing fox, he slammed Billywinkle into an open cage, knocking it completely off the anvil. The tiny prison crashed onto the ground, and the cage door slammed shut with the white silver fox trapped inside.

The glider's altitude subtracted to zero. Bystanders jumped for cover as Jules crashed through a wooden door of a building nearby. Both the door and the glider shattered to pieces.

Cheers erupted from the crowd gathered around the courtyard and surrounding buildings, followed by the groans from the members of the competing gangs who weren't out hunting. As it was, they weren't all young and athletic and ready-to-rumble. Scallywag Alvin was a top-notch account-ant. Cogs Carl was a dandy puppeteer. Ripper Robert had little medical training but tons of medical practice due to all of the accidental, self-inflicted wounds by his compatriots.

It was he who first stepped inside the broken doorway. A piece of the glider crunched under his foot. Jules laid still, collapsed in a heap on the floor. Ripper Robert approached. Gang lines be darned if that was going to stop a medical not-really-professional from doing the medical things with the bandages and the alcohols and the needles and whatnots. If Jules was conscious, he probably would have wished he would have been unconscious, so that was really quite fortunate all around.

With a look of astonishment, Enoch Kaylock stomped over to the upturned cage. Billywinkle, the white silver fox, flailed its legs about with its rear still pointed toward the sky. Enoch snorted in surprise. His weathered, scarred cheeks grinned.

"The first point," his deep voice boomed, "goes to the Steampunks!"

Chapter 13

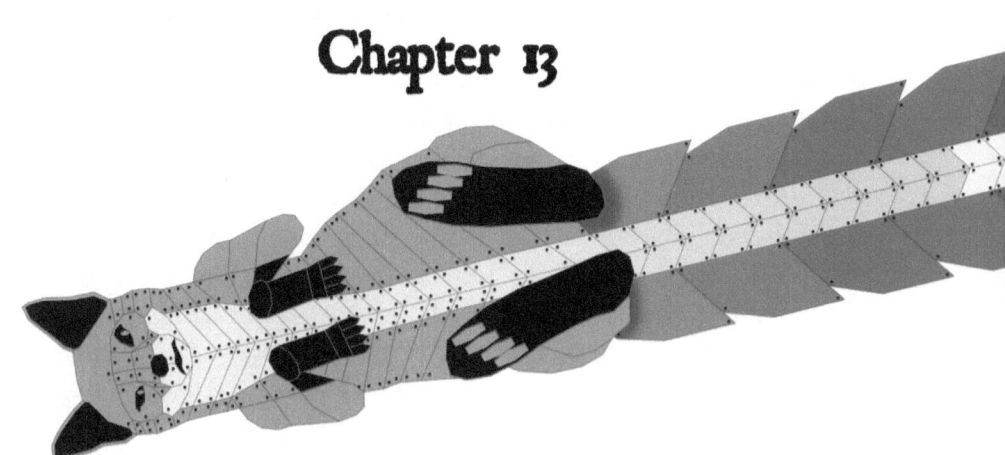

The Great Train Foxery

adie and Adelaide sprinted across a rocky outcropping alongside the cliff face of the Gorge. They ran into the outer railing protecting the common-sense-challenged from falling off the cliff. The girls looked out over the railways and bridges crossing both over and under their heads in the chaotic hodgepodge that was the Gorge transportation.

"Do you see it?" Adelaide asked as they both panted for breath.

"No," Zadie grunted. "I thought we could cut it off."

Their eyes scoured the rooftops and outcroppings and bridges below. Just then, the wee form of a mechanical creature fell out of the sky from a pedestrian bridge above and flopped onto a railway bridge spanning the chasm, level with the girls but several dozen feet away. Adelaide spotted Fizzlesticks, the red copper fox, as it rolled over, found its feet again, and galloped out further onto the bridge.

"There it is!"

The girls chased after it. They rounded the railing, sprinted over the outcropping, and climbed up the wooden beam supports leading to the bridge. Zadie reached the top first, and she stopped dead in her tracks on the tracks.

Adelaide climbed up second and immediately sprinted off after Fizzlesticks as it scarpered down the rails away from the cliffside. Zadie felt rumbling vibrations beneath her feet. She followed her ears to search for a sound behind them. The railway tracks led out from a pitch-black tunnel onto the bridge. A screeching noise echoed through the ominous tunnel and grew louder. As Zadie's trepidatious[64] eyes looked, a train came roaring out of the darkness. Zadie immediately turned and ran away after Adelaide.

"Fingers!"

Intent on capturing the fox, the girl with the mechanical arm was oblivious to Zadie's cries behind her.

"Addy!"

Adelaide finally slowed and looked back. Her eyes widened. The train closed the distance. This was it. This was how she was going to die. Or probably lose her one good, remaining arm. Such a shame. She liked that arm.

Zadie tackled Adelaide, knocking them both off the bridge. The train bulldozed past and missed their feet by mere feet. The girls both smacked their torsos into a horizontal brace running between a vertical support and the railway platform.

Adelaide fell. Zadie caught the wooden brace with her left hand while her right grabbed Adelaide's shirt sleeve. Zadie's right hand slipped, but Adelaide snatched and clutched onto Zadie's waist with her good arm. They dangled over empty air underneath the bridge with the valley floor a long, long way below. The train shook the entire platform as it roared past.

---

64 That's probably a word.

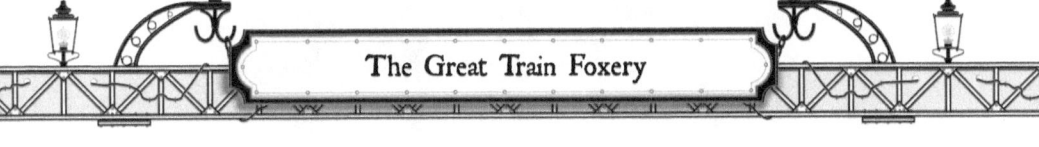

"Climb up!" Zadie implored with her head angled strangely beneath the wooden brace.

Adelaide gained her bearings and looked around Zadie's body to the tracks above. "The train hit the fox!"

"Better it than us!" Zadie pulled them both up just enough for her to grab the horizontal brace with her other hand as well. She grunted, her strong arms still unable to lift them both up.

"I think it got stuck on the grill!" Adelaide surmised.

"I don't care right now!" Zadie grunted. "Smoke it all, you're heavy!"

Adelaide tried to shuffle upwards on Zadie's back with her one good hand and semi-useless metal arm hanging down her side, but she didn't make much progress. She wrapped her legs around Zadie's ankles. Adelaide closed her eyes and calmed her breathing. She pushed her mechanical arm forward around Zadie's waist and controlled it with her good hand.

"Come on!" Zadie grunted. "Climb up before we both fall and die!"

Adelaide pointed her metal hand up just underneath the metal support Zadie was holding onto for their dear lives. Her left hand fiddled with the metal forearm's lever and twisted it. Her metal fingers clanked into hooks. She shifted the lever forward. Adelaide looked from the bridge to the train. From the train to the bridge.

"What are you doing?" Zadie blustered.

"Improvising!" Adelaide shouted.

Adelaide fired her grappling hook hand with a cable trailing behind. It soared through the air and clanked onto the top of the passing train overhead. The hooked fingers caught the short, ankle-high, metal railing encompassing the roof of a passenger car.

"Let go!"

"What?!"

"Now! Let go!"

Zadie's hands let go of the plank. They fell through the air.

Adelaide's arm cable snapped taut with one end on the passing train and the other attached to her arm. Adelaide's good arm and legs held tight onto Zadie as the cable pulled. The train dragged them along, and they swung through the open air below the tracks. Adelaide tilted her body so they swung away from the bridge as much as possible so as not to get caught on the platform.

Zadie slid down and grabbed onto Adelaide's shoulders. Adelaide reached her good arm around Zadie's waist and pressed the button on her mechanical forearm's lever. Her arm cable retracted. Their swinging arc began to rise. As the cable retracted, the train pulled them along and swung them up alongside. The two girls flew up past the tracks, the windows, the flabbergasted passengers inside, and the roof. Adelaide rotated both of their flying bodies as her cable zipped her mechanical wrist back into her grappling-hook hand. With a final swing of momentum and a strange barrel roll through the air, Adelaide and Zadie flopped themselves onto the moving train's passenger car roof.

Zadie's arms and legs splayed out on the metal roof in pure shock as Adelaide's arm and legs were still tightly wrapped around her friend that was now lying on top of her. Adelaide's mechanical hook hand fully retracted and locked back into her wrist.

Both of them stared at the dark, smoggy sky above for several moments before bursting into laughter. Half of that was from the relief of survival, a quarter from sheer shock, and a third of that was from genuine enjoyment.[65] It took the better part of a minute for Adelaide to finally let go of Zadie and for the two girls to separate themselves into a sitting position.

"Alright," Zadie said as she gathered her bearings, "where's the fox?"

---

65 Math is hard.

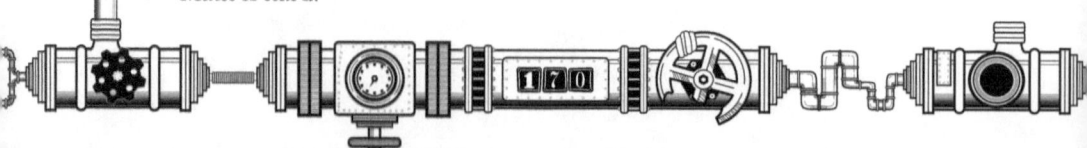

"Unless it got knocked off," Adelaide reasoned, "I think it got stuck on the pilot?"

"Like the driver?"

"No, the grill thing at the front. Looks like a snowplow."

"The cowcatcher?"

"Well," Adelaide uttered, "it doesn't catch cows so much as make them explode."

Zadie chuckled. "Awesome."

Zadie held Adelaide's good hand and helped her to her feet. Smoke billowed over the heads of the two girls as they reached the front edge of the first passenger car. They kneeled down on the unsteady surface and overlooked the tender and engine. The engine cab was completely open in the back for easy access to the tender, which was half-filled with coal. An engineer and fireman operated the steam locomotive from the cab.

The engine powered into a tunnel built into the Gorge's side. At this point, Adelaide had completely lost track of where they were in the city. Were they on the Stacks side or the Lowers side? For reasons that were unknown to time itself, these particular train tracks liked to weave around the Gorge instead of taking straight lines in any logical direction. The train tracks turned to the left and climbed upwards.

"Look!" Adelaide exclaimed. "There it is!"

Visible on the turning engine, Fizzlesticks, the red copper fox, dangled off the front, its tail wedged and caught in the pilot/grill/snowplow/cowcatcher. The trapped head and body flopped and bonked up and down on the tracks.

"It's stuck alright," Zadie said.

"Let's go get it!" Adelaide rose to her feet.

Zadie pulled her back down. "Slow your motor, crazy boots. Wait 'till the train stops again. No reason to climb down the engine while it's movin'. That's how you lose an arm."

Adelaide frowned. "I feel like that comment was directed at me."

"That's a good feelin'. Go with it."

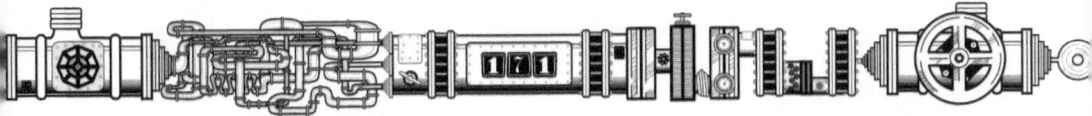

The train exited the tunnel, roared onto the valley cliff face, turned, and climbed. The locomotive leveled off and ran parallel next to a dirt road carved into the cliff. Vehicles passed by and motored up next to the engine. Cogs gang members dangled off the back of two automobiles. They whooped and hollered as they gave chase. The Cog closest to the edge angled his body, ready for a jump.

The train tracks dove downwards, leaving the adjacent road behind. The two automobiles ground their tires into the dirt, skidding to a halt. Both of them reversed. Adelaide and Zadie could just see them over the caboose. One by one, the automobiles bumped their unsure tires up onto the train tracks. They followed the train and rolled down the slope. Their tires bonked back and forth, hugging around the tracks in an unsolicited embrace.

"That's okay," Zadie assured Adelaide. "We still got time."

The locomotive entered a tunnel. The two Cogs cars followed close behind the caboose. Ahead of the train, other tunnels and tracks merged together. A third vehicle with another mentally unstable Cogs member hanging on the back rocketed out from a side tunnel. It pulled in front of the train and rocked back and forth until it finally settled on the tracks. This unwarranted rubber touching is not what the metal tracks signed up for. Didn't even buy it a drink first. The third vehicle slowed and angled before the engine.

"Bollocks," Zadie said. "Alright, I got the fox. You slow down the ones in the back."

Adelaide turned around. Climbing up the back of the caboose were three Cogs members.

"Slow down?" Adelaide blustered. "How?"

"I don't know. Challenge them to a smart test or something. Figure it out!"

Zadie hopped onto the tender. Her feet balanced on the mountain of loose coals. With a running leap, she caught the train engine cab's roof and pulled herself up.

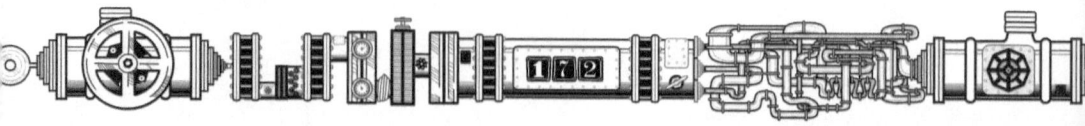

"What in blazes?" the engineer exasperated at Zadie's legs dangling from the roof before vanishing above.

Adelaide stood up on top of the trains' first passenger car. The three Cogs members jumped over the gaps between the cars and approached. Adelaide outstretched her metal hand.

"Halt!" she commanded.

Surprisingly, even to Adelaide, they all slowed to a stop. None of them were quite sure as to why. Perhaps it was the shock of finding another person standing on top of a moving train. Maybe it was her intricately designed, mechanical appendage. Or possibly it was because her commanding voice reminded them of their mothers and how they haven't called her lately.

Nicknamed Teeth, the older Cogs member in his forties shook those thoughts out of his head and grinned. His actual teeth were fairly normal. He just liked the symbolism with cogs being the teeth on a gear wheel. He pulled out a revolver and pointed the weapon at Adelaide.

"Hey!" Adelaide protested. "You can't shoot me! It's against the rules! I don't have a fox!"

The well-dressed, fifteen-year-old Silas Griggs,[66] a young man with a heap of flair and an attitude to match, reached out his hand and lowered Teeth's gun. "She's right. The boss wouldn't be happy."

Teeth holstered his gun and growled. "Guess we'll just have to rough her up then."

The third Cogs member was known as Red Shirt, for reasons that will soon become apparent. He shrugged and went along with the other two because why not? Life was too short for making a fuss.

Adelaide kept her mechanical arm raised. Her left hand withdrew the metal forearm lever. After a short twist, the metal

---

66 He has a last name, so he's going to be important later. That's a subtle-but-not-really writing trick.

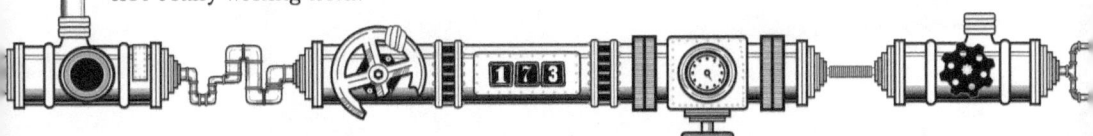

fingers clanked and reshaped into hooks. She shoved her lever forward toward her wrist.

"I'm warning you!" Adelaide warned with her warning.

The three Cogs approached anyway. Her motherly command did not affect them twice. The train emerged into the massive tunnels and underground communities forming the Lower District below the Uppers, sandwiched between a rock and a haughty place.

Adelaide fired her grappling hook hand with compressed air. It smashed into the belly of the third Cog known as Red Shirt and knocked him backwards. He slid across the roof and fell beside the gap in between the first passenger car and the second. Her hook hand caught on the edge. Teeth stalked after her. Adelaide quickly tried to retract her arm's cable to prepare another shot. The cable snapped taut between her arm and the roof's edge.

With a yelp, Adelaide was inadvertently yanked off her feet by her arm's retracting cable. Her flying body barreled into Teeth and knocked out Silas' legs from beneath him. Teeth and Adelaide slid across the roof. They barreled into the Red Shirt Cog, and both he and Teeth fell into the gap between the cars. The two men crashed into the open gangway connecting the two cars below. Adelaide caught herself and withdrew her hooked, metal fingers from the roof's ankle-high railing.

Meanwhile, Zadie climbed onto the engine and maneuvered herself around the smokestack. She hopped down near the large headlamp that shone a blinding beam of flickering illumination. The vehicle in front with the crazy Cog on the back matched speed with the train. It slowed a bit then slowed a bit more until the Cog was within grabbing distance of the pilot. The crazy fellow reached back and yanked on the stuck fox to no avail.

Zadie leaped off the headlamp and kicked the Cog. He slammed back into his vehicle and grabbed hold before he

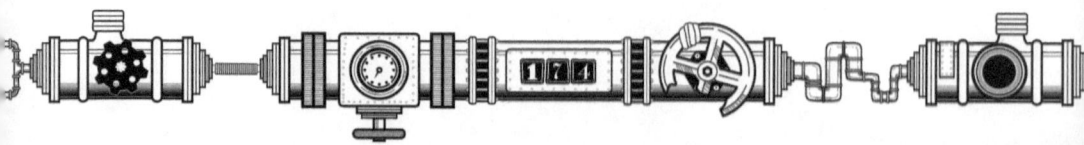

fell. Zadie grabbed hold of the pilot before she fell. They stared each other down. Both of their eyes blazed with the crazy.

Reverse-Meanwhile, Silas rose to his feet on the passenger car and withdrew a police-style baton. He wasn't a bobby, but he sure liked to whack people with sticks anyway. Adelaide grunted herself to a kneeling position. Silas stalked toward her as the train dove down into a tunnel that had grown increasingly unstable over the years. More braces than usual attempted to hold the dirt and rock ceiling. Some braces even doubled up, making the clearance even shorter.

Looking to the front of the car, Adelaide saw the low ceiling. Looking to the back of the car, Silas saw nothing but the need to swing his baton at Adelaide's head. She ducked as her left hand grabbed Silas by his blue silk tie. She yanked his face right next to her face just as a tripled-up brace built across the tunnel ceiling flew dangerously close and over the train's roof. The low ceiling tore the air just over their heads. Silas glanced up in surprise, realizing just how close he came to decapitation.

"Mind your head," Adelaide panted.

"I'm sorry..." he began.

"You should be."

"But I can't let you get the fox."

RudeWhile,[67] on the train engine's front, the crazy Cog leapt from his moving car. He grabbed hold of the pilot and wrestled with Zadie over Fizzlestick's stuck tail.

ConfusedWhile, in the engine's cab, the absentminded engineer finally noticed that there was an automobile driving in front of the locomotive.

"Hey, you!" he shouted. "What are you doing up there?! Get off the tracks!"

NiceWhile, on the passenger car roof, Adelaide looked around, trying to get a view of Zadie. Silas shoved Adelaide aside. She slid to the right and caught herself on the metal rail.

---

67 Because *Meanwhile* is boring.

SurprisedWhile, in the cab, the fireman looked at the tracks and gawked. The train exited the tunnel into the Gorge only to take an abrupt turn along the cliffside.

"Sharp turn!" he yelled at the engineer. "We're too fast!"

The engineer gasped and pulled on the engine's brake lever. The train rocketed around the right-hand curve. The engine brakes squealed and sparked globs of light into the darkness.

Zadie and Crazy Cog held onto the pilot for dear life. The force made Zadie swing off the left side, still holding the vertical brace. Her feet slammed into the supports just over the wheels.

Up top, Silas lost his feet and fell off the train's left side. One hand managed to grab hold of the rail. His fall snapped to a stop, but he dangled precariously off the edge. The force of the turning train simply made Adelaide slide back to the middle of the roof. She scrambled over on all fours and reached her metal arm down toward Silas.

"Grab on!"

He did. Adelaide attempted to pull him up, but he was heavy, and she had difficulty gaining enough leverage with her feet as the train's brakes shoved her forward. His feet slipped on the glass windows below. The passengers inside stared in confusion at the dangling shoes.

TerribleWhile, in the gangway between the train's passenger cars, Teeth held on easily to the handrails built next to the car doors. Red Shirt Cog held on and looked none too eager to release his grip anytime soon. Teeth snorted at his fearful fellow. He extended a switchblade and put the handle in his mouth. His calloused hands climbed up.

Ahead of the moving train, the entire tunnel squished down into a small opening, barely wide or tall enough for a single locomotive to speed through. Adelaide saw it and came to the conclusion that this tight fit looked a bit too tight for the boy hanging off the side. Unable to just simply lift

him up, she instead decided to squish her knees downward. His grip slid down from her metal elbow to her metal forearm.

"What are you doing?!" he yelled.

Adelaide laid her body sideways against the roof with her feet against the rail. Her feet churned and pushed herself along. Her good arm helped push her along as well. Her mechanical arm with Silas dangling off it followed and scraped behind. She dragged Silas along the side of the train, back toward the gap between the cars.

Teeth's head popped up from the gap. The switchblade sparkled in Teeth's teeth. Adelaide pulled and shoved Silas into the gap, knocking Teeth back down to the gangway and avoiding the tight tunnel entrance just in time as the train veered inside.

Silas' feet found purchase by stepping on the top of Red Shirt's head, kicking the fellow back down on top of Teeth. Silas climbed up out of the gap. Both he and Adelaide laid flat on their backs on the roof. They panted for breath and stared at the tunnel ceiling flying overhead.

"Why did..." Silas exhaled, "you save me? Again?"

"I wanna win a race, not kill people."

"Station ahead!" the fireman yelled over the din of metal wheels on metal tracks.

The train tracks straightened leading toward the station. The engineer pulled on all the brake levers, including the emergency brake, for a full stop. The tender's and the passenger cars' brakes all screeched in protest. The passengers inside must have had quite a ride because, on the roof, Adelaide and Silas slid on their backs all the way to the front of the car.

On the engine's front, one of the pilot's vertical supports snapped. Hanging onto it for dear life, deer life, and stag life too, the crazy Cog had no choice but to fall off with it. He landed on the tracks as the engine passed right over him.[68]

---

68 Don't worry. He survived. In case you were wondering.

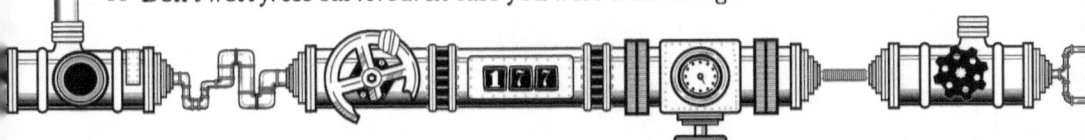

Zadie's body swung forward. Her left hand lost its grip. She reached out and held onto the mechanical fox's body with its tail stuck in the pilot.

Behind the caboose, the leading Cogs vehicle crashed into the back of the train. The trailing vehicle crashed into the other one, making a train/Cog sandwich.

Within the massive tunnel, the pedestrians waiting at the open train station in the Lower District screamed as the leading automobile drove past on the tracks and screeched to a stop far ahead of the station. One moment later, the train squealed to an abrupt halt with two more vehicles rammed up all uncomfortable-like into its caboose.[69]

Zadie kept both of her eyes clamped shut. With the locomotive being loco-stopped, Zadie clamped both of her hands onto Fizzlesticks, the red copper fox, and pulled. The metal, exhaust pipe tail finally just snapped off, and Zadie fell back onto the tracks. Fizzlesticks spun its legs about in her hands.

The flustered engineer wiped sweat from his brow. "Next stop!" he yelled into the train's speaker box, "umm... wherever we are now!"

Panicked passengers pushed each other out of the train cars' doors, down the short steps, and onto the platform. The patient, station pedestrians looked unsure as to whether or not they wanted to board. Most of them couldn't seem to remember where they wanted to go in the first place. Teeth and Red Shirt Cog hopped down from the gangway and pushed through the crowds toward the engine.

The engineer and fireman looked back in surprise to see Adelaide and Silas lying atop the first passenger car. "What is this nonsense?!" the engineer demanded. "What's going on?!"

"Don't worry about it, old man," Silas said. "It's Cogs business."

---

69 Usually, you have to pay for that kind of service.

"Oh, for the love of... gangs?! I hate gangs!"

Ahead of the engine along the tracks, the Cogs driver of the first automobile ran back toward them. The man's eyes were naught for anyone but Zadie holding the fox. The engineer turned his furious gaze to the approaching driver and the parked car in the way.

"I'm tired of you dirty criminals!" the engineer yelled at the Cogs driver and everyone else. "Get off my tracks, or get flattened!"

The engineer released the brakes and pushed up on the throttle. The flabbergasted pedestrians didn't have time to second guess their decisions as the train lurched forward, away from the platform. The fireman simply shrugged and shoveled coal from the tender into the fire box. The locomotive's smokestack sputtered.

With the fox in hand, Zadie faced down the Cogs driver and approached him on the tracks, ready for a fight and oblivious to the moving train behind her. Crazy Cog's hand reached out from beneath the train and yanked her down.[70] That was quite fortunate as the engine slowly rolled forward over Zadie, who looked quite surprised for more reasons than one. She was mainly shocked at how much room there was underneath the train. Unfortunately, that meant Crazy Cog was able to crawl from underneath and grab her legs.

The Cogs driver just missed grabbing Zadie's hair and jumped back away from the slow roll of the engine. He skipped a few steps backwards until he remembered to check on the thing that was a part of his improper name. "My car!" the Cogs driver yelled as though he was somehow surprised that parking a vehicle in front of a train was a poor idea. The panicked automobile owner ran after it.

---

70 See. He didn't die. How did he survive? Apologies, but all questions must be submitted in writing.

On top of the first passenger car, Adelaide gained her balance as the train below moved. She glanced from Silas to the platform and back. She shoved Silas hard, clear off the roof. He fell into a heap right on top of the approaching Teeth jogging on the platform beside the tracks.

"Sorry!" she called after him. "Just trying to win and all!"

The Cogs driver jumped inside his vehicle and attempted to start the engine. The rolling locomotive bonked into the parked vehicle and slowly pushed it aside. The cowcatcher turned into a carcatcher and caught the car just as well as it caught cows, which was to say it shoved the Cogs car off the tracks and onto the adjoining sidewalk. It flipped over with the driver inside.

With the train rolling over her head, Zadie struggled with the crazy Cog on the tracks. He grabbed her metal boot, and his fingers found purchase on the many pipes and engineered additions. Fizzlesticks, the red copper fox, scratched up Zadie's face for good measure.

"Would you…" Zadie struggled with her words and everything else, "just… stop it?!"

She slammed her other metal boot into the crazy Cog's face. Once. Twice. Thrice. He let go as the crunched caboose finally cleared overhead and the dim lights from the tunnel ceiling far above shimmered upon them. Zadie rose to her knees and finally to her feet. Gasps and awes sounded from the remaining pedestrians scattered around the train platform, all of whom were too shocked from the train's departure to even move a single step.

Zadie looked around at her unsuspecting audience. The crazy Cog wiped the trickle of blood from his nose and clambered up to his feet. Teeth pushed Silas off of him and stood. His eyes lit up as he saw Zadie and the scrabbling fox in her arms. Red Shirt Cog helped Silas to his feet. Cogs drivers and passengers from the two wrecked cars behind

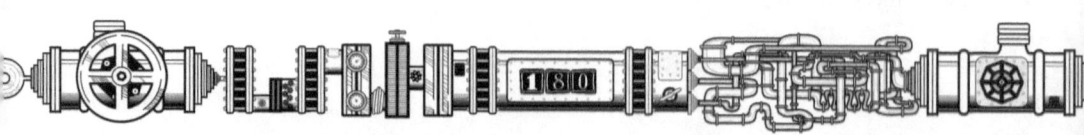

them slowly stalked their way over. Every single one of them stared at Zadie.

Zadie tried to find a word to properly convey her feelings at the situation. "Umm..."

She ran off after the train. All of the Cogs gathered their wits and gave chase right behind. Zadie crutched the energetic fox against her chest with one arm as the other turned the dial on her chest plate. The attached wires running to her backpack told the generator to whir and power up. The Cogs began to catch up to her. The train began to gain speed and outpace them all. Zadie's steam generator whistled through the exhaust pipe poking out just behind her neck.

Zadie planted one boot onto one of the train tracks. The metal braces enclosing the boot with retracted roller skates clanked onto the rail. Steam pressure burst through the boots' nozzles. Her left boot took off. She slammed her right behind her left and onto the rail. The escaping steam propelled her along as the metal boots *screeched* on the metal tracks. The old *fingernails-on-a-chalkboard* didn't have nothin' on that noise. The pursuing Cogs slowed, not just from the hot steam assaulting their skin, but from the grinding noise that grinded into their brains. Silas stopped a ways back, looked at the strange situation he found himself in, and smiled.

The train pushed onwards as the tunnel sloped downwards. Zadie's boots screeched down behind it, and she smacked her face hard into the slightly-damaged-from-the-car-wreck-but-still-okay caboose. She grabbed onto the door and hand rail as her boots' nozzles shot out of control. Her left boot wanted to travel up to the roof. Her right boot found the bottom quite interesting.

On the caboose's roof, Adelaide slid over to the edge and reached down with her mechanical arm. Not wanting to let go while her boots felt like doing splits in mid-air, Zadie just growled and nodded at the red copper fox in her hand.

"Just take frickinstamps here."

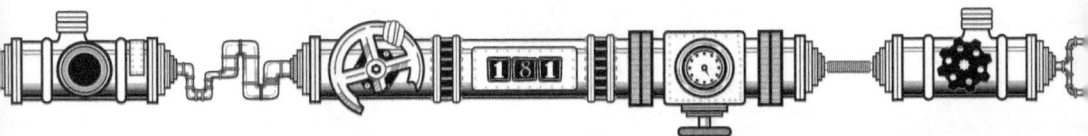

"Fizzlesticks," Adelaide corrected.

"Whatever."

Adelaide withdrew her mechanical arm, repositioned, locked her legs against the roof's rail, reached her good arm down, and grabbed the rambunctious creature.[71] Zadie's boots finally sputtered and whistled to a stop. Her legs settled underneath herself in a more normal position and helped her climb the caboose. Zadie pulled herself up to the roof and laid down next to Adelaide. They both stared at the tunnel ceiling above as the train careened up a slope.

"I don't like trains as much anymore," Adelaide admitted.

Zadie glanced at her. She scoffed. Then she burst out in laughter. Adelaide's giggles joined her as the two girls couldn't contain themselves. Fizzlesticks, the red copper fox, would have laughed as well, but it didn't have vocal chords, a working mouth, or the ability to feel joy at experiencing anything other than the complete destruction of humankind.[72]

---

71 The fox, not Zadie.

72 It's always the quiet ones, isn't it?

Chapter 14

To the Winner...

Ripper monocycles roared down Papin Street in the Stacks. Riptide clutched the dazed-looking Idgit, the black iron fox, in a muscled arm and sped up down a straightaway. He was feeling quite pleased with himself. Pushing kids around, stealing random stuff, driving over the speed limit; these were the things that made his heart sing. Taking the fox from the children was like taking candy from a baby, something that he also enjoyed doing. Because really, why in the world would a baby want to eat caramel toffee, anyways?

A gunshot ripped through Riptide's concentration and also, and more importantly, through his monocycle's tire. The already-unstable, single-tire vehicle jerked and crashed into a bus stop. Riptide fell off and smacked his head onto the pavement. The second Ripper monocycle was also hit by gunfire and crashed. The third didn't appreciate the situation and decided to just take off down an alley.

Golden gang members perched on the rooftops. They continued to fire their rifles down at the street below even though all sense of retaliation had evaporated.

"Oi!" a tall Golden with gold-plated goggles yelled at the others, "Stop yer firin'! Wastin' ammo is like wastin' money, ye dern fangled kinnits!"

"But we like wastin' money, ye frizzled can eater!" another Golden yelled back.

"It's like our whole thing!" a third added.

On the asphalt below, Idgit, the black iron fox, wriggled out from beneath Riptide's fallen form and scratched its claws into the street once again. Only this time, it ran right into the waiting arms of Plated, a thirty-something, lavishly-dressed Golden lieutenant with jewelry on every inch of skin.[73] This narcissistic knob sparkled more than the stars, not that anyone could see the stars through all of the smog.

A few blocks and a few minutes later, Plated waltzed into the Cogs' Courtyard to great cheers and whoops, though most of those originated from his fellow Goldens surrounding him. The sparkly showman placed Idgit into the second cage atop the great anvil. Enoch applauded while he was silently wondering if this guy wanted to take his throne as the most ostentatious gang leader.[74]

Enoch called to the crowd gathered, "Looks like camping *is* a legitimate strategy! Second point goes to the Goldens!"

The hornswagglers whooped and cheered and hollered. A middle-aged man yelled so much that foam started to drip out of his mouth. Those nearby stepped away until they were no longer nearby.

"Two down!" Enoch showboated. "One to go!"

---

73 If anyone was overcompensating for anything, it was this guy.

74 *Ostentatious*: intended to attract notice and impress others. So basically, anything and everything that humans ever did in the presence of another human, ever. Also the primary ingredient for any good mating ritual. Peacocks know what's up. Those birds get all the ladies.

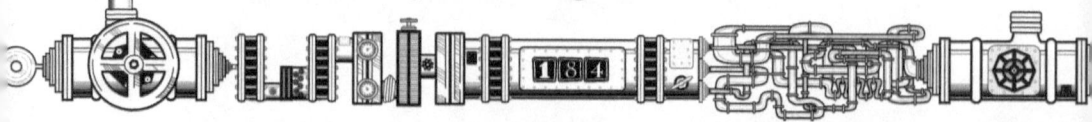

Fizzlesticks, the red copper fox, wriggled its damaged body in Adelaide's secure grasp. Its snapped, exhaust-pipe tail tooted continual wisps of smoke from it now. Adelaide readjusted Fizzlesticks in the crook of her mechanical elbow to compensate. There were only so many toots in the face once could take.[75]

"I can fix it," she said more to herself than anyone else.

"Don't worry with that," Zadie said. "We just gotta turn it in. Without dying."

"That would be preferable."

Adelaide and Zadie kneeled down on top of the moving train's caboose. The locomotive slowed to a stop in front of an open-air train station on the edge of the Stacks. No one inside the train departed. There was no one in the station to board either.

Zadie and Adelaide climbed down the crunched caboose and hopped onto the tracks. The train chugged, spun up its wheels, and sputtered black clouds from its smokestack once again. As the locomotive left them behind, the two girls looked around at just how empty the place was. No other souls were in sight.

"Where is everyone?" Adelaide asked.

"I don't know," Zadie whispered. "Keep your peepers open, yeah?"

They cautiously made their way through the Stacks, sticking to the shadows and peeking around corners whenever possible. The emptiness made that all rather unnecessary. They turned at an intersection and edged up Papin Street. Two blocks later, the two girls could just make out an accident scene ahead. Debris surrounded two crashed monocycles.

---

75 Common consensus is six.

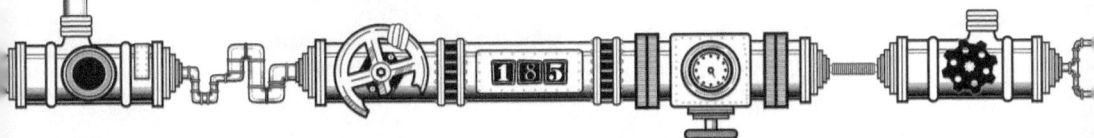

"What is that?" Adelaide asked. "Oh, calm down, Fizzlesticks." She readjusted the mechanical fox in her mechanical elbow as its legs spun and scratched her in the ribs. She wrestled with it and lifted it up to readjust the squirming thing.

A gunshot pierced the silence. A bullet ripped into the fox's dangling neck and tore it open before slicing through Adelaide's metal arm. Fragments exploded and cut Adelaide's face.

Bullets fired overhead. Zadie pulled Adelaide down and took cover behind a parked vehicle. Two small but fast figures sprinted out from the darkness of a cross street and tackled Zadie and Adelaide into an alley. The four of them sprawled onto the concrete in a cluster of appendages. Zadie ripped her arm free and punched Baxter in the face. She looked apologetic as she finally recognized the tackling two as Baxter and Harriet.

"Ow!" Baxter moaned. "We're saving you, numbnuts!"

True enough, the alley provided more than adequate cover from the final spattering of gunfire. Harriet rolled off of Adelaide as they all untangled themselves.

"They got a killzone goin' on up there," Harriet said. "We've been hiding out, hoping to find you guys."

"My eye," Adelaide whimpered. "Did they get my eye?"

Zadie nudged Harriet aside and checked Adelaide's face. She wiped away some blood. With two small cuts on her cheek and one deep cut across her eyebrow, Adelaide appeared to be fine otherwise, despite the blood running over her eyelid.

"Just a cut," Zadie said. "You're okay. You're okay." She pulled out a handkerchief and put pressure on it.

"You got a fox!" Baxter exclaimed.

"Is it still alive?" Adelaide wondered. She craned her neck and tried to look over with her un-handkerchiefed eye.

"Alive is a strong word," Zadie said.

"Look at its neck," Harriet said.

The bullet had torn open the semi-useless gears and hinges holding the top of its head to the body. Fizzlesticks' head flopped down and around from a loose bit of metal.[76] Within the neckhole, an oscillating engine inside sparked with electricity.

"Did they shoot off its tail too?" Baxter asked.

"No, a train ate that," Zadie replied.

"What?"

"How's your arm?" Harriet asked Adelaide.

Adelaide moved her right arm nub and directed her mechanical appendage. The outer rods and chassis were sliced open in two places near the elbow, but it otherwise seemed to function properly.

"Seems okay."

Zadie removed the handkerchief from Adelaide's face. The bleeding had mostly stopped.

"You're a quick clotter," Zadie commented.

"Thanks?"

Zadie licked part of the handkerchief and wiped the fabric over some drying portions of the blood on Adelaide's face.

"Gross," Adelaide groaned. "Stop."

"You're welcome," Zadie said as she cleaned her up much like a mother cat licks the nostrils of her kittens.

"Where's Jules?" Adelaide asked.

"Haven't seen him since we split up," Harriet replied.

Zadie folded the handkerchief, pressed it against Adelaide's eyelid, grabbed Adelaide's good hand, and placed it on the fabric. "Keep pressure on it for a little longer."

Zadie stood and slid to the edge of the building overlooking the street. A bullet whizzed past. She ducked her head back.

"They're all over the roofs," Harriet said. "Hmm. Rooves? Wait, is it roofs or rooves?"

"Is that really important right now?" Baxter blustered.

---

76 *Nearly* headless? How can you be *nearly* headless?

"Language is always important!" Harriet rebutted. "If I don't get my spelling and grammar right, my dad will pull out his belt and... oh... woah..." Her eyes stared off into space.

"Just now connected those dots, eh?" Zadie said.

"I thought we weren't supposed to kill each other," Adelaide commented.

"I was just asking a question," Baxter said.

"I meant the other gangs," Adelaide clarified.

"Maybe no one has actually died yet?" Harriet suggested.

"From a gunshot wound?" Baxter asked.

"My leg!" the fallen form of Riptide groaned out from the nearby street. "Oh gods, I can't feel my leg!"

"It's the Goldens," Zadie said as she knelt back beside the others. "Stupid, goaltending, butt lickers."

Baxter nudged toward the corner and shoved Zadie aside. He slid his forearm's air cannon around the edge and shot out a potato, breaking a window somewhere beyond.

Zadie stared at him and asked, "What was that?"

"Covering fire?" Baxter shrugged.

Zadie snorted. "Can't stay here. They'll surround us."

"What do we do?" Harriet asked.

The other three looked to Zadie. Zadie sighed and looked to the other three. An unusually large spark shot out from inside Fizzlesticks' open neckhole as its head flopped around. They all studied it as it twitched and twerked.[77]

"Do you know how that frankenfurter thing works?" Zadie asked Adelaide.

"Fizzlesticks," Harriet corrected.

"Eat me."

Adelaide looked inside Fizzlesticks' neckhole. The damaged oscillating generator inside sparked but functioned.

"In theory," Adelaide replied.

---

77 In some cultures, fox twerking is a sign of good fortune. Those cultures have since died out due to famine, poverty, and excessive dancing.

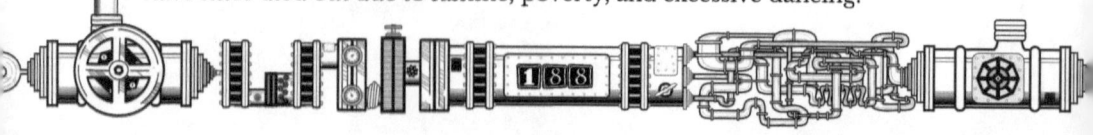

"Do you know how to make it *not* work?"

Adelaide arched her wounded eyebrow then winced. "Don't confuse me. My eyebrow hurts."

Plated and several other Golden cronies marched down Papin Street a block before the alley. On the road running parallel, another group of Goldens stalked toward the alley from the other side. Their rifles were raised. Their blood pressure was high. Their stomachs were gassy. Plated had told Paul not to use the expired milk in their asparagus casserole, but he didn't want to approach too quickly anyways. A flying potato had nearly knocked the golden monocle off his face earlier.

A white handkerchief splotched with blood waved out from the corner of the alley. "Don't shoot!" Zadie's voice called out. "We surrender!"

"Give us the fox, punks!" Plated snorted. "And you can keep living your pathetic lives!"

"Okay! Here!" Zadie's hands tossed out Fizzlesticks, the red copper fox, from the alley onto the street. It scrambled up the road. Plated and his cronies chased it down before he pinned the fox to the ground himself. His expression of triumph quickly turned to one of confusion.

"What the..." he muttered.

The group of Goldens on the other street entered the alleyway. It was empty. Though there were only two entrances into this narrow passage between two buildings, none of them saw the kids escape. Built into the concrete ground, a manhole cover was slightly crooked.

Plated studied Fizzlesticks. Its head was missing. Through the open neckhole, the oscillating engine inside the body rattled and wobbled violently. Sparks and currents of electricity shot out, giving Plated a shock. He dropped the fox in surprise.

"Get back!"

Plated and the others jumped away. The red copper fox's legs stopped moving. Every part of it stopped moving. Then Fizzlesticks exploded.

In the Cogs' courtyard, Enoch Kaylock and the crowd of various members from every gang in the city gathered 'round and looked down the street as a plume of black smoke poured into the sky.

"Too bad we missed the show," Enoch said. "They should have been closer so we could watch." He looked up to yell at a Cogs member patrolling the rooftops. "Hey, Leo! What was that? The Goldens blow up somebody?"

Leo the Cog made hand gestures to communicate with a fellow Cog standing guard closer to the blast zone. "We're not sure yet, boss!" Leo translated and called down. "Still looking in to what caused the explosion!"

Enoch frowned. That's strange. His boys could usually tell how much powder was in a grenade that exploded four blocks away. What could it have been? And did anyone die that wasn't carrying a fox? He would hate to have to punish a rule breaker tonight. Well, that wasn't entirely true. A wicked smile curled his lips. Punishing always put on a good show.

From the opposite direction, in an alleyway just off the courtyard, a manhole[78] cover popped up and slowly scraped off to the side. From within, Zadie pushed her back and shoulders up against the cover until she was free. She inhaled the glorious sense of freedom, not just from the confining quarters, but from the incredible smell she discovered. That particular escape route was through the sewers.

---

78 Why isn't it a womanhole? Wait, that sounds weird. Well, so does manhole. Also, it's taken from the old Middle-English loanword of human, taken from the Latin word: hūmānus. So it's not gender related anyway. Humanhole?

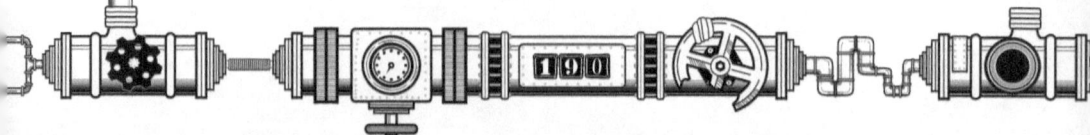

Zadie climbed out of the manhole with Fizzlesticks' red copper fox head in her hands. Baxter followed her and climbed up. Near the top, he coughed at the rancid smell and gagged.

"Don't you throw up on me!" Harriet commanded from beneath him on the ladder within the sewers.

Zadie jogged into the courtyard. The surrounding crowd turned around and looked at her in surprise. As Baxter panted for breath on the asphalt, Harriet helped Adelaide out of the manhole. Behind Enoch, Zadie ran up to the anvil pulpit and slammed the fox's head inside the third and final cage.

"Booyah!" she yelled.

Enoch looked around in surprise. His heavy boots clomped over to the anvil. His wild eyes gazed at the head of the mechanical fox.

"What... what did you do to my poor Fizzlesticks?" he pleaded.

"Uhh..." Zadie searched for an explanation, "it was already like that?"

"My dear, sweet Fizzlesticks. You were so young."

"Jules!" Harriet exclaimed from behind them.

Zadie turned around. Jules was lying on the ground near an outer building. Ripper Robert was tending to him. The Steampunks gathered around Jules.

"What did you do to him?" Zadie demanded.

Ripper Robert perked up, smiled, and replied, "Patched him up. One round, through and through. Lower torso, left side. Not bad. Not pleasant either. Derndest thing I ever saw. Flew out the air like some kind a' bat but also a man. Threw a fox into a cage then threw himself into this wall. Why, that reminds me of the time I courted this dame by making a derned fool outta meself. She was worth it though. Goodness me, I remember she had the biggest pair of—"

"Knock it off." Zadie ignored Ripper Robert by speaking directly to Jules. "You okay?"

Jules nodded.

"You really nabbed a fox?"

Jules nodded.

"So…" Baxter counted on his fingers, "that's two?"

"We won!" Harriet exclaimed.

"We won?" Adelaide asked.

"We won," Zadie confirmed. "Right? Did we win?"

Zadie looked to Enoch. He held the decapitated fox head in his gigantic hands. The gang leader turned his own head in their direction. "You killed my poor Fizzlesticks."

Zadie blanched. As she was searching for some kind of excuse, one arrived in the scorched and burned forms of Plated and other Goldens marching into the courtyard.

"He shot it!" Zadie explained. "It wasn't us! They started shooting and… and I didn't even have the fox, and they shot at me and—"

"Us too!" Baxter added. "They shot at us too!"

"But did you die?" Plated asked. He and the other Goldens dumped handfuls of metal scraps and pieces upon the great anvil.

"What is this?" Enoch questioned.

"The rest of the fox," Plated said. "I believe the combined remains are greater than the weight of the beast's skull that these punks stole from us."

Enoch studied the chunks of the mechanical fox's body.

"We didn't steal it," Zadie protested. "We caught it. You were the ones trying to steal it!"

"You can't steal from each other in a fox hunt," Harriet corrected.

"And that doesn't even count anyway!" Baxter added. "We got here first!"

"Be grateful we don't kill you on the spot for what you did to us!" Plated threatened the lot of them. He removed the extravagant, golden monocle from his burned cheek. Black scorch marks decorated the broken lens. "Do you ingrates have any idea what this cost me?!"

"Your pride?" Zadie postured.

"Dignity?" Baxter suggested.

"Sense of style?" Harriet proposed.

The sensible theories quickly turned into a shouting match between the kids and the much louder and much larger gang of Goldens.

"Enough!" Enoch's voice commanded.

They all obeyed. They all stared at him, waiting for additional instructions.

"My creations, my babies..." Enoch's grating voice gave a soft whimper, "you killed my Fizzlesticks." He turned a fierce glare upon the Steampunks and the Goldens. All of them refused to meet his fiery eyes.

"I declare this hunt to be..."[79] Enoch held the decapitated fox head in his hand, "a tie!"

Echoes of the word "What?" echoed through the courtyard.

"And that means..." Enoch paused, returning to fine form as he leaped atop the great anvil. With a decapitated head in one hand, his other made a grand, sweeping motion over the crowd. "A tiebreak is in order!"

Whoops and cheers erupted upon the populace. The Steampunks and Goldens glared at each other.

Enoch yelled above the din, "As the first to return a fox..." he paused and muttered under his breath, "*at least, a whole one anyways...*" Enoch grunted and shook himself back to stateliness. "The Steampunks shall choose the tiebreak event!"

Zadie and the other punks looked taken aback.

"You may choose any sort of competitive event you wish. To the death or otherwise!"

At that, a great roar of approval erupted from the crowd. Zadie, Baxter, and Harriet gathered around Jules by the building with the broken door as the Goldens grouped together across the courtyard.

---

79 Or not to be.

"Smoke it," Baxter said. "What do we do? What could we beat them in?"

"Could we not do anything to the death, please?" Adelaide asked.

"Youngest member competition?" Zadie suggested.

Baxter answered, "Knowin' them, they'll just go out and buy a baby."

"We got Adelaide," Harriet thought aloud. "Some kind of engineering question quiz?"

"They're pretty smart too, Harrie," Baxter said.

"I don't hear you coming up with suggestions," Harriet harrumphed.

"We *do* have Adelaide," Zadie said. They looked at her as she looked at Adelaide's mechanical arm. Her cheeks creased with a mischievous grin. Her eyes studied the metal pistons.

"What are you thinking?" Adelaide asked.

Zadie turned back to Enoch. "We have chosen!" she called out over the noise. With Enoch's attention grabbed, she continued, "The event will be arm wrestling!"

Roars, laughter, and cheers echoed throughout the night.

"One-on-one!" Zadie yelled. "No rules! First to go down loses!"

Adelaide yanked on Zadie's sleeve until her face was next to her face. "Zadie!" Adelaide madly whispered. "What are you doing?!"

"You got this," Zadie smiled.

"My arm barely has any horizontal torque!"

"What does that mean?"

"It means that this is a bad idea!"

Enoch stepped down from the great anvil. Cogs gang members cleared the cages and mechanical foxes away. Two more dragged over two barrels and set them in place on opposite sides as makeshift stools.

"Steampunks!" Enoch called them out. "Who do you select as your champion?!"

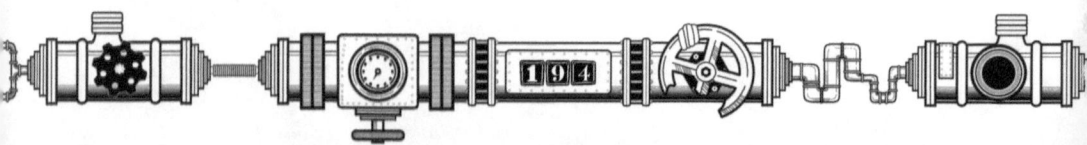

Zadie and Harriet shoved Adelaide forward.

Enoch laughed. "Of course! And the Goldens?!"

The crowd of Goldens parted to allow a gargantuan colossus of a human forward. This outrageously muscular man, whom the others called Beefstick for fairly obvious reasons, stood taller than the tall Enoch Kaylock himself. He flexed his biceps. Just the image of his sheer strength caused the eyeglasses of a Scallywags onlooker to crack.

"This..." Zadie started, "may have been a bad idea."

Adelaide glared at her.

The crowd grabbed Adelaide and Beefstick and shoved them to sit on the barrels by the anvil. The large stick of beef placed his rump on the old barrel's wooden top. His knees only had to bend slightly. Adelaide struggled to hop up on top of her barrel. Two Cogs behind Adelaide hoisted her and planted her in place.

"You heard the lady!" Enoch showboated. "No rules! First one down loses!"

"Good luck!" Zadie yelled.

"I hate you!" Adelaide replied.

Beefstick slammed his beefy arm on the anvil with an earthshaking rumble. With an exasperated sigh, Adelaide clonked her mechanical arm on the anvil with a clang. She was pretty sure that just his wrist weighed more than her entire clump of metal. Adelaide's good left hand dialed her chestplate's primary control panel. Her engine pack sputtered and spit out a wisp of steam.

The two contestants clasped their metal and human hands together. After Adelaide fiddled with her controls, her metal fingers wrapped around his fleshy palm. Adelaide had to lean over awkwardly from her barrel stool. She wriggled and adjusted to find some comfort.

Beefstick slammed his arm forward, pinning Adelaide's mechanical hand to the anvil, which did a full rotation without even pulling on the girl's shoulder. A great roar erupted from the Goldens' side.

Enoch laughed. "Hold on! Hold on! Wait until everyone's positioned and ready to go!" Enoch pretended to whisper behind his hand. "Not that it'll help her too much, anyway!"

His hearty guffaws proved contagious. Adelaide proved to be immune. She slid off of her barrel and stood up straight. This more natural position allowed her to stare at the seated Beefstick just a bit closer to her own eye level. Though, he still had to look down at her.

They clasped metal and skin hands together again. Beefstick wrapped his left fingers around his right arm, bracing himself. Adelaide withdrew the lever from her mechanical forearm and held it tight with her left hand. The crowd hooted and roared and pounded their feet. Enoch approached close and placed his massive hand on the even more massive hand of Beefstick plus Adelaide's smaller one.

"For the tiebreak!" Enoch smiled his sparkly chompers. "Get ready! Three…" Beefstick clenched. "Two…" Adelaide clenched. "One…" Adelaide's butt cheeks clenched.

"GO!"

Adelaide struggled and pushed with all her might. Beefstick simply held still and laughed. The crowd joined in.

"It's adorable!" Beefstick's voice sounded much like a box of nails being thrown down a flight of stairs.

Beefstick pushed. Adelaide's metal elbow dug into the anvil. Her damaged chassis splintered, but she managed to hold his progress.

"You wanna play?!" Beefstick shouted.

He pushed with a second effort. The metal rods near her elbow bent. The crowd hooted and yelled. Zadie bit her nails. Harriet grabbed onto Baxter's head. Jules napped.

"You don't belong here, little girl!" the mound of flesh taunted.

Adelaide strained. The force from Beefstick's push made her accidentally shift her arm lever forward toward her wrist. Her engine backpack chuffed out steam in a conti-nuous

stream. The standing-too-close-for-comfort watchers behind her had to take a step back away from the hot air.

"It's time for you to go back home and play with your—"

Adelaide's finger slipped onto the lever's button. Incredible air pressure blew out from behind her metal hand and shot it from her arm. The force knocked Beefstick clear off his seat.

He flew through the air, knocking over some bystanders before his head smacked onto the ground, along with the back of his huge hand. Adelaide's metal hand clanked into the asphalt a few inches from his face. Her trailing arm cable spooled everywhere.

The crowd quieted in sheer shock. Silence enveloped the entire courtyard.

One could hear a pin drop with cotton swabs shoved in their ears. One Blood Claw actually did have cotton swabs shoved in his ears. He finally remembered to take them out.

Suddenly, the crowd roared in unison. Cheers and jeers and boos and applause erupted in a great cacophony of sound. The foaming-mouth-guy foamed at the mouth again.

"The winner of tonight's Gear Games..." Enoch shouted over the multitude of bellows and hollers, "the Steampunks!"

Zadie shifted through the stomping crowd over next to Enoch. "I told you, our gang name is the *Grinders*."

Enoch chortled at her. "Not anymore!"[80]

---

80 It's too late, Zadie. The book already has a title.

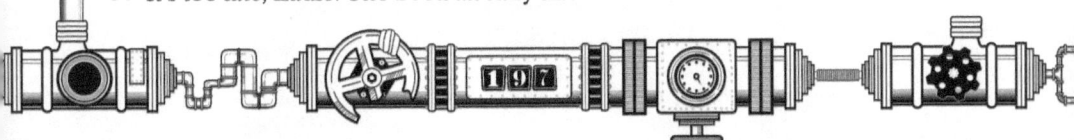

Chapter 15

...Goes the Spoils

Excited gang members lifted Adelaide onto their shoulders and bobbed her around in triumph, taking a tour of the single sight and sound of the Cogs courtyard. Adelaide realized that her mechanical arm was still missing her hand as it spooled cable everywhere. Her good hand pulled on the forearm lever. As her retracting cable zipped back, the attached metal hand smacked several bystanders' faces in the process. With a clank, her metal hand locked back into her metal wrist. The skullduggers realized they much didn't like carrying her around after that.

"Your prize!" the legend known as Enoch Kaylock called over the din.

He slammed a large cashbox onto the great anvil right in front of Zadie. His hands opened the lid, revealing stacks of pound currency. Zadie's eyes widened far beyond what anyone would call healthy.

"Cops! Cops!" a few Blood Claws yelled.

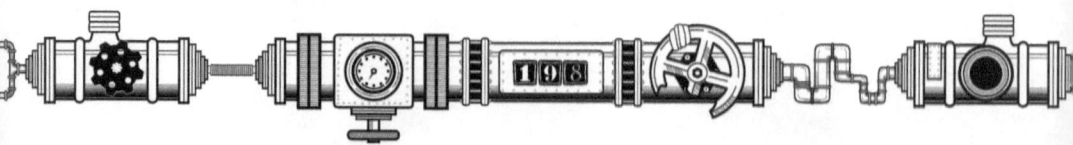

The crowd scattered. Adelaide was nonchalantly and unceremoniously plopped down onto the concrete. Some anti-do-gooders ran through side streets. Others dived down alleyways. A few barged into the surrounding homes and buildings, which they may or may not have had permission to enter. Fewer unwittingly ran into and past the three police officers approaching.

Far more than mere bobbies, these warriors wore full-face, metal knight helmets. Metal body armor and riot gear clasped their imposing figures. Numerous weapons were strapped across their waists and chests. Luckily for those few educationally challenged that ran past, these officers cared not at all. They just marched forward at a snail's pace. And since they were certainly as well protected as snails were, it made sense that they couldn't walk much faster than a brisk jaunt.

"We won't forget this, punks!" Plated yelled as his gang retreated down an alley. He pointed his finger at Zadie in what was supposed to be a threatening gesture. It had the effect of looking like a spoiled child pointing at a toy that he wanted his father to buy him at the store.

"Good!" Zadie yelled back. "Why don't you engrave it on your monocle, frilly Mary!"

Plated's face squished with a mixture of disgust and confusion as he and his gang ran away.

Baxter looked at the approaching officers and pulled on Zadie's sleeve. "Should we book it?"

"Not without the booty," Zadie said.

"Ha, booty," Baxter chuckled.

Zadie reached her hand toward the open cashbox. Enoch slammed it closed as the officers stood before him. He stood tall and faced them. In fact, a slight smile seemed to crease his cheeks. Only a few Cogs members and the highly uncertain Steampunks remained in the courtyard, along with the heavily armed police officers, of course. With a hand on his hip injury, Jules rose and joined the group by the anvil pulpit.

"Enoch Kaylock," the officer in front spoke.

"Officer Halbard," Enoch spoke.

Officer Halbard lifted his metal visor, revealing his tough, grizzled, and mustached face. "The Gear Games?" he asked.

Enoch shrugged. "The usual fee?" He opened the cashbox and dug into the funds. As he was counting, Halbard added another point.

"Your men crashed autos into a train over by the Lowers. Caused quite a ruckus."

"Sorry to hear that."

Enoch added to the pile in his hands. He forked over a sizeable stack of pounds to Officer Halbard. The mustachioed mullet flipped his thick-gloved hands through the currency until he was satisfied.

"Good evening, Mister Kaylock."

"Good evening, Officer Halbard."

With that, the three heavily-armed police officers simply walked away.

"You take that from our winnings?" Zadie asked.

"Your *net* winnings," Enoch corrected. "Not gross."

Baxter whispered under his breath, "*You're* gross."

Enoch retrieved the much-smaller stack of pounds remaining in the cashbox. Zadie reached out for it.

"Ah ah ah," Enoch chastised. "Must withdraw a fee for all of the world-class medical attention provided to the flying masked wonder over there."

"That nurse guy was a Ripper," Harriet protested.

"Using *our* first aid supplies," Enoch said.

"And I'm pretty sure he was only a wet nurse," Baxter added with a huff of superiority.

"That's not what that means, Bax," Harriet subtracted.

Enoch took out a few pounds from the stack. "And let's not forget the location fee." He took out some more. "And hosting fee, of course." He took out even more than that. "Not to mention, repair costs for my beloved foxes. My dear,

sweet Fizzlesticks..." With not much left, he just took away most of the stack. Enoch handed Zadie the few pathetic pounds that remained.

"That's less than the ante! Surely you can't be serious!"[81] Zadie blustered. "We won! Fair and square!"

"Yes, you did," Enoch's calm, cool voice belied his underlying menace. "And those are your winnings. And this is when you are supposed to be grateful to your glorious host."

"You wouldn't pull this garbage on the other gangs!"

"No," Enoch snorted. A wicked smile curled his lips. "I wouldn't. But you're not exactly a gang, are you? Just a group of orphaned children who stumbled onto some luck."

Zadie gritted her teeth in rage. She pulled back for a punch. Harriet grabbed onto her. The small yet surprisingly strong girl struggled against Harriet. Jules and Baxter helped, and the three of them were finally able to hold Zadie back.

"Do you think I am unaware of the various items disappearing from our stores?" Enoch asked.

Zadie and the others paused to look at him.

"Do you think I am oblivious when copper wiring, steel modulators, or chocolate éclairs vanish into thin air? Do not consider me a fool, child. I allow such *minor* thefts because you are *minors*. Go home with your winnings, and know that the only reason I allow you to breathe my air is purely because of my overwhelming generosity."

"We ain't stole from you," Zadie protested.

"You steal from anyone in the Stacks, you steal from me."

He held out the puny pile of money at the Steampunks. Zadie slumped, and the others cautiously released her. Harriet looked ready to hold her back again if needed. Adelaide could only watch, unsure what to do or if anything could be done.

Zadie snatched the pounds out of his hand and growled, "We won. We deserve respect."

---

81 I am Shirley. And don't call me serious.

"You want respect, you join one of the actual gangs. Until then..." he nonchalantly brushed his fingers in a "go away" gesture.

With one final glare at him, Zadie stomped away.

Enoch sniffed and called after her, "And perhaps, in future, you will think twice before you destroy a man's foxy companions!"

Harriet, Adelaide, Baxter, and Jules followed the quickly departing Zadie. Baxter muttered along the way, "That sounded wrong. Right? Am I the only one?"

Adelaide touched Jules' shoulder. "Are you okay?"

Jules nodded and patted her hand as he limped along with the rest of them.

The gang of friends trod their way through the darkened streets in depressed silence. Zadie marched on far ahead of them, rumbling with the occasional grumbling and mumbling. The others gave her space, not just because of the grumbling and mumbling and general air of enraged flatulence, but also because it was difficult to keep up with the speeding teenager.

They soon reached one of the many bridges spanning the width of the Gorge. This particular one had a pedestrian-only bridge suspended beneath the vehicle-only bridge portion over their heads. A pair of opposing conveyor belts ferried the many feet from one end of the pedestrian crossing to the other.

Zadie clomped onto the moving conveyor belt and kicked her metal boot into a vertical support beam as she rolled past. The resulting clang would have been the audio cue that she had broken a toe, but her boot was well protected. In fact, she couldn't feel a thing, which was something that had angered her even more for some reason.

"No good, rotten, horse spanker!" she yelled to no one in particular.

The rest of the Steampunks hopped onto the conveyor belt. Adelaide glanced below the belt to the wobbly, metal-grated floor with no handrails suspended over a thousand foot drop into the valley below, and her brain just tried to keep her eyes ahead of her. She wasn't afraid of heights, but she was afraid of poor construction dangling off of a lethal drop. She didn't think her heart could take another free-falling swing over the Gorge.

"Cantankerous, fart-fried, toe-gunked, half-witted, crank pusher!"

The metal grates supporting the vehicle bridge above clanked and shifted as an automobile drove by. Adelaide wished the structure was more solid and less perforated by holes. As it was, oil droplets could rain down on the pedestrians with no cover whatsoever. She was more angered by the lackluster engineering than the loss of their well-deserved winnings. In fact, Adelaide had nearly forgotten about it already. The Games themselves would be burned into her memory for a very, very long time though. Her adrenaline was still kicking around. With enough time, she wanted to figure out if she found the event fun or utterly terrifying. She hadn't decided yet. Maybe it was both.

"Fracking, butt-faced, stink-brained, no-good, grandma licker!"

Overhead, a squad of three automobiles with gold rims and bumpers roared across the grates. Adelaide thought the gold was a little too extravagant. It was likely gold paint, but what if it was actually made of gold? Had she tested the strength of gold alloy? Wasn't it more pliable?

Behind Adelaide at the beginning of the pedestrian bridge, four Goldens gang members stepped onto the conveyor belt. Their glittering, lovingly-painted faces stood in silence and coasted along far behind them. While they made no threatening moves, Adelaide didn't like their faces. More than the strangely-alluring gold paint on their cheeks or the upturned noses that reminded her of her parents, there was something else about them that made her uneasy. Malice.

"Zadie," Adelaide called.

"Smokin', slimy, skunk-butt, crap-headed... *what*?!"

Zadie turned around and followed Adelaide's gaze. Her eyes squinted at the Goldens. Meanwhile, at the end of the bridge above, the gold-adorned automobiles screeched to a stop. A cadre of ill-intentioned illegitimates marched out of the doors and filed down the stairs built beside the bridge.

Adelaide shoved Baxter over and analyzed his backpack engine.

"Oi!" he protested.

"How's your water supply?" she asked.

"I don't know. I still feel some sloshing around, I guess."

"Is the boiler still working?"

"Umm... it's warm?"

Plated and five other Goldens stomped onto the end of the pedestrian bridge, facing down the Steampunks. Zadie looked from the group of four Goldens blocking the way they came then up to the other group of Goldens blocking the way forward. They were trapped between a Golden rock and a Golden other rock.

"No need to kill them," Plated said with nothing resembling a whisper, "but break some bones. I want them to limp around for the rest of their pathetic lives."

Zadie sighed at Jules and put a hand on his shoulder. "Ready to run?" she asked.

Jules shrugged as if to say, *'Tis the life of a Steampunk.*

Adelaide cranked valves on Baxter's pack and air cannon. She waved Harriet over and did the same for her gear. All the while, the rolling conveyor belt slid them ever closer to the exit and to the waiting Goldens. The Goldens waiting behind them looked content enough to let the belt move them along in the slowest chase scene ever.

"No one insults the Goldens, punks!" Plated yelled.

"Everyone does behind your back, sparkles!" Zadie shouted.

"Well... that's the proper way to insult people!" Plated countered. "You are improper! And dirty! And smelly! And I hate you!"

"Like I haven't heard that one before!"

"Okay, good to go," Adelaide said quietly.

"I don't think we have that many potatoes left," Harriet added as she looked at all the unpleasant grownups.

"They're not for shooting anymore."

Harriet and Baxter looked at her in confusion. Zadie stepped over. A curious hope put the slightest of springs in her step.

"What you got, fingers?"

"Cover," Adelaide replied.

Zadie smiled. Their minds connected at that moment. Without another word, Zadie knew what Adelaide was thinking, and a plan instantly formed.

"Harriet, aim ahead," Zadie's voice softly commanded. "Baxter, aim behind."

"Aim what?" Baxter asked in a whisper.

"Your cannon," Adelaide clarified.

"Slip me a potato," he said.

"No potatoes. Just fire it."

"No potatoes?"

"No potatoes."

"Stop saying *potatoes*," Harriet interrupted.

"Time to pay the toll, punks!" Plated called them out. "You've got nowhere to go!"

Zadie strutted ahead of the group and smirked at the waiting Plated, twenty feet of remaining conveyor belt ahead. "That's your problem, twinkles!" she taunted. "You're too surface level!" Zadie turned back to her friends, nodded, and said, "Now!"

The Steampunks hopped off the conveyor belt and onto the slim sidewalk of metal-grated supports. Harriet unleashed her air cannon toward Plated. Plumes of obscuring steam shot out and blanketed everything in front of them. Baxter turned around and tooted out a semi-opaque envelope of white fog.

"Get them!" Plated's voice called from the other side.

His group of Goldens stepped forward only to stop almost immediately. The boiling-hot vapor clouded their vision and assaulted their eyes.

In the eye of the steam storm, Zadie pulled up one of the slim, metal grates and hopped down inside the opening. An even slimmer, utility repair catwalk was suspended beneath the conveyor belt, dangling over the open Gorge. If Adelaide thought the pedestrian bridge was sketchy, this was another level below that. The catwalk was little more than a pipe and some handholds.[82] Jules slid inside the grate behind Zadie.

Adelaide shivered. The fall from such a great height wouldn't kill her. It would be the sudden stop. And if she fell, she probably wouldn't die on the bottom of the Gorge. She would hit the many crisscrossing bridges and rails and settlements far before that. Not seeing any better options, however, Adelaide followed Zadie anyway.

Harriet's air cannon ran out of steam first, followed closely by Baxter.

"Come on!" she yelled at him. "Go!"

Baxter perked up and noticed the open grate for the first time. He dived down just behind Harriet. Zadie tip-toed and crawled and shimmied her way down the precarious pipe catwalk that not even a cat would dare walk. The various pipes, cables, and wires connecting to, from, and around the rolling conveyor belt above her head snaked their way into a carved opening in the cliff face leading toward the Lower District. Zadie's arms pulled her body inside, and she hopped down into a tight utility tunnel.

---

82 Given that mechanical devices tended to break down and need repair, the original bridge builders wanted to create proper access for workers below the belt. Their twelve and three quarters bosses refused the extra funds, and so handholds were built onto the existing pipes, cables, and framework. Subsequently, all repair workers sent below said, "Ah hell no," and the bridge had not seen any maintenance in seventeen years.

Harriet and Baxter caught up to the much-slower-moving Adelaide. Harriet put a guiding hand on Adelaide's waist as she maneuvered over a stretch of pipe with her good hand jumping from one handhold to the next as her metal-booted feet slipped, readjusted, and barely found the pipe below to walk on.

Plated's head popped down through the opening in the metal grates behind them. "You can't escape my wrath!" he yelled. "I will find—*oh, my monocle!*" His grumbling voice jumped several octaves and squeaked as his scorched and cracked monocle slipped and fell off his face. The damaged piece of ostentation floated for a moment before careening down into the dark Gorge below.

Adelaide squished her torso inside the small cliffside opening with pipes and cables crawling from the bridge and snaking through. Zadie and Jules pulled Adelaide's good arm and metal appendage inside. Harriet slid herself through. Baxter dove in right behind her. And behind him, Plated scrambled down to the makeshift catwalk.

Zadie and the others squeezed in between a cluster of pipes jutting out from the walls, ceiling, floor, and somewhere undefined. Wires and cables formed curtains of electrical power. They eased through, foot by foot, until Zadie's feet turned a corner and promptly slid down a steep tunnel. She didn't bother with the handrail running down the side of the slide. It was more efficient to let her butt do the traveling for once.

She slid her bottom down to the bottom. Jules crashed down behind her and held onto his injured side. Zadie helped him up just before Adelaide, Harriet, and Baxter piled on top of each other. They dusted themselves off, gathered themselves up, and wished themselves elsewhere.

"Think they're still following us?" Harriet asked.

"To me, my nuggets!" the distant sound of Plated's shouting voice echoed. "We'll cut our way through if we have to!"

"Yep," Baxter said. "And did he say *'my nuggets'*?"

"Pick up the pace!" Zadie called back.

Baxter pointed out, "Fine, but we're discussing the Goldens calling each other '*nuggets*' later. Ohh... wait, I get it. Wait. Nope, still weird."

The Steampunks sprinted off among the sounds of sliding adults crashing into the bottom of the tunnel behind them. The teenagers took a turn at an intersection. Then another. Then another. This tunnel went up. The next went down. They took stairs. They rammed through doors. They leaped over pipes. The topsy-turvey tunnels turned and twisted and flipped upside-down.

"Where are we?" Harriet panted.

"I'm not sure!" Zadie gasped.

The latest tunnel ended at a T-intersection with a colossally thick, metal door built into a massively bodacious, metal wall. The door was open. Zadie and the others ran inside.

A monumental, underground chamber spread out before them. Four large pipes extended vertically in the middle of the otherwise empty floor. A spiderweb's collection of pipes and tubes and devices and handwheels and levers decorated the metal walls. The chamber extended upward for an incredible distance. Adelaide couldn't even see the ceiling, partly due to the height, partly due to the fact that no one had bothered to put lights all the way up there. Every foot of the way, crisscrossing pipes and platforms covered the many-storied chamber.

Jules collapsed. He grasped his side with one hand while the other clutched at the floor. Harriet ran to him. Zadie turned back and shoved against the massive, metal door. It barely even moved.

"Help me!" Zadie cried.

Adelaide and Baxter sprang to her aid. The three of them squished their bodies against the heavy, hung-completely-off-center-oh-why-did-they-do-this-it-was-so-so-poorly-fit door. The Goldens fast approached outside.

"Punks!" Plated screamed. His wild, monocle-less eyes glared as he ran toward them. Fifty yards away. Forty. Thirty.

"Phineas!" Harriet exclaimed.

Adelaide glanced back to see Phineas Vinge monkey-bar-swinging himself with his massive, mechanical arm harness on the huge pipes overhead. He flung himself out of the darkness. One giant hand landed next to Zadie as his other slammed the giant door closed, right in Plated's face. Phineas' metal hand cranked the handwheel locking mechanism closed. The Goldens gang members banged the watertight door from the other side.

"Open up!" Plated's muffled voice squeezed through, "Or we'll break it down!"

Phineas snorted. His gnarled human hands reached out from his mechanical harness and pulled open a heavy, multi-layered speakeasy slide in the door. He glared at Plated staring in from the opposite side.

"Good luck, twerps," Phineas said. "That's reinforced steel. Git' goin' back to yer porcelain thrones. I'm workin' here."

"Get out of it, old man. We're here for the punks, not you."

"Who?"

"The punks! Those little turds that just ran in there!"

"Only turds in me tunnels I see is youse."

A short Goldens gang member wearing no less than thirty poorly-crafted necklaces hopped up beside Plated and said, "That's because you're facing the door."

"Speakin' a' which, I gotta evacuate the pipes. Wanna guess where the vents are?"

Plated glanced at the many, various pipes running across the sides of the tunnel outside and over their heads. Many of the metal tubes contained nozzles, vents, releases, and buttflaps.

"I don't care," Plated grumbled. "Just give us—"

What he wanted to say was lost to time as Phineas cranked a large valve by the door. Hot jets of steam exploded from the pipes' nozzles outside and showered the Goldens. They screamed in agony and ran for their lives.

Phineas slammed the speakeasy shut, locked it shut, and shut off the valve. He turned to address the Steampunks.

"You kids been makin' friends, I see."

Jules clumped down against one of the vertical pipes traversing the middle. Red splotches darkened his torn clothing. Harriet kneeled next to him, unsure what to do. Zadie slid on her knees over to him and tended his wound. His bandages were soaked with blood.

"Looks like you popped your front stitches," Zadie said. "Back looks okay, at least."

Phineas mechanical-hand-walked himself over. His real arms reached beneath his seat harness into a compartment tucked away and withdrew a first aid kit. Inside, and aside the usual accoutrements, laid a bottle of rubbing alcohol.

"Gotta clean the wound again," Phineas noted. He grabbed the bottle and pointed at the injury. "Grunt against the pain, lad. This ain't gonna tickle."

Phineas poured some of the rubbing alcohol over Jules' bloody stitches. Jules grunted against the pain, as ordered. Phineas nodded at Zadie and handed her the first aid kit.

"Needle and thread in there, girl. Hands ain't much for delicate work no more. Now first, ye'll wanna..."

Zadie pulled out a needle and thread from the kit. She activated a lighter and hovered the needle over the flame.

"Done this before, eh? Shoulda guessed. Shame. Kids shouldn't need to know this stuff."

Zadie cut the loose stitches free and cleaned him up before putting her own stitches in. The others could only watch. Phineas, however, watched Adelaide.

"You okay, lass?" he asked. "Got cut above your eye."

"It's fine," she replied as she wiped a trickle of blood and a trundle of scab away.

"How are you?" Baxter asked Harriet.

Harriet had to do a double take to realize that she was the center of attention for someone else. "What?"

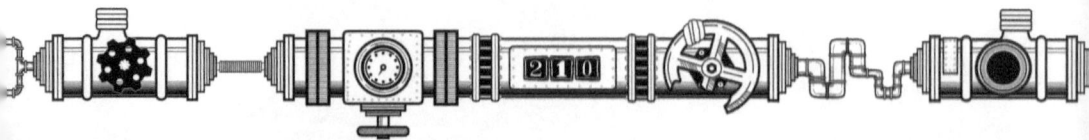

Baxter pointed at her many cuts, bruises, and owwies. "Should clean that up too," he said.

He pointed at the cut on her neck, courtesy of Riptide's knife. The trickle of blood had long dried, but being that it was where her head was attached, Baxter thought they should take a look at it. He took a cloth from the first aid kit and dabbed it with the alcohol. One hand held the side of Harriet's neck to steady her. His other dabbed at the clotted cut with the moist cloth. Harriet winced against the sting, but she relaxed against his touch. She looked into his eyes. He looked into hers.

Jules grunted as Zadie finished stitching him up. Adelaide stood and stepped away. Her adrenaline was finally wearing off. Pain and anxiety flooded into the empty spaces.

Phineas swung his mechanical arms away and opened a small door in the wall leading to a little hideaway. He pulled out a wooden-framed cot and a ratty old blanket. His huge, metal hand clutched them in one. His other propelled him back over like it was a gigantic, frightening pogo stick. He unfolded the cot near the middle of the chamber.

With surprising gentleness, his massive metal hands scooped up Jules and placed him down onto the makeshift bed. After some grunting and groaning, Jules laid back. It was difficult to tell in the sparse light, but it looked as though his eyes behind his visor had closed almost immediately.

"Don't got any more cots," Phineas said, "but I got a couple extra blankets."

"You sleep here?" Zadie asked.

"Sometimes. Depends on what needs work. Got a teapot. I'll make some. Seems ye all could use some calmin' down."

Zadie took off her generator backpack and unhooked herself from the various instruments. Baxter and Harriet did the same. Phineas hand-walked back over to his little cubby. His real hands pulled out an old, cracked teapot with pink flowers. He dug into a frayed box that probably contained tea leaves at one point and nonchalantly tossed whatever was in the box inside the pot. After

his real hands grabbed a couple of mugs that were missing handles, Phineas glanced back.

Baxter and Harriet were sleeping soundly with their heads and shoulders resting on each other and their backs leaned up against the main vertical pipes. Jules' breathing was steady and relaxed on the cot. Phineas had to search for Zadie and found her lying back against a horizontal pipe crossing over Jules. Her head laid on another pipe running perpendicular. While it didn't look particularly comfortable, she looked perfectly content against the hard metal.

Phineas grabbed a couple blankets, placed the entire pile on his seated lap in the harness, and swung over. He draped a stained, holey blanket over both over Baxter and Harriet. He handed a second blanket up to Zadie. She hopped down and placed it over Jules instead.

"I'm good," Zadie said. "This pipe's rather warm anyway."

"As ye wish."

She hopped up to her pipe bed, laid back, and slid her hat over her eyes. She lifted it up for a moment to say, "Thanks, old coot," and placed her hat back down.

"Welcome, young snot."

Clanking and clonking noises caused Phineas to look to the platforms overhead. His mechanical, gorilla arms swung his seat harness and frail legs into the ordered chaos above. On a metal platform suspended between two banks of levers and pipes and thingamabobs, Adelaide had her mechanical arm wedged in between a vertical pipe and two horizontals. She yanked on the curved, damaged metal of her arm with the elbow viced in place. She grunted in frustration. Phineas' huge metal arms pulled on hers and straightened the chassis back into relative shape, more or less.

"Thanks," Adelaide said.

"Took some damage?" Phineas observed.

Adelaide snorted at the bent elbow and sliced rods.

"In more ways than one, eh?" Phineas snorted back.

She nodded and sat down on the platform. Her eyes scanned the many pipes and devices all over the massive chamber. "What is this place?" she asked.

Phineas held his teapot under a nozzle protruding from a nearby pipe. He released the valve, and boiling water shot inside the pot. "Call it the Junction," he replied. "Nearly all the major pipes this side of the Gorge intersect here. Why it's so heavily reinforced." Phineas poured the sort-of-but-not-quite tea into the pair of chipped, sharp, handle-less mugs and handed one to Adelaide. "Incredible pressure could explode any moment and kill us all. Tea?" He sat next to her, or to be more specific, his metal arms placed his chair harness on the platform next to her.

Adelaide took a sip of the brown water with leaf chunks floating around. She smacked her lips and scrunched her face. "Mmm," she hummed almost reassuringly, "crunchy."

"What ye doin' here, girl?"

"We were running away from—"

"Yer parents?"

His wrinkled, weathered face studied her cut and bruised face. Adelaide looked confused, then taken aback, then resigned. She couldn't find the words, so she simply shrugged her reply.

"Why would ye choose this life when ye got family?" Phineas asked with more warmness than she expected.

"Family's about more than blood," Adelaide replied.

"Aye. And once ye feel like ye rebelled enough, ye gon' go back home?"

"That place was never home."

"And this is?"

Adelaide's mouth opened to say something, but it just hung open in the air like a frog who saw a fly then lost where it went.

"So ye got a sob story. Family ye don't like. Jules hadn't spoken a word since the fire. I think he can, but he won't. He hides his scars, but so does Baxter. There a reason he always wears long sleeves. Harriet ain't got scars on the outside I know

of, but she jokes to hide the ones inside. And Zadie? Well... let's just say, those kids down there don't need any more trouble."

"You care a lot for them, don't you?"

"Eh," Phineas began and waved her off. "I used to have a family of me own. Now I got the pipes. And these brats scurrying around the place, messing it up just reminds me of..." his voice trailed off.

They sat in silence and chewed their semi-liquid tea. Adelaide stared down at her new friends. She was so wrapped up in all the new shiny things and her own problems that she never really asked about the others. Was she only causing them trouble? Were they better off without her?

"I never wanted to hurt anybody," Adelaide whispered.

"What *do* ye want?"

That question stumped her more than anything else. She breathed and tried to silence the many voices in her head shouting about all the bad things she had ever done. What did she want? What did she run away for, anyway?

"I don't know," Adelaide said. "All I ever wanted was to go to school, learn engineering. But they don't allow girls."

"Since when did ye need a school to learn anything?"

Adelaide turned her confused face toward him.

"Ye got eyes, don't ye?" Phineas said simply. With that, Phineas' mechanical, gorilla arms hoisted and swung him off the platform.

Adelaide sat with her tea, thinking in the silence. She took a sip and crunched her teeth on it.[83]

---

83 Fun Fact #38: old tea leaves that consumers accidentally ate while drinking tea were the inspiration behind Boba Tea, the liquid sensation which liked to put oddly-shaped crunchy bits in their drinks. This idea was derived by an unemployed bounty hunter just before he was eaten by a creature that, funnily enough, thought he was an oddly-shaped crunchy bit.

Chapter 16

The Mad Happy Scientist

With her hair stuck out wildly at all angles; face covered with grease, oil, and soot; and slightly fractured, mechanical arm flopping loosely by her side, Adelaide busied herself with a new project. Dark-tinted goggles protected her eyes as her good hand gripped a welding torch and melted a strangely-shaped piston to a metal plate. Once she finished, her dirty fingers lifted her goggles and inadvertently wiped more grease on her face.

She tried scraping any gooey residue from her hand onto her pants before she flipped through the piles of books on her workbench/stove/nightstand creation. She had installed plenty of lights in the stash, so much so that the hordes of lamps and dangling bulbs from the cylindrical ceiling cast strange shadows upon the cylindrical walls. If Adelaide had a mind for anything else at the moment, she could have put on a killer shadow-puppet show.

Flipping through the fast-filling-up pages, her journal was blanketed with scribbles and notes and doodles and bullet points clumping together in an inkbath that only made sense to Adelaide. She frowned, took out a measuring tape, and approached her incomplete, welded creation on the floor. She held one end of the tape by the piston with her foot as her hand measured the distance to the end of the crankshaft, right next to the bits of rope covering the hole in the metal plate she accidentally cut three variations ago. She grunted and sat back in her chair.

"Bah, it's too small," she muttered to herself.

"That's what she said?" came a voice by the door.

Adelaide jerked back in surprise so hard that she nearly fell from her seat. Baxter stood in the circular doorway of the stash and smiled.

"You could have announced yourself, you know," Adelaide said, her hand on her heart.

"Thought I did," Baxter replied with a short chuckle. "You alright?"

"Yeah... just frustrated."

"Yeah, everybody's in a bit of a funk these days, it seems."

Adelaide nodded at him. Nearly a week had passed since the sheer excitement and immediate disappointment of the Gear Games, but the adrenaline and hyper-charged emotions still seemed to linger here and there. The gang of friends had kept themselves to themselves mostly with everyone dealing with the aftermath in their own way. Clearly Adelaide's method of coping was to build strange devices that mostly worked. Though, that was also her method of simply existing.

"Whatcha workin' on?" he asked. "Need a hand? Oh... sorry. I didn't mean..."

Adelaide snorted and waved her hand. "You're good, and I'm not sure yet." She sat on the floor next to her welded nonsense, pushed it aside, and rummaged through a basket

full of disassembled pistons, cranks, rods, and one, confused rubber duck.[84] "I'm trying out ideas for a new type of generator."

"Really? How do you do that?"

"Here, open up my copy of *Centrifugal Force and the Power Within*. There's a diagram on page three hundred and ninety four." Her finger lazily pointed up toward her desk above her and the stack of books on top.

"Which one is that?"

"The one that has *Centrifugal Force and the Power Within* on the spine."

Baxter stopped and stared at the books. "Oh uhh... nevermind. I gotta... go do a thing." He shuffled to the doorway.

Adelaide scooched back and looked up at him. "Bax?"

He stopped and turned. "Yeah?"

Adelaide stood and stepped beside him. "Bax," she whispered to him, "I never thought to ask before but... do you know how to read?"

"Uhh, what? Pssh. Yeah. 'Course. Why'd you ask? 'Course I can." His pouted lip jutted toward Adelaide. He glanced around for escape. "Hey, don't judge me, alright!"

"I'm not judging," Adelaide said.

"I learned how. Sorta. It just gets a bit blurry after a minute, and I can't always make out the letters and stuff..." He trailed off as he looked back to the silent Adelaide. "Hey, I don't got the best learnin' or know hows, but I'm darn good at fixin' and getting' outta scrapes and whatever, so I don't need no judgin'!" He looked away.

"I'm not judging," she finally said.

Baxter dismissively waved his hand in her direction and stomped away outside the stash.

"Wait. Bax. Maybe I can help!"

He marched down the tunnel without glancing back.

---

84 Contrary to popular belief, the first rubber duck was not a toy, but was, in fact, the result of a love affair between a curious mallard and an offroad tire.

Standing in the doorway as she became alone once again, Adelaide muttered quietly to herself, "Maybe I can help."

She trudged back to her workbench and slumped into her chair. Adelaide glanced at the array of books open on the desk. A sigh stumbled from her lips. Her eyes darted from her books to her journal and back again, but she couldn't focus. Her hand picked up her quill and dabbed the tip into the ink bottle. Just before she set it down onto a journal page, she forgot what she wanted to write. She looked back up to the doorway.

Adelaide packed up her satchel with her books and journal. She stood and walked out, following the tunnel. After a few turns and a trek over the broken trough of flowing water, Adelaide found Harriet painting the concrete tunnel next to the hideout entrance. She stood next to the taller girl in the tunnel offshoot and gazed at the curved wall. Harriet was putting the finishing touches on a painting of a massive, fluffy bunny sitting in a tuft of grass.

"Cute," Adelaide remarked.

Harriet tilted her head and absentmindedly pressed her wet paintbrush against her chin. "But with a dark side," she said with a spooky wiggle of her brush-holding fingers.

Red droplets traced down from the hare's mouth.[85] Adelaide just noticed it had surprisingly sharp teeth. She also just noticed that there was a severed, human hand sticking out from the grass.

Heavy boots clomped by on the carpeted grate comprising the hideout floor. Zadie marched into view. She looked at the painting and grunted. "You tryin' to give away the location of our hideout?"

"It's right next to it," Harriet replied. "If they can see my painting, they can see the hideout."

---

85 Not to be confused with hairs, which always somehow get stuck in your mouth.

"And how are we supposed to make anyone respect us with paintings of bunnies?"

"That's why she has blood dripping from her mouth."

Zadie grunted and flopped herself into her broken recliner. "Ugh. Not like we have to worry about anyone respecting us anyway, I guess. Paint away."

Adelaide and Harriet looked at each other and shrugged. "Hey, have you seen Baxter?"

"Not in a while," Harriet said. "Why?"

"Oh... no reason."

Jules slept in his hammock, swinging softly over the platform edge. Adelaide couldn't blame him for sleeping so much lately. He definitely needed the extra rest to recuperate. Zadie shoved her fedora over her eyes and laid back in her chair.

"Zadie," Adelaide said as she approached, "did we ever divvy up the winnings?"

Zadie grunted, took out a bag from her coat pocket, and tossed it on the nearby coffee table. "Take what you want."

"You don't want to count and divide it evenly?"

"Doesn't matter. None of it matters."

Adelaide looked at the bag then back to Zadie. "Do you wanna talk about it?"

"I want you to shut yer gob." Zadie shoved her fedora fully over her entire face and crossed her arms over her chest.

Adelaide sighed. She opened the drawstring bag, picked out a few shillings from the meager pile of coins and crushed balls of paper pounds, and put them in her own pockets. She stepped over to Harriet, and the two girls shared a shrug.

"I'm gonna head out. Be back after a while."

"Okay. Be careful. Don't forget to eat."

Adelaide smiled and waved at Harriet before she made her way through the tunnels. She decided to take the scenic route up through the steam tunnels, stairwells, and old, rickety elevators, firstly because she wanted to make an extra stop at The Book Wyrm. After purchasing another book she wasn't looking for

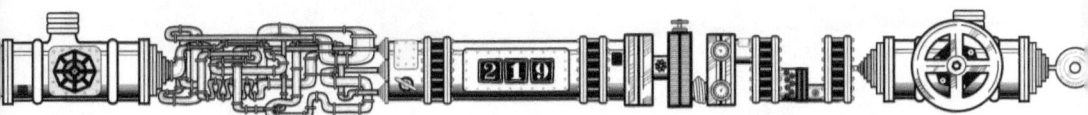

and shoving it inside her already packed-full satchel, she pursued her second reason for the scenic route, which was to ride the train over to the Gorge. More importantly, she wanted to be inside the passenger car this time, which would make for a much simpler and much less frantic journey. She paid for a ticket, skipped inside, and hopped onto a window seat along the right side.

The train chugged and puffed and clackity clacked along the tracks. Overhead, the smoke flew by and mingled with the clouds above, dancing together like a group of awkward middle schoolers. Adelaide's forehead bonked on the glass with every bump of the tracks. The other passengers gave her dirty, greasy face no mind as they shuffled in and out on the various platformed stops. Adelaide just sat and rode along, watching the world roll by, stop, roll by, and stop once more.

At every right turn in the tracks, the girl sitting against the right-side windows gazed at the rolling wheels outside. The eccentric cranks turned the eccentric rods. Adelaide thought they were perfectly centric, to be honest. The cross links pushed the anchor links, and the combination levers pushed the radius bars. All the parts and pieces worked together in harmony in order to drive the whole into greater heights. She thought about that a lot. How much better would the city be if the people worked the same way, with each other in harmony rather than without?

The wheels spun round and round in her mind. The oscillating generator within the mechanical foxes came into focus. She gained a good understanding of their inner workings when Fizzlesticks, the red copper fox, was damaged and, consequently, when she overcranked the engine to the point of explosion. A small one like that was too inefficient, in her opinion.

Visions coalesced in Adelaide's mind: massive versions of the oscillating engine, but with far more than just the

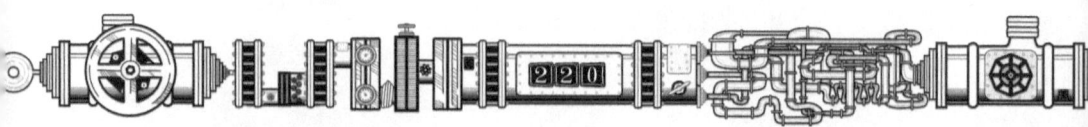

cylinders rotating directly against the crankshaft. Steam pressure could begin the process, but if she was able to properly utilize this new electromagnetic force concept that she read about, perhaps she could rotate an object with far more mass. Maybe over a separate magnetic current. What if she could reduce the air friction to near zero through additional electromagnetic forces? The oscillations could rotate endlessly. That would create... limitless power.

The grin of a mad scientist who spent way too much time alone plastered and slathered all over Adelaide's face. She grew excited just thinking of what such a device could do. She dug into her satchel and pulled out her journal. Struggling to keep it all level, she dabbed her quill into her ink bottle and sketched over another sketch in her journal, balancing the lot on her lap and holding some items with her mechanical elbow. She scratched it all out and began on another page. Then she scratched it all out and began on another page. Several more inkblotted, Rorschach tests later, something began to take shape on the tattered parchment.

In what seemed like no time at all, the train stopped at her stop. Adelaide's overloaded mind ordered her hand to pack away her things and her feet to depart before wandering down the steps. The humid air opened up to the smoggy smells of the Bazaar.

Adelaide squeezed through the crowds and shuffled along until she found a tented shop filled with various goggles and eyed instruments. She stopped as her brain shifted gears. That was why she wanted to come up here in the first place, wasn't it? Adelaide blinked her eyes to focus and entered. A row of goggles laid on the tables and dangled from hooks. Some even had hooks hooked onto them. One of those might be helpful. Probably not the hook one though.

"Oi! It's her!" Winston, with a large group of Caretaker's orphans, called from the tent entrance. "You. Were. Awesome!" He giggled. "The way you guys blew up that fox! And and..."

"Piston punched that guy!" said another.

"And when Jules flew over the Gorge!" said a third.

Adelaide couldn't help but beam at them. "Yeah?"

"Yeah!" Winston punched the air. "Just too bad you guys are still losers though." The others snorted and chuckled.

"What?" Adelaide asked.

"The other gangs all make fun of you. Is it true Enoch didn't give you any of the winnings because you're just a bunch of kids like us?"

"We got some of it."

"*Some of it,*" Winston laughed.

The other kids under eleven chortled and chuckled and sprinkled "Losers" at her as they walked past the entrance. Adelaide thought they were a little haughty for children younger than she was. She made a mental note to think of a comeback that she could yell at them later.

Flanked by his two cronies, Blood Claw Johnny strolled into the tent entrance. His greasy voice uttered, "Only the punks could be winners and losers at the same time."

"Thanks?" said Adelaide as she put on a pair of goggles with pinwheels over her face.

"You won," Johnny began, "but man, oh man, did you piss off absolutely everyone on your way. It's a wonder you're still around. If I were you, I would've skipped town by now."

"If I were you," Adelaide replied as she looked through a pair of goggles to analyze another pair of goggles, "I would have finished last in the games."

"Watch what you say, punk," Johnny said. "You got all the gangs gunning for you now."

"Watch your pockets, claw," Adelaide said with a smirk.

Unbeknownst to Johnny, the orphans shuffled back around and loitered just behind the Blood Claws for a few moments before they took off at a run.

"What?" His smug face turned to confusion.

"Your wallet just got nicked."

Blood Claw Johnny checked his back pocket. Feeling the emptiness on his butt, his eyes widened in shock. Without another word, he bolted and ran down the passageway outside, his two cronies close behind.

After more perusing and without further interruptions, Adelaide made her purchases and left.[86] Perhaps the lenses she found would help Baxter. If not, she could narrow down her parameters and figure something else out, at least.

She was about to make her way back home when the smell of burning coals filled her nostrils. The aroma led her to a blacksmith's shop, one of the very, very few shops in the Bazaar with metal walls, though most of the place was built into a shallow cave along the side of the Gorge. Letters cut out of sheet metal hung above the entryway to spell: "*Jack's Blacksmithery.*"

Inside, the soot-covered, muscular arms of the blacksmith pounded a sheet of glowing-hot metal with a huge hammer. The blistering material bent and shaped to his forceful will, curving around the anvil beneath it. His arms were massive. They looked longer than his entire, stocky body. Adelaide briefly imagined that if she placed her head in the crook of his elbow, he could squeeze his monstrous muscles together until her head popped like a grape. After that bizarre thought in the Bazaar, Adelaide shook her mind clear as he paused and looked up.

"Can I help ye, little lady?" Jack the Blacksmith asked.

"I have a specific design that I was looking to build," Adelaide replied.

She pulled out her journal from her satchel. After flipping through the pages, she showed it to Jack.

His gloved hands put his tools down as his forearm wiped sweat from his brow. He blinked and studied the sketches and nearly illegible, ink splotches that Adelaide called writing. His nostrils puffed.

---

86 She left the shop because it's physically impossible to right the shop. At least, not without a much larger mechanical arm.

"Hmm. Don't think I can help ye there," he said. "Is that a centrifugal governor?"

Adelaide nodded her head, excited that her design sort of made sense to someone else.

"Just that alone is too big to come from my forge." He gestured to the corner and the blazing block of stone with fiery coals on the bottom sizzling and sparkling. "Could we break it down into smaller pieces?"

Adelaide sighed and pointed at her sketches. "I don't think it'll have enough stability if we use welds and bolts. The force will be too great."

"Hmm." His beard was so long it tucked into his apron, but the various wild hairs tickled Adelaide's arm if she stood too close to him. "Best shot ye got would be the Stacks then."

"The Stacks?" she asked.

"Yeh. Got all them factories and industrial plants. Big forges and molds and machines. That's yer best bet."

"Will they do custom builds like this?"

Jack snorted and shrugged. "Beats me. Since the Cogs took over the district, factories still work and provide good jobs. They just build what them Cogs tell them to." He handed Adelaide back her journal. "Good luck."

Adelaide nodded. "Thanks."

He went back to work. Adelaide gripped her journal tightly in her hand as she went into the lower temperatures and higher smells of the Bazaar proper. She trudged over past the shops, to the edge of the outcropping, and to a rusted, metal railing that creaked and bent when she nudged her hip against it.

Across the Gorge, over the railway bridges and ropes and cables and stretches of buildings both abandoned and otherwise, the great smokestacks of the different factories reached up above the Stacks skyline and spewed out black. There were nearly a dozen working factories from what she could see. Surely one of them would have what she needed?

The weight and sheer difficulty of what it would take to build her generator suddenly hit Adelaide like a pile of procrastinating bricks.[87] Still, no time like the present.

From the Bazaar, Adelaide made her way over the Gorge by one of the many, wobbly, unsafe pedestrian bridges and strode into the Stacks. During the Gear Games, she had run all over the district, but she never quite knew where she was at any one given time. Where she should begin her search was still a question in her mind.

With a shrug, Adelaide just pointed her feet in the direction of the nearest active smokestack. The factory the smokestack belonged to encompassed an entire block by itself. Five-story walls of buildings encircled the compound. The only entrance she could see was a wide opening for large vehicles to drive in and out. Adelaide wandered into the entrance before a hand reached out from a side door and pushed her backwards.

"Whoa," said a gangly Cogs member. "Where do you think you're going?"

"I just wanted to—"

The Cog known as Teeth sauntered in from the doorway. "Whatcha doin' here, punk?"

"I was just going to—"

"No one cares," said Teeth. "Get outta here before we get nasty."

Adelaide paused then harrumphed, "One could argue that your breath is already nasty."

The gangly Cog laughed. Teeth cut him off with a glare.

Adelaide continued, "I just wanted to take a look at your forges."

Teeth turned his hateful glare onto Adelaide. "The only thing you're gonna be lookin' at is my boot if you don't git."

"But I—"

"Go on, now."

---

87 A procrastinating brick is really just a pile of clay that's had a long, hard day.

The tall man eye's matched the intensity of the short girl's. The two were locked in a never-ending staring contest of wills, but Adelaide finally ended the never-ender with a teenager-fueled, exasperated sigh of neverendingness. She walked away.

"Worthless punk," he grunted at her departing form.

When she could no longer see them, she muttered to herself, "Rude."

She kicked her feet on the sidewalk, despite the sidewalk having nothing to do with it. Adelaide didn't know what to do. Should she go somewhere else? Should she ask the other Steampunks for help? A sigh raspberried her lips as the sun began to sink below the tall buildings. The faintest hint of starlight glittered off the particles dancing within the smog above.

What would the other Steampunks do in her position? *What would Zadie do? Well, Zadie would have had quite a few more choice words thrown at him, that was for sure, and then she would... oh...*

A mischievous grin creased her cheeks.

Chapter 17

Dumpster Diving

delaide was about as stealthy as anyone would expect of a bouncy girl with bushy, red hair poking out of her purple hat as she adjusted her noisy, mechanical arm. She leaped off the roof of a four-story building. She didn't quite make the jump over to the adjacent building, but her rib cage caught the edge. Adelaide yanked herself up and tried to inflate her lungs again.

Once she could breathe, the curious girl looked out over the skyline of the Stacks. It was difficult to tell directions when leaping from rooftop to rooftop at nighttime for some reason. Her brain drew a mental map[88] and tried to remember where the factory with the possible forge was located, but then, a new contender showed itself in the corner of her eye.

---

88 Mental maps were first trademarked by an investment firm that specialized in hair care products. While initial interest and investments were high, mental maps dropped off because they would inevitably just give directions to the nearest wheel of cheese.

Within a three-story warehouse with open barn doors across the street, she could see what appeared to be a forge. It spread out across one wall and corner in a wide platform. A flue took the fumes straight to the ceiling. It even had a brake drum attached to it. She didn't know if she could spend much time in there without being spotted, but she wanted to check it out first to make sure it was what she needed.

Now, the trick was: how to get in there without being seen. A group of Cogs strolled by on the street below. Adelaide couldn't rooftop jump her way over; it was much too far, and her ribs thanked her for it. She would have to sneak her way on ground level. While a fire escape or set of stairs would have been appropriate, a sneakier idea made her eyes twinkle.

Adelaide adjusted her mechanical appendage's forearm lever. The fingers clanked back and rotated into hooks. With a twist, she released the hand from her wrist and spun out some cable behind it.

Her eyes peeked over the rim of the roof. A large, metal, refuse bin laid below. *That should provide good cover*, she thought. She would just lower herself down, hide behind the garbage bin, and then wait for an opportunity to run across the street. Easy.

Adelaide wedged her hook hand against the roof lip. Once it was secured in place, she gathered the attached cable, slid her legs over the edge, and let go. Her good hand adjusted the forearm lever, and the cable slowly unspooled. She lowered herself down one story. Adelaide felt that she was getting rather good at this sneaking thing.

The fractured fingers of her mechanical hand, however, had another plan in mind. The gear holding the middle finger in place snapped in two and essentially gave Adelaide the middle finger as the entire grappling hook failed. Her hook hand broke free from the roof, and Adelaide fell free through the air.

Luckily, she landed inside the refuse bin. Unluckily, the refuse bin was not nearly as soft as she would have preferred as she landed with a loud, resounding thump followed by an even louder clang. Her metal hand flung itself through the air and crashed into the street.

Best she could tell, her backpack generator impacted on the remains of a broken, wooden pallet, which dampened her fall but made her spine curve at an uncomfortable angle. The edgiest edge of a nail could be felt poking into her right buttock. At least her head appeared to have found a collection of banana peels and whole grapefruit that no one wanted to eat.

She hoped the juices running across the back of her ears were actual juices and not her own blood. Adelaide would have checked, but her body just wanted to lie there. She was not keen on instructing otherwise. As she laid there, staring up at the night sky from within a metal container full of trash after falling from a great height, she found that to be a fitting metaphor for her life's trajectory.[89]

An unpleasant-looking face with almost a full set of teeth peered over the rim of the bin. Five-toothed Freddy held Adelaide's disconnected, metal hand and tapped the metal rim of the bin with it.

A gruff, female voice called behind, "Oi! Issit dead?"

"Dunno," Five-toothed Freddy called back. "You dead?" He poked Adelaide with her own hand.

"Ow," Adelaide replied.

"Oi, it ain't dead yet."

Adelaide used her attached hand to grab her unattached hand from him. The gruff female sporting an impressive mustache peeked over the bin's rim and joined Freddy.

"Better take its to the boss, then," Gruff Gilda muttered.

"You git in dere then."

---

89 Speaking of trajectories, the nearest wheel of cheese is exactly one mile, one point six kilometers, or approximately three hoot nannies away.

Gruff Gilda flashed Freddy a hateful glare.

Freddy shrugged and continued, "I dun' wanna git in dere. Smells right nasty."

"Actually," Adelaide interjected as she retracted the cable and metal hand into her mechanical wrist, "could I just lie here for a moment longer? There's..." Adelaide picked out a shard of glass from her left love handle. "Ah, that's better."

Freddy scoffed. "What kind a' idgit jumps in a trash bin fer? Buncha trash in dere."

"I didn't mean to."

"Buncha sharp an' pokey bits in dere."

"I noticed."

"You gots a weird arm too."

"That is true."

"Why your hand fall off?"

"Come," Gilda grunted. "Get gettin'."

Gilda reached out a hand and pulled on Adelaide's good one. With great effort, Adelaide stood up and bent over the bin's rim. The two adults picked her up and put her on the ground.

"Actually," Adelaide began as she wiped a glob of purplish something from her nose and onto her pants leg, "I think I'm just gonna go home now, thanks."

She stopped abruptly as Gilda pulled out a revolver from her apron. "I wuzn't askin'."

Adelaide gave a sigh and resigned herself to limping along behind Freddy with Gilda close behind. She would have been nervous, but she was too preoccupied by being aggravated with herself. Why didn't she fortify her arm? She knew it was damaged from the games. *So dumb. Bad Adelaide. Bad.*

A hop, skip, and a limp away, they approached a foreboding building lined with metal bars, metal spikes, and metal heads. Literally. There were some sort of metal-looking skulls stuck on some of the spikes. It was obviously

meant to inspire fear into anyone who approached. Adelaide, however, was just curious.

Were those actual skulls? Did they dip them into molten metal and wait for it to cool? Would human bone even survive the process? Or did they sculpt them from metal? That would be rather adorable. The Cogs must have a resident artist and sculptor. Or can you even sculpt metal? Probably need to hammer out a mold then...

Her mind's wanderings were interrupted as Freddy pushed her to the front entrance, making her wandering feet wander inside. A pair of gruff-looking Cogs wielding rifles guarded the dimly-lit foyer. Their heads were also topped with metal caps and Cog eyepieces. Adelaide was sensing a theme here. On the bright side, she was most definitely in the right place for some custom metalwork.

Gruff Gilda shoved her through another doorway and into a spacious room. Pillared supports raised up a balcony that wrapped around the area. Bookshelves above towered up to the tall ceiling, but these were not covered by books. Gold coins, jewels, and all sorts of shiny treasures lined the balcony bookshelves. Below on the main floor, oil paintings and artwork of people, landscapes, and various cheeses covered the walls. Large, marble sculptures of people, automobiles, and cows dotted the corners. One cow statue looked especially proud of her udders and sported a top hat that read, "Moo."

Muscular guards stood stone-faced next to the stones. Expensive rugs lined the room's middle. Glittering chandeliers illuminated the area. And a giant desk took its place at the center of it all, raised even higher than it was designed. And raised even higher than that was a throne-like chair behind it.

Enoch Kaylock fit the throne well. He seemed to enjoy towering over others, though he was already quite tall. Adelaide was curious if it was because he had trouble tilting his neck back.

"Is that a Steampunk you're bringing before me?" Enoch grated.

"Yessir," Gruff Gilda gruffed. "We done caught 'er in the garbage."

"I fell," Adelaide clarified at Enoch's raised eyebrow.

"Interesting," Enoch commented. "And what were you doing in my garbage?"

Adelaide looked around. "Umm... I fell... I just... said that..."

"Were you punks trying to steal something else from my stores?"

Adelaide shifted her feet. "Umm... not steal, exactly. More like... borrow?"

"Borrow? Without my permission? That's called stealing."

"So..." Adelaide averted her eyes. "Can I borrow your forge? I need to make a centrifugal governor."

"Guv'nor?" Five-tooth Freddy asked. "You can't make people, girl."

"Least not that way," Gruff Gilda guffawed.

Freddy joined her guffaws. Enoch Kaylock's cold stare forced them into silence.

"Leave."

Freddy and Gilda shuffled back the way they came, bowing their heads deferentially, which caused Freddy to bump into the table of tiny cow statues. He shuffled back out through the entrance. Enoch's cold stare settled back on Adelaide. Adelaide's warm glance settled everywhere else.

Enoch grumbled, "You Steampunks appear to be under the impression that I provide some kind of free, all-you-can-take marketplace. Full service. No strings attached. Well, let me tell you, in no uncertain terms, that you are mistaken. I have told you this before, yet the message clearly has not quite sunk in."

Two of the muscular guards standing by the door behind Adelaide stepped forth. One grabbed her good arm as the other grabbed her mechanical arm.

"Thievery is normally punished by cutting off the perpetrator's hand. Since you only have one left, your life is about to become quite difficult."

Adelaide's expression turned from frightened to calculating within an instant. "Well, that would be a waste," Adelaide argued.

"I disagree. Your hand would go toward feeding my troops."

Adelaide stopped struggling against the strong hands holding her and simply stared in astonishment at Enoch. "You're cannibals?"

Enoch shrugged and smirked with mischief. "Who's to say?"

"Well, you are. That's disgusting."

"Does that frighten you?"

Adelaide scoffed. "Do you know how many diseases you could get by doing that?"

Enoch tilted his head to the side, pondering. "I don't—"

"If the person had diseases, you would most certainly get them too if you ate him. Why would you even want to do that?"

Enoch shook his head and adjusted his focus. "Destroying evidence is—"

"There are far easier ways to do that. Ways where you don't get scurvy, Lyme disease, and explosive diarrhea."

"I—"

"I suppose you're going for the fear effect to scare your victims, but really I'm just grossed out. And I feel bad for all your underlings." Adelaide looked up to the strong men holding her arms. "Does he make you guys eat people? That's really bad for your health."

The strong men looked at each other.

Enoch sighed, "That's enou—"

"And I wasn't even talking about *wasting* like that. That's so dumb. I was talking about my skills. It would be a waste of my skills."

Enoch stared at her, a little less cold than before. "How so?"

"I'm an engineer."

"You're a little young to be an engineer, don't you think?"

"No." She stared at him for a silent moment just to hammer the point home. "I can build lots of stuff. Stuff that's better than what you got. I just need access to your forge. And some materials. And probably some tools." She sniffed herself. "And a shower wouldn't hurt."

He smirked. "Are you suggesting some sort of trade deal? Little girl, you're in no position to bargain."

Adelaide glanced around. "Why? Should I be sitting down or something?"

"That's not..." Enoch sighed. "The only trade deal would be for me not to kill you outright."

"I mean, you wouldn't get anything out of killing me. That would also be wasteful."

"I would get satisfaction out of shutting you up," he said with a wicked smile.

"Satisfaction? You can't spend that. I thought you were a businessman."

He snorted. "I could keep you here and force you to work for me."

"Slavery? No thanks."

"No thanks?" he scoffed.

"No thanks. Might as well lop my head off. But that would be wasteful, like I said. Besides, I thought you were better than that."

Enoch stroked his chin and studied the girl. "So... I give you access to my facilities, and you build me something? What?" He shook his head and gestured at the many shinies and extravagances and cows around the room. "What could you possibly offer me?"

Adelaide shrugged as much as she could with the strong men holding onto her arms. At first, she thought about blurting out her idea about a perpetually-powered generator, but she wanted to keep that one close to the chest. She wasn't sure if it was going to work, after all, and if it did, she didn't

think she'd want Enoch to have the rights to it. So her whirring brain decided on a simple question instead.

"What do you want?"

Enoch tapped his huge finger on his dimpled chin. He studied the girl. After a few moments, his lips curled into a smile.

"I want to fly."

Chapter 18

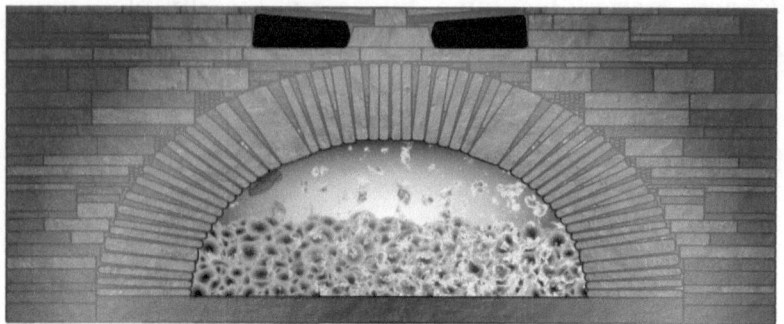

Playing with Fire

Forges were a temperamental lot, that much Adelaide already knew. Some furnaces would fire too hot, some too cold. Some had strange ventilation and air flow, making it difficult to predict proper cooling periods. Still others didn't have the correct equipment, making the forge little more than a large fireplace. And some, as in the case right now, were filled with all manner of garbage that made it difficult to do anything in this stupid place with all these morons putting their doodoo everywhere. *What did they put a tire in here for anyways? Honestly.*

Hours after her own use, Adelaide still found pieces of melted, rubber goo clogging up the vents. These Cogs did not function as precisely as the cogs in a clock, she could tell them that. They were more like a bunch of rusted gears shoved inside a turkey. *And was that a shoe in the flue? Honestly.* No wonder it was getting so smoky in the warehouse. She was both happy and unhappy to be inside the place.

"Leeroy!" Adelaide called out across the busy warehouse. "Why..." she sighed. "Why is there a shoe in the flue?"

A confused-looking man with a metal cogwheel strapped over his eye like an eyepatch lumbered over to her. "Sometimes the feets gets cold," Leeroy said with a shrug.

Adelaide yanked a second boot out of the cylindrical tube reaching toward the three-storied ceiling. She shoved the boots into his arms.

"Your *feets* would be warmer if you kept your boots on," Adelaide grunted. "Keep them out of the forge, please."

Adelaide pointed him away. Leeroy shrugged and lumbered away, clutching his two boots without ever putting them back on his cold feet.[90] It had been a little over a day since she made her deal with Enoch, and she was already tired of dealing with the Cogs.

She glanced back into the depths of the warehouse. Multiple Cogs miscreants were filtered about the place, gathered next to the many workbenches and machines and devices that could turn this old place into a productive factory. These literal gear heads were more interested in drinking and rolling dice.

Adelaide stepped over to the furnace. Her eyes squinted at the funneled opening that led into the fire. Blazing-white coals surrounded a cast-iron container filled with almost-molten metal. It was just about liquid enough for Adelaide to retrieve and mold.

"Silas!" a voiced called from behind her.

Adelaide turned around in confusion. A well-dressed, young man stood a few feet away. He waved his hand and shrugged, sheepishly.

"Griggs," the 15-year-old continued. "Umm, my name... Silas... Griggs... is my name. Yes. That is... my name..."

"Oh," she replied after a moment, "Adelaide Wakefield."

---

90 Turning Leeroy's cold feet into happy feet required several penguins skilled in choreography. Naturally, he just preferred to warm up his boots instead.

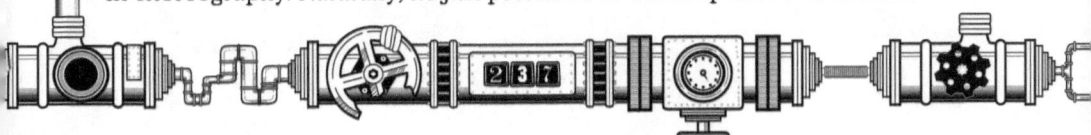

Silas reached out with his right hand, glanced at Adelaide's mechanical hand, withdrew his right, extended his left, and shook her left hand.

"I heard rumors about a girl with a metal arm making waves around here, impressing the boss," he said. "Thought it might be you. Wanted to formally introduce myself."

"I remember you," she said. "From the Gear Games. You were on the train."

Silas straightened his silk tie. "Yes. You saved my life."

"Twice."

"Yes."

Adelaide paused for a moment then smiled. "Then I think I threw you off."

"Yes. Well, I... I landed well enough. And... I just wanted to introduce myself. Say a... proper 'thank you'... and all."

Adelaide nodded. They stared at each other in silence for a few moments. "Well?"

"Hmm?"

"Were you going to thank me?"

"Oh, yes! Yes. Thank you."

Adelaide chuckled. Silas smiled as his cheeks turned red.

"I'm... uhh..." Silas searched for the words that his brain needed to do the speaking with, "I'm usually a lot more... loquacious than this."

"Guess I'll just have to take your word for it," she said with a smirk.

Silas nodded. His hands unconsciously played with his tie. "Well, I'll uhh... just leave you be then. Just wanted to... introduce myself and... say 'thank you' and... yep." He turned around, took a step, then turned back. "Pleasure to make your acquaintance, Miss Adelaide Wakefield."

"And you too, *Mister* Silas Griggs."

He nodded, walked away, had to readjust because he forgot where the door was, then exited. She giggled, quite unsure what to think of the boy. After a few more moments

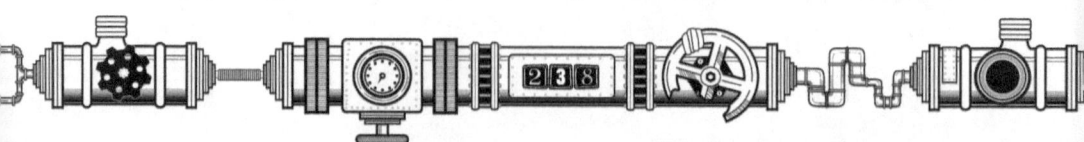

of letting her mind wander the endless plains of teenage angst, Adelaide ignored the many other distractions and dove back into her work.

As the passing hours turned into passing days, the Cogs left her be, for the most part. At least, all of the Cogs except for Silas. He seemed to enjoy dropping by, exchanging a few awkward sentences, then leaving abruptly. Every time, his stuttering improved bit by bit, and he used less ellipses.

She wasn't sure what to think of him. *Was that flirting?* She had not experienced it in person before, just what she read in books. And that was not what it was like in the books.[91] But still, Adelaide's initial confusion at Silas' interest in her quickly turned into flattery. She still wasn't sure what to think of him, but she found herself glancing around, wondering when he would drop by again.

Adelaide's calm corner of the warehouse did not last, however. Impressed by Jules' flying performance in the Gear Games, Enoch desired a glider above all else; though, he wasn't keen on being the first to test it. After fiddling with her initial design, Adelaide decided on scrapping the original concept of collapsible wings for a much larger, more stable design. She just didn't have any confidence that Enoch or any of the other Cogs to handle any kind of delicate device, especially if they were going to be hundreds of feet in the air. Additionally, it was easier to build, which was Adelaide's personal preference. She wanted to get this out of the way so she could work on her own project.

On day five, Adelaide finally finished the massive, twenty-foot-long monstrosity of a glider for Enoch, but she didn't think he even had a chance to try it out before he ordered mass production for the Cogs. Since Adelaide had agreed to build only the one, he had instructed the best and brightest of his lot, which used those terms rather loosely, to build the additional

---

91 Insert *non-sequitur* here, which is probably just when someone doesn't like sequins or other shiny things on their jacket. The Cogs and Goldens didn't like to associate with those people.

gliders. Adelaide kept the one she built up on display in the center of the grand space for study and replication. The Cogs had been not-so-hard-at-work building exact copies of her glider design, to little success, and they tended to blunder into her workspace, which littled her success.

"Miss Engineer Girl," a timid, male voice called from several feet away.

She turned to see Dougy Flopsweat pointing at a display on the workbench. At least, that's what she thought his name was. It would be too awkward to ask now.

"Is this good enough?" he asked.

Adelaide stepped over. Part of a glider wing was beginning to take shape. The metal rods that Adelaide had forged formed the skeleton structure. Dougy had been working on sewing the canvas stretching across to form the wing. The stitching was subpar at best, dangerously unstable at worst. It was as though he had started attentive at the beginning with close, airtight wrappings, then gave up and tried to finish it as quickly as possible.

"That depends, Dougy," Adelaide said. "If I strapped this on your back and told you to jump off into the Gorge, would you want to?"

The man looked at his work then looked to Adelaide then back again. "Uhh, I guess... maybe... no."

"Then that would be a no, it's not good enough. If you don't trust what you make with your life, then it's not good enough. Work on your stitching. You don't want any weak points that could rip the fabric while it's flying. Or you will abruptly stop flying and start crashing."

Adelaide patted the man on the back and stepped away. Dougy stared at his creation and shivered uncontrollably. Adelaide sighed again. She fully intended to build the one glider and only the one, but every time she saw the minions doing something wrong in their own builds, she had to step over and correct it. Adelaide just couldn't let them build it

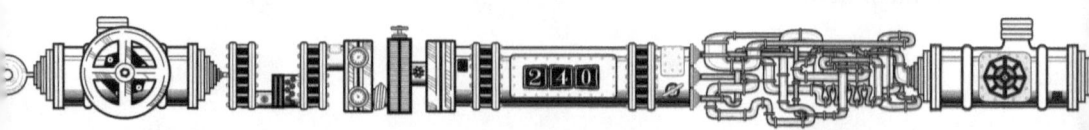

wrong, of course, but she was correcting so much that she didn't have much time in the day for her own experiments.

The not-so-bouncy-anymore girl stepped over to the furnace. The blazing-white coals complimented the molten metal in the cast-iron container within. She enjoyed watching the furnace do its thing for as long as her eyes could take it. Her mind envisioned all of the molecules and particles mixing and molding together into her desired designs. It helped her think, but it didn't help as much as she would like. These last few batches were not strong enough for her own personal project. She kept experimenting, but none of it was quite right for the machine.[92] Not yet anyway.

A falling object slammed onto the brick protrusion of the forge's corner beside Adelaide and made her jump back in shock.

"Gargoyle!" Adelaide yelled for absolutely no discernible reason. After Adelaide's eyes slowly remembered how to focus again, the falling object shaped into the form of a young girl. "Zadie!" Adelaide blustered. "You nearly gave me a heart attack!"

"Quit yer screechin'," Zadie shushed her. "I'm breakin' you outta here."

"Break me out?"

"Come on. There's a hole in the wall up there. You should be able to climb it."

"No, no. Zadie. I'm working."

"You're what?"

"Working. I made a deal with Enoch. I build him a glider; I get to use his forge as much as I want."

"You're…" Zadie scoffed, shocked, slopped, dripped, and her eyes rolled out of her head and back again. "What? Have I taught you nothing?"

"I don't think it's possible to *teach* nothing. That's like a positive and a negative…"

---

92 Forged in the fires of Mount Spoon.

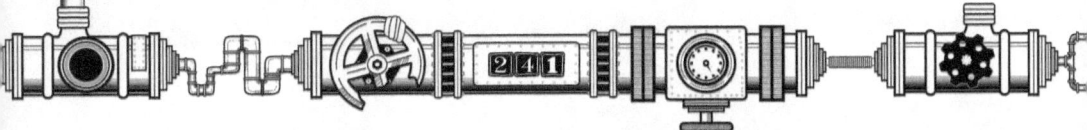

Zadie hopped down and pointed her finger at Adelaide's nose. "You do not work with Cogs. You do not deal with any other gangs. They will backstab you every day of the week."

"Even on Sundays?" Adelaide smirked.

"I'm serious," Zadie's serious face serioused. "What've you been making him?"

"Ah!" a deep, guttural voice called out from the warehouse entrance. "How is my favorite little engineer doing today?"

Enoch Kaylock strolled into view of the two girls. A pair of muscular bodyguards flanked him on both sides, though, considering the fact that Enoch was outfitted in his body armor and retracted, shoulder-mounted chain guns, he scarcely needed any help in that regard.

"And Zadie!" Enoch's voice boomed. "You are so very talented at sneaking into places where you are not invited."

"It's a skill, really," Zadie said.

"To what do I owe the pleasure?"

Enoch's fake smile faded as he pointed his goons toward Zadie. Zadie sighed and spread her arms out in a T-pose, clearly used to the procedure. Goons One and Two checked all of Zadie's numerous pockets in her trench coat and patted her down. Adelaide was sure those two beefy gentlemen had actual names, but she just called them goons. After all, it had been far too long to ask for their real names now. That would just be awkward.

"Clean," Goon One reported.

"Are you actually behaving yourself?" Enoch wondered aloud. "Or did we just catch you early this time?"

"I don't know what you're referring to," Zadie said in her most practiced voice of denial, denial, denial.

"Oh?" Enoch grated as he clomped beside her. "Didn't come to steal anything today?"

"I'm just here to see my friend, ole' what's-her-face here."

"Hmm. I'm sure you are." Enoch's eyes studied her for any sign of weakness. Zadie showed none. Enoch frowned before he turned with a wide smile to Adelaide. "Engineer Adelaide! Progress report. How goes the glider assembly?"

Adelaide shrugged. "Could be faster."

She looked in the direction of the slacker workers. At that moment, they just noticed the presence of Enoch Kaylock and his unwavering gaze. They jumped up from their game of dice and sprinted back to work, each one of them hammering or sewing away on whatever they forgot they were supposed to be doing. A couple of them even managed to hammer the correct object and not just the worktable in front of them. Or their neighbor. Freddy Snotdripper squealed in pain. No one seemed to care about his mutterings of, "Aye yai yai..."

"I only agreed to build the one, of course," she continued.

"Of course," he agreed with a sly smirk.

"But I've been helping them correct course when necessary."

Enoch's gaze settled on the glider hanging on a rack in the middle of the warehouse. "Excellent," he said. "I've been meaning to ask, does that turn into a backpack as well?"

"No," Adelaide replied, "but I'm satisfied with the new design. I went for a larger version that isn't collapsible for many reasons. The primary of which being that it's far more efficient and—"

A loud clang noise from deep within the warehouse followed by a "Yowie!" caused Adelaide and Enoch to pause.

"Far easier to control," Adelaide finished unabated. "This way, you can catch more wind and be less reliant on finding hot air currents to remain aloft. Though, I would still highly recommend you map out potential flight paths before jumping off anything of height. Trying to figure that out mid-glide is a good way to crash into a rock and die."

"Good to know," Enoch tilted his head and smiled. "You are a treasure, my dear. This will be the pathway to many exciting opportunities."

"Like what?" Zadie asked.

Enoch smiled and gritted his silver teeth. "When opportunity knocks, one does not need to question why."

"But I questioned *what*," Zadie commented.

Enoch ignored the comment and tilted his top hat deferentially toward Adelaide. "Engineer Adelaide." He glanced at Zadie and frowned. "Zadie. Good day."

With that, he turned and marched away. Goons One and Two followed close behind. At a wave of his hand, the Goons stopped at the entrance, turned, and stood stock still with their arms crossed. They stared at Zadie much as a chef stares at a cat prowling next to a freshly-baked turkey, which is, to say, meow.

"Do you have any idea what you've done?" Zadie's calm-but-not voice asked.

"What?" Adelaide replied, followed immediately by, "Gargoyle!"

The falling form of Harriet jumped down onto the furnace's brick protrusion above. "Hey! What's the hold up?" Harriet asked.

"Would you stop doing that?!" Adelaide panted.

"I just got here."

Adelaide glanced up at the hole in the wall. Baxter's hind end dangled from it as he lightly wrangled himself through it before slipping and falling down completely. He flopped down onto the concrete floor below with an, "Ow."

Silent as a cat prowling next to a freshly-baked turkey, Jules slid into view on the other side of the warehouse entrance, behind the two Goons. He caught Zadie's eye and pointed two fingers from one hand at the two Goons. Zadie softly shook her head. Jules nodded and slipped back out of sight. Goons One and Two glanced back to see nothing.

"What're we doin'?" Harriet asked as she slid off the furnace. "Were you talking to Enoch?"

"Stumpy's working for him," Zadie grunted.

"Working *with* him," Adelaide corrected.

"Don't answer to *Stumpy*," Harriet chastised.

"We're trading services, like normal folk," Adelaide continued.

"Oh," Harriet's voice was laced with concern, "don't tell me you're a Cog now."

"No, no," Adelaide waved her down, "I built him a glider, and now I can use his forge. It's just a trade."

Baxter limped over. "So are we breaking out or what?"

"No," Zadie crossed her arms. "Adelaide's a sellout."

"Am not," Adelaide defended. "We're trading services."

"That sounds wrong," Baxter said.

"You guys," Adelaide sighed, "thank you for your concern, but I'm okay. I built him a thing, now I can use his stuff. It's an honest trade. No thievery involved."

"Sounds way less interesting." Harriet smirked.

"It is!" Adelaide smiled. "*And* it's far less dangerous."

"Oh," Baxter said, "so it's like one of those squid pro bros."

Everyone stared at him.

Harriet paused before she said, "I'm sorry. What?"

"Squid pro bros. Where you trade something. Like between two squid bros."

"Do you mean *quid pro quo*?" Harriet shook her head.

"The frag is that?" Baxter asked.

"Enough, you too," Zadie said. She turned a fierce glare and wagging finger toward Adelaide. "Mark my words, fingers, this will all blow up in your face. You can't trust the other gangs. You can't trust nobody. Whatever you make them, they will turn it into something terrible and use it against you. Every time."

"Oh, come on," Adelaide exasperated. "You're so pessimistic."

"Ew," Baxter added, "go to the bathroom."

Adelaide continued, "It's just a glider."

Zadie stepped up and put her nose in front of Adelaide's. "Mark my words," Zadie said. "You will regret this."

"Is that a threat?"

"I'm not talkin' 'bout from me."

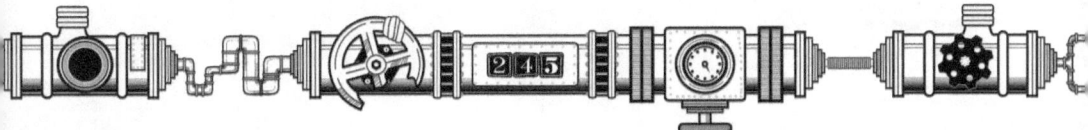

With that, Zadie turned and walked away. Baxter looked at Adelaide, shrugged, and followed. Harriet looked to Adelaide and smiled.

"Need anything?" Harriet asked.

"No." Adelaide smiled back. "Thank you. I have everything I need right here."

"Alrighty. Come back home soon. Unless the Cogs stab you in the back or whatnot."

Harriet skipped away. Zadie glared at Goons One and Two standing by the entrance and marched right between them. The Goons turned to follow and watch Zadie until she vacated the property. Baxter and Harriet followed close behind.

Adelaide sighed. They were all just overreacting. This was a more efficient way to do business. Everyone was safe. Everyone was happy. Nothing could go wrong.

Chapter 19

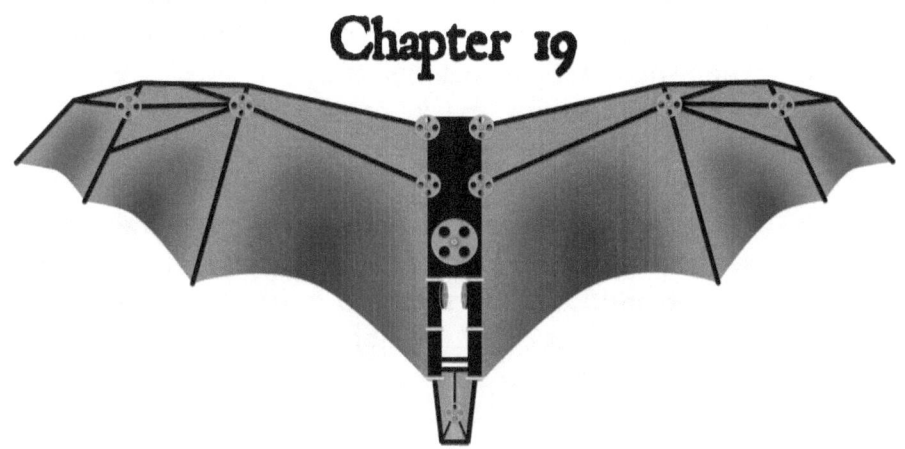

Falling with Style

Everything was going wrong. Adelaide's first metallurgy[93] failed in the stress test for her personal project, and so did metallurgies two through nineteen. That meant that she had to stay in Cogs territory far longer than she planned. And that meant that she had to help these poor buggers with just about every aspect of their glider replications, which slowed down her own project designs even more. And now, Enoch Kaylock told-more-than-asked her to accompany a great, big group of them in a practical demonstration of the glider designs. So she was wasting even more time by trudging along next to Enoch and a pile of other Cogs transporting the transports.

Adelaide glanced back to see Silas trudging along behind the pack of glider-toting gang members. He carried what looked like two, very heavy satchels. As their eyes met, he smiled at her.

---

93 That looks like a made-up word, doesn't it? Metallurgy. Like what happens when a piece of steel has a baby with a member of the clergy. They call that immetalculate conception.

Adelaide returned the expression. She had grown to quite like Silas, but she wasn't sure how to feel about her feelings when she felt those feelings.

Her mind wandering back to her wandering feet, Adelaide didn't even know why they were testing the gliders a second time. She had already tested her initial design with a semi-willing Cog last week. The design worked. It flew well. The test subject landed on his face. All in all, a good run. She thought they would have the ability to finish the rest of the gliders on their own. Alas, that was not the case.

"You seem distracted, little engineer," Enoch's grating voice grated as softly as it could. "It's a beautiful night with a nice, warm breeze. Perfect weather for flying."[94]

Adelaide looked up at him and sighed. "I'm just frustrated with my design."

"The gliders?" He looked back at the gang members hoisting the flying contraptions over their shoulders and following them through the silent streets.

"No, no. My personal project."

"Oh, good. I would hate to lose all this valuable material on only the second demonstration." He glanced back at the concerned faces behind him and added, "And all of my friends, of course. The most... *valuable* material of all." He coughed and looked forward.

"I think I'll experiment on your blast furnace next," Adelaide continued, mostly to herself. "Maybe add some kind of carbon to the iron ore. The limestone in the bottom of the furnace helps pull out impurities, right?"

Her curious eyes looked up to him. Enoch's less-than-curious eyes looked down to her, then they looked around.

"Hmm, excellent question," Enoch said. "The key to knowledge is the understanding of the what and why. And look there, here we are. After you, my dear."

---

94 Nighttime flying? Hmm, mysterious.

Enoch stood before a tall, five-storied building with an outer, merchandise lift leading up to the roof. He gestured to the platform and ushered Adelaide onto it. Cogs members standing by raised them up the side of the building through use of the turn crank.

Adelaide marveled at all of the people working for Enoch in unison, reacting to his every will. It seemed like a luxury. Luxuries reminded her of her parents. As a result, she didn't think all the gang member attention was quite right for her. Adelaide unconsciously fiddled with her mechanical arm.

The lift clanked to maximum height. Adelaide stepped off onto the building's roof and gazed off into the dark, night sky. The Gorge dove down before them, its many repurposed factories and dwellings disappearing beneath the darkness. Only bits of illumination from streetlamps, bridge lights, and exterior bulbs attempted to penetrate the overwhelming blackness. They did not succeed.

"Why are we doing this at night?" Adelaide just now thought to ask.

"Why not?" Enoch smiled as he stepped next to her.

"Because it's more difficult to see what you're doing than in the daytime. Obviously. And it's even a new moon out tonight. Did you want the testers to crash into the Gorge?"

"I planned for this specific time."

"Why? Did you not want us to see?"

"Actually, I did not want *anyone* to see."

She stared at him, completely unable to comprehend what he just said. "I don't..."

"My dear, some activities are best performed under the cover of darkness."

With a simple wave of his hand, a small army of Cogs fanned out below. Gliders and test pilots got into position on rooftops of shorter buildings all around. More poured onto the edge of the street below, all of them peering into the Gorge.

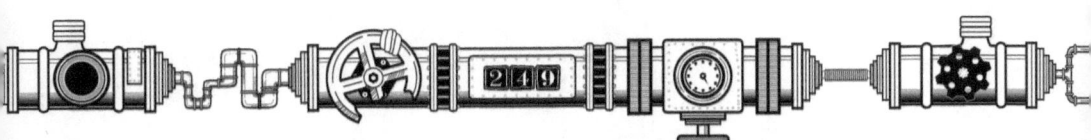

"My Cogs don't have the technical know-how that you do," Enoch cooed[95] to Adelaide while staring off into the dark abyss, "but I wanted to demonstrate to you what we are very, very good at."

With another simple wave of his hand, the Cogs gliders leapt off into the dark night. Adelaide's mind was twisted with concern, curiosity, trepidation, fear, hunger, and trying to restrain herself from telling Enoch that ending a sentence with a preposition was poor grammar. Enoch's face was pure confidence watching the show below, so Adelaide decided to put a pin in her concern and turn to her curiosity. That was her stronger trait anyhow.

She could barely make out the gliding forms swirling around the open air in between the cliffsides. The most she could discern were their silhouettes against the ineffective lights that did exist within the Gorge.

"Do they have flight plans?" Adelaide asked. "They have to find heat currents to stay aloft. Most of them can find smokestack exhaust for that. How about landing? Do they—"

"Relax, little engineer," Enoch cut her off. "Just watch."

"That's rather difficult. Being night and all."

Enoch pointed a massive finger toward a specific location on the dark cliffside opposite them. "There. The abandoned pump station. Do you see?"

Adelaide squinted her eyes, though that didn't exactly help with her vision. She could just make out silhouettes landing upon the roof of a gigantic building built into the rock wall. At least, a few of the glider silhouettes landed. She winced as some seemed to career off elsewhere or disappear into the cliffside of the Gorge below.

"Are they landing there?" she asked.

"Yes."

---

95 *Cooed* as in he spoke softly to her. Not that he cooed like a baby. That would be... rather strange.

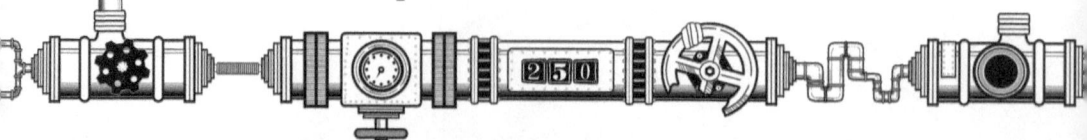

"Why? What's over there?"

"That is the location of the Blood Claws' headquarters." Enoch smiled and propped his foot up on the rooftop edge, peering into the dark.

"Do they know you're landing people on their roof?" Adelaide asked and immediately realized what his answer was going to be.

Sure enough, his incredulous smirk was his only response. The gliding party also gave a response of their own. The sonic *boom* of a minor explosion rocked the Gorge. The concussive blast eliminated some of the lights shining around the headquarters while the ensuing dust obscured the rest. Muzzle flashes from gunfire sparked into the night.

"The Blood Claws have been extending their influence for weeks now, into the Uppers, and into my own territory. They thought they were subtle, picking marks here and there, shaking down key merchants. They were wrong."

Headlights from Cogs vehicles shined into the Gorge as they traveled along the cliffside roads toward the commotion. Within moments, a coordinated effort saw the entire place surrounded.

"Despite their blatant disregard for claim rights," Enoch continued, "the Blood Claws had fortified their headquarters well. Numerous choke points blocked the only two approaches, making a head-on raid quite costly."

His massive finger pointed out locations. Adelaide's cluttered mind couldn't contemplate any of it.

"But then you came along, gifting me the ability to send in my soldiers from above. Air superiority. Remarkable really. You made all of this possible."

Any color that was in Adelaide's face drained completely. The remaining sounds of battle and gunfire died as quickly as it began.

"And now you see the power of the Cogs," Enoch said as his overwhelming presence gazed down upon her. "I allow the other gangs to conduct their business as long as they do not interfere

with my own. We all have our place in order to keep the gears moving, but the Blood Claws overstepped. They no longer fit within the other moving pieces. And now, they are no more."

Enoch placed his paw on Adelaide's shoulder, turning her to look up at him.

"Zadie and her little band of Steampunks are amusing, for the most part, but her rebellious tendencies are beginning to irritate the machinations of the Cogs' moving parts. If she oversteps much more, well..."

Enoch glanced down into the Gorge. Flames blazed into life, throwing the distant pump station into sharp relief for the first time, though, there didn't seem to be much of the building left. Fires spread behind a collapsed wall and several broken windows.

"A sinking ship is no place to call home. I would offer you a position within the Cogs. You would be safe here with all the food, clothing, and shelter you would ever need. Full access to all of our forges. All of the equipment and materials you want for all of your experiments and inventions. You could have a life here. Safe from all reprisals."

Enoch's giant hand squeezed Adelaide's shoulder. It was both endearing and comforting with an underlying hint of utterly terrifying. Adelaide's addled brain understood and comprehended all of his words, but she could scarce process any of it.

"Think it over," Enoch said.

He marched away. His boots clomped onto the nearby merchandise lift. A wave of his hand sent the Cogs below working to lower him.

Adelaide finally remembered how to breathe. Her eyes tried to focus on the flames, but it was just a hazy collection of dancing lights. She made all of this possible. All the death and destruction. Just because she thought it would be neat to see if she could make a glider fly.

After waiting to be lowered down from the roof, Adelaide found her feet walking a familiar path. While her initial intention was to go back to the forge warehouse to sleep, she headed over a bridge crossing the Gorge. She blinked her eyes, shrugged, and let her toes lead her down into the tunnels beneath the Lowers.

Even so, she didn't feel ready to go back to the Steampunks hideout. She didn't know how to talk about how she was feeling yet. She didn't really know how she was feeling quite yet. So her feet wandered. Her mind whirled. Her stomach burbled.

Some time later, Adelaide found herself in a large chamber. Pipes poured water out from all sides into a metal channel in the bottom where it all funneled into one pipe. A thirty-foot water wheel built into one wall splashed water every which way as the poor design lazily forced it to spin correctly.

She remembered chasing Zadie into this chamber on their first encounter. The chain Zadie swung off of was still dangling from the ceiling. Adelaide stood where Zadie had landed, on the metal grate platform far above the churning water below.

Adelaide sat and shoved her feet and arms through the railing in a not-quite-comfortable-but-not-quite-uncomfortable position resting against the cool, metal bars. Her eyes gazed at the water wheel and churning water below, but her mind was fully elsewhere. So elsewhere, in fact, that she barely registered the loud clanging and clomping noises in the distance growing closer by the second. In the back of her mind, she recognized those noises anyway, and it put her more at ease.

Phineas and his gigantic, gorilla arm harness clanked onto the metal platform and propped himself up next to Adelaide.

"Well, ye're up early," Phineas' craggy voice greeted.

"Never went to bed," Adelaide sighed as she stared into the water below.

"Late then." Phineas looked her up and down, studying her posture. "Looks like ye got some brain farts clogging up the exit pipes."

Adelaide nodded and shrugged. Phineas plopped his chair harness down next to her. His huge mechanical arms mimicked Adelaide's by crossing over the railing and setting his chin on top. The effect did not look comfortable, and his larger two mechanical arms compared to Adelaide's one caused the railing to bend and buckle slightly.

"I'd offer ye some tea," he said, "but I'm all out. I can offer ye some whiskey though."

His human hand shook a flask in between his fingers toward Adelaide.

"Are you offering alcohol to a minor?"

"I won't tell if ye won't."

She smiled but shook her head. Phineas shrugged and took a swig from his flask.

"Isn't it early for that, anyway?" Adelaide asked.

"Early one place is right on time someplace else. 'Sides, it's only water."

Adelaide chortled, "You lied to me then?"

"I ain't telled ye I had some. Just that I could offer ye some."

"Isn't that the same thing? Can you offer something you don't have?"

"Banks do it. Why can't I?"

Adelaide snorted, "I never know what to make of you."

"Makes two of us," Phineas said as he chugged some water from his flask.

The two of them sat in silence for a while. They stared at the water below and listened to the splashes upon the wheel. Adelaide kicked her feet.

"Phineas, you make things, right?" she asked.

"Whatcha mean, *make*?"

"Like... build things. Invent things."

"No, not really."

"You didn't build your arms?"

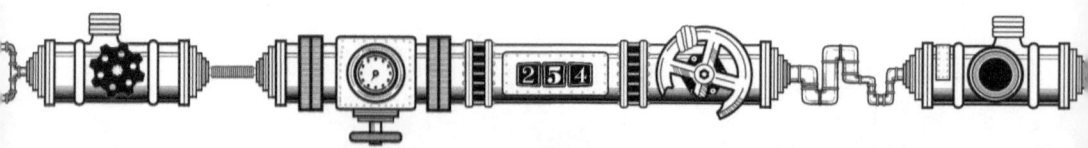

"No, no. Got these out of a scrap yard and fixed 'em up. These made some waves back in the day fer the handicapped community, but they're notoriously difficult to use and even harder to control. Didn't deter me none. I just practiced and trained and now they're second nature. Couldn't do me job without 'em. Why ye ask?"

"I just... I built something for the Cogs. Gliders, like I made for Jules. And then, they immediately used them to attack the Blood Claws."

"Ah."

"And I just... that wouldn't have happened if I hadn't made that for them. It's my fault those people got hurt or... oh my goodness, they might have died. And that's on me."

Adelaide buried her face in the skin of her good arm and tried to stifle the sudden wave of nausea washing over her. She caught her breath and heard Phineas smacking his lips. She turned her face slightly for one eye to look at him.

"What?" Phineas asked in response. "Ye want me to say something?"

She nodded her head against her arm.

"Then yeah. It's your fault."

Adelaide groaned and buried both her eyes back into her arm. That was not the answer she was hoping to hear.

"They used what ye made to hurt people, and that's on you. But then again, ye gotta ask yerself the question, would they have hurt each other if ye hadn't been there at all?"

Adelaide lifted her head up at that.

"Ye think those gang heads wouldn't clobber each other if they didn't have gliders to glide around or whatnot? Pssh. What ye're really askin' is the age-old question: is the creator responsible for what others do with their creations? Well, there ain't no easy answer to that, cuz there ain't no answer at all." His lips smacked together as his brain contemplated. "Take this for example..."

One of Phineas' gigantic gorilla hands grabbed Adelaide's generator backpack and nonchalantly yanked her upwards. Her chest and arm and the rest of her went along for the ride, on account of the straps and all. Without another word, Phineas tossed her into the air. With several choice words and a short screech, Adelaide fell from the platform and splashed into the water far below.

Her backpack clonked onto the metal channel five feet within the warm liquid. The waterfalls from the pipes and water wheel churned and forced the current toward the one exit pipe. Adelaide floundered up and gasped for breath as the current swept her down the pipe. The limited illumination from the chamber vanished as she was flushed down into the pure blackness.

Seconds later in the water slide of terror, Adelaide smacked into the side of a metal grate built vertically inside the pipe. She felt around and found herself wedged against it from the current. A bundle of foliage, hay, and strangely squishy items gathered around her. Just as Adelaide started to understand that the grate acted as some sort of water filter, and as she started to not understand what the strangely squishy bits were, she felt herself being lifted upwards out of the current.

She could see traces of light from above. A metal-woven basket in a vertical conveyor box lift scooped up Adelaide and the other debris from the water. Just as she started to study the chain pulley system, the basket flipped over and dumped her onto a horizontal conveyor belt that rolled and bumped along in its own metal channel. This area had a lot of light to see, and Adelaide realized why. The conveyor belt fed directly into a monumental furnace, eating up all of the unwanted things clogging the pipes below. The fires within danced and skipped happily as more debris stoked the blaze.

Before she had time to think of an exit strategy from her impending doom, her mechanical arm moved of its own

accord. The metal slammed against a rotating, metal device built into the channel's wall. Her generator backpack pulled her backwards and hugged the device with all its might, as though they were long lost friends. Adelaide recognized the pull of a surprisingly strong magnet.

Large, electromagnetic plates attached to four sides of the rotating cube. It pulled anything metal out of the conveyor belt trough rolling toward the furnace and plucked them right out. As it flipped Adelaide up, out, and over, a diagonal slide came into her upside-down view. Built next to the rotating cube with some sort of spring-pressure system, it shoved into the magnetized plates and scraped against the surface. Adelaide felt herself being scraped off and shoved onto the diagonal slide. She rode down the concrete scraper into a smooth, metal slide until a gigantic, mechanical hand grabbed her backpack and plucked her right out.

Fortuitous timing, Adelaide thought as she got a view of where the slide ended. The chute poured into a massive vat of metal pieces and debris. The huge, circular container did not look like a comfortable landing spot for her already sore bottom.

Phineas' hand plopped her onto a concrete walkway spanning in between the conveyor belt furnace and metal slide of doom. After Adelaide gained her bearings once again, she turned her tired, wet, and bleary countenance upon the older gentleman.

"What the what?" was all Adelaide could piece together to say. "Why?"

"Fire is a great example for yer question," Phineas said.

"I don't remember what the question was," Adelaide gasped.

"The first iteration was meant for warmth. To cook food. To keep folks alive. Didn't take long to use that warmth as a weapon. Unchecked, it'd catch everything on fire, causing untold devastation. Even here, controlled, it burns up all the debris caught in the pipes, both getting rid of it and using it as fuel to power the steam generators." Phineas pointed at the furnace.

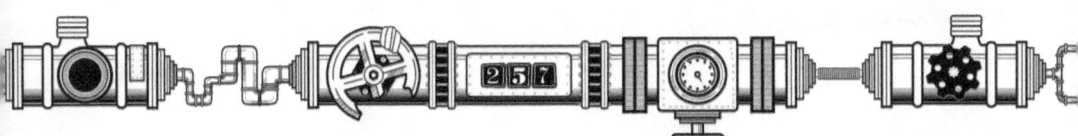

"This is only a minor generator in the system, but still, an important one. But don't need me to tell ye how dangerous fire can be. At best, it's a source 'a life. Worst, it'll kill ye."

"Did you throw me into the pipes just to talk about fire as an example?" Adelaide blustered.

"Well," Phineas shrugged and smirked, "I do like to entertain meself."

Adelaide bristled to the point where she almost turned into a porcupine.

"But everything ye look at here is an example. Take that, for instance. Those conveyor belts shovel stuff along real nice. Good for bridges and such too. But know what else they do? Same idea powers the treads in a tank. Weapon o' war."

Adelaide nodded.

"Pipes? Good for water. Also good design for the barrel of a gun. Metal? Well that's good for all sorts, good and bad. Oh, check out them magnets there. Seem harmless. Made natural like. Point north for compasses and the like. Picks up metal, and metal girls." He nudged Adelaide.

She simply shook her head at him.

"Now they're using it for them rail guns, making bullets go faster or some such nonsense. Like they needed that. But ye know, they're also puttin' them on rails for trains. Making them go really fast too."

"Really?" Adelaide perked up. "Magnetized rails? That's super interesting. Like... you could run an electrical current through them at certain times to accelerate the metal of a train passing over?"

"Ah, see there. That's that creative spark ye got."

Adelaide shrugged like a fluffy little sheep and smirked like a fuzzy little fox.

"Point is: people can take anything and hurt each other with it. Makers' job is to try and be responsible with what ye make and keep it in the right hands for as long as ye can, but no matter how hard ye try, bad people will eventually find a

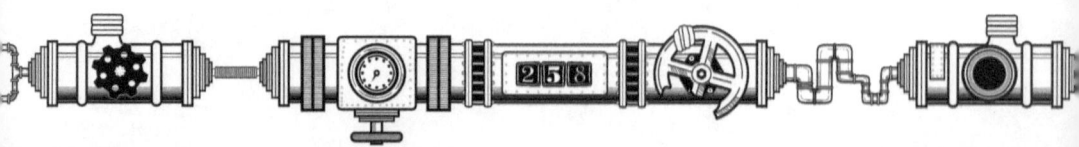

way to ruin what ye built. Ye make somethin' for someone other than yerself, and it'll end up happenin' no matter what. Ye can't control what other people do. That's not failin'. That's not yer fault. That's life."

He gave a great sigh and looked her over. "Now, whether or not that stops ye from makin' stuff is up to you, but most important... is the heart."

Phineas' large, human finger poked Adelaide's chest plate and control panel. Her wet, mechanical fingers spun around in response. "Ye got a good heart on ya, girl," Phineas continued. "Ye make what ye want to help people. Go about it smart, and ye'll be alright."

Adelaide glanced from Phineas to the furnace to the magnets and back again. She smiled and said, "Thank you, Phineas."

"Yep," Phineas said as his mechanical arm harness hoisted him up. "But if ye make anything that might blow up the city, ye just let me know ahead a' time. So I can get outta town."

Adelaide giggled. "Sure thing."[96]

With that, Phineas swung and hand-walked his way off into the chamber and disappeared down a side exit. Adelaide felt surprisingly better, despite the wet clothes, sore muscles, bumps, bruises, and the swelling knot on the back of her head. But the knots inside of her head were much more relaxed now. Having good intentions and being smart about it seemed like a good way to live since she had no control about how other people would live their own lives.

Not yet anyway.[97]

---

96 Adelaide had trouble keeping certain promises. She also had trouble keeping change in her pocket. Little did she know that her pocket was actually a door to another dimension, one in which made great change.

97 The first mind control device was created by Quarich Fadlov during his experiments on his own dog. His last recorded experiment backfired, and Fadlov spent the rest of his days giving belly rubs and playing fetch.

Chapter 20

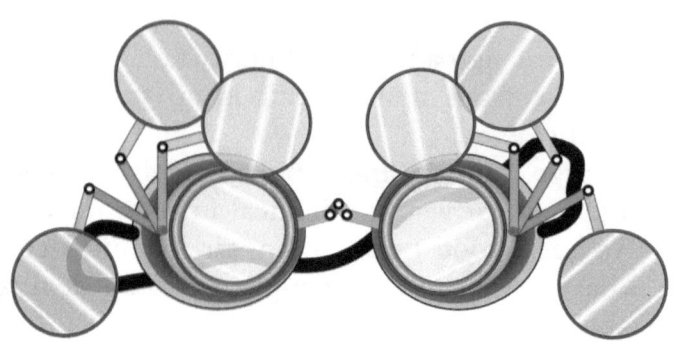

How to Win Gangs and Influence Burglars

Much like everyone else, Adelaide did not enjoy the taste of failure.[98] While she didn't fail herself exactly, she did feel the Cogs had taken advantage of her, despite Zadie's warnings. That was not a conversation Adelaide was looking forward to having. Without speaking to Leeroy, Dougy Flopsweat, Five-toothed Freddy, Gruff Gilda, or even Enoch Kaylock, Adelaide packed up her stuff from the Cogs' forge warehouse. She screwed castor wheels on the bottom of a metal frame and piled her creations, devices, and tools on top. With a heave, she rolled her makeshift cart out of Cogs territory. Her eyes kept glancing back, thinking she might catch a glimpse of Silas, but she never did.

There were a few side-eyed glances at her, however, as she rolled her way across a bridge and down toward the Lowers, but Adelaide was far more preoccupied thinking of

---

98 Unsurprisingly, failure tends to taste like canned beets with just a hint of flatulence.

how much she wished she had welded a chest-level support bar for her to push her cart. As of now, she had to bend over and crab-walk the wheeled slab every step of the way.

After a long journey filled with breaks and swearing, Adelaide rolled, heaved, dragged, and clonked her valuables back to the Steampunks stash. She had to take a longer, more roundabout way to avoid the broken trough of water and the curving flight of stairs and the too-small elevator, but she made it. Her entire body tried to shove her makeshift cart over the bumpy threshold into the stash, but the circular hatch door was too circular at the bottom for her square clump of junk, so she left it in the tunnel and unpacked from there.

Adelaide paused when she started unpacking her satchel. Her fingers flipped over the goggles she purchased at the Gorge. That felt like a lifetime ago. The reason why she bought them in the first place sparked the synapses in her brain. That project was long overdue.

First things first. She rummaged through a chest of drawers sitting underneath the broken, horse carriage with one wheel attached. Several scratched and scuffed reading glasses sat at the bottom of the second shelf. One of those would do. Or maybe all of them. She popped the lenses free from the goggles. New lenses were too small. Needed to adjust the securing ring. There were some more goggles. Pried out the wire. Needed more adjusting. Minor welding. Attached separate pieces to separate adjusters. Ooh, have all the lenses separated from the goggles, then reattached when ready. That would work.

After that, she worked on her second idea. Then her third. Then her fourth. While the day and night cycle mattered not at all to the denizens who dwelt in the tunnels below the city, the early night cycle passed full on into the daytime when Adelaide finally popped up for breath. Having several, somewhat random projects to work on utilized her scatterbrained noggin to its fullest extent, and strangely enough, it helped her focus once all was said and done.

It was time. She packed up her satchel, strapped it around her neck and shoulder, shoved a clump of wooden pieces in her armpit, and held onto a wooden frame before she trekked to the hideout. The stringed lights were lit, so it wasn't too early for everyone else.

Jules had taken up a bit of knitting in his hammock swinging gently over the platform's edge. Zadie was lying back in her chair with her fedora over her face. Harriet was sprawled on the couch and reading a book about dragons falling in love with fairies. Baxter was sitting on the rug-strewn floor next to the platform edge, trying to fix the broken pulley system yet again. They were all either engrossed in their own things or sleeping, so no one even noticed Adelaide approaching.

"Hello there," Adelaide said.

"Addy!" Harriet greeted.

Harriet jumped off the couch and embraced the shorter girl, shoving her neck into Adelaide's face. Harriet's arms wrapped around Adelaide's shoulders, causing her to lose grip on all the pieces she held in her good arm's pit.

"You alright?" Harriet asked. "Oh, what all you got here?"

Adelaide released herself from the face-squishing hug and replied, "This one's for you." She released the hinged, wooden, frame pieces from her hand, which flipped over and plopped onto the rug. "Whoops. Hold on. Don't worry, it's supposed to do that. It's collapsible."

"What does that mean?" Baxter asked.

"It means she broke it," Harriet replied with a giggle.

"No, no," Adelaide said, "It's all good."

Adelaide wrestled her good arm with the multiple pieces of circular rods, rectangular braces, and long, wooden planks. Some were connected and flopped over her shoulder. Some just flopped around. She managed to wrangle the pieces together into a semi-supportive shape. Adelaide added additional accessories to the triangular A-frame.

"It's an easel," Adelaide said. "For painting."

Harriet tilted her head to see what Adelaide was still in the process of assembling.

"Got a little tray for putting paints," Adelaide said. She unfolded a rectangular piece. "Brush holders." Small cylinders popped out. "Brush cleaning station in the middle." She hung a bucket with a metal rod stretching across the inside. "And here's a canvas for painting happy little trees." She placed the wooden frame with an inverted canvas banner stapled onto it. "I'm not sure if it's great quality, and I wasn't sure what you liked to—"

Harriet's enclosing arms muffled Adelaide's voice, and she squeezed Adelaide in a tight embrace. "Thank you!" Harriet beamed. "That's so sweet! I love it!"

Adelaide pulled back for air and smiled up at Harriet. After a moment, she wriggled out of the embrace and looked toward the boy on the floor. "And for Baxter..."

She dug into her satchel and withdrew a pair of leather-strapped, copper eye wear that vaguely resembled the goggles she bought from the Bazaar. Baxter stood up as she approached, and she draped the goggles around his head and over his eyes.

"Now, these are special, so don't go smashing your face into stuff."

"Then what's the point of goggles?" he asked.

A collection of glass lenses protruded out from the eyepieces in different layers.[99] Each lens could flip up and down separately. Adelaide swung two of the lenses down over his eyes and turned the other six out of his sight. She grabbed the side of his head while her eyes stared at the device with her face very close to Baxter's. Before he could communicate just how uncomfortable that was, Adelaide released him and stepped back. She picked up Harriet's discarded dragon book from the couch and handed it back to Harriet.

---

99 Much like an onion. Or an ogre.

"Could you hold this up for me, please?" Adelaide asked her as she placed the book in the taller girl's hands and opened it up to a random page in the middle. She stepped back to Baxter, stepped out of his line of sight to the book, and said, "Now read the letters."

Baxter grunted.

"No really. Look for me, and tell me which is clearer: one... or two?"

Adelaide flipped the lenses up and slid another set down. Baxter squinted.

"Umm..." he pondered, "two?"

"Okay, one..." Adelaide flipped more lenses down and up, "or two?"

Baxter was much more sure when he replied, "Two."

"Once more."

"One, I think?"

Adelaide adjusted the lenses before unceremoniously yanking the entire goggled contraption off his skull. Baxter blinked and readjusted his blushed face and wild hair. Adelaide unscrewed one part of the goggles, screwed in one lens, adjusted a thingy, tightened a whatsit, and slid the goggles back over Baxter's eyes.

"How about this?" Adelaide asked.

Baxter blinked his eyes. His bottom lip slowly hung open. "How..." Baxter had trouble finding the words, "you... everything is so much clearer."

Adelaide smiled with pure, unadulterated[100] triumph. "Sounded like your vision was a little fuzzy," she said. "These are corrective lenses. Much more fragile than the protective ones in your other goggles, but they should help with, you know, not eating beetles instead of raisins."

"That was *one* time."

Adelaide and Harriet chortled at his expense.

---

100 Of course it was unadulterated. They were still teenagers.

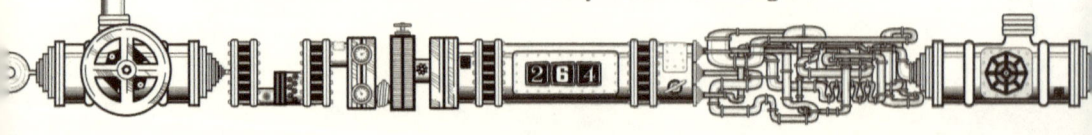

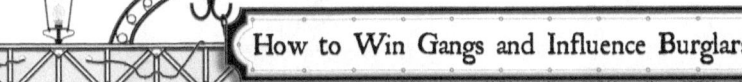 

"Wow," Baxter said and gazed around. "Thanks."

"And," Adelaide continued, "these will probably help when we start our reading lessons."

"Reading lessons?"

"Yep."

Baxter shrugged. "Guess it wouldn't be the worst thing in the world."

"Oh my goodness," Harriet interjected. "I've been trying to get him into reading for the longest time."

Baxter blinked his eyes multiple times as he adjusted and readjusted his focus. He gazed around the hideout. His eyes landed on Harriet still holding open the book.

"Wow," he muttered aloud.

"What?" Harriet asked, a look of concern crossing her features.

"Oh, nothing... it's just... your... face is just... very symmetrical."

Harriet's eyebrow raised. "Umm, is that a good thing?"

"Yeah, you're just... very pretty... or whatever."

Her eyes squinted with mistrust, but her cheeks turned into a grin and flushed red. "Yeah, I know."

"What's all this for?" Zadie asked. Her fedora was back on top of her head. She stared at them with her arms crossed over her chest.

The others quieted. Adelaide didn't even realize Zadie had woken up.

Adelaide replied, "I just wanted to make stuff to make your lives better. As opposed to the opposite. And for you, Zadie..."

Adelaide withdrew a clump of metal from her bag of goodies. She presented it to Zadie. A collection of metal bits and pieces were screwed and welded together.

"I made you a multi-tool." Adelaide narrated while she extended out various instruments, all of which looked like they were repurposed from their past lives. "It's got a knife," which was just a sharpened metal shard, "pliers," were welded tongs,

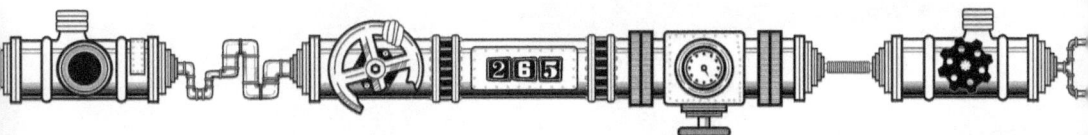

"can opener," was a sharpened wrench, "nail file," was leftover sanding paper glued to a metal stick, "flathead screwdriver," which actually was a flathead screwdriver, "and..." the final metal piece shot out of the casing like a bullet. Adelaide tilted her head then shrugged her shoulders. "Oh well. I don't think you needed a corkscrew anyway."

"Was that an old spring?"

"Yeah."

"I don't think that would've screwed a cork," Harriet commented.

"Definitely not now," Baxter added.

Adelaide folded the foldable package and handed it to Zadie.

"Thanks, I guess?" Zadie said with a bit of trepidation. "I can use... some of these."

"And Jules..."

Jules slightly lifted his head from his relaxed hammock lounging. Adelaide scrounged around in her bag.

"This will need some adjusting." She withdrew a full face mask. A wide, clear-glassed visor covered the top. A nose-piece and lightweight mask contained slots for air filters. "I scrounged together some silk and sewed all the parts and pieces together, which should make a breathable and comfortable covering for your face." Adelaide skipped over to Jules' hammock and presented her prized creation with a beaming smile.

Jules extended his hand, not in acceptance, but with his palm raised vertically. He gently shook his head.

"No?" Adelaide asked. "You don't like it?"

"He doesn't wear his mask because he likes it," Zadie interrupted.

Adelaide and the others turned to look at her.

"He wears it as penance."

Baxter leaned over to Harriet and whispered, "What does that mean?"

She whispered back, "Trying to make up for something wrong you did."

"What do—" Adelaide began.

"You can't fix everyone's problems, gimpy," Zadie interrupted again and sat up with her elbows on her knees. "Some things can't be fixed. This messed-up world can't all be fixed. Some things are broken and will forever be broken."

"Well," Adelaide decided, "that doesn't mean I'm going to stop trying."

She placed her good hand on Jules' forearm.

"I won't bother you about your mask again, but if there's anything else you want or need or… think would be fun… you communicate that to me how best you can. I can help make you whatever you want. Okay?"

Jules snorted and nodded his head in acceptance. He patted her hand with his own.

Zadie snorted, but not with acceptance. "Like you made stuff for the Cogs? You think handing out gifts will make us forget how you abandoned us and went to build flying death machines for *the Cogs*?!"

"I…"

"Yeah, we heard about how they wiped out the Blood Claws with those. An entire gang, gone. Cogs took over the Gorge now too. All cuz of you."

"I… I made a mistake."

"No spit."

"But they were going to fight each other whether I was there or not. Whether I made them gliders or not."

Zadie snorted. "Your nigh-levity has gotten ridiculous."

Harriet tapped her lips and asked, "Naiveté?"

"Don't you French at me."

Adelaide continued, "I regret my part in it. I shouldn't have done it. I shouldn't have been there, but I'm not gonna stop trying to build things. I'm not gonna stop trying to make the world a better place."

Zadie scoffed, "You're in for a *world* of disappointment then, rich girl."

"I... I just..." Adelaide looked to the others, "I just wanted to do something nice for you guys. My new family. You don't... you don't have to use them if you don't like them." Adelaide sighed before turning a determined stare at Zadie. "And just because you're upset and mad doesn't mean you have to take your frustrations out on us."

Zadie gritted her teeth and grunted, "Bah." She didn't intend to sound like a sheep, but that was all that her aggravation would allow from her mouth. Zadie waved her hand in frustration and marched out of the hideout and into an adjoining tunnel. She glanced at Harriet's painting of the bloody bunny and gave another "Bah" before disappearing down the bend.

Harriet and Adelaide shared a glance. Harriet gave a shrug and skipped over to her gift. "Don't worry about her. I, for one, appreciate my present." She adjusted the canvas frame atop the easel and said, "Now what should I paint? Oh, where did I leave all my paints?"

Adelaide smiled. She found Harriet's discarded book, picked it up, and glanced at Baxter. "Come have a seat with me," she said as she strolled over to the couch. She patted the cushions beside her.

Baxter looked apprehensive, but after he blinked his goggled eyes a few more times, he accepted. "Feels like I'm straining my eyes."

"Yeah, I've heard it can take a while for your eyes to adjust. Hopefully it doesn't give you a headache or anything. Here," Adelaide said while she opened the book and pointed to the beginning of chapter one, "let's see where you are, reading level."

"I remember a bit," he said, "but the whole 'before E except after P' thing always confused me."

"It's 'I before E except after C.'"

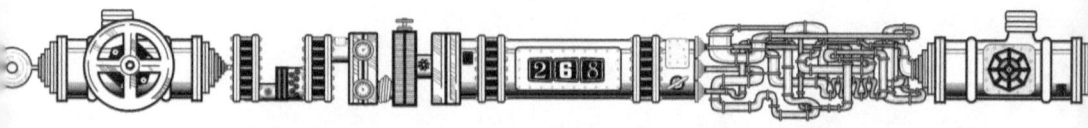

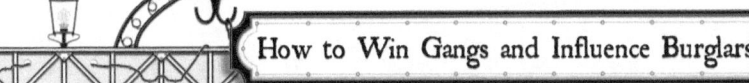

"Yeah, that."

Harriet chimed in, "Except for when the rule doesn't apply. Which happens a lot." She dabbed blue on her brush and spread it across the canvas with a twirl and flourish. "Like science! And weird. And weigh. And neighbor…"

"Language is stupid," Baxter said.

"Language is a puzzle that only makes sense after you solved it," Harriet altered.

"Puzzles are supposed to make sense and provide clues to solve."

"I didn't say it was a good puzzle."

"You'll get it," Adelaide encouraged. "It just takes time and practice."

"You know I hate both of those, right?"

Chapter 21

The Machine

Sparks smacked into the darkened goggles of the girl who was not wearing enough protection on her face to be welding metal. The mini fires lit up the Steampunks stash chamber. Adelaide winced as a minuscule piece of molten metal seared her cheek above her makeshift mask, which was little more than a folded up apron she wrapped about her noggin. She regretted not searching out for a full-face welder's mask before starting this, but such was the price of progress. Her hair may have gotten singed a bit, but she was almost done.

Adelaide didn't notice as Zadie peeked around the open hatch and stepped into the stash's cluttered chamber. Much like she did weeks ago, Zadie entered into a completely upgraded area from what it was before. More than organized, the stash was actually functional. Adelaide was sitting at a sprawling workspace with tables, desks, and machinery. All the lamps had bulbs. All the bulbs were lit. A

machine with a bowl shook and sorted a bunch of screws. A conveyor belt shuttled bolts from one device to another. Zadie didn't understand what half of this stuff did, and she was rather iffy on the other half as well.

Adelaide welded a thick, metal chassis together on top of the worktable. The blowtorch in her hand blazed with fiery light. Wires and tubes connected the tool to a generator of Adelaide's own design. Nearly every free inch of every table, desk, object top, dresser, and floor was filled with thick books opened and bookmarked on specific pages. There were pencil marks and notes all over the pages of the book directly next to Adelaide. Zadie leaned over to read the book title printed on the header: "*The Shocking Truth About Electrical Currents* by Zacharias Thundercrack."

Adelaide worked and hummed and tapped her foot in an improvised percussion song. As always, she was almost, but not quite, on the beat, which was a difficult feat to accomplish in a song of her own creation. Her head just happened to tilt back enough for her eyes to glance at Zadie's head quite close to her own. Adelaide jumped in surprise.

"You scared me," Adelaide said, hand on her heart.

"Sorry," Zadie replied. Her eyes darted around the stash, and her feet dug into the floor. "For uh... a few things, I guess."

Adelaide pulled up her goggles and nodded.

"I didn't like how uh... then you uh... and I got kinda... anyways. We good?"

Adelaide smiled and nodded. "Yeah."

Zadie's sheepish expression glanced at everything other than Adelaide. Her eyes finally landed on the worktable.[101] A shiny, new mechanical arm laid on top. It looked upgraded from the current version dangling off of Adelaide's arm nub. A thicker chassis frame wrapped around a mishmash of heavy-duty pistons, gears, and tubes.

---

101 Metaphorically. She didn't have detachable eyes. Or did she?

"You made a new arm," Zadie observed.

"Working on it. It's got a pressure leak somewhere."

A bunched collection of copper wires led from the arm to a new backpack as well. An open casing contained an unusual oscillating engine inside, similar but different to the generators powering the mechanical foxes.

"What's with all this wiring?" Zadie asked. "Does it got new tricks?"

"Of course!" Adelaide beamed. "But I can't show it off yet. Not ready."

"That's like one of them fox engines, yeah?"

"Maybe."

Zadie followed Adelaide's eyes to a metal object on the worktable next to her. A one-eyed, decapitated, mechanical fox head stared into her very soul.

"Geez." Zadie jumped. "You stole one of those?"

"No!" Adelaide defended herself, but then she shrugged. "Yes. Little bit. I needed to borrow a concept or two from the fox design during my rebuild. Then I expanded the snot out of that to build this."

Adelaide gestured to the five-foot-tall by eight-foot-wide metal monstrosity a few yards away. Inside the massive chassis and heavy braces forming a strong, skeletal box, an amalgamation of pipes, pistons, gears, centrifugal governors, and thingamabobs laid suspended in a spherical, oval structure in between the chassis' heavy metal bars.

"What is it?"

"The most powerful engine ever made. In theory. I think. Probably."

Adelaide pushed up a throttle lever on the outer control panel. The engine chugged to life. The inner spherical structure within the skeletal box flipped and rotated. It operated like a bizarre rotisserie spit mixed with a yo-yo of pure terror. The entire engine's structure vibrated and shook violently on the concrete floor. Adelaide powered it down.

"It supposed to quake like that?" Zadie wondered.

"Only a little bit. It's an oscillating engine, but the idea is that it levels out once it gets to full speed. Probably. In theory."[102]

"Didn't you just test it right now?"

"No, no, no, no. It doesn't have enough power by itself to get up to full speed. Have to hook it up to another generator for a full test."

"You gotta hook up your generator to another generator for it to work?" Zadie snorted. "Seems kinda lame."

"No, once it gets to full power, it should provide enough energy to not only power itself, but also the power of like..." Adelaide crossed her eyes as she did inside-brain-math, "thirty full-sized, steam-powered generators."

"Huh." Zadie nodded in appreciation. "So you wanna plug it into one of the generators below the hideout?"

Adelaide shook her head. "I'm not sure I want to test on something important. It's a completely new design, you know. New technology. I mean, what if there's blowback? Or feedback? I don't wanna damage the machines. That could cut power to a whole city block or something. Actually, I don't even know what those old generators are connected to."

"Not sure Phineas does anymore either," Zadie agreed. "So... is this thing important to you, or what?"

"Well, yeah. I think it'd be really helpful."

"Why? It's just a more powerful generator, right? What's the difference between that and a bunch of the older ones downstairs?"

"So much!" Adelaide grew excited. "If I can reduce the friction and adjust the oscillations to rotate endlessly, we're talking potentially limitless power. A series of them could reduce pollution. There would be no more need for coal or coal mining injuries and deaths. The Stacks could expand, not as a slum

---

102 Oscillating engines were, strangely enough, not run by ocelots running on hamster wheels.

where factories churned out harmful smoke and toxins over its working populace, but as a clean, charged place that could rival the Uppers. People could break free out of Cogs territory. Maybe the generators could be installed on trains too, providing perpetual powered transport as well!"[103]

Zadie wiped a bit of enthusiastic spit off of her cheek, collateral damage from Adelaide's fast-talking word explosion. After a moment for her brain to adjust and catch up, Zadie couldn't help but grin at the mad scientist. "You really think this clump of metal could do all that?"

"I do!" Adelaide sat back and shrugged, "Or at least, I hope so. That's why it needs testing. Probably lots and lots of testing. And access to some high-grade generators. Or some kind of power station, maybe."

"Hmm," Zadie hmmed as she took a rather old biscuit out of her trench coat pocket and munched on it. After a few moments, she smiled. "Today's your lucky day," she said while spewing bits of biscuit everywhere.

Adelaide raised an eyebrow and brushed enthusiastic biscuit crumbs off of her shirt. "How so?"

"I know where to go."

Traveling with a three-hundred-pound, metal, wired cluster of engineered chaos went smoother than Adelaide would have guessed, after she remembered to put wheels on the heavy thing, of course. Trying to scrape it across the floor was not a good start. The two girls took the longer-but-stairless route through the tunnels. The metal monstrosity banged and clacked and screeched every chug of the way.

"Where are we going exactly?" Adelaide asked.

"Don't worry about it," Zadie replied. "It's a surprise."

---

103 Sufferin' succotash!

Adelaide wasn't fond of that answer. Zadie's surprises tended to require bandages afterwards. As they huffed and puffed their way up a slope, a thought occurred to Adelaide.

"Should we have gotten the others to help?" she asked.

"Nah, we got this," panted Zadie. "Besides... I think... they went off... doing... a scam... or something..."

"A scam?"

Zadie pushed and Adelaide pulled the wheeled generator to the precipice. Zadie flopped on top and took a breather.

"Yeah. Harriet's got some good ones." Zadie chuckled. "Judging from their clothes this mornin', think they're pulling the debutante ball trick. She goes all dressed up and fancy. Jules is the hired bodyguard. They make distractions for Bax to sneak in and steal stuff."

"Someone's hosting a ball in the morning?"

"No clue. Could be a fancy brunch. I don't know. Rich folk like their balls all over. I don't feel left out or anything. *You* feel left out. Whatever."

Zadie pushed and Adelaide pulled. The concrete floor gave way to hard-packed dirt. The tunnel curved around and around. They turned at one intersection then another. Finally, they ended up at a large, cargo lift built into the wall.

The wheels carved into the packed dirt before bumping into the metal floor of the elevator and scraping inside. The two girls took a breath, got situated, and clanged the metal gate closed. Zadie tugged on the control lever, and the lift lifted upwards.

"We took the nice entrance route last time," Zadie said. "Now, I figured we'd best stick to the back entrance. More hidden. Where they make all their blue collar folk go in."

"This place has different entrances for different people?" Adelaide asked.

"Most places do in this town."

"I never understood that."

"That's because you're a good person."

"Well, you're one too," Adelaide smiled and shrugged. "Good, I mean. Not just a person. Though you're also a person. You... you know what I mean."

Zadie smirked and shook her head. "Nah, I ain't good. I ain't bad. I'm just..." she sighed a great big sigh, "livin'."

The lift clanked at the top. Zadie pulled open the gate, revealing an alleyway tucked between a nondescript building behind them and a long, tall, brick wall in front. The late afternoon sunlight glinted off the metal bars forming the side gate built into the brick. Adelaide's face drooped as she recognized the campus beyond. Newcomen University.

Adelaide groaned. "You're taking me to the school?"

"Right?" Zadie smirked.

"I didn't want to come back to the school."

"They ain't gonna make you do homework or nuthin'. Actually, you'd like that, wouldn't you?" Zadie put her hands on her hips. "Nerd."

"But we..." Adelaide began, "we messed up the building. I don't want to mess up any place where students go to learn."

"*Male* students."

"Still." Adelaide frowned and stared up at the brick wall. "It's sacred ground."

"Hey, you'd be runnin' this place if they'd let you in. 'Sides, where better to test out a revolutionary thingamajig than a school where they build revolutionary thingamajigs? Right?"

After a moment, Adelaide shrugged. "But I don't wanna get caught."

Zadie sighed, tapping a finger on her chin. After several moments, she said, "Ain't nobody here. It's Steam Day."

"Steam Day?"

"Yeah. You ain't heard a' Steam Day? Holiday for when they invented steam power or some such. Got a big ole' celebration at the park down by the oceanside cliff. Like to set off fireworks and junk. School's closed."

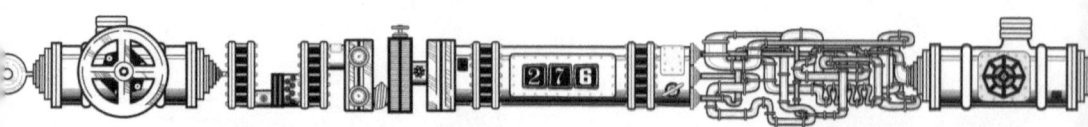

"You sure?"

"Yeah."

Zadie pushed the iron-barred gate open. Struggling to keep the generator moving, the castor roller wheels clacked and clanked and shook their way down the smooth pavement weaving in between tall buildings, patches of grass, decorative benches, and sculptures displaying, what appeared to be, abstract art pieces.

With her wary eyes sharpened by years of getting into trouble, Zadie spotted a security guard making the rounds around a building far ahead. She pulled back on the generator's horizontal support bar, stopping Adelaide in her tracks. She waved her over to a metal sculpture and pulled the generator in close.

"I thought you said the school was empty," Adelaide furiously whispered.

"Shh," Zadie shushed.

The two girls hid inside the tall, sheets of folded metal in what Adelaide could only describe as a giant, rotten banana wearing a prom dress. Pulling the generator right up next to them, Zadie thought the clump of metal blended well with the other clump of metal. Sure enough, the mustachioed security guard patrolling thirty-feet away on the opposite side of the sculpture took no notice of anything awry. The two clumps of metal must have combined together to form one, camouflaged piece of abstract creativity. Adelaide thought that the feeling derived from the piece must represent the variety of life's dangers that can hide within the ordinary. Or it was a banana. Also, the yawning guard could do little to keep the sheer boredom from clouding his eyes, so he was not all that attentive in the first place.

Once he had rounded the corner around another building and was safely out of earshot, Zadie whispered, "I said the school was closed, not empty. Always bound to be security guards. Why we just gotta be careful and quiet-like."

Adelaide simply shrugged as Zadie pulled her and the generator out of their artistic hiding spot.[104] They strolled and rumbled along toward the Science building just as the sun began to lower itself behind the tallest skyscraper. After a feat of lockpicking skill by Zadie, the two girls went inside through the side door. The wheels clanked especially loud against the grouted, uneven, tile floor. Their many noises echoed throughout the empty hallways.

"Shh," Adelaide shushed.

Zadie whispered, "You tell me how to push this thing silent-like, then you can shush me."

Zadie pushed the generator down hard toward a ramp leading to a lower floor. The slope caused the rolling monstrosity to speed up. Zadie and Adelaide's eyebrows jumped as they had to sprint to keep up. The hallway curved to the left, and the rolling generator slammed into the wall and scratched its way down. Adelaide and Zadie grabbed onto the back just as it crashed through a pair of swinging doors. Beyond, they slammed into a giant, metal something and stopped instantly. Adelaide and Zadie bounced off the back and fell off.

Zadie giggled, "The wheels were a good addition."

"Probably should've installed brakes though," Adelaide admitted.

"Nah. Other stuff stops us fine."

"Do you think anybody heard us?"

Zadie held up a finger. The two girls listened to the silence. "I think that guard went to the other side of campus. We should be clear."

Adelaide studied their current surroundings. They landed inside a massive basement turned power station plus boiler room. Ten-feet-high and twenty-feet-long, these

---

104 Avante-garde keeps many things hidden, like meaning and purpose and is that a nose or a horse?

cylindrical boilers were industrial grade. Three of them powered a fleet of steam-turbine generators around eight-feet-tall each. Adelaide could practically see in her head how the turbine blades within the metal casings spun vertically and rotated the output shaft to create electrical power. All Zadie could see in her head was what looked like a collection of hubcaps with hotdogs stuck horizontally on the edge with everything wrapped up in chunks of metal. In theory, she wasn't too far off.

A set of windows at the top of the tall walls overlooked the grounds from ground level and shone sunlight into the musty room. Adelaide's oscillating generator had face-planted into one of the ten steam-turbine generators. Zadie glanced from the seven-foot-tall turbines to Adelaide's four-foot version.

"Theirs are bigger than yours," Zadie said.

"Mine's thirty times more powerful," Adelaide boasted. "In theory. Probably."

"Be careful with that," Zadie warned. "People who get a taste of power will change. Usually for the worse."

"You're just full of random knowledge, aren't you?"

"Friendo, I *am* random knowledge."

Adelaide pulled out a jack stuck inside her generator. She cranked it up beneath the bottom support and lifted the entire structure up a foot. Adelaide pulled out a screwdriver from her pocket and began unscrewing the castor wheels from the base. Zadie leaned her elbow against the generator and watched Adelaide work.

"So," Zadie muttered, "after we get this thing going, you think they'll take you in?"

"Who? The school?"

"Yeah. Isn't that what you wanted?"

"Is this a test?" Adelaide asked. "Is this why you brought us here?"

Zadie shrugged. "Answer the question."

"I..." Adelaide stuttered while she unscrewed the stuck screws. "I forgot what the question was."

"Do you want the school to take you in?"

Adelaide tossed the loose wheel to the floor and gave a great sigh before working on the second one. "That's what I wanted before. Now? I don't know. I just wanted to learn and make new things. Things to help people, whether they like it or not. But... I can do that without them. I can build anything I want."

"Why did you build this thing then? And not all that bollocks about making the world a better place or what-the-snot-ever. Why did *you* build it?"

"I don't know." Adelaide tossed aside the second wheel and dropped the jack down. With some extra effort, she tilted it out of the way and pulled the jack free. "I just had the idea and had to make it. It's just... making stuff makes me happy. And who knows? Maybe it'll be like you said. They'll be begging me to run this place once we get the machine running." Adelaide worked on the other set of two wheels. "How about you?"

"Me? I don't wanna go to this stupid school."

"No, I mean, what do you want?"

Zadie simply smirked and said, "To grind the gears."

Adelaide shook her head. "That's a terrible noise."

"If you're gonna build stuff, I wanna break all the old stuff first. Give you room to improve." Zadie winked.

"Well, I guess that is required for upgrading."

"Teamwork!"

Adelaide sighed but couldn't help a smile. She unspooled loops of cables from inside her machine and spliced them into the outputting power lines from the various turbines. Fairly soon, it looked like someone spilled spaghetti noodles all over the place, or at least, that's how Zadie looked at the cluster of wires.

"Mmm, pasta," Zadie said to no one in particular.

"Well," Adelaide said aloud while thinking of other things, "I think that's it. Let me just... hmm... carry the five..."

Adelaide closed her eyes and started counting imaginary numbers with her finger.

"What are you doing?"

"Mental checklist."

"You mental?"

"I don't have any paper. Alright." Adelaide shuffled up next to her oscillating generator's control panel bolted into the upper support beam. "You ready?"

Zadie smirked and raised her fist. "Here's to girl power." The two girls bumped their knuckles together.

Adelaide closed her eyes and took a deep breath. Her good hand hovered over the control panel. "Here we go."

Adelaide pushed up on the throttle and stepped back. The machine whirred and clanked to life. A hum began in the pit of its metal stomach and vibrated outward. The oscillating engine turned and whipped around in a circle. The yo-yo of terror stopped. It whipped around again. It stopped. It whipped around again. And again. And again.

The yo-yo/tetherball/rotisserie spit of electricity-crackling force picked up speed. Violent shifts in momentum shook the entire generator. The bottom of the heavy chassis lifted and smacked back down into the concrete floor. Every molecule of the machine vibrated. The shaking became more and more violent. It slammed into the floor so hard, the concrete cracked.

Adelaide and Zadie took another step backwards.

Finally, the shaking relented as the spinning engine picked up near top speed. The generator leveled itself out. A blur was all that Adelaide could make out of the rotating oscillation. The support braces dug into the floor with extreme force.

After a few moments of the machine spinning smoothly at high speed, Adelaide gingerly stepped toward the control panel. Her eyes peeked over at the display.

"It's working," she said, her voice barely above the loud humming. "Smokes, look at that power output. That's even higher than I calculated."

A metallic, harmonic echo erupted from the machine. It billowed and rang throughout the entire room. The ear-splitting noise rose to a screech. The larger, steam-turbine generators hummed and screeched with the same exact sound, almost as though the machines came to life and began imitating each other. The machines hummed at each other in a perfect echo.

"What is that?!" Zadie yelled above the din.

The entire building shook and quaked. Zadie and Adelaide had to adjust their footing to stay upright. They could feel the air itself pushing them around. Branching out from the machine, a spider's web of fractures ripped open the floor and cracked into the walls. The windows above splintered and shattered to pieces. The girls took cover. Most of the razor-sharp shards missed them, but Adelaide felt a sharp pain tear into her shoulder.

"Turn it off!" Zadie shouted.

Adelaide pulled down the throttle, which did precisely zilch. She pressed buttons. Nothing. She flipped switches. Nada. She finally just started pounding her fingers into the control panel. All the while, above all the noise, rang the incessant, echoing, all-encompassing hum that resonated deep from within the machine.

"It's too late!" Adelaide yelled. "The reciprocating rotations are self-sustaining now!"

"What does that mean?!"

"It means: *Run!*" she screamed as the ceiling shook apart above them.

Chapter 22

Aftershock

Crumbles are delightful additions in many different ways. Some are delicious, such as the variety within: cookies, coffee cake, chocolate, and broccoli ketchup pudding. Others are useful, like breadcrumbs. Some can be artistic in oil paintings and great, big, marble sculptures. Still, others can be quite dangerous, much like the crumbling ceiling collapsing above the heads of Adelaide and Zadie.

The debris was fairly simple for the agile girls to avoid, for the most part. A simple sidestep cleared them from a baseball-sized chunk of concrete ceiling. The only exit in the room, however, was not as lucky. Contrary to the advice of "the safest place during an earthquake is in a doorway," this particular doorway collapsed. The ceiling caved in above it, and their only exit had been blocked off. Luckily for Adelaide, Zadie was good at finding alternate escape routes.

"Come on!" Zadie yelled as she grabbed Adelaide by the hand.

She pulled the shocked engineer to the windows. Zadie hopped on a table and used her small crowbar (that she always keeps in her back pocket for just such a situation) to clear away the remaining glass shards within the broken window pane several feet above the floor of the basement. She jumped up and pulled herself through the now-empty frame. Adelaide stared at the cracks spreading through the walls, tearing lines into the corner of the ceiling. Zadie's hand shot down, grabbed Adelaide by the shoulder strap, and pulled her up.

On the small, grass lawn outside, the two girls crawled free from the shaking and quaking building. Windows on the second and third floors shattered. Zadie and Adelaide took cover from the raining shards and staggered farther away.

The entire wall acted like a banana on the run from the ice cream mafia, which is to say, it split. A gargantuan chunk of the wall ripped free from the roof and fell over. Zadie pushed Adelaide out of harm's way as the wall crashed into the grass. The entire building collapsed within an impenetrable cloud of dust.

Waves of thick, obscuring air washed over them. Adelaide snorted a sinus full, and she immediately began coughing her lungs out of her body. The problem was, the air she tried to inhale was also enveloped by dust. She covered her mouth with her hand and buried her face in her shirt, trying desperately to find oxygen she wouldn't have to cough out again.

The quaking stopped. The last bit of rubble from what used to be a beautiful building crashed and settled into the other mounds of rubble. The last rays of sunset pierced through the cloud. The dust finally began to settle along with everything else. After the agonizing, ear-splitting noises, the dead silence felt even more overwhelming.

Adelaide rubbed her eyes somewhat clear and coughed in somewhat clean air. The Science building had shaken

itself into pieces. It looked like sections of the top floor had simply slid off, mostly intact. From what she could determine, the basement and first floor took the brunt. Many pieces of concrete wall and rebar supports were broken into bite-sized chunks. The basement must have been nearly vaporized for everything to sink into the ground-carved hole that much.

Yet the earthquake, strangely enough, did not quake the earth much at all. The grass and dirt had risen and fallen in circular patterns away from the building. It looked like earthen ripples in a pond. Adelaide's mind wrinkled, trying to figure out what that meant.

From the corner of her twitching eye, Adelaide saw Zadie stepping over rubble. She coughed and spit and hawked up a loogie.

"Are you okay?" Adelaide asked.

"Yeah," Zadie replied. "You?"

"I can't stop shaking."

"Let's get out of here."

Zadie grabbed Adelaide by the hand and pulled her away. Adelaide stopped dead in her tracks at sounds coming from the collapsed building. It sounded like... people.

"Someone's in there!" Adelaide cried.

She ran back to the remnants. Her good hand dug at the rubble, dust, and dirt. Making very little progress, Adelaide turned the dial and raised the sliders on her chest control panel. Her metal fingers straightened and locked into place. She used her mechanical arm as a shovel and dug deeper into the debris. Her desperation grew as the sound of crying grew louder.

"We gotta go!" Zadie warned as she scanned their surroundings.

Another chunk of debris removed, a human hand was visible, reaching out toward the sunlight and air. Adelaide pulled rocks and shoveled dirt beneath it.

"Help me!" Adelaide exclaimed.

"We're gonna get caught!" Zadie argued.

"I'm not leaving!"

"Someone else will get them out! Let's get outta here!"

"Either help me or go!"

Zadie shuffled her feet and glanced from Adelaide to the road. Sounds of sirens echoed in the distance. Concerned or curious pedestrians made their way onto the campus. The gears turning in Zadie's head ground to a halt. With one last look at Adelaide, Zadie turned and ran away, disappearing beyond the gates.

Adelaide pulled free a large piece of debris. The owner of the hand was below. The young man in his late teens to early twenties was covered in all manner of dust and dirt and debris. His head and torso were free, but the rest of him was not as lucky.

"I've got you!" Adelaide said.

A groan from his lips was his reply. Adelaide dug around his torso and noticed that his waist and legs were pinned beneath a single, massive piece of the wall.

"Okay, hang on."

She straightened her metal arm and locked her elbow in place. Her arm nub shoved it toward the ground. Her metal hand dug into the dirt as her metal bicep wedged against the debris. Awkwardly tilted, the lever was nevertheless effective. Adelaide heaved her shoulder up. Her arm lever tilted up the debris a couple of inches.

"Can you move?" she grunted.

The young man groaned in pain and crawled. Adelaide's good hand grabbed him by the belt and helped pull him out. Once his sneakers were free, her tired shoulders released her mechanical arm lever. The wall debris lowered back, and Adelaide bent down to check on the young man. More muffled cries echoed from beneath the debris.

"How many more are in there?" Adelaide gasped.

"We..." the young man began, "were doing labs... about... five of us..."

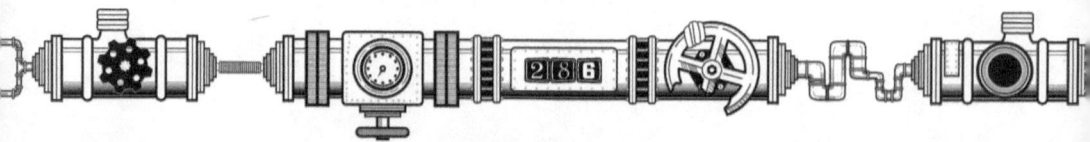

Adelaide dove onto the dirt. She wedged her face in between the debris and the ground, trying to gain a look. Through the sparse bits of dusty, ambient light, she could see a small alcove inside. Largely intact pieces of wall seemed to collapse together and hold themselves up, leaning against desks and chairs. Huddled beneath were more heads and hands reaching out from beneath the desks.

"In here!" a voice called out.

Adelaide analyzed the debris. She didn't like the stability of the wall she just lifted. It could cause a collapse on the other pieces holding up the house of cards. As she looked, some of the debris shifted and settled further into the dirt, causing rocks and chunks to slide off the top and topple into the grass. Adelaide backed off.

"Hold on! Let me look around!" Adelaide called to them.

The young man collapsed on the ground and coughed, not wanting to rise from his knees again. Adelaide walked the perimeter, studying every inch. Her whirling mind finally decided on one, massive, solid piece of wall lying on top, near horizontal. Her shovel hand scraped free several pieces and cleared away an access near the bottom.

"I'm gonna lift this piece! See if that's enough to crawl out!"

Adelaide laid her back flat on the ground, or at least as flat as her generator backpack would allow. Her good fingers worked the sliders on her chest control panel. The straightened palm of her mechanical hand shovel pointed backwards, perpendicular to her forearm, and her elbow bent once more. She shoved her mechanical arm underneath the wall debris. Her metal elbow scraped across the dirt, rocks, and random chunks of metal and rebar. She shoved her weight against her arm, again and again. Slowly and with many scrapes of metal on concrete, she was able to raise her forearm vertically, pinned between the debris and the ground. Her metal palm sank into her wrist. Her elbow dug into the dirt, but she both cautiously and foolhardily forced it into position.

Adelaide's good fingers worked her control panel. Her backpack engine chugged to life and whirred beneath her. It cranked to full power and shook her whole body. She extended her metal forearm lever and turned it before shifting it into another gear. Her right shoulder and arm nub dug into her generator backpack. Pistons and air pressure pushed her engineered creation.

Her metal bicep lifted her metal elbow. Every single piston strained. A leak in the line sprang from somewhere. A screw shot out from anotherwhere. Finally, her mechanical arm extended straight and her elbow locked in place. The vast majority of the weight was centered on the metal arm, digging into her generator backpack with her fleshy shoulder wedged between, but an uncomfortable portion still pierced her skin. She shifted as much of her arm nub out as she could, but she needed it in place to steer her mechanical creation. She just had to bear the weight. And pain.

"This is as far as I can go!"

"Dig!" came the muffled voice of an older man inside.

A boy's hands reached out from the hole that Adelaide's mechanical arm jack created. His fingers shoved aside dirt, throwing it forward and backward. Adelaide turned her control panel. The palm of her metal hand slowly raised the wall. Her fingers bent back as her palm straightened vertically for a few more centimeters. Her ring finger bent so far back that the metal supports snapped off.

"Go! See if you can crawl out!" came the older voice.

A pair of chubby arms extended out.

"Not you, Thomas! Someone skinny go!"

The arms withdrew and a thin, young man crawled his body through the gap, shimmying himself past Adelaide. She stared at her arm. The already cut, fractured, and split pieces of metal and chassis bent. The gap she strained to create between the debris and dirt lessened and lost a centimeter. A second boy managed to crawl out to freedom.

298

"Take him! He's unconscious!"

The two boys pulled the sleeping arms of a third and dragged him free. Adelaide tried not to look at the boy's head wound that was bleeding profusely, despite the haphazard bandages wrapped around his forehead.

The fourth boy, Thomas, crawled out to his large torso and appeared stuck. The other two grabbed his arms and tugged. The wall debris overhead splintered before Adelaide's eyes, but it held. For now. They pulled Thomas free.

One of the metal supports on Adelaide's forearm crumpled and snapped. Two more centimeters lost.

The owner of the older voice crawled through. Their faces close together, Adelaide's glance at the man's mustache kicked her memory into gear. It was Dean Douglas.

The metal on Adelaide's wrist collapsed, crushing her palm into her forearm and losing a few more centimeters. Dean Douglas stopped, wedged in between debris and dirt. He gasped in pain and surprise.

"Hurry!" Adelaide yelled.

The two boys grabbed him by the arms and pulled. Thomas dug out the dirt and debris around his chest. Adelaide's arm splintered. The boys pulled Dean Douglas free as her mechanical arm collapsed. She moved her shoulder as the debris fell and crushed her metal arm.

She groaned in agony at the twisting metal smashing and piercing her arm nub and shoulder. Adelaide ripped open her outer shirt, revealing her chest harness and undershirt beneath. Her remaining hand began unhooking herself from the many horizontal, vertical, and diagonal straps.

Among the curious pedestrians simply looking on, a wave of people approached. Uniformed police officers and firefighters ran with equipment and scanned the scene before them. Several people checked on the injured boys.

The man known as Officer Adams asked, "Did everyone make it out okay?"

Dean Douglas counted the boys. "One, two, three, four... I think that's all. Yes. I don't know if anyone else was in the building. Just our rescuer..."

Adelaide ripped herself free from her backpack, harness, and crushed mechanical arm. She rolled to her knees, and after a few, steadying breaths, rose to her feet. Her shoulder and arm remnant were scraped and bleeding, but it looked fine overall, or at least, still attached and whole. Dean Douglas looked at Adelaide's face for the first time. His face shifted from panicked and thankful to something else entirely. His eyebrows dropped.

"The Wakefield girl?" he said, aghast. "What are you doing here?!"

"Umm..."

"Seize her!" Dean Douglas commanded the officer.

Officer Adams, bemused,[105] nevertheless grabbed onto Adelaide's single, remaining arm.

"What were you... you did this, didn't you?" Dean Douglas accused.

Adelaide simply stared at the ground.

"Come now, Dean," Officer Adams began, "this little girl could not have caused an earthquake."

"Parsons City does not lie on a fault line, Officer," Dean Douglas countered. "We do not encounter earthquakes. No, no. This was man-made. Or should I say... *woman*-made."[106]

Officer Adams furrowed his brow. "Do you have any evidence to corroborate your claim?"

"Sir," Thomas piped up, "she just saved our lives."

"Silence yourself, Thomas," Dean Douglas frothed. "As for evidence? Evidence?! The evidence is all around us! Buried beneath rubble! If nothing else, you can arrest her for trespassing on private property." He glared at Adelaide for

---

105 B-mused, not to be mistaken for A-mused. Confused versus happy.

106 We already covered that joke, silly Dean.

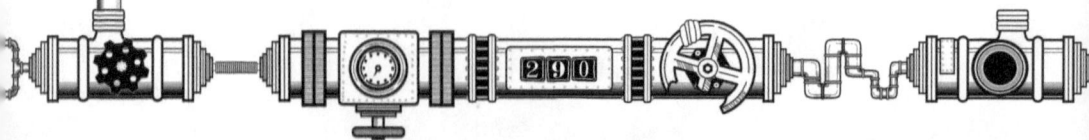

several moments before adding, "I will discover how you did this. Mark my words."

Adelaide said nothing. Her eyes continued to find the ground fascinating.

"Very well," Officer Adams said.

He pulled Adelaide away. The Dean's voice caused them to stop.

"Miss Wakefield!" He stomped over to them. "You asked me once why we did not allow women in our school." He gestured back at the wreckage. "*This* is why."

Adelaide studied the collapsed building. She could not speak. She could not think. Her eyes were happy to water themselves, however. Her gray matter twisted and clenched. Bile rose in her throat. Her mind retreated inside her skull, unable to cope quite yet as Officer Adams took her away.

Chapter 23

Behind Bars

delaide became vaguely aware of being put inside a horse-drawn carriage. She liked horses. Horses were nice. Why did they use horses instead of automobiles? Oh, it was cheaper. Government salaries, she guessed. She wondered if she could make a cheaper automobile. With a more efficient engine, maybe. Engine. Generator. Earthquake. Rubble. Nausea. Heartburn. Indigestion. Adelaide felt woozy.

Officer Adams pulled her out of the carriage. They were in front of the police station. She couldn't remember the carriage moving. Doors. Rooms. People. He sat her down in a chair next to a single table in the interrogation room. Adelaide pressed her arm against the table and laid her head atop it. Seconds... minutes... weeks... months... passed by. Or maybe it was just the minutes. Adelaide just tried to keep herself from vomiting.

The door opened. The imposing presence of her father, Franklin Wakefield, encompassed the exit. A squirrel of a man skittered around behind him.

"Trespassing?" the squirrel man asked. "You are holding the daughter of my client, one of the most wealthy and influential men in the city, over a case of mere trespassing?"

Officer Adams stepped into the doorway. "The dean of the university seemed to think it was her fault."

"Oh ho!" the lawyer squeaked. "So people can make the earth quake now, can they? What did she do? Play hopscotch until the ground opened up beneath her? Preposterous!"

The officer and the lawyer continued their banter behind Mister Wakefield. He paid them no mind. He continued to stare at Adelaide. His stone-like expression never wavered. Adelaide thought it felt both familiar and brutal at the same time.

"Come along," he ordered.

With a simple wave of his hand, Adelaide was on her feet and following him out the door. The officer and the lawyer kept talking behind them, but Adelaide's befuddled brain couldn't translate their words. Her eyes just kept glancing from the floor to the back of her father's jacket.

Outside the station, she climbed up into the family car behind him. Luther sat behind the wheel and cranked the engine to life. The exhaust bellowed black, and the massive wheels turned.

The two sat in perfect silence. Well, perfect aside from the chugging engine, loud traffic, bustling city dwellers, and Luther's occasional bout of unrequited gas coming from the driver's seat outside the cabin. Mister Wakefield looked away from his daughter, gazing outside the window and to the darkened, nighttime city. Adelaide knew not to hope that was because something interesting flopped around on the sidewalk beyond.

Feeling slowly started to creep back into her hand. She could even feel her face again. Her heart pumped normally for the first time in hours. Adelaide took a deep breath. Something about

being in the old Wakefield tradition of her dad being incredibly disappointed in her made Adelaide find her voice once again.

"Aren't you going to ask?" she asked.

"Ask what?" he asked in return.

"If I actually did it?"

Silence. For several moments, Mister Wakefield stared through the window. Finally, he turned a severe, highly unfavorable gaze upon Adelaide.

"Of course I know you did it," he barked. "How could I expect anything less from my disappointment of a child?"

He turned back toward the window. Adelaide turned away as well. She lost the feeling in her face again.

Questions arose over the next several hours in the cluttered mind of Adelaide Wakefield. None were answered. It was easier to just numb herself, mentally and physically. Her father marched her through their family home. Her mother doted on her with the frequent addition of criticism. Adelaide was aware of it but did not absorb anything. She was like a wrench that was covered in grease. Slippery and hard to hold. Or was she like a tire rolling down a hill? An endless hill sloping down into the deepest, darkest pits of the earth. Yeah, that was better. She was a tire.

A freshly-bathed Adelaide in a pure, white nightgown sat on her pink, polka-dot bedspread. She gazed out at the black night through her barred window. Her mother, Margaret Wakefield, ran a brush through Adelaide's tangle of hair.

"So good to have you back, my darling," her mother cooed with an air of pomp. "I can't imagine the horrors you must have experienced out there with those... *people*."

Missus Wakefield gave a slight shudder. She checked the bandages on Adelaide's right shoulder and arm nub before she pulled her daughter's sleeve down to cover it.

"But you're back home now," she said. "Safe and sound."

She kissed Adelaide on the forehead and walked away. Her mother did not look back as she exited the bedroom, closed the door, and locked it from the other side. Adelaide laid back in her bed, watching the illumination from her lamp on the ceiling. The gas-lit flame danced upon the white paint.

Her plush, expensive bed was extremely comfortable on her sore and aching body. She didn't feel like she deserved such comfort, but she also didn't feel like moving. Adelaide was sure she deserved punishment though. Being imprisoned in her room technically counted. Treated well. Fed well. But unable to leave and hurt anyone else. Yep, that seemed about right.

Adelaide had hurt people. It was unintentional, of course, but the image of the bloodied boy being pulled from the wreckage haunted her mind. Of her fuzzy recollections afterwards, she did remember asking her father about the boys. He confirmed that they were doing well at the medical center and were going to make a full recovery. That eased Adelaide's mind quite a bit. Yet even though Dean Douglas confirmed that no one else was in the building at the time of collapse, Adelaide wouldn't feel right until they were able to dig through the rubble and thoroughly search the debris.

When Adelaide first began staying over at the Steampunks hideout, she had the most immense trouble sleeping. But now? She found herself unable to sleep without the sound of Baxter's snoring, Harriet's tossing and turning, and Zadie occasionally waking herself up with a single, loud snort before going right back to sleep. Even Jules' silent companionship was incredibly comforting.

She turned at the sound of knocking against her window. Her bleary eyes gazed through the glass and bars. *Oh great*, she thought to herself. *I missed them so much, I'm hallucinating now.*

"Oi! Oi!" came Zadie's voice in a harsh whisper through the glass. "Demo girl!"

Adelaide blinked her eyes. Zadie, Harriet, Baxter, and Jules stood on the other side of her window. Adelaide slid the pane open.

"You okay?" Zadie asked in a softer whisper.

"What are you doing here?" Adelaide wondered aloud.

"What are we..." Zadie scoffed and shook her head, "we're here to bust you out, nubbin'! Again. We're always doin' that. You realize that, yeah?"

Baxter raised a crowbar and displayed it to Adelaide. He wedged the tool in between the window bars and the wall.

"No," Adelaide said. "No."

Baxter stopped. The punks all looked at her, curiously.

"I... I can't..."

"What do you mean?" Harriet asked.

"I..." Adelaide struggled to say the words, "I hurt all those people. I could have killed someone. Maybe I..." Adelaide struggled with the words as her fingers found the bars, "maybe I should just stay here."

Zadie scoffed again. "You're jokin'!"

"You don't wanna come back with us?" Baxter's sad expression melted into his words.

"But you hate it here," Harriet said.

Adelaide sat back on her bed, refusing to face them.

"They'll never let you be yourself," Zadie argued.

"Maybe..." Adelaide said, "maybe that's for the best."

Zadie turned away. Her boots stomped into the well-kept grass. She paced back and forth, making the other punks look from her to the window to Adelaide and back again. Zadie suddenly rushed back to the bars and grabbed hold.

"Your brain is gonna be *wasted* in there," Zadie said. "Your inventions... your creations... your generator could be the greatest thing ever made!"

"I collapsed a building."

"Exactly! That kind of power..." Zadie's eyes blazed with life and possibilities and her arms waved in the air, "it's incredible! Do you realize what we could do with it?"

"What?" Adelaide's expression transformed from dejected to bewildered to abject confusion. "Wait... wait..." Her eyes squinted as her brain tried to connect the dots. She pointed at Zadie. "Why... Why... Why were people there? The school was supposed to be empty for Steam Day."

"Steam what?" Harriet asked.

"Steam Day. The holiday?"

Harriet shook her head. Baxter shrugged. Jules remained still. Zadie looked the perfect mix of sheepish and mischievous, like a lamb who enjoyed robbing banks. She held it in for a moment more before she squeezed out a short laugh.

"Sorry," Zadie chortled. "I made that up."

"What?" Adelaide asked.

"Such a dumb name too. Can't believe you bought that."

"Why..."

"Bah, you were being all wishy washy. Who cares if anyone else was there?" Zadie turned on a devious grin. "I think you should build another machine."

"Another one? Are you serious?"

"Don't you get it? You built an earthquake machine! We could make everyone do what we wanted, because if they didn't," her hand dipped in a falling gesture, "off into the Gorge they go."

"That's dark, Zadie," Harriet said.

"You guys," Zadie argued, "this is exactly the opportunity we've been waiting for! We don't have to get beat down or ridiculed or struggle just to survive anymore! We can be the ones in charge. We can finally be the ones on top! Jules, back me up here, mate."

Jules tilted his masked head.

"No!" Adelaide yelled in a harsh whisper. "I'm never going to build another generator again. I'm never going to build anything ever again."

"Come on!" Zadie argued. Her hands clutched onto the bars. "Think of everything we could do."

"Like hurting people? No. My ideas... they're just too dangerous. I deserve to be locked up for what I did. Alone. Away from everyone else. Like... like penance."

"Oh, I see." Zadie let go of the bars and stepped back. She frowned and studied her friend on the other side. "So you got your taste back for fancy food and fluffy pillows and fine clothes and decided you're better than us?"

"That's not what I—"

"I see how it is," Zadie's voice cut off Adelaide. "You enjoy being a rich girl. We'll just go back into the steam tunnels and eat your scraps."

"That's not what I... Zadie..."

Zadie stomped away. Adelaide wanted to yell at her to come back but didn't think she could without alerting her parents and any nighttime guards wandering the grounds. Harriet, Baxter, and Jules studied Adelaide for a few moments. Harriet looked like she had just lost her best friend. Baxter looked like his favorite toy had just been smashed in front of his eyes. Jules was as unreadable as always, but Adelaide thought his posture was more slumped than usual.

Adelaide's friends turned away from her and followed Zadie out of the grounds. Adelaide's heart clenched onto her rib cage before falling into her lower intestines.[107] This was for the best. She was sure of it. Adelaide didn't like it, but she couldn't be allowed to wander free, for everyone's sakes. This was for the best. She was sure of it. Her eyes just felt that her cheeks were too dry and needed to be watered, that was all.

She dove back into her squishy mattress and silky sheets. Minutes ticked by. Hours. The first rays of the rising sun pierced the smog and floated into her bedroom.

---

107 Biology is gross.

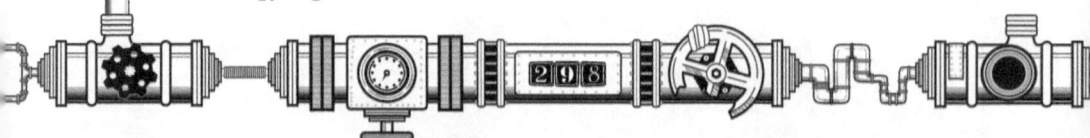

Adelaide was gaining a greater understanding of the science behind her generator and what happened, but she was losing much of everything else. Zadie had called it an earthquake machine, but it wasn't though. The ground. The ground had that ripple pattern. And that noise it made. The other generators made that noise too. It had something to do with sound. It was like... no... the other generators didn't make that sound too. It was an echo. That was it. Her generator vibrated through sound. Harmonic resonance. It oscillated at the resonance frequency of the building around it as the engine spun at top speed. So that wasn't an earthquake. Well, Adelaide guessed it sort of was, but it also wasn't. Just the concept of it was unheard of... at least, for a machine to generate, at any rate. She had never read about anything doing that before.

A sharp knock on her bedroom door broke her out of her troubled reverie.[108] The deadbolt unlocked from the other side. Her father's stern expression appeared through the small opening.

"Breakfast," he said. "Come along."

"I'm not hungry," Adelaide replied.

"Fine."

Mister Wakefield closed the door and locked it from the other side. Adelaide thought that was the most pleasant conversation she's had with her father in a long time. She sank back into her bed. It was too much to hope for sleep. Her eyes attempted to rest but gave up after a few minutes and stared at the ceiling for another hour. They gave up on that too after another knock on her bedroom door, but this particular knock was soft with a happy little rhythm.

"Miss Adelaide?" came the familiar hearty yet bubbly voice of Chef Charlemagne from the other side. "May I come in?"

Adelaide gave a soft smile and said, "Yes."

---

108 Absentminded dreaming. Much more laid back than revelry, which is when a bunch of people in horseback come charging in with their muskets blazing. Or is that cavalry? Chivalry?

After the deadbolt unlocked, the hearty yet bubbly big man himself entered. His outrageous toque[109] tickled the top of the doorframe as he sauntered into her bedroom.

"You did not arrive at breakfast this morning," Chef Charlemagne noted, "and so, breakfast now arrives at you."

His hands carried a massive, silver tray of scrambled eggs, toast, sausage, bacon, and flapjacks. While Adelaide wasn't hungry before, the aromas wafting in her nostrils begged her to reconsider. Chef Charlemagne gently placed the tray over Adelaide's lap.

"Is this to your liking?" his kind and heavily-accented-from-somewhere-Adelaide-wasn't-familiar-with voice asked. "I would be happy to return to the kitchen and prepare whatever meal the little miss desires."

"This is lovely. Thank you."

"But of course!"

"Would you like to join me?" Adelaide asked as she gestured to the foot of her bed.

"Oh," his rosy cheeks turned rosier, "the little miss is so kind, but the chef never dines with his guests. It is bad form."

"You can have my bacon."

"But... then again... Chef Charlemagne is unable to resist such a kind offer when it comes to bacon."

He sat on the corner of her bed. Adelaide steadied her tray as his bulk tilted the mattress. Chef Charlemagne lightly selected a piece and longingly savored the perfectly-cooked meat in his mouth.

"Ahh," Chef Charlemagne exuded. "Magnifique. If I do say so myself."

He chuckled at himself. Adelaide chuckled too amidst a mouthful of eggs. The two sat in relative silence aside from the chewing noises. Chef Charlemagne happily ate bacon

---

109 You're not a true chef unless you have a fancy, made-up word to describe your top hat.

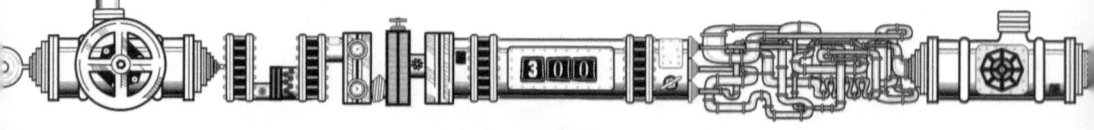

and contented himself with a contented guest eating his food. Adelaide could feel the warmth of the nutrients spreading through her bloodstream and easing her relentless headache. After a few more moments, Adelaide realized that, while she liked Chef Charlemagne very much, she didn't actually know very much about him.

"Are you happy here?" she asked.

"Very much, little miss," he replied. "All the kitchen equipment and materials I could ever want for. Satisfied guests. Following my passion! What else could Chef Charlemagne ask?"

He smiled. Adelaide lightly returned the smile then looked introspective. Charlemagne also turned introspective.

"What about you, little miss? How was your trip? Did you follow your passion?"

"I did, but... it ended with people getting hurt because of it."

"Ahh," Chef Charlemagne tapped a slice of bacon on his bottom lip, "but such is the price of passion, eh? I know that pain all too well."

"Your cooking hurt people?" Adelaide's confused voice asked.

Chef Charlemagne nodded. "Oh yes. My family."

Adelaide's inadvertent, judgmental attitude melted.

He continued, "I pursued my passion with such ferocity! Traveled all over the world! Cooked meals in nearly every country. Learned so much from all different cultures. But my family..." He sighed with abject loss and sadness. "My family... I neglected them. My wife, Luciana. My little daughter, Eva." He turned a longing expression toward Adelaide. "She left me, you see. My wife. And I have not seen my darling Eva in... oh... a very long time."

"I'm sorry."

He nodded. "I am torn, you see. Driven to pursue my passion but losing all that makes that passion worthwhile. If I may, little miss, I would give you advice from my own personal experiences."

Adelaide nodded.

"Pursue your passion. Pursue it will all your heart! But not at the cost of family. For family is the greatest adventure your life will ever find. And if you can find a balance between the two, well, that is the greatest embodiment of happiness you shall ever discover. But if you cannot find that balance, well then, perhaps that passion will not lead to any sort of happiness at all. Perhaps it will just lead... away from the things that matter most. Take it from me. I have led a good life, but if I could do it all over again, I would."

He patted Adelaide's foot buried beneath the blankets and rose to his feet. Chef Charlemagne gave a great sigh and rubbed the bit of bacon grease from his fingers on his protruding belly. With one last look at Adelaide and her tray of food, he snatched the last slice of bacon.

"One more for the road, I think." He winked.

Adelaide smiled. "Thank you, Charlemagne. I hope you get to see your daughter again soon."

"Ahh, yet the little miss still so kind. You have a good heart. Follow it."

He tilted his toque toward her in a deferential bow. With bacon in his mouth, he bounced toward the door. He stopped at the frame and turned back toward her.

"I do apologize, little miss," he began, "but I am required to lock this behind me."

"It's okay. I understand."

Chef Charlemagne glanced at the door frame and the hinges and added, "But, judging from your previous trip, I daresay that would not stop you, if you so chose."

He winked, exited, closed and locked the door behind him.[110] He gave her a lot to ponder. He also gave her a lot of food to digest. Adelaide's stomach grumbled, but it wasn't from the eggs.

---

110 You know what has more water than a pond? A ponder! Not nearly as much as a pondest, but still quite liquidy.

Chapter 24

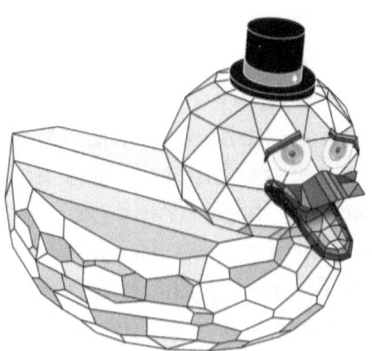

A Familiar Sensation

Days had passed since Adelaide's first night of confinement. Days since she last saw her friends at her barred window. A window that looked quite empty on the other side now. Adelaide untangled herself from the blankets and rose to her feet. Her hand turned on the gas lamp, shining a bit of illumination on the dark bedroom. Strangely enough, Adelaide preferred her bedroom in the pitch black. At least then, she wouldn't have to stare at the pink polka dots and doilies strewn about. Maybe she should redecorate. No, that was part of her well-earned punishment: the pink polka dot torture.

Adelaide glanced around for the jewelry box she made for Lillian, but she must have left it back at the hideout. Suddenly, she felt even more alone.

Morning arrived, as did a knock at her door. A key turned the lock. Her father's stern face appeared through the opening.

"Breakfast," he said. "Come along."

"Okay," Adelaide replied.

Mister Wakefield left the door open a crack. Adelaide's good arm tugged a robe over her nightgown. She glanced over at her dresser.

Adelaide's mother had brought her a new prosthetic arm the day before. Adelaide had been loath to try it out. The arm was comprised entirely of leather with some kind of feathers or something stuffed inside. Adelaide thought it looked completely useless, but still she fitted it to her arm remnant and attached the straps across her chest and shoulder. Yep, she thought to herself, it was completely useless. The pillow-like-thing just hung there. It didn't even appear like an actual arm. It was just a thing dangling from her shoulder.

Her parents probably thought that a regular wooden prosthetic would be too problematic for her to wield. Maybe they thought that she would hurt herself with it. Adelaide shrugged her shoulders, causing the pillow arm to flop along. Maybe her parents were right.

She stuffed the arm-thing through her robe, adjusted herself, and left her bedroom. As much as she didn't like the rest of the house, Adelaide did enjoy being outside her room. It was amazing how interesting everything looked when she wasn't allowed to see it normally.

Luther stood guard in the hallway. He nodded politely to Adelaide as she passed, but he watched her, as he always did, making sure she didn't get into anywhere she didn't belong, which seemed to be everywhere now.

Adelaide's feet shuffled along the expensive rug and entered the grand dining room with the paintings of her grandparents staring disapprovingly upon all.

Mister Wakefield opened the newspaper before him and read the headlines. "Good," he mentioned aloud. "Mayor Stanbury won his re-election."

"Wonderful," Missus Wakefield added. "I could think of no better candidate."

"I should hope not. I spent much toward his campaign. He knows the rails will benefit his standing as much as our own."

Adelaide's eyes crossed. She was desperate for conversation, but she was not desperate enough to talk about politics. With her elbow on the table and her head in hand, she stared at the decorative, glass cabinets housing all of her mother's expensive china and exorbitant collection of crystal ducks. Adelaide wasn't sure how many crystal ducks were too many crystal ducks, but her mother must have passed that line long ago.

Chef Charlemagne entered and set down fine bowls filled with soup in front of the parents, who did not acknowledge him.

Missus Wakefield looked to Adelaide and asked, "How do you like your new prosthetic, dear?"

"It's..." Adelaide struggled to find the right word, "squishy."

Missus Wakefield beamed and said, "The finest leather filled with the most exquisite goose down."

Charlemagne set down a bowl before Adelaide.

"Thank you," she said.

He bowed his outrageous toque, winked, then took his leave.

The Wakefield family dipped their silver spoons into their soup and ate in silence. The exquisitely-crafted silverware made Adelaide think of Zadie and the other Steampunks. She smiled at the memories. Her parents didn't notice that she was in a more jovial mood this morning. Though, it wouldn't have mattered with what happened next.

Slurping a spoonful, Adelaide noticed that her soup was vibrating. Ripples rushed across the liquid, softly at first, as though a treaded machine was rumbling along outside, but then the ripples grew larger. Then... the sound came.

A soft hum echoed in the distance. Adelaide knew that hum. Her memory kicked into overdrive as the hum grew in volume. Her parents looked up. Clearly they could hear it too. Before either of them could speak, a rumble sounded in the distance and grew. Adelaide's soup vacated the bowl.

An earthquake washed through the house like a single, powerful, ocean wave on the beach. The earthquake shook everything in one, strong pass and then vanished. Adelaide's parents gripped onto the table and gasped. Adelaide stood and studied the house as the tremors subsided. A couple of spilled glasses and one upturned china plate in the cabinet were the only casualties.

"Goodness gracious!" Mister Wakefield exclaimed. "I wasn't aware this area was prone to earthquakes."

"It's not," Adelaide said, simply.

"Oh, that was frightening," Missus Wakefield said.

Adelaide marched to the window and peered at the cloudy sky outside.

The hum returned. The rumble returned. The quake emerged from the bellows of the deep, enveloping everything within an instant. The entire house shook again, far more violently than before. The crystal chandelier overhead swung to inaudible swing music.

Several small crystals fell to the table below. Their silverware and bowls vibrated and fell to the floor. Paintings dropped from the walls. Adelaide staggered away from the window as the glass cracked and pieces smashed.

Her parents leaned over and grabbed their dining chairs for support as the ground wavered beneath their feet. The glass, china display cabinet tilted. Adelaide pushed herself off the wall and tackled her mother to the floor as the cabinet fell and crashed into a million pieces right where she was previously standing. The most expensive ceramics her mother could buy exploded onto the table.

Franklin grabbed his wife and daughter and pulled them into the doorway. The other glass cabinet maintained its footing,[111] but the door ended up swinging open anyway. All

---

111 Mainly to spite its sister cabinet who always thought it was better than it was. "Who was the subpar furniture now, Bernice?" the cabinet would have thought had it could think.

of the crystal ducks vibrated and waddled out to shatter upon the floor. Franklin clutched his two girls against his chest. They kneeled down and took cover beneath the doorframe as the ceiling split by the outer wall.

As abruptly as it erupted, the earthquakes subsided. A few last sneezes of vibration coursed through the grounds, then silence. The house settled, aside from the crystal chandelier swinging to and fro in more of a subdued waltz now, stubbornly holding on to the ceiling.

"Margaret, are you all right?" Franklin asked his wife.

"Y-yes," she replied.

"Adelaide?"

"Still here."

"Oh, that was so dreadful," Margaret said.

"Luther?!" Franklin called down the hall.

"Sir!" came Luther's pained voice.

The Wakefields stood and peered down the darkened hallway. Luther was trapped beneath a fallen armoire. They rushed over to his side. The three of them had difficulty lifting up the solid rectangle of wood.

A familiar voice exclaimed from the kitchen, "Ça alors! Je n'y crois pas! Is everyone all right?"

Chef Charlemagne staggered out into the hallway, clutching a cloth napkin to a deep cut across his forehead. His outrageous toque was nowhere to be found.

"Charlemagne! Can you help?" Franklin asked the approaching chef.

The four of them heaved the furniture off of Luther and shoved it back against the wall. Margaret checked on Luther.

"Are you injured?" she asked. "Where does it hurt?"

"I'm okay, milady," Luther replied. "I... ah..." he winced, "don't think anything's broken."

"I will have to have a word with the contractor about this house," Franklin said.

"Goodness, is it over?" Margaret asked.

"No," Adelaide declared. The others looked to her, surprised at her deciding tone-of-voice. "I'm afraid it's not."

Adelaide rose to her feet and marched to her bedroom. Her room was in about the same state as the rest of the house, which was to say, trashed. Her window was shattered. Cracks had ripped across the outer wall. The pink, polka-dot dresser had been toppled onto the floor. *No great loss,* Adelaide thought to herself. She traversed across the fallen dresser and hopped off in front of her closet.

Franklin and Margaret appeared at the doorway.

"Good," he said. "Stay here where it is safe. Mind the glass and sit on your bed. We will speak to the brigade and ascertain what needs to be done."

He closed and locked the door from the other side. Unconcerned that her father wanted her to stay inside a building that had been compromised from an earthquake instead of exiting the structure to the safer grounds outside, Adelaide pulled on a pair of cloth pants underneath her nightgown followed by a pair of heavy-duty boots over her feet. She shoved her useless prosthetic arm through the sleeve of a leather jacket and put it on.

Adelaide climbed back onto the toppled dresser. Her boots clomped onto the wood. She hopped off, strolled over to her bedroom door, turned the knob, and swung it open, apparently unlocked. Deep in conversation on the other side, her parents, Luther, and Charlemagne gazed at her, shocked.

"What?" Franklin sputtered. "I could have sworn I just locked it."

Adelaide shrugged and said, "I disengaged the tumblers from the bolt days ago. You've been locking an unattached latch."[112]

---

112   Unattached latches were really just locks who were afraid of commitment.

Adelaide trudged down the hall, past the lot of them. Her father blinked his eyes several times, trying to process what she just said.

"What are you doing? You are not to leave this house."

"I have to go," Adelaide said.

Mister Wakefield caught up to Adelaide and grabbed her good arm. "That's enough, young lady. You will listen to your father."

Adelaide rotated her forearm in his grasp, turned the grab around by grabbing his wrist instead, pulled him forward, and shoved his own elbow into his gut with a simple, flawlessly-executed arm lock. Mister Wakefield looked shocked and helpless as Adelaide bent his shoulder down through a subtle turn of the arm lock. He wobbled and had to bend his knee to prevent the leverage from tilting him completely over.

"I've learned a lot from all those people you think are beneath you, father."

A quiet aftershock vibrated the house and stopped. Adelaide released the arm lock and pushed them apart.

"You feel that?" Adelaide implored her father. "Those aren't natural."

"What nonsense is this?" he asked, trying to put on an appearance of consternation, but his look of shock was still fresh as he massaged his elbow.

"Why do you say that?" Missus Wakefield asked as she approached the pair.

"Because I built the machine that's doing this. It's my responsibility."

"You..." Mister Wakefield started then stopped then blustered, "of course it's your fault. How could it be anyone else's? You're just like..." He grunted and growled and turned away.

"I don't understand," Missus Wakefield said. "It's not your obligation. Let someone else take care of it."

Her mother reached a hand out toward her. Adelaide pulled her hand away.

"I don't think anyone else can. Not in time. I feel like... it's my responsibility. Even if someone else is doing this. Even if my family is disappointed in me. "I can fix it. I... *have* to fix it. I will not leave a wrong when I can make it right."

Adelaide turned and walked away. She entered the foyer with cracked walls and broken furniture. Mister Wakefield followed and pointed a wagging finger at her.

"Wait! Adelaide! Wait! You... you..." he searched for something to say, "you walk out that door... you can never come back!"

Adelaide stopped at the open front door. Her determined eyes gazed into the bewildered eyes of her parents. "You do whatever you have to do. I love you."

Adelaide's heavy boots stomped out the door, and she slammed it closed behind her. Her toes paused ever so slightly for a few moments before they turned back. She meekly opened the door again, poked her head inside, and spoke to the surprised group at large.

"And be sure to exit the house as soon as you can. The walls and ceiling are bound to be unstable. It's much safer to stay outside until you can figure out the structural damage... and whatnots..." Adelaide's eyes looked around at the mixture of shocked, depressed, and quaintly curious faces. Her own sheepish face stuttered out, "Umm... yeah... anyways..."

Adelaide threw her own embarrassed self out of the house. She made it quite a few steps down the driveway before she heard the door open behind her, as expected. Unexpectedly, however, it was not her father in the opening.

"Good luck, little miss!" Chef Charlemagne yelled and waved at her from the front door. "I believe in you!"

Adelaide stopped, taken aback. She smiled and nodded at Charlemagne before continuing forward. Her eyes caught a glimpse of Charlemagne stepping to safety outside, briefly

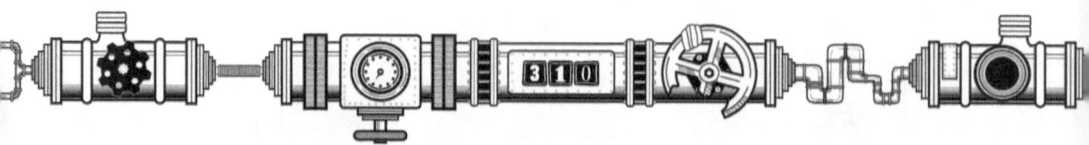

followed by the others, which gave the smallest sense of relief into the shivering girl. Her father stared at her, but amongst the rage and frustration that was clearly etched on his face, there was something else. Something softer. Something... curious. Before Adelaide could think on it any further, she gathered her strength and broke into a run.

The streets beyond were even more chaotic than Adelaide had even imagined. Automobiles had crashed into each other. Panicked horses ran free of their carriages. Street lamps had fallen. Glass fragments sparkled everywhere. A building's brick facade had broken free and smashed into the asphalt. Walls that were upright were now downleft.

Adelaide kept her brisk pace, but she had to take her steps carefully. Her feet hopped and skipped in between debris. Bricks, glass, and other pieces of broken things turned the streets into a minefield. Gobsmacked[113] at the destruction, Adelaide was nevertheless pleased to see that all of the buildings watching the streets had survived. Some were missing their walls and bricks, of course, but they still stood.

Adelaide tried to continue looking on the bright side of things as she rushed her way down the sidewalks. People seemed to be pulling through this disaster. They helped each other and pulled each other up. She ran past groups of them as they filtered about, standing outside their compromised buildings, gazing at the devastation. Then she saw others that weren't as lucky. Some were being pulled out of the wreckage, bloodied and bruised.

Was this Adelaide's fault? Was her machine really the cause of all this? She ran all the harder toward where she believed ground zero to be.

The sign for Newcomen University had cracked into pieces and fallen to the ground. Adelaide stepped over it and ran to the

---

113 Surprised. On another note, have you ever tried to smack a Gob? They really don't like that.

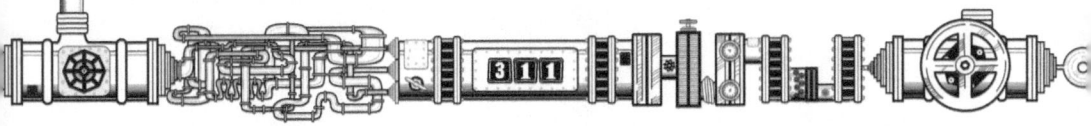

wreckage of the Science building she had inadvertently destroyed. She ignored the stitch pounding painfully in her side and stopped before the rubble. Most of the debris had been cleared off. A hole was where the basement used to be.

Adelaide couldn't see any evidence that her generator had survived the destruction, or that it had been running anytime afterwards. There were no noticeable cracks or damage in the earth, at least no more than the rest of the city. No ripples in the dirt. No marks that this was the center of it all. If her generator did survive, it was no longer here. Either the broken remains were carted off with the rest of the debris, or... could someone have taken it? Could it have been...

Adelaide shook her head of the thoughts she didn't like thinking. Regardless, first things first: she needed to find out where the earthquakes were coming from in the city, then she could find out if her machine was truly the cause.

Newcomen University was not ground zero like she had thought it was. It wasn't likely that the quakes had originated above ground, even if the remains of her machine had been carted off and dumped somewhere along with the rest of the debris from the Science building. Adelaide held out hope, just a teeny, tiny slice of hope, that her machine might not be the cause. Perhaps she could find clues underground, if there was still an underground around to bound around in.

Her boots clomped into the grass and sprinted away from the campus. She turned past *The Book Wyrm*, thanked the dragon gods above that the store and dragon statue still stood, then found an elevator built into the sidewalk. Adelaide wasn't sure if the lift was still working after the earthquakes, but she had no idea where a set of stairs might be. She didn't need to search either, for the lift dinged into place. Adelaide scraped open the doors and scraped them back closed behind her. Through the gate, she saw the outline of a mustached someone running toward her, but the

lift lowered into the depths. The cables snapped, crackled, popped, and wiggle wobbled, but it functioned. It lowered her into the Lowers.

Adelaide gazed through the protective gate. A massive monopoly of naturally-formed caverns lied beyond along with all of the complexes of homes, apartments, and dwellings that comprised Lower Central. She studied the cavern walls beyond as the lift descended. She couldn't see any ripples or carvings in the earth that indicated a direction of the quakes.

As the lift clanged at the bottom, Adelaide scraped open the doors and jumped out. Lower Central survived better than the surface, but chunks of tile and concrete supports had fallen onto the little wooden buildings below. People were picking up the broken remains of their livelihoods. Adelaide didn't know where to look or where to go. She ran forward, took a turn, then stopped before one of the many tunnel entrances.

"Steampunks," a voice called from just off to the side.

Adelaide looked around, searching for the sound. It was a man she recognized. "Blood Claw Johnny," she greeted with more than a little hesitation.

"Oh, it's just Johnny now. Ain't no more Blood Claws." His ragged, skinny face looked pale. He was sitting on the dirt, leaning back against the curving wall of the tunnel entrance. Where there was indignant life oozing out of the young man's pores before, now there was just solemn acceptance. "Enoch saw to that."

Adelaide winced and muttered, "I'm sorry."

"He let a few of us live if we pledged our loyalty to him. Easy choice, really."

Adelaide kneeled down next to Johnny and looked into his eyes. While she had no love for the man, she couldn't help but feel sorry for the broken shell wrapped in tattered rags that sat before her now. "Are you okay?"

Johnny shrugged. "I got my scars. Fared better than others. Probably better than you, now that I think about it."

Adelaide stood, defensive. "How do you mean?"

"Goldens put out a bounty on your heads. All the punks. If you haven't met anybody tryin' to collect yet, you will soon."

Adelaide's muscles tightened. "Are you a bounty hunter now, Johnny?"

Johnny let out a wheezing scoff. "Nah. I ain't got the energy for that no more." Adelaide relaxed, but Johnny's tired face flashed her a devious smile. "Some of my buddies that made it through though," he said in a grating tone, "they were happy to take the job."

Johnny nodded to his side. Adelaide noticed figures moving toward them through the maze of buildings. She recognized the two former Blood Claws who used to flank Johnny like his own personal cronies. In the tunnel behind her, two more dangerous-looking fellows appeared around the bend. Adelaide didn't recognize them, but she did recognize the Blood Claw tattoos on their necks. Both had recent scars and black marks crossing out the ink, but the red stubbornly shone through.

"Run, run, little Steampunk," Johnny said. "Run."

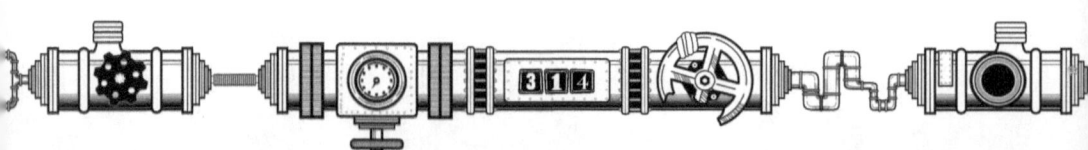

Chapter 25

Losing Ground

Unexpectedly, even to herself, Adelaide took the advice of the dullard[114] formerly known as Blood Claw Johnny. She ran. The four, former Blood Claws gave chase. Adelaide jumped over chunks of rocks and debris fallen onto the streets and alleyways in Lower Central. She dashed in between the homes and buildings then pushed between a group of surprised folks. Through the crowds she ran. It was at this moment that Adelaide became incredibly aware of the stitch pounding in her side, and she quite regretted her earlier run to the University campus above.

"Oi!" Winston called. He was sitting on the side of a fence alongside some of his friends. They shoved sunflower seeds into their hungry mouths and spit the shells at anyone close by, including each other.

---

114 Contrary to popular belief, the first dullard was not a slow or stupid person, but was, in fact, the result of a love affair between a curious mallard and a doorknob.

Adelaide didn't have time to give him so much as a glance before she sprinted past, but Winston did as he glanced from her to her pursuers. Without another moment's hesitation, Winston kicked over a garbage can into the street. The front two Blood Claws plowed right into it and fell over with a thud. The back two were tripped up and slowed down over their fellows.

Winston and the orphans cackled. When the former Blood Claws glared up at them, they scarpered every which way. The adults attempted chasing after them, but they couldn't even think of who to go after first before all the kids vanished behind doors and alleyways. The Blood Claws changed targets again and chased Adelaide's trail.

A mustachioed shadow lurched out from an alleyway and shoulder-tackled the last Blood Claw that was trailing behind. "Away with you, scoundrel!"

Far ahead, Adelaide couldn't hear the extra commotion from the mysterious rescuer and ran down a tunnel carved into the cavern wall. The concrete-reinforced corridors gave way to earthen cylinders. Adelaide took a left then a right then a middle. Her attempt at trying to lose her pursuers got her a little lost too.

She squeezed through a doorway and stopped to listen for any signs of pursuit. Nothing. Winston had made for an excellent distraction. She would have to buy him a bunch of éclairs[115] at some point. The earth vibrated beneath her feet again. The pastry buying would have to wait.

The real question now was: where should she go? *The quakes were stronger on the surface than underground. Did that mean the machine was up top? But that didn't make any sense. Any*

---

115 Contrary to popular belief, the first éclair was unaccented, but it always felt cuter than all the other pastries, thus it treated itself to an acute. Not to be outdone, bear claws began wearing top hats until the Great Dough Rebellion, which led to a shortage crisis on fashionable headwear. The economy never fully recovered.

above ground earth shaking would be fairly limited to the area around it, right? It had to be under the ground to expand in such devastation, right? It just had to be. But where?

The sounds of heavy feet pounding into the dirt echoed up the tunnel, and three former Blood Claws came into view. She heard someone calling her name from far behind, but she paid no attention to it. The chase was on again.

Adelaide took off and tried to lose them in the twists and turns. After the eighteenth twist and/or turn down in the labyrinth of tunnels that Adelaide was barely cognizant she was running around in, a few of the various odds and ends became familiar to her. The loud sound of rushing water echoed as she reached the end of an odd intersection, which was really more of a hole in the floor. She remembered this place very well and didn't stop before hopping inside the hole.

She landed in a metal trough with a fast current of one-foot-deep water, rushing down a slope. She expertly balanced on her feet and slid down the current. The trough twisted and turned and topsyed and turveyed and ended abruptly with a steep drop into a massive chamber. After a jump off the end of the tunnel into open air, her lone hand grabbed onto a metal chain hanging from the ceiling of the tall chamber. Adelaide swung over the empty space and hopped off onto a raised platform three stories up on the chamber's side.

Adelaide didn't even have to look to know what would happen next, but a smile creased her cheeks all the same. The former Blood Claws' flailing bottoms flew out of the pipe and dropped three stories into a five-foot, metal channel of water. They clonked onto the channel's bottom and flushed into the exit pipe.

Adelaide couldn't help but smirk before she ran off. Soon, she entered a gigantic, five-story chamber serving as an intersection of steam pipes. Massive machines built into the walls and bolted to the floor whirred, clanked, and issued forth puffs of heated air. Adelaide looked up and gazed at the covered

platform comprising the Steampunks hideout five stories above. She wondered if she would find her friends up there, waiting for her.

Adelaide's useless, feather-filled prosthetic wouldn't grapple her way up this time around, so she stepped toward a generator tooting out steam two rows in, retrieved the long, metal cable with the loop on the end, put her foot inside, and tugged hard on the cable extending all the way up to the hideout, hoping that Baxter had repaired it. The motor overhead whirred and retracted the cable, pulling her along with it up high into the chamber. She breathed in the even warmer air as she dangled above the generators.

Her mind tried to stamp out expectations, but her heart filled with hope and anticipation of finally seeing her adopted family again. Even more so, she wanted her faith in her friends to be vindicated. She wanted Zadie to be sitting in her recliner, just as grumpy as always and just as confused about the earthquakes as much as everyone else.

The cable retracted into the spool. Adelaide's foot in the cable loop dangled at equal height right next to the hideout's platform. She opened her eyes to give her friends a warm welcome. She wanted to think of some clever speech to say, but all Adelaide could think to say was, "Howdy-yuhhh..."

The response to her presence was not what she expected. The people she met at the Steampunks hideout were also not whom she expected. They also were not Steampunks.

"Well, it's about time," said a scratchy, high-pitched, male voice. His skin sparkled from the array of gaudy jewelry pasted on every inch of him, and his eye bulged behind a single, and quite unnecessary, golden monocle. Plated, the screechy yet formidable leader of the Goldens gang, sat in Zadie's plushy chair with his arms crossed.

His eyes gazed at the sudden appearance of Adelaide in the Steampunks hideout. His golden monocle would have made it appear that he was studying her closely, except that

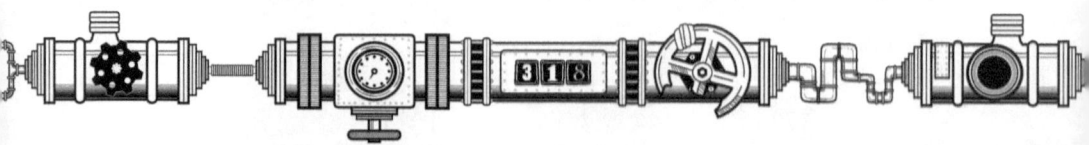

everyone in attendance knew that he could barely see with that gaudy thing on his face. "Nice of you to join us."

Beefstick, the colossal monstrosity of a man that Adelaide was still surprised she managed to beat in an arm wrestling contest, grabbed Adelaide by the scruff of her neck. She suppressed a meow as he yanked her out of the cable transport and shoved her onto the platform proper. She fell at the feet of Plated. However, she couldn't suppress a scoff as her face fell close to Plated's shoes. Even his sneakers were gold-painted and ridiculous-looking. His toes must have been suffocating in the now-opposite-of-breathable fabric.

Another glint of gold caught her eye. The jewelry box she made for Lillian sparkled on the coffee table beside Plated. A sudden longing filled her thoughts and distracted her from her current predicament.

"Where are the others?" Plated asked.

Adelaide tried to think of something dry and wry to reply, but all she could do was stare at his gaudily painted shoes. Even the other Goldens gang members, who were too unimportant for Adelaide to give nicknames to, wore different pairs of painted plops. Although, once her attention shifted past the shoes, she noticed that there was another figure on the floor.

"Phineas!" Adelaide said.

She crawled over to the collapsed, elderly man lying near the edge of the platform, close to the hammocks suspended beyond. His monstrous, metal arms and chair harness were nowhere to be seen. He looked so helpless without them and with just his skinny, frail legs that were unable to support him. Phineas opened his eyes. As she embraced him, he returned the gesture and wrapped his arms around her.

Phineas grunted, "What ye doin' here, girl?"

"What happened?" she asked. "Where are your mechanical arms? Did they take them?"

"Outrageous!" Plated huffed. "We would never pick on a cripple. Well, besides you, of course. And I suppose the old man,

a bit. But still, the Goldens have standards. He was like that when we found him, crawling around the tunnels. Lost and useless. Well, not entirely, I suppose. He did lead us here. Didn't even take that much convincing."

Adelaide felt that the cuts and bruises across Phineas' face communicated otherwise, but Phineas' face also hinted that there was perhaps more to the story. He didn't look ashamed or hurt. His expression looked like Zadie's when she was calling someone's bluff at cards. The same face she made before she won the pot.

"And now we've found you at your own hideout," Plated continued. "Not so hidden anymore, is it? And... you actually *live* here? Like... *live* here?"

"That's what I first thought too," Adelaide replied.

"How dreadful. I'd almost feel sorry for you, if I didn't want to kill you already. No wonder it was so hard to find this place before. Couldn't imagine anyone would want to live in such a place on purpose."

"It has its charms."

"Yes, I imagine tetanus can be quite charming to a gutter rat. Still, I only have one of the five. I'd like to complete the whole set."

"I don't know where the others are."

"Why don't I believe you?"

Adelaide's face screwed up in confusion. "How would I know? I'm not in your brain."

"Aren't you?"

"Aren't I... what?"

"I..." Plated's face screwed up in confusion, "I lost where I was going with that."

"Can't blame you."

"*You're* going to be lost when I'm done with you."

Adelaide sighed. "You're really not good at this intimidation thing, are you?"

"I..." Plated glanced at Beefstick and continued, "I thought I was doing pretty well, wasn't I?"

"Yeah, boss," Beefstick replied. "Very scary. Super shiny."

"Thank you. I am the shiniest."

"Is that slang for strange?" Adelaide asked.

Beefstick picked her up by the scuff of the neck and shook. Adelaide couldn't help but uttering out a "meow" this time.

"Release her, cretin!" came a voice. Everyone turned in surprise to see an enraged Franklin Wakefield wagging a finger and marching out of a side tunnel. "If you scallywags know what is good for you, you shall put my daughter down and cease this nonsense."

Everyone stared at him.

"I am not a man prone to violence," he continued while moving his fists around in circles close to his face, "but I am no stranger to the art of fisticuffs."

Beefstick looked at his dangling prisoner, Adelaide, and silently mouthed, "*Fisticuffs?*" Adelaide simply shrugged to the best of her dangling ability.

Franklin's feet did a little jig and pointed outwards which clearly communicated that he knew how to float like a bee, but that didn't help him much as a Goldens thug stepped up behind him and clocked Franklin over the head with a lead pipe. His lips kissed the rug.

"Stop!" Adelaide cried. "Don't hurt him!"

Plated scoffed as his eyes glanced from Adelaide to Franklin and back. "So you're his daughter? You know, somehow, I didn't think this street rat even had a father. I thought she was just spawned out of the sewers."

"Rude."

"Quite so," Franklin added from his position on the floor. He held on to the carpet as stars shone in his eyes, and his dizziness made the ground appear to rock back and forth. Then the ground really did rock back and forth.

An overwhelming hum echoed as the entire chamber shook beneath their feet. Beefstick let go of Adelaide, and she flopped down to the carpeted platform. The shaking and quaking forced the big man down to his knees as well.

A single, tremendous crack ripped through the ceiling and raced down the right wall. A steam pipe running across split open, spilling its boiling vapor over the two Goldens standing by. They screamed and crawled away. The platform's supports, welded into the chamber wall, split along the right side.

Adelaide reached for Phineas' hand, and Franklin made slow and shaky progress in crawling toward his daughter.

"Father! What are you doing here?"

"I... well, I could not very well let my child race off toward unknown dangers alone, or... at least... not again."

As the earthquake quieted and the shaking stopped, Adelaide looked from the edge of the platform to the hammocks swinging freely from the chains attached to the ceiling above. Small splits in the concrete ran along the left wall and side supports. Adelaide's mind raced with worry. Pretty soon with that damage, only the back edge of the platformed hideout would be supported. After a few more moments of ponderings, Adelaide's expression turned from frightened to calculating within an instant.

"What in the blazes is happening with these earthquakes?!" Plated screeched at no one in particular.

Beefstick still took it upon himself to answer though. "Seismic vibrations occur when the earth's tectonic plates shift against each other, sometimes causing extreme quakes or movement above."

Plated turned his incredulous monocle on the man. "What?"

Adelaide raised herself to her knees. She took Phineas' strong hand and placed his fingers around one of the chain supports connecting the suspended hammocks to the ceiling.

She patted his hand, silently communicating for him to stay there.

She did the same for her father on the next hammock. His expression was far less agreeable, but she whispered to him, "Trust me." Slowly, very slowly, he nodded and kept his hand on the hammock chain. His other hand rubbed the growing knot on the back of his head.

"Alright," Adelaide called to the Goldens, "I give up. I'll tell you everything you want to know." She got to her feet and began jumping up and down near the platform's edge.

"Finally," Plated said. "You're starting to see reason and understand my—why are you hopping up and down?"

"Because..." Adelaide's lungs squeezed out a couple of syllables every time her feet landed on the carpet, "I'm just... so in... awe of... your... presence... you're so... magni... ficent... and... shiny..."

"Why thank you. I try."

Franklin Wakefield's eyes glanced from his daughter to the floor she was bouncing on. The entire platform creaked and groaned. The left corner bent and lowered ever so slightly. His eyebrows widened in recognition.

"Oh, yes," Franklin said. "I agree." He stood up and started bouncing up and down on the balls of his feet. "He is... very... shiny... perhaps... the... shiniest..."

"How nice of you to say. I... wait, just stop that. It's annoying." His eyes widened in shock as the entire platform clonked and scraped along the concrete bricks. "Stop them from doing that."

Beefstick grabbed Adelaide by the arm.

"Unhand... me!" Adelaide cried.

Beefstick neither understood the pun nor seemed to notice that he gripped onto a fake, leathery hand. He pulled back with all his might as Adelaide jumped. The dainty prosthetic did not care for the situation at all and decided it would rather detach entirely. The straps pulled apart, and the entire arm slipped out of Adelaide's sleeve.

Apparently, Beefstick had completely forgotten that Adelaide wore a prosthetic, and the big, tough, burly man let out a shriek of shock. Not a manly, bassy shout of defiance, it was shrill and ear-piercing, like a soprano choir of mice squeaking into the opera's third act crescendo.

She fell backwards, and he fell backwards. They both crashed onto the platform at the same time. The resultant bounce forced Franklin to collapse to his knees. The combined force ripped the fragile supports out of the left side wall, and the platform fell.

The Steampunks hideout, with all of the carpets, furniture, machines, bits and bobs, and unfriendly gang members, suddenly had no front supports holding it up against the force of gravity. With one, burly hand still gripping onto the hammock, Phineas grabbed the scruff of Adelaide's neck with his other as Adelaide meowed. He held them both up onto the chain swinging from the ceiling. Franklin gripped both hands onto his hammock as the floor beneath them fell away. His mustache nearly curled itself back into his nostrils in shock.

With a stubbornness that exemplified the spirit of the Steampunks, the hideout floor remained attached on one corner of the wall, making the large, metal grate tilt downwards in a violent slope three stories below until it crashed into the tops of the tallest generators at the chamber's bottom. Several of the Goldens gang members slid and fell into the darkness below, along with the furniture, devices, and other random Punks' belongings.

Adelaide winced. A glint of gold flashed before her eyes. Her jewelry box that was sitting on the coffee table fell through the air along with the coffee table itself. The last surviving bit of her memorabilia with Lillian fell. The box shattered upon the dark floor far below. A tremendous sense of loss flooded through her as Phineas lifted her up with one arm and threw her into the hammock.

Plated, Beefstick, and three of the unimportant Goldens hung on to the tilted, metal-grated floor. Their fingers dug into the small holes, holding themselves up as their heads dodged falling pieces of furniture and debris.

"Punks!" Plated yelled.

Phineas pulled Adelaide's arm onto his shoulder. Face-to-face, he whispered, "Zadie and the others are holed up in the Junction. Get them out. Quick as ye can."

"What about you?" Adelaide asked.

"I'll be fine from here, but they need you. Get goin', before it's too late," he said as he began swinging across. With a yank, a pull, a heave, and a squeak, he tossed Adelaide's body through the air. She crash landed onto the opening of a small, maintenance tunnel entrance in the chamber's fourth floor.

"Adelaide!" her father yelled after her. "Are you all right?!"

She turned back to both of the older gentlemen swinging from the ceiling. "Yes, but... I can't leave you two!"

"Punks!" Plated shouted as his jewelry-laden fingers dug into the metal grated floor below them and climbed upwards.

Phineas snorted in the direction of Franklin. "I've got the mustache. Go!"

She looked to her father, aka *the mustache*. He nodded. "Get to safety! I will find you later!"

Adelaide nodded, staggered to her feet, and ran down the tunnel.

Chapter 26

Brass Brawls

The ever-so-familiar shout of "Punks" followed Adelaide through the tunnels. This direction was somewhat familiar to her as well, but the Steampunks had rarely traveled through these passages before. They normally stuck to the ones attached directly to their hideout one story above. Still, with one intersection rising upwards, she felt that they were going to intersect eventually. And now she knew where to go.

Twisting, turning tunnels led Adelaide to passages more traveled, except that this time, she had uninvited solicitors. Plated, Beefstick, and three extra Goldens panted and peered out from a tunnel intersection several dozen feet ahead.

"She's here!" Plated shouted. "To me, my nuggets!"

An earthquake rippled through the tunnel. Strangely enough, Adelaide felt it vibrating through the steam pipes more than the earth itself. She thought about that for a second as the solid, reverberating hum echoed so loudly she could nearly feel it inside her own brain. Steampunk and

Goldens alike staggered and struggled to find their footing. The tunnel, while it felt like it was dancing of its own volition, remained quite intact. The moment the humming and vibrating subsided, Adelaide took off. A moment later, the Goldens were in pursuit.

Adelaide climbed inside a hastily cut-open section of the wall with pipes and cables diverted within where the passage traversed over an uneven, unlevel, unsafe, metal-grated floor, which looked down on a flowing trough of water below. Adelaide ducked under a broken pipe and crawled along the creaking metal. She chanced a glance back to see the Goldens following, all crawling over the metal grate and ducking underneath pipes, cables, and jagged rocks.

Unimportant Golden number three, traveling in the back of the pack, got his foot stuck in a broken piece of the metal-grated floor. He tugged and ripped it free, ripping a chunk out of the floor in the process. The portion of the grate around his crawling body collapsed. He fell into the metal trough of water and disappeared in the rushing current below.

Adelaide hopped down from the passage and into an intersecting utility tunnel. The pipes led out from the passage and out and around and eventually over to a circular chamber built into the circular wall. She scraped open the stash's massive door and closed it behind her.

Inside the watertight chamber, Adelaide could just barely hear the pounding of fists on the other side, as well as a loud, disappointed voice shouting, "You can't hide in there forever!" Which was ironic because Adelaide had no intention of hiding.

Her muscle memory reached out into the dark and found the switch of a desk lamp she must have turned on and off a thousand times before. The flickering bulb shone upon a workbench with her upgraded, mechanical arm lying on top. Brass, steel, copper, and iron melded together in an even more impressive display of engineering than her previous appendage. Copper wiring and steel pipes and clear tubes led from the arm

to a slimmed down yet even more bulbous generator backpack, equipped with an oscillating engine of Adelaide's own design.

Several feet away, a messy pile of the most random clothing the Steampunks had ever stolen laid on top of a broken desk. Adelaide had never repaired that desk nor found a use for all of the random clothing. That was, until now. More than her arm required an upgrade, as her ripped sleeves and pants and nightdress would attest.

There was a leak in the arm's pressure valve line that Adelaide had struggled to find before when she was working on her creation. The good thing about her solitary confinement was that it gave her a lot of time to think, and she spent that time thinking about how to rebuild her mechanical arm purely by the strength of her imagination. She knew how to fix it. As the angry men outside continued to pound upon the door, the only question left was: did she have enough time?

Beefstick pushed against the stash door's locked hand wheel. Even with his considerable strength, the welded metal remained firmly in place. He picked up a rock from the tunnel floor and slammed it against the spoke. Nothing. They had been at it for fifteen minutes, and the fairly unwrinkled brain of Beefstick had run out of ideas.

Plated stood behind him and tapped his foot impatiently. "Come on! What am I paying you for?!"

Unimportant Golden number one leaned back against the curved tunnel wall with his eyes closed, definitely not asleep and pretending otherwise. Meanwhile, Unimportant

Golden number two stood dumbly by the intersection with his finger up his nose. He retrieved a chunk from inside. Sniff.

Unseen by the others, a mustachioed shadow creeped through the tunnel behind them. Franklin emerged and smashed a metal pipe into the back of Unimportant Golden number two's head. The fodder crumpled, unconscious.

"You leave my daughter alone, you knaves," Franklin growled as he brandished the pipe toward Plated, "or I shall be forced to treat you all with similar consequences forthwith."

Plated stared at him. "What?"

Beefstick shook his meaty head. Unimportant Golden number one blinked himself awake.

"I…" Franklin looked at their confused faces. "I shall be forced to use unsavory levels of force if you three do not vacate yourselves from these premises immediately."

Plated rolled his eyes and nodded toward Beefstick, who promptly slapped the pipe out of Franklin's hands and wrapped a ham-shaped hand around his throat.

Plated smiled and stepped toward the hatch. "Steampunk! You hear this?!" He nodded at Beefstick again, who shook Franklin by the throat until he made gurgling/coughing noises. "We got your daddy out here! Open the door now! The Steampunks owe me a debt, and I demand payment!"

His incessant screeching seemed to work. The muffled sound of metal grinding against metal rang out from within. The door unlocked. The massive, circular portal scraped against the floor and slowly swung open. Lightless, the dark inside seemed to swallow the dim light from the tunnel outside. The overwhelming silence swallowed everything else.

With his hand still wrapped around Franklin's throat, Beefstick took a tentative step inside the pitch-black stash. Mechanical whirring and chugging sounds echoed, bouncing around the metal container. He looked around for the source of the noise. It found him first.

The fist of Adelaide's new, mechanical arm shot out like a rocket from within the darkness. Clenched, metal phalanges smashed into his jaw. His feet stood in place while his head went backwards. Slamming hard on the floor outside the stash, Beefstick laid unconscious and moved no more. Unfortunately, Franklin's throat followed the big man's hand, and he was thrown to the ground as well.

The cable connected to the flying fist retracted. Adelaide stepped out of the darkness. Her frilly dress had been replaced by a pair of black jeans and a t-shirt that had seen its fair share of dirt, grease, grime, and blowtorches. Her ripped, dark leather jacket sleeve had been cut off above the bicep area, showcasing her shiny, new, mechanical arm.

A pair of dark-tinted goggles covered her eyes. Minutes earlier, after she pulled on the goggles and checked out her own reflection, she thought to herself, *she made this look good*.

Her father, once he lifted his bleary head from the ground, could do nothing but gaze upon his daughter.

Adelaide's hand cable stopped retracting with two-feet of cable left. She spun her metal hand around herself like it was a medieval flail, only she traded a stick for her arm, a chain for her unspooled cable, and a spiky ball of death for her metal fingers and palm.[116] She smacked her flail hand into the unsuspecting face of Plated, smashing his nonsensical monocle into a million pieces.

Adelaide wound up her hand flail into a flying spin again and advanced forward. Unimportant Golden number one proved to be as useless as his nickname. Adelaide released more cable and threw her hand at him. The cable wrapped around his neck, and her floating hand caught it in a lock. His look of surprise and fear was the most emotion he had shown all day, but it didn't last long as the cable retracted fast

---

116 Which was more frightening between a medieval flail and a young girl's flying, amputated hand would be a point of discussion amongst scholars for centuries.

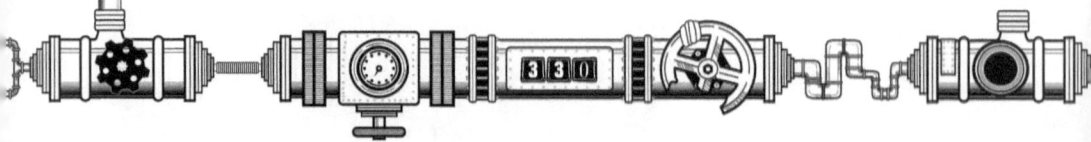

into Adelaide's arm. She turned her arm and forced his face to meet her mechanical elbow at a velocity far more than he would have preferred. He went out like a light. Adelaide released him and retracted her hand into her wrist.

"Punk!" Plated shouted.

Plated began withdrawing a revolver that was, naturally, also painted gold, but it had an absurdly long and unnecessary twelve-inch-long barrel stuck in his trousers. He attempted to point it at her face just as she approached, but Adelaide was faster as her fleshy fingers worked the control panels on her chestplate. Her mechanical fingers wrapped around the long barrel and squeezed, crumpling the barrel.

Plated yelled as her pinky crushed the cylinder against both the trigger and his finger. Adelaide ripped the revolver from his grasp. The destroyed weapon bounced inside the stash to live along with all of the other broken junk.

The monocled menace roared with pain and fury before reaching back with his uninjured hand. He smashed a strong gut punch right into Adelaide's ribs. She collapsed down to her knee, gasping for breath. The many, varied, and gaudy rings adorning each of his fingers made a sizable impression on her sternum. Stars flew before her eyes.

Plated smiled with gleeful vengeance and gave a short, nasally cackle. Adelaide felt he shouldn't have wasted his time gloating until the fight was finished. Now, it was her turn.

Her mechanical arm rotated back before launching forward, giving a steam-powered uppercut of her own right into his ribs. The pistons on her metal arm shot up and extended the forearm from the elbow in a foot of sudden, air-pressured force.

Plated's body flew up into the air. He smacked into the tunnel ceiling before falling to the hard ground at Adelaide's feet. Not quite unconscious, but not quite conscious either, Plated just sort of groaned and wobbled. Adelaide rose to standing height. Her mechanical hand reached down and grabbed Plated by the collar.

"You want payment?" Adelaide asked calmly with a hint of underlying menace.

Her generator-powered arm dragged him along the floor with ease. His limp body and floppy legs gave no opposition. She stopped before the entrance to the stash.

"Here," she continued. "This is everything we've ever owned. You can have it all."

Her mechanical arm locked, cocked, and exploded forward. Plated's body flew inside the darkened chamber. He crashed into a variety of metal, pointy-sounding objects.

Adelaide shut the door and cranked the hand wheel. It spun to a stop, but her mechanical hand continued shoving. The exhaust pipe poking out just above the collar near the back of her neck choked out a puff of steam. The sturdy, welded metal that withstood fifteen minutes of hammering by the man known as Beefstick snapped. In three seconds, Adelaide broke the wheel.

"Consider our debt paid."

After a few moments, Adelaide remembered that her father was watching her. She gently turned around and looked back to him.

Franklin raised himself to his knees on the floor and looked up to his daughter. "Adelaide…"

"Are you all right?" she asked.

"I…" he rubbed the bruise in the shape of a hand along his neck, and then he rubbed the knot on the back of his head, "I believe so, but why on earth are all these gangsters after you? These filthy hooligans are all over the place."

"It's a long story, filled with me doing things you wouldn't approve of." Adelaide grabbed him by the elbow and helped him to his feet. She stared at him as her mouth opened and closed several times. "Father, I… I'm sorry. I'm a *filthy hooligan* too… and dirty and rough and unladylike… and not the daughter I know you wanted—"

"You..." Franklin's eyes studied his daughter's mechanical arm, goggles, and leather jacket. "You are so much more than I ever could have expected. I have been trying desperately to protect you from the world, but... perhaps I had it the wrong way round."

"Look..." She misinterpreted his softened expression. "I know you're disappointed in me. I know I've made mistakes. But I was just hoping that—"

Adelaide's father cut her off by grabbing her shoulders and embracing her in a fierce hug. Adelaide yelped before she realized what was happening.

"My disappointment," he began, "has only been in myself. I thought I lost you, and I... I pushed you away." He pushed her to arm's length to look her in the eyes. "I... you remind me so much of my father. And... of me."

Adelaide's eyes blinked away tears.

"Now," he coughed and shrugged to get rid of all those troublesome emotions before he continued, "where is this machine that is causing such a ruckus?"

She snorted and smiled at him. After staring into his eyes, the kindest she's seen in years, her good hand patted his elbow. "You need to get back to the surface."

"I could not simply leave—"

"I have to do this alone. They won't even talk to us if you're with me. And where's Phineas? Did he get out?"

"We parted ways when he said he could make it on his own."

"Yeah, but he can't walk without his prosthetics. Goodness, he'd have to crawl his way out." She sighed. "He pretends like he doesn't want or need any help, even when he does." Adelaide smirked and snorted. "Maybe we're related to him."

Franklin cocked his head before he gave a near identical snort to his daughter. "I shall find this Phineas fellow while you... you do what you need to do." He snorted again and studied his daughter for perhaps the very first time. "I... I suppose I have not

been much help to you down here after all, have I?" He laughed. "You are far more capable than I could ever dream."

He hugged her close again.

"You stop this," he said with his face buried in her hair, "and I will see you after."

"Can you find your way?" Adelaide asked.

"Ha, that much, I can manage. You stay safe."

"I will."

After a moment, Adelaide tore herself from her father and walked away. He stood there and watched her disappear down a bend.

She heard him softly mutter in the echoing tunnel, "Stay safe. My daughter."

Chapter 27

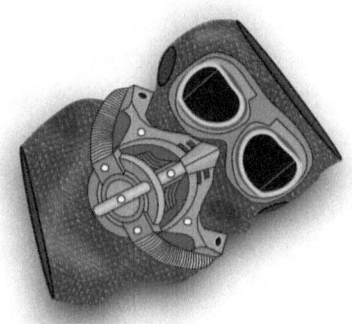

The Junction

Interminable time passed as Adelaide marched through the tunnels. Her feet knew the way, so she let them lead. That let her mind wander and process the colossal number of ponderings, mullings, ruminatings, and various ouchies that she had no time for previously, and she really didn't like what she found. There was really only one answer to the problems facing her, but accepting it was something else.

Adelaide pushed the dark-tinted goggles up on her forehead. Her feet found a tunnel that ended at a T-intersection with a tremendously thick, metal door built into a massively bodacious, metal wall. The door was closed tight with a handwheel locking mechanism. The determined girl with the mechanical arm stepped up to the door and banged her metal fingers against the metal portal. She stared at the heavy, multi-layered speakeasy slide in the door and waited for it to open, which it did. A familiar set of eyes looked around from beyond the slide.

"Adelaide!" came Harriet's muffled voice.

The speakeasy slammed closed before Adelaide could reply. Sounds of the handwheel locking mechanism turning and cranking from the other side echoed within the metal. The door scraped inwards. Chugs, whomps, whirs, screeches, and roars reverberated from within.

Harriet engulfed Adelaide in a bone-squishing hug. "We've missed you so much!"

"I've missed you too," Adelaide mumbled beneath the oppressive affection.

Harriet let Adelaide breathe only long enough to drag her inside and scrape the massive door closed behind them. Adelaide had forgotten how big the Junction was. Every pipe traveling throughout all of Parsons City seemed to meet in this one place, built near perfectly below the center of the Upper District. Despite her limited time spent in this place before, Adelaide remembered it quite well; although, there were several new additions to the chamber, confirming Adelaide's suspicions and plopping a bucket of rocks in her stomach.

Adelaide's oscillating generator, her inadvertent earthquake machine, stared at her. A rebuilt, much larger version had been welded onto the floor as well as to the four, large pipes extending vertically in the center of the chamber. Cables connected her machine to a second generator by the west wall of pipes. More connected to a third generator by the east wall. Even more cables ran overhead and got lost within the spiderweb of pipes and tubes ascending into the infinite blackness of the colossal chamber.

Sitting with his back against the east wall, Jules stood up at Adelaide's presence. He nodded at her and gave a slight bow. Adelaide returned the warm gesture from the silent guardian. Crouching next to and almost inside the vertical pipes in the chamber's middle, Baxter wrestled with a set of cables snaking in between the cylinders. After he happened to glance back, he perked up, sat up, and waved at Adelaide.

"Hey!" Baxter said. "You're back! Did you see what we did? We rebuilt your thing!" He stood up and dusted off his trousers. His jovial expression seemed completely oblivious to Adelaide's disappointment.

"I saw," Adelaide droned.

"Well, not really *rebuilt*," he continued. "We wouldn't know how to fully rebuild it, but we borrowed some of that digging equipment the city crews left over 'round midnight one night. Dug up the machine and everything else that looked important. Got it running again. Welded it to the floor. Hooked it all up. It survived that building collapse super well, so we didn't need to think on it too much."

"I wish you *had* thought on it."

Overhead, a monstrous shape descended down from the crisscrossing pipes. The gargantuan, mechanical arm harness that had previously belonged to Phineas grabbed onto the pipes and swung across. Strapped inside the chair harness and working the arms from inside was the rebellious thief: Adelaide's old friend, Zadie.

Hanging by a monstrous hand from a large pipe twenty feet in the air directly above the group, Zadie looked down at them and said simply, "Adelaide."

She swung down and landed with a slam on one, gargantuan, metal fist before her.

"Zadie," Adelaide greeted with neither warmth nor coldness.

"What are you doing here?" Zadie asked as her mechanical arms set her legs down to the floor before the arms stretched around her, forming a metal, supportive barricade.

Harriet, Baxter, and Jules all gathered 'round. The Steampunks were together once again. Adelaide wished she could feel happy about that.

"I'm here to turn my machine off," Adelaide said.

"Ain't yours no more," Zadie said. "What is scavenged belongs to the scavenger."

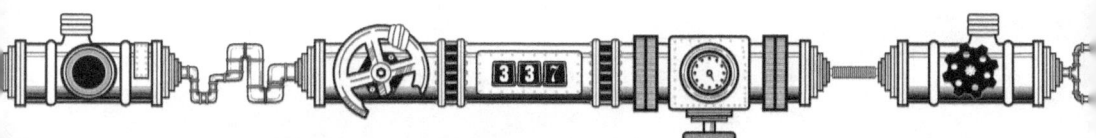

"Not when an earthquake tears through my parents' house," Adelaide said.

Harriet gasped and swatted Zadie on the metal arm. "I thought you said it was just going to mess up the mayor's mansion, and there'd be time to get everyone clear."

Zadie's shoulders shrugged within the harness. "I wasn't trying to hit Stumpy's house, but I'm still figurin' out how to focus it."

"Focus it?" Adelaide asked.

"Yeah. Haven't you noticed how the machine creates the quakes?" Zadie's mechanical hands gorilla-walked her comparatively tiny body over to the machine. Her human hand extended out from the harness and turned a dial on the control panel. "It's not the energy output. It's the vibrations. The harmonics." She pushed up a slider control. The machine hummed with incredible energy and grew louder.

On the one hand, Adelaide was glad that her internal theories were correct about the machine. On the other, she truly wished Zadie had not discovered it too.

"Stop," Adelaide said.

Zadie pulled back. The humming softened. "You can match that frequency to your surroundings," said Zadie. "Or you can widen it, elongate it, and make it travel far away."

"And you matched the frequency to the pipes," Adelaide concluded. "Because the earth itself has too many different kinds of dirt and rocks and layers to share a single, vibrating harmonic."

"Yep. These pipes that carry the energy and lifeblood of the city, the same ones that the snobs above decided were too much of an eyesore to look at all the time, these carry vibrations extremely well."

"Yeah," Adelaide said. "I've seen it. I've seen the earthquakes tearing the city apart."

"W-Wait," Baxter stuttered, "what do you mean? The city? The whole city?"

Adelaide nodded. "The Uppers and the Lowers."

The soft, humming echo reverberating from the machine and through the pipes suddenly rose in volume to an ear-splitting screech. A wave of vibrations washed over them and knocked everyone but Zadie and her stabilizing arm monstrosities to their knees. Within moments, the wave of noise and vibrations vanished.

"We have to turn it off!" Harriet implored.

She rose to her feet and stepped toward the machine, but Zadie barred her way.

"No."

"Zadie?"

"We're not turning it off." Zadie's eyes flashed and stared them all down.

"You're destroying everything," Adelaide said.

"Good," Zadie replied. Her bloodshot eyes seemed to waver as moisture crept in.

"This is too far, Zadie," Harriet argued.

Adelaide interjected, "I thought too far would be hurting Phineas."

Harriet glanced back, her eyes wide with shock and her cheeks sagging with embarrassment. "I... but Zadie said that... we didn't..."

Zadie's tired voice grumbled, "He found us dragging the machine down here. He asked me about it. Asked me a lot of questions. Didn't like my answers. He thought we should destroy it. Tried smashing the machine into pieces." Zadie shook her head. "I couldn't let him do that, you see."

"So you beat him up and took his arms?" Adelaide responded with a look of disgust.

Zadie shrugged. "He didn't put up a fight."

"And you left him to rot outside in the tunnels. Alone."

"That was his own fault."

"He got taken hostage by the Goldens."

That little fact took Zadie aback. "What?"

"They put out a bounty on us," Adelaide explained. "All of us. Plated and his cronies were searching the tunnels when they found Phineas. He led them straight to our hideout. I couldn't wrap my head around why he would do that, but... it was because he was leading them away from you... the whole time. Even after everything you did to him, he... he was still trying to protect you."

"Is he okay?" Harriet asked.

"He's okay now. I got him out. Well, he got *me* out. And my father. But that's a longer story.[117] The hideout is destroyed."

Baxter muttered a whimpering sound.

"It doesn't matter," Zadie said. "Everything will be different after today."

"Everything will be gone after today," Adelaide corrected.

"It will be worth it to get rid of him!" Zadie yelled at the top of her voice. Her eye twitched as she regarded all of their shocked faces.

"*Him?*"

Zadie unconsciously stepped back until she leaned against the vibrating earthquake machine. "Mayor *Stanbury*," her voice oozed with venom. "He gets accused of bribery, forgery, blackmail, murder: and none of it sticks! No matter how much evidence I find! Money gets passed around. All those charges go away. He greases the gears. Makes rich people richer. And then they elect him again to do whatever he wants."

Adelaide studied Zadie's bloodshot, watery eyes, manically darting around. "Even so, what does that have to do with you?"

Zadie snorted and shook her head. "Mayor Stanbury is my father."

---

117 At least a chapter's worth.

Adelaide's eyebrows almost reached her hairline. She looked at Harriet. The girl dragged her foot along the floor and avoided her gaze, which told Adelaide what she needed to know.

Zadie gritted her teeth. "He killed my mom. Almost killed me. You think someone like that deserves to keep on living? Him and all his little murder buddies just like him?"

She didn't even notice as Jules approached her. He leaned in between her mechanical arms holding her up and gently placed his hand on her cheek. She jerked back in shock but relaxed as her eyes found Jules.

All Zadie could think to say in his presence was, "We can't stop now."

He grabbed his gas mask and goggle combo stitched together with a bandana and lifted it away from his face, revealing heavily scarred skin beneath. Adelaide could only surmise that most of his scars were from severe, third-degree burns. His teeth peered out from a gap in his open, torn lip.

All Zadie could see was the pleading in his eyes. "No, we aren't the monsters, Jules," Zadie said to him. "They are. *He* is. He's the monster."

Jules placed his forehead against hers. Their eyes closed as their noses touched.

"He's the monster," she repeated.

The overarching rumbling of the machine lessened. Zadie opened her eyes. Jules' hand reached out past her, behind her back. He flicked a switch on the machine. With one hand on Zadie's waist, Jules stepped beside her and pulled down a slider control with his other hand. The incessant humming quieted.

"No!" Zadie spun around, and her colossal, mechanical arms slammed into Jules' side, knocking his body across the chamber.

"Jules!" Harriet screamed.

Harriet, Baxter, and Adelaide rushed over to his fallen form. Harriet gently rolled him on his back. She checked his head and stabilized his neck. Jules coughed and winced in pain.

"J..." Zadie stammered and blinked her eyes, "I... I'm sorry."

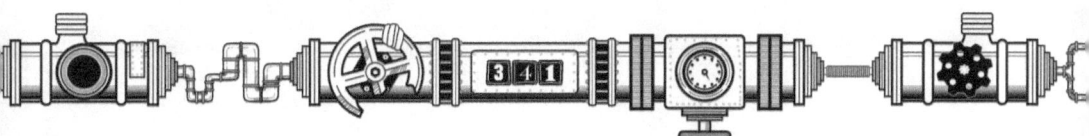

From the floor, Jules' eyes were full of understanding and forgiveness as he gazed into Zadie's strained, unfocused spheres of desperation.

"His arm's broken," Harriet concluded. "I think ribs too."

"Oh, and that's his bad side," Baxter said.

Zadie turned her mechanical arm harness away from them. She faced the generator. Her human hand reached out over the controls. Her fingers hesitated for a moment before she pushed up the sliders.

"We can't stop now," Zadie said, to herself more than anyone else. "It's too late."

Adelaide stared at Zadie. She glanced from her to the others. Her heart felt like it was breaking into pieces. Her stomach might never be whole again. But there was only one way she could move forward.

"You three need to get out of here," Adelaide told the others. "Get Jules to a doctor."

Harriet stared at Adelaide. Their eyes met. No more needed to be said.

"What are you going to do?" Baxter asked.

"I can fix this," Adelaide said. She nodded at him. "Go."

Baxter put Jules' good arm around his shoulders and lifted him up. Harriet steadied his injured side and helped him walk as much as she could. Jules leaned on them both for support.

Harriet glanced back at Adelaide as they hobbled past. "Be safe. Both of you. Please."

Zadie didn't notice or regard any of them. She leaned over the device, her arms and face trembling more than the earthquake machine.

With one last look, Harriet cranked the handwheel and creaked open the door. She, Baxter, and Jules walked together out of the chamber.

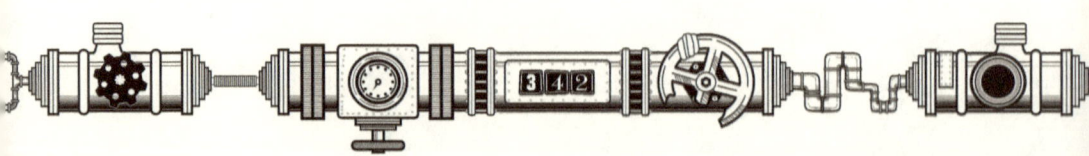

Zadie blinked her eyes until they could focus again and looked back at the empty doorframe. "Wait! You'll die out there!"

"How do you figure the outside is less safe than in here?" Adelaide asked.

Zadie searched Adelaide and shook her head. "Junction's heavily reinforced, meant to bear the weight of the fatcat city up there. And them quakes are radiating outwards. Uppers could collapse, and the Junction'd survive just fine."

Adelaide shook her head. "No matter how you try to balance the vibrations, this chamber is still taking severe damage. The Lowers and the rest of the underground too. It's only a matter of time before you destroy the entire city, not just the Uppers."

Another wave of vibrations and rumbles washed through the machine and into the pipes. Adelaide steadied herself on her feet as the minor earthquake passed. She pointed at a collection of particularly nasty cracks shining through the main, vertical cylinders. Dust rained down from the ceiling far above.

"It doesn't matter," Zadie said as dust fell into her open eyes. She didn't even blink. "It doesn't matter." Her eyebrows suddenly furrowed as she gritted her teeth and growled. "It doesn't matter!" Her mechanical arms reached back and slammed into the heavy, vertical pipes, leaving behind a huge dent. "It will all be worth it!" A bit of steam hissed out from a newly ruptured seal at the top of the pipe.

Adelaide studied her friend before gesturing to the room around them. "Nothing could be worth this."

Zadie stood up straight and stared her down. "You can't stop me, stumpy."

Anger tried to build up in Adelaide, but it just got washed away with a wave of sadness. "Don't make me hurt you, Zadie." Adelaide pulled her dark-tinted goggles down over her eyes. She extended her mechanical forearm's lever out to her elbow and shifted it toward her wrist. Her backpack's steam generator whirred to life.

"Oh, gimpy," Zadie scoffed. "You ain't gonna be the one doin' the hurtin.'"

The two girls stalked around each other in a circle. Zadie's gorilla-arms padded her along the floor. Adelaide's normal walk looked far less imposing.

"I'm sorry, Zadie."

"I am too."

With a snap, Adelaide air-pressure-rocket-launched her metal hand through the air, trailing the cable attachment behind. The mechanical ball of phalanges rocketed toward Zadie's face. With a quick shuffle to the side, powered by her massive, mechanical arms, she dodged it easily.

As the cable trailed past her head, Zadie's own mechanical hand grabbed the cable and pulled hard. The strong, steam-powered arms yanked Adelaide clear off of her feet. Adelaide cradled her metal arm as a shield in front of her before Zadie's other arm slammed into her and knocked Adelaide clear across the room.

She slid on her butt and rolled, saving herself from too much harm. Her shiny, new mechanical arm looked a bit dented though. Her hand and trailing cable zipped back and locked into her wrist.

"You need new tricks, handsy," Zadie said. "Seen that one before."

Adelaide rose to her knees. She studied her no-longer shiny, metal elbow. A needle gauge built inside the joint, right within the crook, read that it was maxed out at 100%. Adelaide rotated the entire metal chassis comprising her forearm. The spring-loaded mechanism inside locked and changed gears. Her forearm popped free. Hinges built within the elbow rotated the metal forearm, folding it backwards, parallel onto the upper arm.

"Weeks ago," Adelaide said, "you asked me what these copper wires do."

The elbow joint exposed itself[118] without the forearm covering it. From within the joint's new opening, a barrel with two prongs extended outwards like a creepy finger with two fingernails. Adelaide dialed her chest's control panel. Her fingers rotated the circular panel and raised the sliders. Both the prongs and the barrel from her elbow device sparked with electricity.

Zadie's eyes widened.

Adelaide's elbow barrel fired a bolt of lightning. The beam of pure electricity struck Zadie in her chest and shoulder. Her body and mechanical arms flew through the air and landed on her back. Zadie gasped and writhed within her harness straps. Her mechanical arms laid still, locked in place.

"That..." Zadie coughed, "was new..."

Adelaide adjusted her chest's control panel. The barrel and prongs sprang back inside her elbow. Her human hand swung her metal forearm back down, twisted it, and locked it back into place, returning the mechanical creation back to normal, as far as it could be called normal anyways. She checked her elbow's needle gauge: 0%... 1%... 2%...

It would take a while for her oscillating steam generator on her back to charge up enough power to unleash that kind of electricity again, but Adelaide hoped she didn't have to worry about that. She stood and approached her machine. She had such hopes for this thing as well. She wanted to change the world. This wasn't what she had in mind.

Adelaide turned the dials on the machine's control panel. Small, colored light bulbs progressed from red to green, high to low. The bulbs shone bright green near the top. Adelaide slid the sliders down. The gauge remained unchanged. The bulbs remained as bright as ever.

"Hey..." Zadie groaned, "you remember when we were at the school, and we couldn't turn off your generator? Re-ci-pro-cating rotations, you said?" Zadie smiled.

---

118 Outrageous! There are children present!

"It's fully self sustaining," Adelaide realized aloud. "Once it got up to speed, we couldn't slow it down."

"Yeah, I never bothered to try and fix that little problem. Good luck turnin' off an otterlateral engine that can't stop."

"Oscillating."

"Sure, that."

Zadie struggled to get up. Her mechanical arms had difficulty responding to her real arms' commands.

Adelaide studied the machine's control panel. Her hand turned all of the dials to max and flipped all of the switches on. All of the sliders slid to max. The generator's whirring and rumbling grew louder as the rotating engine spun so fast that, to her naked eyes, it looked like it wasn't moving at all. It was just a blur. Her eyes could only picture glimpses of the engine frozen in time as it rotated at ludicrous speed.[119]

"What are you doing?" Zadie asked as her mechanical fingers jerked and flexed.

"I can't damage it," Adelaide deduced, "but it sure can damage itself."

Adelaide glanced back just in time to see Zadie's mechanical arms throw her body from the floor and launch herself at Adelaide's face. Zadie swung her monstrous arms at Adelaide's head. Adelaide ducked. Zadie's arms smashed into the heavy pipes, crushing a severe dent in the already fractured metal. The humming and vibrations from within grew even more intense. Adelaide could feel the quaking in her teeth.

Adelaide's piston-powered punch launched her forearm forward and slammed into Zadie's midsection. Her fist impacted the chair harness holding Zadie's legs, but it still launched Zadie's entire body through the air. She crash landed several yards away. Saved from getting her ribs broken, Zadie suffered severe whiplash instead, and she was

---

119 It nearly turned plaid.

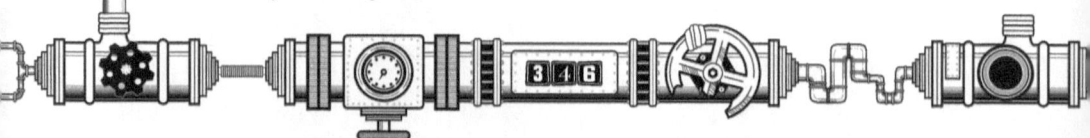

fairly certain that her knees had wound up behind her head at some point.

Zadie coughed and spit before turning a fierce glare at Adelaide. Adelaide ignored her and checked her elbow needle gauge: 70%... 71%...

Zadie's arms raised her harnessed body up to her feet. Adelaide did not want to get in a fist fight with her. Those gigantic arms were too strong. She needed another tactic while she recharged. With pipes and cables crisscrossing all around, the massive chamber was basically a giant jungle gym, and it was time to play. More specifically, it was time to run.

Adelaide jumped and pulled herself up onto a metal-grated platform overhead. Zadie's monstrous arms gave a double-fisted slam against the platform, snapping one side free of the wall and transforming the platform into an uncomfortable slide. Zadie smashed her arms down toward Adelaide's sliding form. Adelaide dodged and rolled off onto the ground.

Adelaide grabbed her forearm's lever and pulled. Her metal hand launched. Her fist grazed Zadie's cheek and disappeared behind her into the pipes and platforms above.

Zadie blinked her eyes and stretched her bruised cheek. Her metal hand reached for Adelaide's trailing arm cable. Just as her phalanges enclosed around it, Adelaide retracted the cable, timing it perfectly. The cable stretched taut, and the powerful, little motor in Adelaide's arm yanked her clear off her feet. Her flying body followed the cable and slammed into Zadie, knocking her over.

The cable reeled Adelaide up, smacking her body into a pipe, another pipe, a platform, and through a web of cables. Her metal hand broke free of whatever it was stuck on and retracted back into her forearm, causing Adelaide to fall onto a platform below. She slammed back, and the sudden increase in weight caused the platform to creak and lower an inch.

The earthquake machine below glowed red hot. Vibrations hummed and shook the entire chamber. The platform Adelaide

was standing on snapped free of its supports. Metal crashed onto a pipe running horizontally below, which cracked open and spewed boiling steam. Adelaide climbed up onto another pipe out of the line of fire.

Zadie's huge, metal hand grasped the cracked pipe and climbed up, giving no heed nor notice to the boiling steam, all so she could chase after Adelaide.

Adelaide squeezed through a pair of pipes built closely together. She hopped off into empty space and swung off a cable, making her way through the playground of chaos. Zadie clomped and gripped and smashed into everything right behind her. Pieces of metal and concrete exploded.

Adelaide slipped through another small opening between several pipes. Zadie's gargantuan arm crunched through the opening, tearing open a bigger hole. The metal fingers found purchase and grasped around Adelaide's foot. Adelaide's free hand directed her mechanical one to grab onto Zadie's metal thumb. Adelaide's pistons pushed as Zadie's pistons pulled. Gears turned. Exhaust pipes tooted. Before Zadie could yank Adelaide's body out through the hole she made, Adelaide was able to pull back the huge thumb and free her foot from the grasp. The problem with that was: Adelaide had nothing to fall back onto.

Adelaide fell through the open air. Cables attempted to slow her fall. They made her spin. A pipe tried to help next. That smashed into her ribs. Her body slammed onto a platform ten feet above the ground. Her harness and backpack snapped her spine upright.

A powerful earthquake shook the entire chamber. More than the pipes vibrated. The dirt itself joined in for the dance party. Pipes broke apart. Steam showered over the two girls. Parts of the walls collapsed and crumbled.

Adelaide's platform broke into pieces. She fell and crashed upon the floor. Groaning from the sudden and painful impact, her eyes opened just in time to tell her body

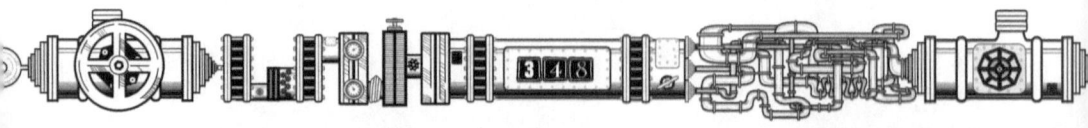

to roll out of the way, narrowly avoiding a falling concrete pipe that smashed into the floor.

Zadie flew down from above and landed on top of Adelaide. Her right mechanical hand pinned Adelaide's human left arm to her own chest just as she was attempting to reach the controls. Adelaide's right mechanical arm reached up, but Zadie's left mechanical arm caught her fist. The two metal appendages pushed against each other. Metal scraped against metal. Pistons pushed. One example of engineering might tested against another.

Adelaide's left hand, nearly crushed as it was, still managed to flick part of her chest's control panel. Her metal forearm launched forth with a piston-powered punch. Zadie's rigid arm and entire body jerked backwards, but she fell back and leaned forward again with her metal fingers still clamped around Adelaide's fist.

Zadie's metal fingers dug in. Adelaide's wrist joints started to bend. Zadie pushed down. Adelaide's metal arm bent and buckled at the elbow. Adelaide immediately realized that a flaw with having her forearm being removable was that it was much more fragile at the hinges.

The tremendous amount of pressure from Zadie's right mechanical arm pressing against Adelaide's human arm and chest made it difficult to breathe. Adelaide thought she felt one of her ribs crack. And she definitely felt her pinky finger break.

Adelaide ripped her mind from the pain and studied her mechanical arm, which was badly losing the contest of engineering might. Her elbow joint was failing. Only one hinge kept it from flying off entirely, and that was about to go. Adelaide's eyes flashed. Her elbow needle gauge read: 100%.

Her unbroken index finger on her left hand flicked her chest's control panel. Part of the sliding controls had been crushed into oblivion. She wasn't sure what worked and what didn't. Adelaide screamed in pain as Zadie crushed the metal arm into her shoulder. Adelaide's mechanical forearm collapsed.

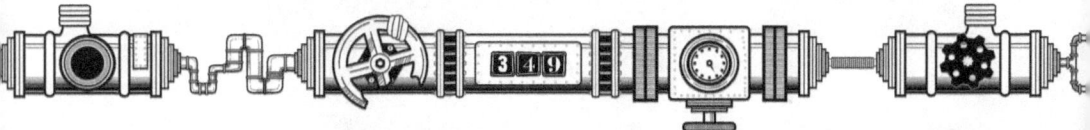

Her metal bicep bent. The cracked elbow split down the middle, revealing a sparking barrel within. Adelaide's finger slid the control panel slider to max.

The young engineer's mechanical arm exploded in a sudden, violent burst of energy.

A bolt of lightning split the air, striking Zadie's face, chest, arm, and backpack generator. The resultant crack of exploding air pressure smashed them both apart. Zadie's harnessed body flew off and landed several feet away. Adelaide skidded along the concrete.

Adelaide's cut and burned face grunted in pain. Her pounding left hand shook of its own volition. Her middle and index fingers still seemed to work, so she focused on using those to unstrap herself from her mangled, mechanical arm harness. She was in too much pain to feel remorse for her brand new prosthetic. She bent the twisted metal away from her shoulder to find a shard stabbing into her arm nub. Adelaide twisted and pulled the metal out of her skin.

Three of the four massive, vertical pipes encompassing the middle of the chamber had survived up until that point, but that point was now over. All three of them broke simultaneously and spewed boiling steam everywhere. Adelaide dove down to the floor as the vapor flowed over her head. The concrete floor cracked.

Adelaide crawled over to Zadie as best she could while nursing a couple of broken ribs. Zadie laid unconscious. Her face and left eyelid suffered severe burns.

Adelaide unstrapped Zadie's chest and legs from the broken chair harness, which was taking much longer than she wanted it to with her just using two fingers and her teeth at a couple of points. She pulled her free just as more earthquakes ripped through the chamber.

Wall debris and pipes and metal destruction crashed down around them. Adelaide calculated the safe zones and pulled herself and Zadie toward them, avoiding most of the

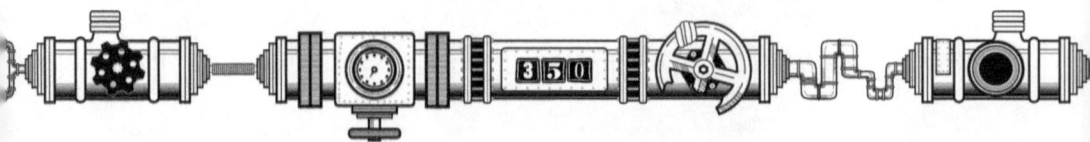

danger. Smaller rocks and debris rained on their heads. A concrete pipe slammed into the ground next to Zadie's foot. Adelaide looked to the entrance. Heavy debris blocked the door.

They needed an exit. Adelaide's cracked goggles performed their job well enough, allowing her to look through the dust and avoid most of the dangerous debris. She ignored the feeling of splintering shards of bone sticking inside her and dragged Zadie by the arm across the hard floor to an open doorway. She had no idea where it led, but it was bound to be an improvement. She was both right and wrong at the same time.

The doorway led into a boiler room. Most of it was intact as rows and rows of massive boilers all worked simultaneously, but Adelaide couldn't find a way out. It was a dead end. Still, she dragged Zadie inside and away from ground zero as more debris rained down outside. Adelaide ducked as a pipe leading from the wall above the door to a nearby boiler snapped and broke free, dumping hot water all over the floor.

As she avoided scalding her feet on the water, Adelaide's eyes followed the current as it traveled along the sloped floor in one, solid direction. It flowed down a metal grated drain built into the middle of the boiler room. The drainage system emptied into a large trough tunnel built beneath the chamber.

Adelaide tried to lift the grate, but it was screwed down tight. Given that she had nothing to screw with, she felt she was rather screwed. But no, there was always a way. Those hapless engineers weren't always so hapless. They must have built access hatches. They always needed hatches to access the things that needed accessing. Sure enough, she looked around and found one such access hatch in the floor near the outer wall.

She dragged Zadie's limp body by the arm over to it. Adelaide lifted the hatch. Inside, currents of brown, disgusting water flowed through the trough tunnel. She had no idea where this led, but the current was flowing, so the tunnel wasn't blocked. Cracks ripped into the wall next to her. No time like the present.

Adelaide pulled on Zadie's belt and nonchalantly dumped her unconscious body inside. Adelaide hopped in as an earthquake shook the area so violently that Adelaide wasn't sure if she entered of her own volition or simply fell in. The old, water trough tunnel curved and sloped through the earth. There were no lights or illumination of any kind. Adelaide felt splashes from intersecting pipes dumping their liquid contents onto her. All of it was warm. None of it smelled nice. She tried her dangedest to keep most of it out of her mouth. She failed.

Light flickered at the end of the tunnel. Adelaide saw it. Then Adelaide fell through it almost immediately afterward. In fact, she kept falling.

She fell for twenty... thirty... forty feet. The evacuating trough tunnel dumped the girls and all of its questionable liquid out through the edge of the Gorge outside.

Water and other things poured out of pipes that jutted from the cliffside and dumped their contents directly into the brown sludge at the very bottom of the Gorge. What must have been a raging river at some point in time was just a thin stream of gunk in the present, and the two girls were in it over their heads.

The beaten forms of Adelaide and Zadie splashed into the muck and churned within the yuck. Adelaide flailed and floated to the shallow surface. She grabbed Zadie by the shirt and waddled over to the almost non-existent beach. Black sand and mud covered a couple feet of rocks, garbage, and debris next to the very bottom of the cliff face.

The black sludge river at the bottom of the Gorge flowed like syrup off toward another cliff, dropping thirty feet in a molasses-style waterfall into the ocean beyond. Adelaide remembered the short beaches at the bottom of the ocean Cliffside were settled a comfortable distance away from the gunk pollution that they themselves created so the citizens from the Uppers could have their nice vacation condos built

into the cliff face. Adelaide saw those beaches once. What a world of difference two thousand yards could make.

Adelaide pulled Zadie's body onto the most comfortable-looking rock she could find within the nearest three feet, which was as far as her tired eyes would allow, and laid the unconscious girl's back on it. Adelaide checked Zadie's face. She was still breathing. Adelaide sat down, adjusted her buttocks around some rocks, and laid back against the cliff face.

Aside from the plops and flushes and various other noises of mild concern, Adelaide did not hear nor feel any quakes or vibrations. Her machine must have stopped. The chamber must have collapsed upon it, smothering the machine underneath tons of rock and earth. It was over.

Her mind shut down, and she passed out.

How long she had remained unconscious was unclear, but what was very clear in Adelaide's vision as she finally opened her eyes was the severely pissed-off form of Zadie standing over her. In the next instant, Zadie slugged Adelaide hard in the face. Adelaide felt her head hit the ground. She couldn't see much else due to the wide array of stars shooting across her eyeballs.

Zadie's knee pinned down Adelaide's remaining arm. One of Zadie's hands grabbed Adelaide by the throat as the other grabbed a rock and raised it over her head, ready for a strike.

Her burned left eyelid remained shut while her angry right eye stared into Adelaide. Zadie gritted her teeth. Her entire body trembled with rage. A single tear streamed from her cheek.

Adelaide just looked into her eye, accepting whatever fate she decided. Zadie dropped the rock and released Adelaide.

"We're even," Zadie grated.

Panting for breath, desperately trying to force blood back into her brain, Zadie stood up over her. After one more glance at Adelaide, Zadie stepped over her fallen body and walked away.

Adelaide watched her old friend wander along the shore, lost and alone, before she disappeared into the mist.

Chapter 28

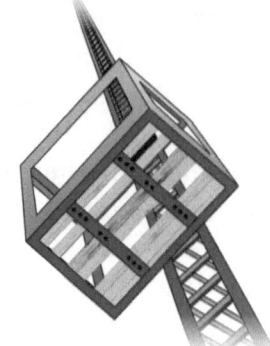

Aftermath[120]

Adelaide's eyes adjusted as the sun set in the sky. She groaned with delayed pain receptors as she stood and leaned against the bottom of the Gorge's sheer cliff face. Dried blood and mud caked over her. Her pinky and ring finger were definitely broken, along with a rib or two or four. That was one thing Adelaide had no idea how to fix.

Adelaide's torn, moist, disgusting clothes clung onto her skin as she shuffled her way down the sticky rocks and across what could be vaguely described as a river shoreline. The sloped pile of gunk and stones were less of a beach and more like whatever boats and large machinery had shoved up against the cliff face in an ever expanding exercise for industrial progress. Adelaide thought this place might be worthwhile if it was cleaned up, and maybe, she was too.

---

120   The chapter title is *Aftermath*. Much to my confusion during my youngster years, this was not the time after class when I was allowed to go play during recess. That was, of course, *AfterEnglish*.

Pipes jutting out of the cliff face spewed various liquids and chunks of hairy things. The third pipe poured out semi-transparent liquid.

Too tired to think about it too much, Adelaide shoved her face into the vertical stream to wash herself off. The impromptu shower was enough to reinvigorate Adelaide, as well as dramatically highlight any cuts, bruises, and various injuries she sustained. Her right shoulder and arm remnant, in particular, felt like it was on fire.

Water logged and sogged and bogged and slightly less smelly, she continued forward. It wasn't too much further until she could see actual settlements. Away from the exit pipes of various substances, various peoples had built makeshift homes and structures either on the jagged cliff face or just above the dubious water line.

A large, wooden-planked dock, filled with the poor, the destitute, and the unemployed, stretched out across the muck river and stopped. Broken pieces of docks long since destroyed over the decades littered the river and vanished beneath the black. In fact, there were so many abandoned and broken structures poking out of the grimy water, it made a sort of walkable crossing. Haphazard and hapless faces belonging to literally the lowest citizens of Parsons City looked upon the limping form of Adelaide with pity.

She paid no notice as she made her way over to the oldest elevator throughout all of the districts.[121] Swaying silently beside the cliff wall, many of the wooden boards comprising the lift's floor had rotted away, and the metal supports and braces looked rusted and worn.

Adelaide's feet found the sturdiest floor boards as her hand, which was two sizes too big now, pushed up on the operating lever. The motorized mechanism above vibrated to life, and the

---

121 The other lifts liked to call him "Pappy," and all of his stories began with "Back in *my* day" or "Lifts these days" or "If I had a mind to, I'd bend you over and paddle your counterweight pulley."

box lifted into the sky. Or, to be more precise, the box scraped along the cliff face, swayed back and forth, tilted on jagged rocks, flung itself free, then slammed back into the cliff. Over and over it went until the lift finally clanked to a stop at the Bazaar, midway up the Gorge.

Stepping off onto the firm ground, Adelaide noticed that the Gorge fared better from the earthquakes than the Upper District above. Some of the rock face had fallen, and debris littered the area, but most of the market was intact. The wide outcropping remained quite solid.

"Hurry along now!" shouted a familiar voice. "We haven't all day!"

A team of what looked like first responders, police officers, and random bystanders cleared rocks and debris from the walkway. Several attended injured persons. Even more scraped and dug into a partially collapsed tunnel entrance, trying to widen it enough to walk through. With a shining helmet and open visor, the lead bobby stood watch over everyone else and yelled instructions. Adelaide recognized him from the Gear Games: the corrupt bobby who demanded bribes from Enoch Kaylock. His huge mustache flapped in the breeze as she approached.

"Officer... Halbard?" Adelaide asked.

"Yes?"

Adelaide wasn't sure if she could trust the overtly dirty cop, but he seemed to have enough authority to do what she required of him. "Officer Halbard, I would like to turn myself in for crimes against the city."

"Is that so?" His dismissive expression slowly turned to interest.

"I caused all these earthquakes. Take me in."

The stern, weathered, wrinkled face of Officer Halbard stared at Adelaide for several moments. He snorted. "Okay, little girl. Move along now."

Adelaide's mouth dropped open. "No, I'm serious."

His impressive mustache curled, and his bulbous nose inhaled before he gave a great, exaggerated sigh.

"I was building a new design for an oscillating engine," Adelaide continued unabated of his bated-ness, "and I needed extra power and we hooked it up to the school and it went crazy and took down the building and I felt horrible and said *never again* but then my friend went crazy too and she took it and hooked my machine up to the Junction down in the tunnels and it was going crazy and was making all those earthquakes and it hit my parents' house so I chased after it and bad guys chased after me but I found them and argued with them so I overloaded it so it's gone and I hurt all those people but I didn't mean to and I feel like I am the worst person in the world so I deserve to be arrested."

Officer Halbard simply stared at her. His mustache, for the first time in years, had no idea what to do.[122]

"Look, little girl," he growled, "I don't know what kind of game you street rats are playing, but I'm not interested." He studied her cut, bruised, and extremely grimy face. His eyes took notice of the long trail of dried blood running down from her scalp. "Go to the first aid tent. They can help you there. Move along now."

The armored bobby pushed Adelaide down the walkway before marching back toward the nearly-cleared tunnel entrance so he could yell at more people doing their jobs. Adelaide stood there in silence. He didn't believe her. Granted, she did a terrible job explaining her story, but he didn't seem to care in the slightest. All these male authoritarian figures would not even comprehend that a thirteen-year-old girl had the ability to create an invention, let alone one that could accidentally destroy the city. Dean Douglas might, but would they still require evidence of her wrongdoing? How could she prove her guilt? All

---

122 It's a strange day indeed when an impressive mustache is left unable to give a proper statement. Normally, a mustache is all the statement one needs to give.

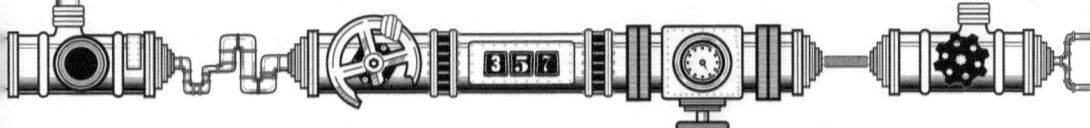

the evidence had been destroyed. They would... they would want her to recreate her machine.

They would want her to recreate her machine.

Adelaide blanched at her realization. That... that she could not allow. Her brain whirled. She wanted to turn herself in, but even if that were possible, she couldn't let any trace of her machine make it out of the collapsed Junction. No matter what. But what should she do now? What could she do now? Too much thinking made her dizzy, so she simply wandered away from the destruction she inadvertently caused.

After a limp, skip, and another limp, Adelaide found the first aid station Officer Halbard mentioned, which was really just a hastily-set-up tent with bent poles and drooping sides. Dozens of people bustled about the tarped construction nestled in a nook of the cliff face. Adelaide peered through the open flap in the front entrance. Bleeding, coughing, hunched, backed, peoples upon peoples waited their turn.

Holding a clipboard, an elderly woman with long, silvery-white hair, who had a very distinctive don't-mess-with-me personality, attended to the various attendees. Adelaide didn't spot an exam room or anything set up privately. The lady doctor was looking at and helping people wherever they sat or stood.

Adelaide plopped herself in a chair with three legs that was closest to the person she figured was in the back of the line. Adelaide felt the tiniest stabbing pain in her buttocks from a possible splinter, but before she decided if she felt like moving her arm enough to pluck it out, the wrinkled face of the stern doctor had Adelaide's chin in her hands.

"Multiple contusions," the doctor said. She lifted Adelaide's hand. "Broken bones." She pressed on Adelaide's chest, whose wince of pain communicated quite well. "Broken ribs. Breathe out for me." Adelaide wheezed. "Lungs intact." She turned to her nurse assistant. "Give me a splint!"

The nurse assistant walked over, and Adelaide recognized Cheryl, the kind-faced woman from the train platform and Lower Central. "Hello again."

"Hi," Adelaide said. "You're okay. How are your boys?"

"We're all okay," Cheryl replied. "Looks like you've seen better days."

"You don't know the quarter of it. Wait. Half of it? Fraction of it? I'm too tired for maths. Or adages. Abages? Abagels?"

"Shush now, baby," Cheryl said.

Cheryl dragged over a rolling, wooden box. The Doc rummaged through and picked out some cloth wrappings and small pieces of wood. She looked back to Adelaide.

"Grit your teeth," Doc said.

"Why?" Adelaide asked.

"Because we're low on painkillers, and I don't want you to bite your tongue off."

Adelaide's eyes widened in panic, but she gritted her teeth as ordered. The Doc dug her fingers into Adelaide's hand. The soft, grinding noises and quick snap made Adelaide's eyes flutter closed. When she opened them again, she found the Doc steadying her by the shoulder.

"You're alright," the Doc said. "Drink." She handed Adelaide a cup of water. "Swallow." She handed Adelaide a couple of pills. "That's all we got. Now keep this on."

Adelaide looked down to find her hand wrapped in cloth with a set of small, wood pieces stabilizing her pinky and ring finger. "Will my hand be okay?"

"You'll be fine, as long as you let it heal and don't injure yourself again until then. Your ribs are just going to have to heal on their own, so take care how you move. I would prefer to wrap up your chest, but we're low on supplies. That's the best we can do down here."

The Doc had already turned away from Adelaide to search for her next patient, but Adelaide's voice drew her attention back.

"What... umm... what do I owe you?" Adelaide's face flushed red beneath all the scratches and bruises. "I don't have any money on me..."

"We don't take payment here," Doc said.[123] "You want to pay someone, pay it forward. Help someone just like I did for you." Doc patted Adelaide on the knee, somehow already knowing that was the one place on Adelaide's body that didn't ache profusely, then she turned away. "Alright, who's next?" Doc asked the tent at large.

"Thank you. Oh, have you seen my friends?" Adelaide asked. "One had a broken arm and... they're about my age..."

"We've seen a lot of kids today. If they're not in here, maybe check outside."

Cheryl brushed Adelaide's bushy hair away from her eyes and said, "Take care, honey." She nodded then bustled back to work, hot on the doctor's heels.

Adelaide didn't see anyone else she recognized in the tent, so she staggered to her feet and limped outside while thinking about what the doctor said. Paying it forward seemed like a nice way to live. Did everyone live like that in the Gorge? Before she could think (ouch) on it further, some familiar shapes came into focus out on the edge of the Bazaar.

"Adelaide!" Harriet ran toward her. She reached out her arms for a hug, looked at the mess that was Adelaide, and decided against it.

Adelaide smiled, but then she wobbled on her feet.

Harriet ended up gently embracing her after all. "I gotcha. Here, have a seat."

Adelaide winced and groaned when Harriet placed her hand on her side.

"Oh," Harriet backed away, "ribs for you too?"

---

123 The health insurance industry would have wept, but their claim for salty tears was denied.

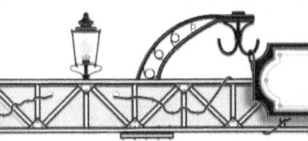

She even more gingerly lowered Adelaide to sit and lean back against the railing surrounding the cliff's edge. The breeze swirling in from the Gorge felt nice on Adelaide's sweating body, and it didn't smell like rotten pickled carrots or forgotten rodent carcass at all.

Baxter approached with his hands in his pockets, smiled at her and said, "Hey, you and Jules are broken rib buddies!"

Jules sat close by and leaned back against the nearest shop, which was mainly a broken picket fence with a tarp for a roof. He nodded his masked head at Adelaide. She waved at him, then regretted the action as the pain followed. Jules' left arm rested in a sling, which Adelaide admitted looked rather comfortable.

"So what happened?" Harriet asked. "Where's Zadie?"

After a deep breath, followed by deeply regretting doing that to her broken insides, Adelaide began to regale her friends with the story. She didn't remember much about the fight itself, but the part about her overloading the machine and dragging Zadie away from the rubble elicited the perfect amount of "ooh's" and "ahh's." The Steampunks made for a good audience.

"Can't say I'm surprised," Harriet said in response to Adelaide recalling how Zadie woke her up on the beach by slugging her in the face.

"But where did she go?" Baxter asked.

"I don't know," Adelaide replied.

They sat together in silence for several moments. Baxter's crossed legs rocked back and forth as he contemplated life to himself. Harriet leaned against the railing and looked out into the winking lights around the moonlit Gorge. Jules had fallen asleep. Adelaide's stomach twisted.

"I tried turning myself in," Adelaide muttered.

"To who?" Baxter asked.

"Whom," Harriet corrected a frowning Baxter.

"The police," Adelaide said.

"What?!" Baxter and Harriet responded in unison. Even Jules turned his dark-tinted goggles toward her.

"I built the machine that hurt all those people." Adelaide paused to catch a breath that refused to come. Harriet and Baxter looked to each other, unsure what to say either. "Don't the victims deserve... I don't know... justice?"

"B-but..." Baxter stuttered, "wasn't it really Zadie's fault?"

"And she's not gonna turn herself in," Harriet said.

"Yeah," Baxter argued, "so that can't be on you. It's Zadie's fault."

"Unless we would be considered accomplices too." Harriet tapped a finger to her lips.

"What?"

"Like we were there and helped. Well, sorta helped. We didn't stop her."

"I... is that bad?"

"That's a crime too, Bax."

"Oh..."

The four of them sat in silence once again. Adelaide thought it felt good to get some of the guilt off of her chest, but she regretted making the others feel it too. She was just trying to relieve her own conscience, but she didn't even realize that they must be going through similar emotions. Their internal torments excreted from their bodies and hung in the air, farting into a fog of despair.[124]

"What should we do?" Baxter asked.

"That was my question," Adelaide said.

"You really tried to turn yourself in to the cops?" Harriet asked.

"He didn't believe me."

"So..." Baxter pondered, "how would that help anyone?"

"What do you mean?"

"Turning yourself in. Say they threw you in prison for twenty years or whatever. How would that help anyone?"

---

124 From "*The Annals of Smelly Poetry*" by Bodentrius Oddment, the number two bestseller in Beatnik Slam Poetry Magazine's list of top collections to read while on the commode.

Adelaide opened her mouth to speak, but nothing came out. She sighed, shrugged, and said, "I don't know. Isn't that what you're supposed to do?"

"I mean, that's to stop folks from doing the same bad things again, right? The machine's gone already. 'Sides, I don't see how lockin' people up is supposed to help anybody anyhow. People don't learn no lessons in the clink. They just get angry and do the same stuff again when they get out."

"So you think everyone should just get away with doing whatever they want?" Harriet asked him.

"No, but if you think lockin' yourself up is gonna make some unhappy person happy, then you don't know how people work. You invented something you thought was neat." He pointed at Adelaide before nodding toward Harriet. "You helped out your friend like you always did. Should we throw ourselves off a bridge now? Would that help anybody?"

"Smokes, Bax," Harriet said.

"I'm just sayin'," he continued. "Me, I think if somebody did something wrong, they should make up for it until they make it right. Some grifter owes you money, you don't chop off his hands. You make him pay you back, or pay for somethin' else, or help someone you like. Me, I like fixin' things. Maybe I can fix enough things around the city to make up for what happened. To me, that's justice right there."

Adelaide gave a slight smile. "So... you don't believe in payback exactly so much as... paying it forward."

"Uhh, yeah, I guess."

The Steampunks took a few moments to ponder life, the universe, and everything.[125]

"We could do a lot for this city," Adelaide thought aloud, "if we wanted to fix it. If we wanted to change things for the better. Maybe I could build a school. One that allowed girls in."

---

125 And the number forty-two.

"That'd be nice," Harriet said. "Maybe I could run an art gallery that would put up works from anybody. Art makes people happy."

"Depends on the art," Baxter said. "Hey, are we... without Zadie, are we still the Steampunks? Are we still a gang?"

"Ugh," Harriet ughed. "Gang life is hard."

"Can we just be friends?" Adelaide asked.

"No," Harriet said immediately. "Not friends." She gave a wide, contagious smile. "Family."

Adelaide laughed. "It's so cheesy. I love it."

"Ugh," Baxter ughed. "Can we not?"

"Why?" Adelaide wondered.

"Because he's got a crush on me," Harriet said with a pair of blushed cheeks.

Baxter's cheeks turned the same shade of embarrassed red, straight from the teenager's fall collection. "I... well... yeah, I do. I said it. So there."

Adelaide laughed at the pair of them. Harriet leaned over and kissed Baxter on his rosy cheek. He sank into such a pool of bliss that Adelaide thought she would have to scoop the poor boy off the floor. Meanwhile, Jules was most definitely taking a nap.

"So now what?" Baxter asked.

Harriet shrugged. "We need a new hideout."

Adelaide slowly rose to her feet and gazed out upon the Gorge. She turned to them and smiled. "Come with me."

They made their way through the streets of the Lower District before climbing a set of stairs into the Uppers. Along with the Lowers and the Gorge, the edge of the Upper District had survived the earthquakes fairly intact. There were some broken windows and toppled street lamps, but for the most part, this area of the city looked fine. The closer they walked toward the epicenter, however, the more damage and destruction they found. Collapsed walls, debris, and splintered concrete ground were everywhere. Massive

chunks of the ground had risen or fallen, leaving miniature cliff faces and valleys of concrete within the city itself.

Roof debris had crushed automobiles into horseshoes. Carriages had fallen into shallow sinkholes. Storefronts had been demolished. Just as the sheer weight of the destruction hit Adelaide, she found herself at the epicenter.

Not so far from the Wakefield home, the intersection, which used to rise up as a geared platform to shuttle trams in different directions, intersected no more. An enormous sinkhole opened the earth below. The circular, geared, street platform had fallen what must have been thirty feet. The platform itself had survived, but it looked like a flipped coin stuck inside a hole that it could never escape.

The glittering wreckage of a broken tram could be seen at the bottom of the hole. Ropes and ladders extended down toward the tram as passengers and innocent bystanders were being helped out of the wreckage. This entire area must have been right above the Junction. When it collapsed, the street above followed the leader.

Standing on the safest part of the edge she could stand on, Adelaide spotted Silas Griggs in the sinkhole, helping others out and moving debris. He spotted Adelaide right back. His dimpled face gave her a half smile as his rough hand gave her a wave. Adelaide's hand could only manage a tiny wave around her waist. He nodded and went back to work. Adelaide thought about joining him, but her limited ability to move or even breathe at the moment made her feel like she would be more of a hindrance than a help.

The Steampunks walked past in silence along the sidewalks until the Wakefield estate loomed before them. On the driveway, illumination shined from gas lamps and stringed light bulbs held above a collection of tables. City blueprints scattered across the tops. Nearly one dozen men gathered around Mister Wakefield pouring over the schematics in the makeshift, mini crisis center.

"The second search party should enter from the west, below city hall," Mister Wakefield ordered. "From there..."

His voice trailed off as the teenagers walked into the light. He pushed aside the men to stride up to his daughter and place both his hands on her cheeks.

"My dear girl," he whispered. "Are you okay?"

"I'm okay," Adelaide replied. "It's all over. It's all over."

After a few moments, Franklin looked back at his personal band of mercenaries. "Ascertain where the nearest fire brigade is and help with whatever they require."

A man with a bowler hat and an impressive pair of mutton chops said, "What of our pay?"

"You will still be paid in full by the hour. Assist wherever you are needed, and I shall foot the bill. Go."

Mutton chops nodded, and the others followed him off the property. After they parted, Adelaide could finally see the slumped, unconscious form of Phineas sitting in a chair next to the farthest table.

"Phineas! Is he okay?" Adelaide asked her father.

"Oh yes," he replied. "Our family doctor did him a once over. After he helped us sketch out the layout of the steam tunnels, he fell asleep posthaste. Could sleep through another earthquake, that one."

"Adelaide." Missus Wakefield appeared at the front doorway. Her wavering gaze studied her daughter, analyzing her filthy clothes, her disgusting hair, and her many cuts, bruises, and injuries. Margaret approached her and smiled with a warmth Adelaide hadn't seen in years. "I..." she began before her nose turned up in a wrinkle. "Truly, you smell something horrible, dear. Come inside now."

Adelaide chuckled. However, she held back as her mother attempted to pull her through the doorway. "Umm..." Adelaide ummed, "these are my friends, by the way."

They all looked back at Harriet smiling brightly, Baxter analyzing the city schematics on the tables, and Jules, whose

darkened visor caused him to walk straight into a table and knock it to the ground. His unbroken arm snatched a flying paper out of the air, and he gently placed it on one of the surviving pieces of furniture.

"They need a place to stay," Adelaide said.

Baxter belched so loud it echoed off the brick walls.

Harriet giggled. "Nice."

"Oh, me too," Phineas piped up with a yawn. "Least 'til I get some more of them arms."

Baxter leaned toward Harriet and loudly whispered, "Is he gonna lock us in and bar the windows?"

Harriet shushed him.

Mister Wakefield's stern eyes studied them all before resting on his daughter. "You wish to turn our home into some sort of orphanage for wayward children?"

"And wayward old farts," Phineas tooted.

Adelaide kicked the dirt. "Well, we did kinda destroy their home."

"*We?*" Her father both dismissed and asked at the same time.

"The hideout in the tunnels."

He had to think for a moment. "You mean the disgusting platform with rotting furniture that collapsed?!"

"Hey!" Baxter protested.

"It was rather disgusting, Bax," Harriet contested.

"I know, but it was *our* disgusting platform with rotting furniture."

Jules nodded his head at Baxter and patted the boy on the shoulder but withdrew his hand quickly to analyze why his fingers were suddenly sticky.

"And they're more than friends really," Adelaide added. "They're my family."

The Steampunks beamed at her words. Mister Wakefield dimmed and pursed his lips.[126]

---

126 Though it was really more of a man bag.

"Family?" he muttered.

Adelaide fluttered her eyelids at her father and smiled the slightest of smirks. "You said we have thirty-two rooms, right?"

"Thirty-three," he couldn't help correcting. Franklin Wakefield sighed like a deflating balloon. He studied all of their faces once again before turning to his wife.

After a few moments, Margaret Wakefield flippantly waved a jewelry-laden hand at her husband and scoffed. "Well, darling, you always said you wanted to have more children."

Epilogue

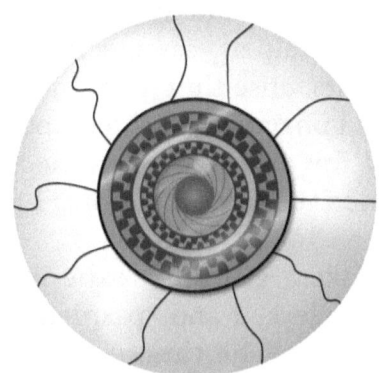

Deep down within the darkest pits of Parsons City, screams seemed to seep through the pores of the hard-packed, earthen walls and ceilings. Far deeper below the surface than even most of the Steampunks had previously dared to explore, there was nothing worth discovering about these dubious tunnel chambers. This was where the most dreadful denizens of the dark concocted their most devious experiments.

Several minutes, or perhaps even hours, passed before the broken, fifteen-year-old girl realized that the screams she kept hearing echo throughout the chamber were her own. The Crone, an elderly, crinkly, creepy, scare-packagey of a woman, hovered over her body. Her long fingernails clicked together like the sharp rap of chalk against a blackboard.

The sparse light attempting-yet-failing to illuminate the small chamber came from a lone filament bulb dangling from the earthen ceiling. Dirt sprinkled into rain overhead as a rhythmic pounding from somewhere deep within the tunnels

shook the walls. Nothing about this chamber was sanitary. Nothing about it needed to be.

"You have such beautiful nerves," the Crone cooed. "The endings were seared perfectly."

Her long fingernails scratched over the surface of the small table nearby. Scalpels, saws, screwdrivers, hammers, and a variety of other unsettling instruments decorated the surface. Her gnarled phalanges decided upon a pair of pliers.

"Should allow for excellent re-connectivity. Never had such a fine specimen to experiment on... I mean... *operate* on before."

Zadie, the broken girl, the experimental operation, grunted as her body jerked and spasmed of its own accord on the examining table. The Crone's claws dug into Zadie's head. A mechanical click reverberated through Zadie's skull. The pain subsided. She gasped for air.

"There," the Crone's scraggy voice whispered in awe. "Does it work?"

Zadie touched her face. Her burned and scarred cheek, courtesy of Adelaide's lightning launcher, greeted her sensitive fingers. Then, she felt something else. Something metal. She felt it inside her skull before her fingers could tell what it was. Where blackness used to rule over her lost left vision, colors began to illuminate.

The mechanical device welded over Zadie's burned eye socket clicked a lens and focused the aperture. The device, fused onto her nerves, shocked electrical impulses back toward her brain. Her brain then interpreted those impulses and transformed them into blurry, disturbing, yet beautiful images.

Colors danced. Dim at first, they grew in light. Almost too bright. Absolutely too bright. As her weary skull adjusted, shapes slowly came into focus.

"Yes," Zadie grated.

"Goooood," the Crone cackled. "Goooood."

The Crone danced in front of Zadie's right eye and the mechanical device inserted in place of her left. She stared into the red orb that flicked a lens closed when it needed to transmit images.

"Now tell me," the Crone's high pitched voice scraped against Zadie's eardrums. "What do you see?"

Zadie's dry mouth swallowed. How could she possibly describe the dulling pain and unbelievable imagery being transmitted directly into her brain right now? It was like nothing she had ever experienced before. Sparks transformed into colors that she had never seen. The air itself seemed to pulse and breathe before her. The ceiling appeared solid then flashed into a great beam of light, crystallizing into glass. Colors and forms and shapes assaulted her mind all at once. Zadie embraced it all.

After several moments of letting the device work, click, and adjust, Zadie decided that only one word could answer her question. Only one word could suffice.

"Everything."

The End[127]

---

127 Book epilogues were doing the Marvel mid-credit scenes far before motion pictures had been invented. The O.G. sequel trailers right there.

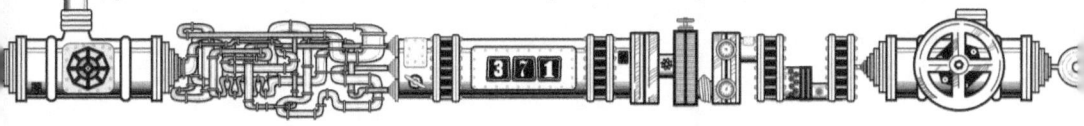

The Steampunks will return!

(if we sell enough copies of this one, that is.)

If you liked the book, please feel free to leave a review!
(If you *didn't* like the book, please feel free to keep it to yourself.)

Reviews will help my small business grow.
Your help in spreading the word
would be most appreciated.
Visit the websites of your favorite retailer(s)
and leave your thoughts.

For updates and more, sign up for the
Steampunks Newsletter
and see new, original illustrations
not shown anywhere else!

Links to all the things can be found at:
SteampunksBooks.com

About the Author

Robert "Bo" Forehand is a staggeringly beautiful man, and this blurb in third person was most definitely not written by him. Robert was named after his grandfather, Robert (go figure), who everyone called Bob instead of Robert, and little Robert's parents didn't want to call a baby Robert, but they couldn't call him Bob either, because that would be confusing to have multiple Bobs. You can't have multiple Bobs. That's just madness. So they called the baby Bo, for little Bob. So Bo (a.k.a. little Bob) [a.k.a. little Robert] —a.k.a. the staggeringly beautiful man— grew up with a love of comic books and art. He studied Computer Animation at Full Sail University for a time until he realized that he didn't quite like studying Computer Animation. The Psychology class where he invented imaginary characters and gave them mental disorders was far more fun, so he gave himself a mental disorder by becoming a writer. An Associate's degree from Gulf Coast State College, a Bachelor's degree in Film - Cinema Studies with a minor in Music from the University of Central Florida, and a Master's degree in Creative Writing from his triumphant (not really) return to Full Sail University gave him both extensive knowledge and expensive debt. He estimates that he will be able to pay back his student loans around the year 2142.

To receive new book updates or just read more nonsense about the man, the myth, the legend; sign up for the newsletter by visiting his website at:

RobertBoForehand.com

Special Acknowledgements

More special thanks (because I do what I want) to Nicole Chapman-Leonard, editor extraordinaire. I've learned so much from you, and I appreciate all of your help.

Special thanks to Kaitlyn Chipps at **Kai Ceramics** for her friendship and gorgeous artwork. View her pottery and sign up for her newsletter at:

KaiCeramics.com

More special thanks to Jenna and Jeremy Chipps at **Quench Your Adventure** for their friendship and fun, compelling escapades. View videos about travel, family, and just being a good person at:

QuenchYourAdventure.com

Organic vs Artificial Intelligence

<u>This novel was created without the use of A.I.</u>

(Although, the current use of A.I. is as much Artificial Intelligence as those hoverboards that have wheels instead of, you know, hover technology; but calling them Advanced-Search-Engines-That-Scrape-Data-To-Steal-Pieces-Of-Works-In-Order-To-Slap-Them-Together-Haphazardly-And-Try-To-Pass-It-Off-As-Original-Works-Of-Art [or A.S.E.T.S.D.T.S.P.O.W.I.O.T.S.T.T.H.A.T.T.P.I.O.A.O.W.O.A., if you will] didn't quite roll off the tongue as much. By the by, this is in reference to the Generative A.I. programs used to replicate writing and art. There are other spaces, such as the medical field, in which this type of technology could be beneficial.)

Creativity and art are an essential part of the human experience. The act of making, with intention and meaning and purpose behind it, is so important for communication and artistic expression. Handmade works with emotional connection behind it just means so much more. The effort behind making the piece is the entire point. If art takes no effort, creativity, or overall purpose, then all you will get is low-effort, unimaginative, meaningless slop that just gets thrown out as content for content's sake. Not to mention, comparing professionally-crafted artwork to Generative A.I. is like comparing a juicy cut of medium-rare porterhouse to a frozen, mystery meat, TV dinner. You'll still be fed, but geez, it is not the same.

All that is why I exclusively use free, open-source software that does not train A.I. with your stolen data and hard work.

Software and Fonts

This text was written using **LibreOffice**, a free and open-source office productivity software suite. It is a project of The Document Foundation (TDF), a non-profit organization that promotes open-source document handling software. LibreOffice Writer is released under the Mozilla Public License v2.0.

All artwork was created by the author using **Inkscape**, a free and open-source vector graphics editor released under a GNU General Public License.

Various images utilized **GIMP**, the GNU Image Manipulation Program, a free and open-source raster graphics editor. It is freely available and licensed under the GNU General Public License.

The book was finalized for print publication using **PDF24 Creator**, an application software released under a proprietary freeware license by Geek Software GmbH.

The font **LibreBaskerville** was used for the Body Text, licensed under the SIL Open Font License, Version 1.1, created by Pablo Impallari and Rodrigo Fuenzalida.

Various other fonts were created by Dieter Steffmann who, from a desire to share fonts as cultural heritage, gave out his fonts to everyone without any restrictions, all of which were licensed under the **1001Fonts** Free For Commercial Use License (FFC). I thank him for his artistry, kindness, and generosity.

Roman Antique (Roman Antique) was used for Headers and various text, including parts of the cover. **College TM** (College TM) was used as a base to make custom designs, such as the drop Caps and parts of the cover. Caslon Antique (Caslon Antique) was used in the cover. *Adine Kirnberg* (Adine Kirnberg) was used for Adelaide's handwriting. Messing Lettern (Messing Lettern) was used for the Newcomen University signage.

Index

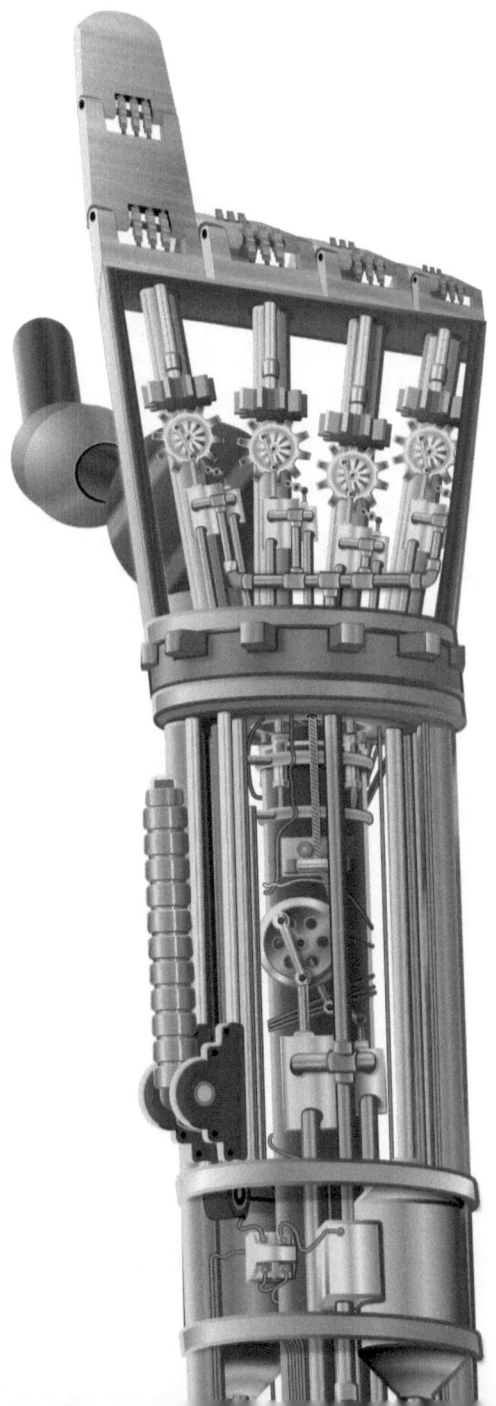